THE DEVIL IS BACK AND THE UNDERWORLD IS GOING TO HELL

THE MAN IN THE DARK

JONATHAN WHITELAW

THE MAN
IN THE
DARK

JONATHAN
WHITELAW

TO
Scott

Hope you have
a DEVILISHLY
good read.

JW

Urbane
PUBLICATIONS

urbanepublications.com

First published in Great Britain in 2019
by Urbane Publications Ltd
Unit E3, The Premier Centre, Premier Way,
Romsey, Hampshire, SO51 9DG
Copyright © Jonathan Whitelaw, 2019

A CIP catalogue record for this book is available
from the British Library.

ISBN 978-1-912666-46-1
MOBI 978-1-912666-47-8

Design and Typeset by Michelle Morgan

Cover by OR8 Design

Printed and bound by 4edge Limited, UK

URBANE
urbanepublications.com

For my darling (now) wife Anne-Marie.
You bring light into my world and make sure I'm
never the real Man in the Dark.

"Treachery is noble
when aimed at tyranny."

Pierre Corneille

THE MAN IN THE DARK

ONE

The Pope's private quarters deep within Vatican City were quiet. Only an old, ticking clock on the mantelpiece disturbed the stillness of the place. It was peaceful, serene even, just what you'd expect from the office of an elderly man of great power.

All the hallmarks were there. The mahogany desk, the lack of computer, a set of reading glasses perched neatly on top of a writing ledger. There was even room for an old-fashioned inkwell, two fountain pens with the Pope's sigil branded up their shaft.

Light was easily flowing into the room from an open window. The sky outside was warm and blue, the first hints of a Roman summer making everything very comfortable. The clock ticked on and on, stopping for no one, even if there was nobody around to hear it. Nobody but the large, ornate crucifix that hung from the opposite wall. It wasn't going to mind the noise.

It was just as well. The second hand ticked over, then over again, then over for a third time. But, where the fourth consecutive tick should have sounded, there was nothing. Ordinarily this would have been cause for concern. However, this was the heart of the Catholic Church. Out of the ordinary wasn't always out of the ordinary. For an institution founded on fable, legend and tradition, the non-ticking of a clock was hardly a reason to think the world was ending.

And besides. The battery had probably just run out. Not that there was anybody around to hear or notice the silence. The crucifix on the wall wasn't going to change the double As.

Only there *was* cause for concern. A pretty big cause for concern. The last time the clocks had stopped in Vatican City, there had been a visitor. In the short time since that incident, the story had become the stuff of myth. This was the Catholic Church, it liked to keep its secrets secret. But this one had, pardon the expression, spread like wildfire.

The Pope had never been the same since that night. His hair had turned whiter, his eyes a little wilder. Gone was the good sense and diplomacy expected of a modern world leader. In its place the rantings and ravings of a Dark Ages fanatic.

He'd spoken of meeting The Devil, coming face to face with the incarnate of evil. He'd even been saved by the creature, his heart stopped from stopping. The foul beast from below had sought his guidance, come to him for advice on matters he'd never been able to divulge.

And as a result of this now fabled meeting, there had been a few changes to the way things were done around the old place. Centuries old rules were brought back in from the cold, the whole institution taking on a more careful, commanding persona to the wider world. The good Catholics, and everyone else, needed protecting from The Devil, who was very much real. Especially now that people were throwing themselves at the feet of a new, amoral business in Scotland that promised to give them the world.

The sweeping reforms weren't without their critics, both inside and out. But The Pope's say was final. He made sure of that.

Now the clock had stopped again. That could only be a bad sign, couldn't it? Don't ask the crucifix on the wall though. There was very little it could do.

THE MAN IN THE DARK

Time had a strange way of repeating itself. Especially if things lasted long enough. That's why the small, swirling cloud of black smoke and ash in the middle of the office was met with all the nonchalance and casual ignorance expected of there being nobody there.

The little cloud grew and grew until it was a large, billowing column. Dirty black smoke and grit spiralled around and around, stretching from the floor to the ceiling. Around and around it went, gathering pace until it was like a tornado, raging violently within the confines of the office.

As quickly as it had appeared, it stopped. The billowing ash and smoke vanished, leaving a dirty black stain on the hardwood floor. Two shoes scuffed through the remnants of the column and stormed over towards the door.

"Look, I know I said I'd probably not be back, but you and I have to talk buck-o."

The Devil was in full flight. He was throwing his arms around all over the place, trying best to show just how angry he was. In days gone by he would have just appeared as a three-headed dragon, spitting fire and meteors, eyes glowing and fangs glistening. But this was the twenty-first century. Nothing he could conjure up would top the special effects wizards in Hollywood. He should know, he was teaching them on a daily basis. Or at least, his company was.

Now he was back in familiar threads, sharp suit, tartan tie, hair slicked back behind his ears. It would have to do. He had bigger fish to fry.

"You're not holding up your end of the bargain," he said. "I thought we'd been through all of this before. You keep Him busy Upstairs while I get on with having the time of my life. It's not hard, it's not even hard-boiled, a child could grasp this concept.

So why am I having to come here, *again*, going back on my word, which I don't like doing by the way, and going through this whole rigmarole again? Really, it has to stop now Sonny Jim, it's not going to do…"

It had taken The Devil an alarming amount of time to realise he was talking to himself. For someone who had an ego the size of half the known universe, he did have a tendency to ramble on. But even *he* was shocked when he noticed he was the only one in the office.

"Hello?" he asked, not sure what answer he was expecting back. "Is there anybody there? Hello? It's me, your mortal enemy, the one you spend your every waking moment trying to defend the Humans against. You know, the other one, the one with the pointy tail and pitchfork - not a good look by the way. Hello? Anybody?"

He stood still for a moment, looking around. The office was almost exactly the same as it had been the last time he was there. Humans, he thought, they loved their consistency.

"Hello?"

He sounded almost apologetic. The Devil didn't mind admitting that he was a little downtrodden that there was nobody there to greet him. He put his hands on his hips and looked about the place again. Sucking on his tongue, he blew a loud raspberry.

"Well this has put a bit of a fly in the ointment," he said loudly. "Here was me getting all geared up for a right good therapy session and there's no bugger here to listen to me. I bet He never has this problem. In fact, I *know* He never has this problem. Or should that be She, I can't remember now."

He sighed. Then he noticed the large crucifix on the wall. A wry smirk came over his face. He sauntered up to the ornament and puffed out his chest.

"I suppose you'll have to do," he said, licking his lips. "You're not quite the real thing, no flesh and blood and all that, but I made the effort, scrubbed up and combed my hair. I don't normally do that for nothing."

The Devil rocked on his heels. He took a deep breath of the stale, dusty air and got fully into ranting mode.

"Here's the rub," he began. "He's getting right up my goat, for want of a better expression. There I was, sitting, relaxing, having a lovely time on a beautiful, sun-kissed beach somewhere in the middle of nowhere, when I get a phone call. Oh, you should have seen that place, I mean, I know all about carnal inhibition and hedonism but this place was absolutely perfect, like something out of a dream. I don't often tip my hat to Him, but he really pulled out all the stops when he created that beach. Simply magnificent. Anyway, where was I, oh yes, the bloody phone goes and out pops a hotel hand, cowering, snivelling, not knowing what to do with himself. I know who it is already, who else would have the fifty-tonne brass bollocks to phone me, *me* of all people when I'm on holiday. That's a holiday that I *earned* by the way, earned more than ten times over."

He rounded and began pacing. Like a judge cross-examining a defenceless, whimpering witness, The Devil was in full flow.

"Which is another thing. I'm a person of great importance, VIP, access all areas. I'm not a bloomin' lackey to be called upon day and night to start running errands. Which is *exactly* what this phone call was. 'I've got another one for you' He has the audacity to say. Another one for you, as if I'm the police, the rozzers, the filth! Now don't get me wrong. I did a bang-up job with that murder. I mean, what else would you expect from me? I'm nothing if not a perfectionist and I knocked that one right out of the park - even though it was beneath me on so many levels.

"I get it, of course I get it! You have to jump through certain hoops to get what you want in this universe. Believe me, it's a ploy

I've used for eons now. But that doesn't mean I'm at His beck and call for any and every little thing, now does it? I mean, He's got people for that sort of thing. There are millions, tens of millions, quite literally, Upstairs *literally* begging for a chance to prove their worth to him. And that's before we get on to this lot down here. So why am I the patsy? Why am I suddenly the go-to guy for any and every piece of garbage that needs to be taken out, put in the bins and parked on the edge of the street ready for collection? It's toxic, a toxic way to treat people. Dignity... where's my... dignity..."

The Devil paused to catch his breath. He puckered his mouth. Suddenly he didn't feel so high and mighty. The more he'd spoken, the less it felt like a good idea to be venting. Therapy was all well and good if your heart and mind were open to hearing all the bad things about yourself. Standing, alone, in the office of The Pope, talking to a wooden crucifix wasn't exactly what he'd had in mind.

"Yes, well, not that I'd expect *you* to understand," he said indignantly. "What answer I was ever going to get out of you was probably going to be a load of old rubbish anyway. You always did have a tendency to go on a bit, didn't you old boy?"

He adjusted the cuffs of his shirt beneath the sleeves of his immaculately pressed suit. Fixing his tie, he ran his hands through his hair.

"You know something," he said. "I don't need this. I don't need any of this. I know who I am. And I don't need to be standing here, talking to some old relic, moaning about how I'm hard done by. That's what *they* do. Out there!"

He threw his hands towards the open window. Gritting his teeth, he snarled at the crucifix.

"And that's another thing!" he bellowed. "Where the hell are they anyway? I'm standing here talking to myself like some attention-starved imbecile while they're off out there, gallivanting, repopulating, breeding like animals. I mean, what could possibly be more important than…"

The Devil reached the window and stopped. Not many things in existence had the ability to take his breath away. What met him outside the window was as close as anything had ever come.

St Peter's Square, awash with colour, spread out before him. The tall, ancient obelisk known as The Witness stood high above a sea of people. Flags from a hundred countries hung perfectly still above the heads, camera flashes stopped in time, perpetually bright amongst the faces.

Row after row of old men in crimson and purple were seated close to the huge entrance of St Peter's Basilica. Flanked by the two huge statues of Paul and Peter, they had their heads bowed respectfully. At the centre of the mass gathering of humanity was a small, humble looking wooden box. The focus of all the attention, the penny dropped like a dead weight in the midst of The Devil's mind.

"Shit," he whispered, taking in the enormity of the funeral that was stuck in time, frozen, out in front of him.

He slowly edged back from the window. The swirling, black cloud that had marked his entrance appeared again, billowing up and around his ankles. He held up his hands, still staring out the open window.

"Maybe I'll come back later," he said. "I can see you're a bit busy with… well… you know."

The smoke engulfed him. It swirled and raged, scattering black ash and dirt all around the room. Then it vanished, leaving everything as still and silent as it had found it.

A few seconds passed before the old clock on the mantelpiece ticked back into life.

TWO

Contrary to popular belief, Hell's bells weren't constantly ringing. In fact, they were in a pretty poor state of decay. Housed in a decrepit, badly maintained tower right in the centre of Hell's busiest quadrant, the bells themselves were all cracked and broken. If anybody tried to ring them, they'd be sorely disappointed. Which in a way was perfectly apt.

The bells dated from a bygone era when The Devil had taken it upon himself to update his kingdom. Cities were all the rage amongst the humans, popping up anywhere and everywhere they had gathered for long enough. And thinking, of course, he could do it so much better, The Devil had sought about reorganising the whole of his landscape.

Gone was the fire and brimstone, in its place oceans of concrete. Tower blocks almost infinitely tall replaced the great lakes of lava, acid rain neatly replaced with jammed motorways and concourses. A monorail network had been installed at one point but The Devil had grown weary of its efficiency and effortless popularity. The souls of the damned were there to be punished, not to enjoy the novelty of getting back and forth from work on a nifty bit of Human engineering.

Hell's bells had been put in place as a sort of constant reminder. They were supposed to ring every six minutes, for exactly six

THE MAN IN THE DARK

times, each bong lasting six seconds. The Devil was, if nothing else, vain. He liked to remind himself of his own little quirks and elements of popularity.

The bells also served as an extra little punishment for those in the immediate vicinity - namely Department J. Home to Humanity's greatest, slimiest, sneakiest traitors. The offices, directly below the tower and surrounding the building, were reserved for a special breed of damned. The Devil took great delight in turning the screw on the unworthy at every chance he got.

It was only his laziness that had seen them let off with the bells falling into disrepair. Not that those snakes were complaining.

Centuries had come and gone in what felt like a Human heartbeat. But the principle of Hell's great architectural upheaval and renaissance had stayed exactly the same, despite the crumbling buildings. Be as inconvenient and space robbing as possible - so as to maximise misery.

Thick smog belched out of factories which were making nothing, clogging up the air. Tired, unreliable little cars peeped and puttered along the cramped, overcrowded streets. Like Jupiter's great raging spot of a storm, there was a perpetual traffic jam around the outskirts of the main city. The damned didn't know how they got there but they sure weren't getting out.

Meanwhile the skyscrapers and tower blocks were so scant that a good wind would blow them down. Thankfully there wasn't any wind in Hell.

Much like how crime and punishment in the Human realm had changed over the years, so too had it Downstairs. It had to; The Devil always made sure of that. In fact, that was one of the many, many reasons that separated him from Him. Embracing change, moving with the times, keeping a finger on the pulse of popular culture. It meant he was always evolving. And that meant the whole ship could run smoothly, keeping the Humans on their toes and, above all else, punished.

So why wasn't he feeling smug about himself? Why was he sitting in the back of his private limousine with nagging worry and doubt eating away at his insides?

Maybe he was just angry. After all this wasn't part of the deal. He wasn't supposed to be back at the office already. This was *his* time - a holiday, for the first time ever. He should have been stretched out, sipping something exotic on a beach in the middle of nowhere. Yet here he was.

Holiday woes aside, there was a big, divine-shaped elephant in the room. The biggest elephant in the biggest room ever. He had been in touch, had requested the pleasure of The Devil's company.

Before He had time to explain, the phone had ended up in the ocean. While it had gotten acquainted with some tropical fish and coral, he had made a hasty retreat to the Vatican, looking for some help. And the less said about that trip the better.

In times of crises, it was the expected norm to go with what one knows. For The Devil, that was procrastination. He was struck by a revelation.

What better way to procrastinate than to turn his wrath on his employees? More importantly, the employees he hated the most.

"Driver!" he shouted excitedly, pleased with his own reasoning.

The window between the back cabin and driver's seat dropped down. A toothy, multi-eyed creature with oozing boils and weeping sores looked around at his master. Its tentacles gripped the steering wheel and a makeshift chauffeur's uniform covered up its lumpy, out of shape body. Not everybody Downstairs had the pleasure of being Human once. And He hadn't gotten the design for them right from the off. The Devil had, of course, put all of the rejects to good use, with a few modifications here and there to make sure children were scared of the dark.

"Yessir," gargled the driver, saliva dripping from its fangs.

The Devil recoiled a little. Even he was affronted by this one.

"Department J," he said. "Sharpish."

"Yessir, right away sir," croaked the driver.

The Devil clicked his fingers and the screen went back up. He didn't have the stomach for that kind of thing just now. He made a mental note to hold back on the sores and boils in the future.

"Department J?" asked Alice.

The Devil had, for his shame, forgotten that his loyal secretary and heartbeat of Downstairs, was sitting beside him. She was sifting through an unimaginably high stack of papers and folders, scribbling signatures with well-rehearsed experience.

"I don't remember seeing that on the schedule."

"No," he said. "A slight detour."

Alice clicked the lid on her pen. She tipped the rim of her glasses down her nose and peered over them at her boss. The Devil felt a little quiver of excitement. He both liked and feared that look. Pain and pleasure all at once.

"Is there a reason for the detour sir?" she asked, her voice as smooth as molten lava.

The Devil cleared his throat. He should know better than to try and fool Alice. She was, after-all, the engine that kept this whole hellish afterlife running.

"No, no reason," he said. "I just thought I should drop into Department J, rally the troops, see how the infantry are doing. It's been a while, I'm sure they're missing me."

Alice smiled. It was that knowing smile The Devil adored. There wasn't very much that he didn't love about her. But the little things were what counted the most.

"I should probably say, for the record and all of that, you've been summoned Upstairs sir," said Alice. "Now you know as much as I do that you don't have to answer every beck and call He throws at you. In fact, I'd say you've been *more* than accommodating in recent history. I mean, if it's not too much of a liberty, you didn't even get to enjoy your holiday."

"Oh Alice," he sighed, feeling a little doe-eyed. "If only I were five thousand years younger or you were five thousand years older..."

She leaned in a little closer to him. He watched her, the cabin of his limousine, the buildings streaming past outside, even the whole of Downstairs dissolving away as he stared into her sharp, intelligent eyes.

"Ifs and buts sir," she said softly. "Ifs and buts."

Alice slowly pushed her glasses back up her nose and sat upright. She uncapped her pen with an expert flick of her blood-red nails and returned to her paperwork. Just like that, The Devil was back in reality. He blew out a puff of air and tried to remember who he was and what he was doing.

After a short lifetime of battling through the endless traffic, The Devil's limousine pulled up outside the main building of Department J. He stepped out and looked around the pavement. A few local denizens gasped, the sight of their overlord altogether too much for them. One woman screamed, half in awe, half in sheer terror. Thankfully there were some staff around to mop her up.

"Lovely," said The Devil, pressing on. "Nothing like meeting the people."

He gave a little wave to the other terrified pedestrians before turning back to the limousine. Alice lowered the back window.

"Better head back to headquarters Alice," he said. "I might take my time with this lot in here. No real rush to answer the big phone is there?"

"Absolutely not sir," she said. "Shall I prepare the latest report on HellCorp for you to look over when you get back?"

"If by that you mean you'll be doing all the work, then yes, of course."

"Do you expect anything less of me sir?" she said.

"Alice, I expect nothing but the highest level of professionalism from you. That and perhaps the occasional peck on the cheek."

"There's a difference between expectation and hope sir. I need not remind you of that."

The Devil realised he was stooping, bending over to get as close to his trusted secretary as possible. He corrected himself and smiled as Alice raised the window of the limo. He watched it drive up the pothole riddled road until it vanished in the miasma of an eternal traffic jam.

The Devil cleared his mind. He marched up to the doors of the big, official looking Department J. He strode confidently into the lobby and the place fell silent as his staff realised they were being paid a surprise visit. A very surprise visit - The Devil hadn't even thought about Department J for at least a century.

There were a few whispers from panicked faces as people scurried about in the shadows. Nobody wanted to greet The Devil first, nobody wanted to be that person. But somebody had to, he was growing impatient.

Just as he was about to start tapping his foot, a snivelling little man came hurrying forward. Tiny round glasses sat perched on top of a big, bulbous nose. He adjusted the high collar of his shirt, late Victorian by The Devil's estimations, and bowed.

"Good afternoon sir," he said, dandruff sprinkled hair making The Devil feel queasy. "We weren't expecting a visit from your good self at all."

"Less of the good," said The Devil. "And you are?"

"Colby," said the man. "Charles Hector Colby."

"New here Colby?"

"No sir… not at all. I arrived in your service in the year of our Lord 1888… that is to say, 1888 sir. I've been a proud member of Department J ever since."

"Proud?" asked The Devil.

"Oh yes sir, very proud, I take my role as a senior clerk very seriously sir. Very seriously."

"And Department J is your home because?"

Colby stood a little stiffer. He adjusted his glasses and fidgeted with his fingers. He was nervous, like most Department J employees. There was a reason they were there - treachery was a tricky animal to tame. The ones who were good at it had to be supremely confident. Those who weren't could only aspire to become senior clerks. Pecking orders, another of The Devil's inventions.

"There was… an unpleasantness with my employer sir," said Colby. "He was an industrialist, a good man, but he was… foolish with his assets. I simply felt that some of his competitors, rivals if you will, would be better served with information on his business and his customers."

The Devil smiled. He clapped Colby on the shoulder as he passed him.

"Well done Colby," he said. "Stand down. I'm here to see your bosses."

"Bosses sir?" Colby followed him as they crossed the lobby.

"Yes, bosses, where are they? I've got a bone to pick with them, about that lovely big bell tower that pokes up from the roof of this building."

"The bells?" asked Colby. "Forgive me sir but what about them?"

"They don't work Colby, they're not ringing. What's the point in having lovely big bells that hang there and don't ring? That's like composing a beautiful, delicate symphony inspired by the wonders of nature and Humanity - only to play it to the deaf."

"Again sir, forgive me. Campanology has never been my strongest suit."

The Devil sighed loudly. He spied a lift on the far side of the lobby and strode purposely towards it. Colby followed him at a safe, respectful distance of a half step, not too far to seem impolite but still far enough away to bolt should the chance present itself.

The clerk ferreted around for the elevator button while The Devil feigned impatience. He had all the time in existence, there was no rush. But he wouldn't let Colby know that. Twist the knife, turn the screw, make the little man sweat that bit more. Lovely stuff.

A pod arrived, its doors squeaking open. A pale-faced bellhop appeared, slovenly dressed and chewing gum. When he saw The Devil standing waiting for him, he swallowed the gum and almost fainted with fright.

"Department J is getting sloppy Colby, real sloppy," he said. "I'll be having strong words with your masters."

He stepped into the lift, Colby joining him. After a short but uncomfortable journey upwards, they stopped. The bellhop slid the rickety doors open and resumed his position cowering in the corner. Colby scurried out first, The Devil strutting as pompously as he could.

A large, decaying office opened up in front of them. Huge windows covered in cobwebs looked out over the city. Row after row of desks sat empty, papers and files scattered across their tops, long abandoned. The Devil ground his teeth. Inefficiency was one of his very worst pet hates. He hated it even more when it was happening on *his* time.

The faint sound of music broke the stillness of the huge, empty room. The Devil stepped out into the office and held up a finger.

"Do you hear that Colby?" he said.

The clerk was sweating profusely now. His face, rather than being white like that of most Humans around The Devil, was blotchy and red, like he was embarrassed.

"Is that music?" he asked. "Party music?"

"I… I'm not sure sir," said Colby, having the nerve to lie. "I… I really don't know."

"I think it is," said The Devil. "And it's coming from next door."

He hurried across the room, moving so quick that papers and files dropped off of the desks and scattered on the floor behind him. Colby tried his best to rearrange them but he was lost in a sea of paper.

The Devil marched up to the head of the room where two large doors stood waiting for him. On each was the Department J logo, carved into the oak with expert precision, craft and care. He pushed them open and a wave of heat and foul-smelling air washed over him.

He had been right. There was a party being held. And what a party.

The first thing he noticed was the nudity. A hundred people, maybe more, were all running around in various states of undress. Naked for the most part, they were drinking, dancing and other unmentionables. The room was a stark contrast to the office behind. Huge golden statues propped up the roof, fountains spewing water at all angles, beautiful frescoes defaced and covered in spray paint and graffiti adorning the walls and the ceiling.

Women tittered and men grunted. They all lounged around without a care in the world. And none of them, The Devil noted, looked like they were working.

Across the vast expanse of hedonistic abandon was what looked like a stage. Elevated from the rest of the place, the precipice was crowned with two chairs, almost throne like in their nature.

Two men slouched lazily on top of the pile, surveying everything. A harem of beautiful, scantily clad women and buff, broad-shouldered men flocked around them, feeding them grapes and pouring wine into goblets. They were both with the party and above it, literally.

Like everything else in the hot, sweaty room, the pair looked, acted and smelled Roman, a waft of superior arrogance pouring from the decadence. The Devil couldn't have asked for anything better really. He never, ever needed an excuse to get mad. When one presented itself though, he always took great delight.

His arrival was signalled by silence. The music stopped and everyone else along with it. Those in the closest vicinity cowered, realising that they were in big, big trouble. The Devil stifled a smile. The Human body could only react in so many ways to fear. Things shrivelled quickly when the lord of darkness was close at hand.

As he approached, the two men noticed him and Colby. They swallowed their wine and raised their hands in greeting.

"Ah! There he is!" said the first.

"Our great and good benefactor. Welcome sir!" added the other.

A path cleared in the ocean of naked flesh and drunken debauchery. The Devil stopped a few feet away from the elevated stage. The harem stopped their feeding and sat or stood to attention, the colour draining from their bronzed bodies. The two Romans remained uninterested, legs dangling over the arms of their makeshift thrones.

"Brutus, Cassius, I wish I could say it was good to see you both," said The Devil sternly. "But I assure you chaps this isn't a social call."

THE MAN IN THE DARK

THREE

The Romans looked at each other. Then they laughed, loudly, proudly, with perfect abandon. They clapped each other on the back, slapping their bare knees. Wiping away tears, they pointed and smiled at The Devil.

"Oh you," said Brutus. "You old trickster you. You had us going for a moment there."

"Yes, you did," wheezed Cassius. "You really did."

They continued to laugh. The Devil remained stoic. He'd set his face purposely neutral in the hope that not knowing how terrifyingly angry he was might put some fear and sense into the Romans. Everyone else in the flashy, glitzy party room seemed to have taken the hint. Colby was very slowly retreating from his side.

"Well gentlemen, I must say this is all a bit of a surprise," he said, stepping forward.

The harem flinched, recoiling a little. Brutus and Cassius weren't phased.

"Surprised sir?" asked Cassius, draining his glass. "What do you mean?"

"Here I am, making a little visit to one of Hell's most important, busiest, famous departments and all I find is a bunch of layabouts enjoying their own importance."

The Devil's voice was growing deeper. It was a neat little trick he'd learned from Him. It usually worked a treat. But not this time.

"I'm sorry," smirked Brutus. "Is there some dissatisfaction with our work sir?"

"Yes, is that the case sir?" Cassius said too. "Because we work very hard for you sir. In fact, we've been breaking our backs for you."

"Oh, don't you mean, stabbing our backs Cassius?" giggled Brutus.

"Oh yes," tittered his friend. "Stabbing our backs, that's a bit more like it, isn't it Brutus?"

The Romans erupted in another fit of hysteria. The Devil would have sworn they were drunk. Only that wasn't a thing Downstairs. One of the advantages of being damned for all eternity was the prospect of never being drunk. The Devil never, ever wanted Human senses to be dulled to just how miserable and awful their eternal damnation would be. Not even for a second.

Not that Brutus and Cassius were noticing that. The Devil almost thought they were enjoying themselves.

"Yes, very funny," he cleared his throat. "All joking aside gentlemen, I'm expecting an explanation, at the very least, as to why this place seems to be a bollock-hair away from falling apart? The bells aren't ringing, there seems to be no order or any work being done. And I'm stood downstairs waiting like a naughty schoolboy to be seen by the headmaster! Me! Come on, who's first, what excuses are on the table this time? Anything? Anyone?"

He pointed a finger at the nearest broad chested, semi-naked man. He shook his head, cowering a little behind his plate of grapes.

"What about you?" asked The Devil. "You, there, with the hair covering your boobs? Any idea what's going on here?"

THE MAN IN THE DARK

The woman shook her head too. Her eyes filled with tears, hands shaking uncontrollably. The Devil ground his teeth.

"Right, I see," he said. "It's like that, is it?"

Brutus and Cassius stopped laughing. They gave each other a sly look and pushed themselves up from their thrones. Wiping away crumbs and seeds, they fixed their togas, straightening their shoulders to stand with equal pomp to The Devil. They stepped down from their stage, a few naked bodies scuttling out of their way as they did so. They sidled up to The Devil, one on each side of him.

"I'm sorry sir, truly I am," said Brutus. "We both are, aren't we Cassius?"

"Yes sir, truly sorry."

"Sorry?" The Devil said. "You're *sorry*? That's it? That's the best you're going to come up with?"

"We're sorry sir," said Brutus again.

"Yes sir, absolutely sorry," said Cassius. "But you see, we thought we'd have a bit of a party. A celebration even."

The Devil smelled a rat. He was good at that, he had to be. And in this building it wasn't hard. Still, there was something particularly fishy about these two. They were, after all, two of Humanity's very worst examples.

"Party?" he said cautiously. "What do you mean party? This is Department J. Which reminds me. Where's your boss? Is he not even bothering to show up to work now? Or let me guess, he's at the bottom of an orgy pile, with a beer bong shoved down his throat and a penis drawn over his face."

The Romans darted each other a quick look across The Devil.

"He's indisposed at the moment," said Cassius sharply.

"Yes, indisposed," Brutus repeated. "He's having one of his turns unfortunately, an attack of conscience you see. And as you well know, that really doesn't play very well to the troops down here, does it sir?"

The Devil's patience was wearing thinner and thinner with every second he spent with the Romans. He'd never really liked them - or any Romans for that matter. Unfortunately, the truth was they were far too good at what they did.

Somehow, despite his best efforts, they'd muddied the waters on his existence. Filling Human heads with all kinds of daft imagery, the very notion there might be other deities was actually very clever. A little too clever for The Devil's liking. He'd taken great delight in bringing them down, piece by piece, brick by brick, until all that was left of their once endless empire was dust and tourist destinations.

"One of his turns?" he asked. "This is Department J - *his* department. It's not a bloody book club meeting, he can't just scurry off into a dark corner when he's got a bit of a headache. He has a job to do!"

"Yes, we thought so too, didn't we Cassius?"

"Absolutely Brutus, we did."

"But you know what he's like sir, you just can't trust him!" said the Roman. "But to answer your question about this place falling to the dogs a little. We might have let the old office go a bit astray, but it's all for good reason."

"A good reason, a great reason even," said Cassius.

"A good reason? Not to do work? Is that what you're saying to me?" asked The Devil. "You're telling me you have a good reason why one of my biggest departments is being turned into some nostalgic, retro holiday camp for you two?"

"Yes sir," Cassius continued.

"Absolutely," said Brutus.

The Devil took a long, controlled, angry breath. He hadn't been

THE MAN IN THE DARK

expecting this. He was at Department J to kick some backsides and push people about. He didn't think he'd actually have to do some work. That's not what procrastination is all about.

"Gentlemen, you have about three seconds to tell me what's going on here before I really lose my temper," he said. "And believe me, you don't want that to happen. Not today, not when I'm supposed to be on my holidays."

"We can sir," said Cassius. "We can even show you."

The Roman clapped his hands twice. There was a shuffle from a far corner of the room, the silent stillness broken. An elderly man, with a long, white, straggly beard that reached down to his saggy belly button pushed his way through the crowds. He stood to a hunched attention in front of The Devil, Cassius, Brutus and Colby.

"You've got to be kidding me," said The Devil. "This better be good."

"Oh it is," smiled Brutus,

"Come on then," said Cassius, addressing the naked old man like he was a dog. "Hand it over, there's a good boy."

"Hand it over?" asked The Devil. "Hand what over, he's completely naked. Unless he's hiding something in his beard then I don't want to…"

The Devil shook his head. The old man winced a little as he reached around and behind him. Producing a tightly bound scroll he handed it over to Cassius, bowed a little then returned to the corner of the party he'd first appeared from. The Devil looked on in disgust as Cassius unfurled the scroll.

"Safe keeping," winked Brutus.

"I'll bet," droned The Devil. "Like I said, this better be good."

"Better than good sir," said Cassius. "Amazing in fact."

"It's about your approval rating sir," said Brutus, throwing his arm around The Devil's shoulders.

"I beg your pardon?"

"Your approval ratings sir, the way *you're* perceived by the people of Hell," said Cassius.

"I know what approval ratings are Cassius! And I know that I don't need any rating to know I'm approved of."

"Ah, but you see sir, it's better than that!" said the Roman.

"Much better than that!" chimed Brutus. "Your approval is through the roof!"

Cassius turned the scroll around to show The Devil a graph. Even with his Human illiteracy The Devil could understand what was going on. A great big, red arrow was shooting straight upwards, off and out of the box it was supposed to be contained in. He looked at it while the Romans hovered about him.

"What is this?" he asked. "Where did these numbers come from?"

Cassius and Brutus smiled. They shrugged a little, feigning modesty.

"We did a little extra homework sir," said Brutus.

"Yes, a little bit of extra work to help you out sir," said Cassius. "We just thought you might like to know how well you're doing, you know, since you opened up HellCorp."

"HellCorp?" asked The Devil. "This approval rating is because of *HellCorp*?"

He snatched the scroll from Cassius. There were numbers and writing he didn't understand. He knew he should probably pay more attention to them. But with such a stark rise it was hard not to feel a little proud, his ego well and truly massaged by the graph.

"Not just HellCorp sir," Cassius also put his arm around The Devil's shoulder. "But the way you handled that trial. It was just, well how can I put this? Superb."

"Trial? What trial?" asked The Devil suspiciously.

"You know," said Brutus, raising his eyes to the graffiti covered ceiling. "Him, Her, whatever They are calling themselves now. The trial, your test, the murder. All of that sir, your people thought you did a wonderful job."

"Yes, wonderful is the word," said Cassius. "In fact, I'd say your decorum, dignity and sheer intelligence in having to deal with everything that was thrown at you was nothing short of astounding. Amazing."

He began to clap. Brutus joined with him, followed by Colby. Then the whole room erupted in one long, raucous applause. The Devil looked about, seeing the naked partygoers getting to their feet, smiling, cheering, lavishing him with praise and attention.

"You're an inspiration sir, truly you are," said Brutus over the din. "An absolute inspiration to all of us. You faced down every twist and turn that He threw at you, beat every cheat He could come up with. You won sir, a well-deserved victory, and one we just wanted to celebrate."

"This little shindig sir, it's a celebration of you!" shouted Cassius.

The Devil smiled. He turned around and around, looking at everybody in turn. It had felt like a long time since he had been exalted like this. He'd forgotten what it was like to be appreciated.

But something irked him. He knew what these two rats were capable of. That's why they were with him instead of Upstairs.

"And what do you two get out of all this?" he asked, still smiling at the adoring crowd. "You Romans never do anything that doesn't suit yourselves first and foremost. Tell me what you're up to."

"Absolutely nothing," said Brutus.

"Not a thing," said Cassius.

They guided The Devil towards the stage. They sat him down on one of the thrones, the harem flocking about him as the music started up again and the party resumed. The carnal hedonism didn't take long to get back into full flow and the guests were once again engaged in their sordid frolicking and explicit antics.

"Of course, it could always be better," said Cassius, leaning in closer to The Devil as he helped himself to a grape.

"There's always room for improvement sir," said Brutus, doing the same on the other side.

"What do you mean?" he asked.

The Romans eased themselves onto the armrests of the throne. They leaned around The Devil, perched on either side of him like a pair of Human wings.

"This is just the tip of the iceberg sir," said Brutus. "These numbers, they're only the start."

"Start of what?" he asked.

"Start of something very special," said Cassius. "Think about it sir, if we could be so pertinent to be casual for a moment."

"I'll allow it," said The Devil, scoffing another handful of grapes.

"The people love you, they *adore* you sir," said Cassius. "We all saw what happened with the Humans, how you handled Him and brought Him down a peg or two. We were all supporting you sir, we here at Department J, everyone Downstairs, we all rooted for you, wanted you to win."

"We did sir, really we did," said Brutus. "Your foresight, your acumen, even the way you dealt with that Human woman, what was she called?"

"Gideon," said The Devil.

"Yes, her. You were tested sir, put on trial, forced against your own free will to do His bidding and you came out of it better, stronger, more powerful than ever."

"This is true," said The Devil nodding. "This is very, very true. But not something I didn't already know."

"Of course not sir," said Cassius. "But we've been thinking, plotting if you will."

"I see," he said sceptically. "I recall the last time you two plotted. It didn't end very well for old Caesar."

"Ah, halcyon days," said Brutus fondly.

"We've been thinking sir, how wonderful it would be, how timely it would be, if you were to strike while the proverbial iron was hot."

"I don't understand," said The Devil. "Strike what?"

The Romans paused for a dramatic moment. Then they huddled in closer to him, almost whispering.

"Everything," they said together.

"Everything?" asked The Devil.

"Yes," said Brutus.

"Everything," said Cassius.

"Your people love you," he continued. "HellCorp is going from strength to strength sir, the Humans can't get *enough* of the place."

"It's true," said Cassius. "Recruitment has quadrupled since opening; they want more and more."

"Momentum is in your favour sir," said Brutus. "Throughout eternity there's never been a better time for *you* to be in charge. For *you* to dictate matters. For *you* to be calling the shots."

"It's all there sir, just waiting for you," said Cassius. "You're on the cusp of something wonderful here sir. All you have to do is take it."

The Devil's head was spinning. He hadn't thought about any of this before. And he didn't know why. As the orgy writhed and wriggled about in front of him, he began to feel his mind slowly whirring back up to speed.

The Romans were rats, he knew that. But they were also clever. And if there were any two lowlifes in Hell who could see an opportunity, it was them.

"And what do you two get out of this?" he asked, trying to inject some control back into the conversation. "I know you two. What do you get if I decide to launch into an insurrection that could tear the very fabric of reality apart at its seams. What's in it for you?"

Brutus and Cassius both clasped their hands. They smiled amicably and stared at The Devil.

"We are but loyal servants in your service," said Brutus.

"Knowing you were being rewarded for your hard work, toil and effort would be reward enough."

"Ha!" The Devil pushed himself free of them. "Don't make me laugh. Never cheat a cheater lads. You almost had me there."

He straightened his tartan tie and looked out across the party. Brutus and Cassius reappeared beside him, their chests pushed out, nostrils flaring, drinking in the mayhem and madness they had created.

"We merely thought we'd bring it to your attention sir, that was all," said Brutus.

"We know we have reputations as debauchers and traitors," said Cassius. "But we also know politics sir, we were masters of that when we walked among the living."

"Everyone has the seed of evil and wickedness in them sir."

"They long for it, obsess over it! And all it takes is a little nudge from us. From you."

"Just think," said Brutus wilfully. "Just think what you could do sir with a whole world of those people at your command."

"Yes sir, listen to Brutus," said Cassius. "Just think about that."

"All it would take is for you and HellCorp to bring it out in them. And what wonderful work you could do if you were given but half a chance."

"You have the backing, our backing, their backing, should you ever wish to act on this."

"And we would support you in any way we could."

The Devil surveyed the anarchy. This was what Brutus and Cassius did. Hedonistic abandon and treachery. He had to admit they were experts in both fields. If you ever wanted a party thrown and somebody stabbed in the back, they were the go-to guys.

Somehow they'd managed to plant something. They'd said the right things, coaxed him just the right way, appealed to his vanity and given him a little taste of something that was altogether irresistible.

Absolute power and control over existence. Could he really have it? Did he even want it? He didn't know. But where was the harm in asking?

"Okay," he said at length, as the party continued. "You've got my attention."

FOUR

The quiet of the abandoned office was a welcome change from the party. For one thing the lack of writhing, naked Human beings meant The Devil could clear his mind. If there was anything uglier in all of existence - he hadn't found it.

He stood at the panoramic windows, staring out through a clearing in the dust at the city beyond. This was *his* domain, *his* kingdom, a place he had presided over since the very beginning of what Humanity called time. He had worked hard, put a lot of love and devotion into creating the worst place imaginable for the most loathsome, hated people ever to be born. And he thought he'd done a pretty good job of it.

Now he was being tempted. It was nothing new for The Devil. Temptation was in his DNA - or it would have been if he had any. Offering that little bit more than you've already got, that tease of gaining, it was both brilliant and devastating in equal measure. That's why he loved it so. Of all the things he had invented across the millennia, temptation always ranked near the top of his list. It did the trick almost every time. What wasn't there to love about it?

And like all good inventions of his, it had been weaponized. Only this time he was the victim.

"Do you two know what natural order is?" he asked the room.

Brutus and Cassius were pacing about between the desks. Their

THE MAN IN THE DARK

hands were tucked behind their backs and they walked with the stately pomposity of career politicians.

"Natural order?" asked Cassius.

"We do not, no," said Brutus.

"Natural order, it does what it says," said The Devil, turning to them. "It's a theme, it's *the* theme, that runs through everything - and has done forever. A sort of safety net that keeps me and Him in a job. It's a handy little trick He employs to ensure the whole shooting match ticks over nicely. In short gentlemen, it keeps the good staying good and the bad... well, you know what happens to the bad."

The Romans stared blankly at him.

"What you're asking me to do is to upset the natural order," he continued. "You're asking me to go against millions of years of existence, of the status quo, of a system that's so fragile in its balance that all it takes to tip it either way is the breath of a new-born child. And believe me guys, that example is spot on."

Brutus and Cassius remained silent. The Devil waved them away.

"So I guess what I'm asking is... why?"

"Why?" asked Brutus.

"Yes, why?"

"Surely you understand why sir? Surely *you* of all people understand why this is the time to strike," said Cassius. "The approval ratings, the success of HellCorp, you're at the height of your powers sir. If not now, then *when*?"

"Never," said The Devil. "Maybe never is when. Maybe that's how it's supposed to be."

"We don't believe you," said Brutus, wagging his finger. "We *refuse* to believe you sir. The creature we saw staring Him down amongst the Humans, the person we aspire to be, he wouldn't say never. He wouldn't give up, resign himself to forever being in second place. We *know* you want more than that sir. And we think we know how to help you."

"You *think*," said The Devil, turning back to face the window. "There's a big difference in thinking and doing Brutus. I would have thought of all people *you* would have known that by now."

"What he's saying sir, if I could interject," said Cassius. "Is that you're on the crest of a wave at the moment. You could do anything you wanted and the people, *your* people, and the majority of the Humans, would back you to the hilt. Isn't that something that should be capitalised upon? Is that not something that you should *want* to explore? I mean, I know I would. But I'm a mere servant."

"Yes, yes, Cassius is right my lord," said Brutus. "If we mere mortals are excited and confident by your power, then what must you be thinking?"

"You two will never know what I think," he said, a sliver of sadness in his voice. "But that's not the point. You're asking me to wage war. *The* war, the biggest war that existence is ever likely to know. One doesn't just drop into the apocalypse because of a few good reviews."

Brutus and Cassius erupted into fits of laughter. The Devil wasn't quite sure what he'd said that was so funny. The pair of them wiped tears from their eyes and put their hands on their hips.

"Oh you," said Brutus. "You're such a joker."

"Apocalypse indeed, very good," said Cassius.

"I'm not kidding," said The Devil.

The Romans stopped their pacing. They walked over to be on either side of The Devil and they all looked out of the window.

"There are many ways to fight and win a war," said Brutus.

"It's not always done on a battlefield," said Cassius.

"Yes, I'm aware of that," said The Devil. "I do have some

    THE MAN IN THE DARK

experience when it comes to winning a fight. I got you two taken care of, remember?"

Neither of them answered that. Instead they pressed on, deliberately ignoring their own failures.

"We aren't proposing an all-out war with Him," said Cassius.

"No, no, that would be madness, strategic incompetence," said Brutus.

"Instead, we suggest something a little more subtle."

"Yes, tailormade, debonair, everything you've come to embody sir. Everything."

"Such as?" asked The Devil.

The Romans exchanged a look across him. He was starting to tire of that.

"Your momentum sir, your popularity, it could always be *more*," said Brutus.

"Yes, *more*," said Cassius. "You can never have enough when it comes to the backing of the public."

"That's why we suggest another show of strength."

"Show of strength?" The Devil sneered. "I'm not a bloody performing seal, I don't jump through hoops."

"Of course not sir," bleated Cassius.

"Definitely not sir, definitely not," pleaded Brutus. "Play along with Him, lure Him into a false sense of security, appease His good nature and willingness to trust almost anything and everything."

"Why?" asked The Devil. "What do I gain except giving Him a sense of satisfaction that'll last a million years? Do you know how utterly degrading it is to have Him know He's right? Of course you don't, you're down here for a reason."

Brutus and Cassius chuckled a little. The Devil growled. Just thinking about Him being on His moral high horse made his proverbial teeth itch.

"Your performance as a Human was astounding sir," said Cassius. "It redefined who you were to new audiences, new followers, it won over millions who, for want of a better expression, didn't know - didn't *care* you existed."

"It's the same with HellCorp," said Brutus. "Your work is reaching new heights we could all only have dreamed of. And it's all because you stood up to Him. Now imagine, for just a second," he paused. "If you did it *again*. You wouldn't just double your standing; you'd blow it out of the water."

He made an eruption with his hands. There was a glistening ambition in his eyes. It was a hunger, a Human hunger The Devil recognised as nothing more than total and complete obsession. He turned to Cassius.

"I take it you agree with him then?" said The Devil. "I take it you're on side with me going crawling back to Him and asking him for another challenge. That's what you're saying yeah?"

"Not begging or crawling sir," Cassius steepled his fingers. "Merely accepting anything that He may ask of you."

"And what if I'm to go back into Human form? What if I have to leave here again? You don't think people would get the wrong impression, think I was taking the piss a bit?"

"We would be here to steady the ship," said Cassius.

"Not just us of course," said Brutus quickly. "All of your department heads, your senior consorts and ministers. And Alice of course."

A tingle of excitement ran through The Devil just at the mention of her name. He did his best not to smile but he thought he might have failed.

"Oh yes, Alice of course," said Cassius. "What a wonderful woman, she did such a great job before. I'm sure her talents and her dedication will be put to good use for any absence."

THE MAN IN THE DARK

The Devil tapped his finger against the end of his nose. The swirling cloud of smog was growing thicker above the city. The lights of the cars in the eternal traffic jam snaked around the outskirts like two rivers of white and red. Down amongst the concrete he knew there were billions of people, all walking around going from one punishment to another, day in, day out, for all eternity. And he knew, somewhere high above them, HellCorp was pumping in fresh candidates as soon as they shuffled out of the mortal realm.

It was the perfect system, he had mastered everything he could. He didn't need statistics, numbers, graphs or pie charts to tell him that. And he certainly didn't need two Roman backstabbers whispering in his ear. The Devil knew just how good he was.

Could he really have more though? That was the question. Sure he'd thought about it a few times down the years. Who wouldn't? Yet every time he'd always just let his lethargy get the better of him. Why bother going to war when you could sit back and lap up the misery, destruction and chaos the Humans made for themselves anyway?

But he'd never been tested before, never put through the ringer the way He had put him last time. In fact He was still at it, calling him up while he was on holiday. A flash of anger came over The Devil as he remembered why he was back Downstairs in the first place. He was avoiding Him, going out of his way to make sure He didn't think he was at His beck and call, anytime, anywhere.

Like a petulant child, The Devil turned around quickly and stormed towards the lift. He managed to stop just short of stamping his foot.

"Sir?" asked Cassius.

"Where are you going sir?" asked Brutus.

"I'm going to see Him," The Devil called back over his shoulder.

The lift arrived, the bellhop still cowering in the corner. The Devil fumed as he stepped in. Brutus and Cassius hurried over towards him, their togas billowing in the dusty, stagnant air. They caught their breath at the entrance to the lift.

"What are you going to do?" asked Brutus.

"Are you going to accept His challenge?" asked Cassius hopefully.

"I'm going to tell Him I'll do whatever it is He wants me to!" snarled The Devil.

"And what would you like us to do?" asked Brutus.

The Devil mashed the bottom button on the lift control and squared his shoulders.

"Prepare for war," he said firmly.

The doors closed automatically and as they did so, The Devil caught sight of the two Romans smirking. The lift began to descend away from them. He was fuming, spurred on by his anger. He wanted to punch something. He thought about hitting the bellhop but it wasn't worth it. There was no use in wasting energy on somebody so lowly.

"Come on, come on," he said, watching the numbers tick down. "Can't this thing go any quicker?"

"I'm... I'm sorry sir," croaked the bellhop.

The Devil's head was thumping with pain. What was supposed to be a quick bullying session to people he didn't like had spiralled way out of control. He had only popped into Department J for a nice distraction. Now he was getting ready to start a full-scale coup.

He let out a long and frustrated breath of hot air. He unfastened his top button and loosened his tie. Staring down at his feet, he flexed his hands into little balls over and over again.

"Hold on," he said, looking up at the terrified bellhop. "Is it just

THE MAN IN THE DARK

me or are things getting a bit lighter in here?"

He looked around the cramped lift, the walls glowing a little. The light got stronger and stronger.

"I... I don't know sir," said the bellhop.

He tried pressing the buttons but nothing happened. Gradually the whole pod filled with a piercing, blinding white glow.

The Devil gritted his teeth.

"Great," he said. "Right on cue."

The lift reached the bottom floor. The doors clanked open to reveal the bellhop, his hair scorched a brilliant white. The Devil was nowhere to be seen.

FIVE

Much to his surprise, and relief, The Devil wasn't met with the blinding, piercing light that normally induced a migraine. Instead it was dark. Dead dark. Unsettlingly dark.

He stood for a moment, not sure what to do with himself. Was this right? He was going Upstairs wasn't he? He'd been summoned in the usual way - out of the blue and at the most inopportune time. If history had taught him anything, if it looked, smelled and tasted like dog food it was usually dog food.

Only this was out of the ordinary. He stood a little moment longer. Everything was black. And befitting Upstairs, there was an eternal permanence to just how black it was. He looked around, trying to find some semblance of what was going on.

"Hello?" he said. "Are You there? Is anybody there?"

The Devil smelled a rat. If anybody knew how to lay a trap, it was him. Only he had suspected better of Him and that lot Upstairs. While being left in the dark was nothing new, this was altogether a bit amateurish when it came to pranks.

"Alright," he said aloud. "Very funny. Ha bloody ha. You got me. What are we, pensioners trying to give each other a surprise party? Come on, let's be having you, I'm really not in the mood. The sort of day I've had already I'm about ready to throw myself under a bus. Only You and I both know that would be about as useful as a chocolate kettle. So come on, let's have it out."

Silence. Oppressing silence. The type of silence that made The Devil shiver.

"Enough's enough now," he said aloud, his voice sounding cramped and confined. "If you don't want me here then I'll happily go home. I've got a list of things the length of my arm that need done. And then there's the little matter of what You want me for. I'm afraid that's just going to have to wait. So… come on then. Stop the mucking around, jokes were never Your forte and this is about one of the worst."

He stepped forward but something, unseen in the darkness, stopped him. He rubbed his nose.

"Hold on," he said to himself. "That's not right."

The unmistakable sensation of pain spread out from the end of his nose to his cheeks. He rubbed his face but something wasn't right. It felt squidgy, soft and a little greasy.

His teeth clamped together, except they weren't *his* teeth. A boiling hot rage started to fill him, from the very tips of his toes right the way up his legs until it made his buttocks clench. This was all very odd, very real, very Human.

"No," he grumbled, his voice low and gravelly. "Please, please, please tell me You didn't. You *wouldn't* do this to me. Not even *You* would be so underhanded and cheap."

Prodding blindly, he could feel a hard surface just ahead. He clapped it with his palms until he came across what felt like a doorknob. Pressing it, a creak of hinges filled his head, although the sound was denser, more dulled than usual.

A crack of light appeared, about a foot taller than him. He pulled the handle, more and more light engulfing him. The smell of stale smoke and fish filled his nostrils, bringing a gulp of sick up his throat.

"No," he said again, as if by repeating his protest it would change things. "You've got to be kidding me. Really?"

He pulled the door open to reveal a dank hallway. A pale, sickly looking bulb made the whole place look like the inside of an empty jar of mustard. There were stains on the carpets, marks and thumbprints on the walls. A radiator was giving off a pulsing heat, making the whole place uncomfortably dry.

The Devil poked his head out the door. He looked around and growled.

"An airing cupboard, fantastic," he said. "You sure know how to treat a girl on a night out."

There was a thump from somewhere beyond the hall. The Devil looked about. The thump came again, this time harder, angrier. It echoed down the dank little hall and he realised it was coming from the front door.

Dark shapes moved about on the other side of the frosted glass window. The banging got louder, as did the voices. They were angry, very angry. He'd learned over the millennia to tell when somebody was angry and when they were ballistic. This was the latter.

"Hello!" he shouted back into the flat. "Is there anybody here? Hello! You know you should probably answer that door. Otherwise it's going to end up getting kicked in!"

The words weren't out of his mouth when the hinges gave way, tiny screws pinging off the walls like bullets. The wood buckled and splintered around the frame and the frosted glass window cracked as the door was booted open.

The Devil froze in the dingy hallway as a dozen armour-clad, screaming riot police officers charged in all at once. They came storming towards him, shields raised and batons ready and waiting to do a bit of damage.

 THE MAN IN THE DARK

"Oh come on-"

They hammered into him hard. He didn't put up a fight - what was the use? He slammed hard onto the floor with a meaty thud, the cops piling on top of him one after the other. The whole world went black as he squirmed beneath the mass of Humanity. Then the crushing weight started to painfully choke the air from his lungs.

Lungs - he just realised. Human lungs. Human eyes, legs, hands and feet. Human dulled senses and Human slowness and reflexes. Human.

"Human!" he shouted, getting a mouth full of Kevlar vest. "Bloody Human again!"

"Shut up!" barked a voice close to his ear.

"Keep your trap shut creep!" said another somewhere near his navel.

"Belt him one!" shouted another, this time in the region of his right armpit.

"I'd rather you didn't, if you don't mind," he shouted back. "While I'm sure being at the bottom of a big pile of bruising police officers is some of you people's wet dream, pardon the expression but it's my form of Hell."

Then nobody said anything. Through the blanket of bodies The Devil could hear doors opening then angrily being slammed shut. Glass broke and heavy thuds came from all about the flat as it was, he assumed, turned over. Footsteps tapped and shuffled around him, more angry voices shouting instructions and complaints. What had he been dropped into?

The shouting stopped abruptly and with it the clatter of the search. There was a short pause before a single pair of feet echoed from somewhere below him. They came to a halt close to where he was pinned down.

"Well?" came a woman's voice, English, London somewhere.

"It's not a pretty sight ma'am," replied a man. "But we've got him."

"Him?" asked the woman again. "You've got *him*?"

"Well," said the man, sounding a little unsure. "We have someone."

"Better than nobody I suppose. What do you mean not a pretty sight? I'm looking for a kidnapper, not a shag Cohannon."

There were a few titters of laughter, some from around The Devil. He rolled his eyes in the darkness.

"Yes ma'am, of course," said Cohannon. "You want to… you know… see him Detective Sergeant?"

"That would be delightful," she said sarcastically. "Come on then lads, on your feet."

There was another grunt of an order and the bodies began to peel themselves off The Devil. One by one the light appeared around him and he winced as he was pulled to his feet. When the dizziness stopped he saw a short woman standing in front of him, her round little eyes staring intently at his face.

Her hair was neatly cut around her ears, making her ruddy round face look like a ball. She wore a washed-out look of scepticism - a policewoman, he thought. She was the only one not in uniform - the Detective Sergeant then, if The Devil could remember his ranks. Beside her was a tall, gangly riot cop, the chin strap of his helmet bobbing off his Adam's apple. Cohannon, he assumed. They both stared at him expectantly, waiting to see what he said.

"See," said Cohannon. "I told you it wasn't pretty."

"No," said the DS. "Although it's nothing I haven't seen before unfortunately."

"Eh…" The Devil interrupted her. "I can assure you madam

that you have most certainly *never* seen anything even close to me before. For you see I am…"

He looked down at himself and stopped. The realisation that he was naked hit him like the gong of his beloved Hell's bells. Not only that but the body he'd been shoved into was hardly a prime specimen. Blotchy, pale skin, a bit of a paunch and a dirty blonde coating of hair made for a rather unimpressive spectacle.

"Oh," he said. "Right, yes, average I assume. At best maybe?"

"Bang average," said the DS, walking up to him.

She had to crane her neck to catch his eyeline. He refrained from meeting hers, seething silently at being handed yet *another* lemon of a body.

"So," she said sharply. "You want to tell me what this is all about then?"

The Devil looked about the flat. Riot cops stood in every doorway, uniformed officers on guard at the broken-down entrance. He peered into the rooms and saw the place was a tip - open cupboards, upturned tables, the TV in pieces on the floor. He looked for some inspiration from the cops slapping handcuffs on his wrists as he thought of something smart to say.

"Kidnapping," he said, suddenly remembering what he'd heard. "Have I been kidnapped? Is that it?"

The DS puckered her mouth enough that it looked like the knot of a balloon. She put her hands on her round hips and shook her head.

"No," she said angrily. "That's not it sunshine."

"Okay," said The Devil sarcastically. "How many guesses do I have to get it right?"

A nervous tension went around the big, burly riot cops when they heard his flippancy. He felt their grip on his arms tighten just a little bit. What did they know that he didn't?

"None," said the DS. "And you've already had your chance to come out with it."

"Ah right, I see," The Devil nodded. "Well I suppose you'll just have to fit me up then. That's how these things go isn't it? Did You hear that?"

He shouted up at the ceiling.

"That's how these things usually go yeah?" No answer. "Yeah."

The DS smiled, looking like she'd just been given the best news possible. She nodded and rubbed her hands excitedly.

"You bet sunshine," she said. "You bet. I'm Detective Sergeant Laurie. And you're nicked."

SIX

A cramped space, caged walls all around him and an overbearing sense of oppression. This should have been The Devil's dream. Or at the very least a retirement home. So why did he feel so out of sorts, so unhinged?

He knew exactly why. He was stuck in another Human body, festering away while it decomposed all around him. He felt like his head was stuffed with thick, itchy wool. Every sense was dulled, every sensation that little bit fuzzy. The eyes didn't work properly, distance infuriatingly blurry. And the taste in his mouth was wretched, all tinny and bitter. He tried to cough it up but there was nothing. Only the boring pain in his ribs when it got too much.

The two police officers in the front cabin of the van didn't seem to care. Why would they? He was just another criminal to them. Probably not even that - the nudity marking him out as a crazy.

And that was another thing that made him fume. The Devil knew that He knew only too well Humans had a big thing against nakedness. They were so against it they had even made a cottage industry for themselves in trying to cover everything that drooped, sagged, dangled and wafted up.

"A cheap shot," he mumbled to himself.

"Eh?" asked one of the cops, turning awkwardly and staring at him through the lattice of the cage. "You say something?"

"I said it was a cheap shot," The Devil said. "Dropping me in there like that with no clothes on. Totally unnecessary."

The policeman had big, white eyes staring out from a young, dark face. He was new, The Devil could tell. There was that moment's hesitation where he'd let fear and curiosity get the better of him, stopping him from saying anything. Then the training kicked in and he blinked.

"Keep it down back there," he said boringly, turning back to his colleague.

"Right," said The Devil.

He groaned and looked down at his feet. He knew the cold metal of the police van's floor should be making him shiver. But the sensory system of this Human body was so shot he felt next to nothing. He wriggled his big, meaty toes around, hoping to spark them into life. Nothing.

Mercifully the police had insisted on making him put some clothes on - a pair of ill-fitting jogging trousers and an itchy jumper. He shuddered at the thought of what he looked like to the wider world. If they only knew who walked amongst them... again.

"Oi, oi, what's all this about then?" asked the young cop.

"Oh shit," said his companion, driving the van.

The vehicle came to a sudden stop. There was a growing sound from outside. The Devil had been around enough angry crowds to know when there was unrest. He leaned forward and stared out from his cage in the back of the van.

The road outside was filled with people. They weren't ordinary people, The Devil could tell that much. Sweaty, slightly overweight, they had the air of journalists about them. The cameras and video recorders slung about their necks and shoulders were also a bit of a giveaway.

THE MAN IN THE DARK

A barrage of flashes erupted when they spotted the van. Like a huge wave crashing against the beach, they swarmed towards them. Scuttling about, it wasn't long before the whole van was swamped by the media.

"Shit!" shouted the young cop. "Get moving Wilson, put your foot down!"

"I can't run them over!" cried Wilson. "The Super would have my arse!"

"We can't let them get a picture. Get a move on!"

He reached over and slammed his hand into the horn. The cop car gave out a bit of a damp wail. Unsurprisingly none of the baying journalists and photographers moved.

"Just go!"

"I can't!" Wilson shouted. "What if I run over one of them?"

"They shouldn't be here in the first place!"

"It's a public highway."

"But we're the police!"

The arguing went back and forth. The Devil could hear the voices outside the walls of his pen. There was thumping now on the sides, at the back door. He could see the shapes moving around beyond the blacked out back windows. Flashes went off with the cameras, everybody trying to get a shot of him.

"Excuse me," he said, rattling the cage.

The two cops looked about at him, their faces blank.

"You want to tell me what's going on out there?" he said. "Because I'm pretty sure they don't know I'm here. That is, this is a bit of an undercover visit, nothing personal mind. I just don't think the Human press would be clever enough to have cottoned on to the fact I'm back amongst you all."

The policemen looked at each other. There was a long, silent moment between them before they turned back to the task at hand. Revving the engine, Wilson decided he'd had enough.

"Right," he said. "We're off."

He nudged the van forward. Three photographers shuffled back before banging their hands on the bonnet, a torrent of abuse launched at the policemen. Despite their protest, Wilson's subtle signal seemed to do the trick. The van picked up momentum and a path began to clear.

"There!" shouted Wilson. "Down there, the underground car park."

"Thank God," said his companion, wiping sweat from his forehead.

The van pulled off the street, swallowed by a big, red sandstone building that yawned like an ancient monster. Security waved them in and the distant din of the pack faded. Wilson parked the van and opened the back doors, The Devil stepping out, his wrists in cuffs.

"Nothing?" he asked the two cops. "I'm getting no explanation what that was about then?"

"Mate, you'll be lucky if you get a phone call to your lawyer at this rate," said the black officer, pushing him around the van.

A small army of uniformed cops were waiting for The Devil there. They climbed out of their squad cars, puffed out their chests and in general tried to look intimidating. They lined a path that led into the station from the underground car park. He was beginning to suspect he was something of a big deal.

"A welcome party then," he said. "I've had worse."

He was led through the station. Everybody seemed to stop when they saw him. Police were posted at every door he passed, the whole station coming to a standstill as he was directed, shoved and nudged in the right direction. The journey into the bowels of the building came to a stop at a drab little interview room. Laurie was waiting for him there.

"Sit down," she said.

The Devil spied two seats on either side of a table. In the middle was what he assumed was a recording device. Along the far wall was a mirror. He knew there would be an audience behind it. One plastic cup filled with coffee steamed on the table. He sat down and reached for it.

"What do you think you're doing?" asked Laurie, closing the door behind her, two cops on guard outside. "That's mine."

"I have a dreadful taste in my mouth," he said, nursing the cup. "It's like I've had mercury poured down my throat."

"I don't care what you've been putting down your throat," she said angrily. "That's mine!"

She snatched the cup away from him, spilling some on her hand. It was boiling hot, scalding, but she didn't flinch. She wiped her skin, a red blotch left behind, and sat down. She pressed a button on the device and leaned forward.

"Interview number one, Tuesday July fifth, Detective Sergeant Laurie in charge," she said. "So, what do you know of Medina Cade's disappearance?"

The Devil sat still for a moment. Laurie stared at him, her little dark eyes an image of total concentration. He looked over his shoulders to make sure he was the only other person in the room.

"Are you talking to me?" he asked sincerely.

"Who else would I be talking to?" she asked.

"Oh right, sorry," he said, sitting up. "What was the question?"

"Medina Cade," she said. "What do you know about her disappearance?"

"Who or what is Medina Cade?" he asked.

Laurie's nostrils flared, doubling in size.

"Come on sunshine, I don't have time for this," she said. "I've got a husband with a bad back and a seven-year-old who wants her tea. Let's not mess around here. You tell me what you know and we can crack on. Sound good?"

"Crack on?" he asked. "Crack on with what?"

"Medina Cade," said Laurie. "What do you know about her disappearance?"

"You're a police officer, right?" The Devil asked.

Laurie faltered for a brief second. The Devil cocked his new eyebrow.

"You're a copper, a Rozzer, one of the Old Bill, as you lot seem to say," he pressed.

"Yes," she said firmly. "Of course I am."

"Right, good, I'm glad we've established that. Tell me then, Detective Sergeant Laurie, why does an officer of Her Maj's constabulary persist in asking questions that she's already been told the answer to?"

"I've been given *an* answer," she said.

"It's *the* answer."

"And how do I know that?"

"Because I've just told you."

Laurie's face suddenly lit up. Her eyes widened and the washed-out defeat was chased away. She leaned back in her chair, the plastic creaking, and held her hands up to the ceiling.

"Right!" she said, getting up. "Brilliant, fantastic. That's the best bit of news I've had in a fortnight. Maybe even longer. Terrific."

She marched over to the door and opened it. The two cops outside looked over their shoulders at her and grunted. The Devil was a little more suspicious.

"Come on then," she said. "Up, on your feet. Let's be having you, as my ancestors used to say."

The Devil hesitated. He could smell something fishy. And it wasn't just the questionable hygiene of his clothes.

                    THE MAN IN THE DARK

"This is a trick," he said. "What are you up to Laurie?"

"Nothing," she shrugged. "Absolutely nothing at all. You said you didn't know what I was talking about. You said you don't know who Medina Cade is. You said you don't know anything about her kidnapping."

"Yes," he said.

"Well then you better go," she nodded out the door.

"Just like that?"

"Just like that," she smiled. "After all, I'm a policewoman, a member of Her Maj's constabulary, as you so rightly put it. I should know that when a punter is found at a suspected crime scene, doesn't resist arrest and then lies through his teeth about any involvement that he's clearly innocent. Yes?"

She slammed the door as hard as she could. The bang was so loud it cleared some of the fuzziness from The Devil's new ears.

Laurie angrily stomped back to the table. She sat down with a thud and wagged a finger at him angrily.

"Don't jerk me around sunshine," she said firmly. "I've got more senior officers coming down on me than I've had hot dinners in the past two weeks. You're caught bang-to-rights here son and if you don't start talking then there's going to be trouble."

"Trouble?" The Devil asked. "What more kind of trouble could there possibly be?"

"I've got a computer that's aching at the seams out there with unsolved crimes. If you don't start helping me then you'll find yourself banged up in the Tower of London forever with a charge sheet as long as your arm."

The Devil yawned lazily. Laurie slammed her fists down onto the table hard. She leaned forward a little, her face a little more crimson than before.

"Hey! I'm talking to you! Do you hear me!"

"Yes, I can hear you," he said. "But you'll have to forgive me, I'm not paying attention. I don't have time for empty threats."

"Empty?" she squealed. "What's so empty about what I've just said?"

"Well, for starters, you can't just fit somebody up with crimes they have no connection to," he droned. "Even with my petty understanding of how you Humans work I know that won't fly."

"You Humans?" she pounced. "What do you mean by that?"

"Laurie, even in my distressed, post temporal hangover I'm still the smartest person you're ever likely to meet."

"Really?" she said sarcastically. "And how did you figure that one out?"

"It's hardly difficult is it?" he gloated. "Your clothes, the technology, that lovely cramped cage your pals put me in earlier, it all smacks very much of the twenty-first century. Even this strange less than passive aggressive feigned masculinity you seem to insist upon, it's all a bit dated. Hardly a vintage era for Humanity but then again, when was?"

He laughed smugly. Laurie remained firm.

"Okay," she said. "Are you saying there's a chance this isn't the twenty-first century?"

"Of course there's a chance," said The Devil. "Admittedly you're not seeing me in my best light, although that best light is worryingly sporadic and lacklustre these days. But I would have thought a professional policewoman, a detective no less, would have been able to work out who or what I am by now."

He levelled a straight, plain look at her. Laurie stared back, her expression shifting from one of anger to a more placid intrigue. She didn't answer him. Instead she sipped at the coffee and then remained silent. When nothing was forthcoming, The Devil decided to offer her an olive branch.

"Look," he said, leaning in conspiratorially. "I'll be on the level with you Laurie. This is all a bit of a sham."

"A sham?" she said, never taking her eyes from him. "It's a sham?"

"Yeah, it is," he said. "Whatever is going on here, whatever I've been dropped right into the middle of, it's all part of His big plan."

"His plan? And who's that exactly?"

"You know, Him. The Big Man Upstairs, The Boss, Numero Uno."

"You mean…"

She raised her eyebrows followed by her eyes. Then her face looked back up to the ceiling and its damp, nicotine-stained tiles. She turned back to The Devil and he smiled.

"Yeah, Him," he continued. "See we've got a bit of a thing going on at the moment. He goads me, I try and outdo Him, it's all a bit of fun until one of us drops the ball. You know that HellCorp company that's opened up?"

"In Edinburgh?" she asked. "The one with all those daft adverts, dancing cat videos and annoying pop-ups on the internet?"

"Sounds about right yeah," he smirked. "That's what I got so I could go on holiday you see. But Him being Him didn't think it was enough that I jumped through His hoops once before. So here I am, doing it all over again. It's good for morale Downstairs though, I have *that* on good authority."

"And who's authority would that be?"

"Cassius and Brutus," he said. "Department J, good men, clever, just the type of chaps you want working for you. Throw one hell of a party too it has to be said."

"I see," said the policewoman.

"So what we have here is fairly simple," he said. "You fill me in on what this Medina Cade situation is and I'll get to work on sorting it out. Sound good?"

He leaned back and she did the same. She thought about it for a moment before draining her coffee.

"Okay, let me see if I've got this right," she said, drumming her fingers on the table. "You want me to hand over all the information on an active criminal investigation. Hand over leads, details, back history, checks, calls, interviews all that stuff to you - somebody who's been detained as part of that probe?"

"Yes."

"And you're going to solve the case yeah? Did I hear that part right?" she asked.

"That's right."

"And this is all because He," she pointed upwards. "He gets you to do all this so you can own and operate a multi-national company. Am I in the right ball-park?"

"It's not so I can run HellCorp, it's so I can go on holiday," he sucked his tongue. "Keep up Laurie."

"Ah, I see. Sorry."

She put her hands behind her head and rocked on her chair. Puffing out her ruddy cheeks, she looked across at The Devil and shook her head.

"Well, it's original, I'll give you that," she said. "I can honestly say in all my time as a policewoman I've never been propositioned quite like that before."

"No," said The Devil, sneering at her. "I wouldn't have thought you get much propositioning Laurie."

"Thanks," she seethed.

"So we have a deal?" he asked.

As Laurie was about to answer him, the door opened. In walked a tall, broad shouldered man wearing a long raincoat, cheap suit and a look of permanent anger. Sweat had beaded on his flat forehead, two vulture-like eyes poking out from underneath its ridge.

THE MAN IN THE DARK

When Laurie saw who it was, she stopped rocking on her chair. The man took one look at her and then over to The Devil.

"This him?" he snarled.

"Yeah, it's him Lister," she said. "But this is my collar. I'm doing the interview and-"

"Save it Laurie," he said. "Why don't you stop fannying around and go make me a cup of tea or something. Be useful for the first time in your life, eh?"

The Devil looked back and forth between Laurie and Lister. Neither cop was happy, neither looked like they were backing down. And he was in the middle.

"Alright then," he said, clasping his hands. "Any chance of something to drink?

SEVEN

"Who the hell do you think you are?" Laurie shouted.

"Watch it Laurie," said Lister. "I'm your superior now. You don't talk to me like that."

"I'll talk to you however I choose!" she screamed. "Who do you think you are barging in here when I'm interviewing a suspect. You didn't even knock!"

"I don't have to knock Laurie. I'm a Detective Chief Inspector. DCIs don't need to knock!"

He smirked at her to reveal a row of yellowed, uncared for teeth. The Devil felt his Human stomach turning over. Whoever this DCI Lister was, he clearly thought he was in charge. Although he suspected Laurie had other ideas.

"You… you can't just…" she held her forehead, walking around the room in a trance.

Lister watched her then looked at The Devil. He eyed him up and down, snorting to himself.

"What have you got from him then?" asked the DCI. "Nothing I assume?"

"Don't be so bloody patronising," sneered Laurie. "This is my collar, my investigation."

"And you're *my* officer," spat Lister. "Sergeant."

The word hung in the stale air of the interview room. The Devil could see Laurie wincing a little. She seemed to take umbrage at her title, like it was a burden rather than a compliment. Lister was all powerful, a little man in charge of his own little kingdom. The Devil had seen a billion of those men pass through time. They rarely made a difference and all ended up in the same place in the end.

"Well?" asked Lister. "Has he said anything?"

"Why don't you ask him. Sir," said Laurie. "If you don't think I'm doing a good enough job then please, feel free to show me the error of my ways."

"I'm warning you Laurie!"

Lister's eyes bulged from his dark face. He pointed across the little interview room, his arm long and menacing like a cannon. She stood up to him though, The Devil liked that. Laurie appeared to be of some substance, he thought. If she was intimidated, she was hiding it well.

"I've been following procedure sir, as I *always* do," she said. "The interview has been recorded, everything the suspect has said will be on file. Like I said, if you want to show me how best to improve my interrogation skills, I am, of course, more than happy to learn from my senior and get better. As it says on all those colourful posters in the canteen, we're here to learn."

Lister choked down something unpleasant. He flexed his big, calloused hands and grunted. Turning his attention to The Devil, he shoved the free chair out of the way, leaning down on him like a prowling lion.

"What were you doing in that flat?" he barked. "Where's Medina Cade?"

"As I explained to your colleague DS Laurie."

"She's not my colleague," Lister said angrily. "She's my inferior."

He took the time to turn and face Laurie when he said that.

She stood in the corner of the interview room, arms folded, lips puckered, anger bubbling up inside of her.

"You talk to me now, understand?" said Lister.

"I understand," said The Devil. "But I don't repeat myself. I don't have to. Never have."

"What do you mean you don't repeat yourself?" asked Lister angrily. "Do you know who you're talking to son? I'm the law here, I'm the law in London, you'll answer me if I ask you a question. And you'll do it sharpish."

The Devil leaned to the side so he could see Laurie. Cocking his eyebrow, he called over to her.

"Is he always like this?" he asked.

A little smirk crept into Laurie's mouth. She bowed her head, shaking it away.

"Hey!"

Lister banged his hands down on the desk. The Devil sat upright. The DCI wasn't happy, a large vein pulsing in his gnarled, wrinkled forehead.

"Are you listening to me?" he said, leaning in closer. "You're looking at very, very serious charges here son. And I want answers. I'm not a patient man, I don't hang around like a fart in the wind waiting on namby pamby welfare reports and slimy lawyers to come in here and get snowflakes like you off the hook. I get results."

"I'm sure you do," said The Devil. "But I can assure you, you won't get them this time. This is altogether bigger and better than your pay grade Detective Chief Inspector."

"Is that so?"

Lister stood back up. He pushed his raincoat past his hips, his pot belly stretching his trousers and belt to their very limit. He poked his tongue into his cheek, staring down at The Devil.

"Sir," said Laurie. "I should tell you that I think you might want

 THE MAN IN THE DARK

to get psych down here."

"Psych?" Lister grunted. "Why would I want those university toss-pots in to tell this twat that there's something wrong with him when he's perfectly fine."

"That might be the case sir, but you still need them down here," Laurie insisted.

"I can assure you both that my mental health is in tip top condition," said The Devil. "But time is pressing on and I really need to get to work."

Laurie stepped out from the corner and stopped at Lister's side. She seemed to take extra care with her next words, thinking them over while the DCI stood fuming.

"He's been talking sir, saying some things that are, well, less than usual," she said. "I think before we do anything else we should at least let the doctors take a look at him."

"What's he been saying?" asked Lister.

The two police officers stood watching The Devil like he was an exhibit in a museum. It made him a little angry.

"I can hear you both you know," he said. "I might not be used to these Human ears yet and the fact they make everything sound as though I'm being waterboarded. But I can understand everything you're saying. You're five feet away from me."

"Yeah," said Laurie. "Stuff like that. And more to boot."

"More?" Lister was pretending he wasn't confused. "What kind of more?"

"Oh, I don't know, just stuff about being on a mission from God. Being sent here to solve the kidnapping case."

"Those are all true," said The Devil. "And while you two are bickering I'm wasting valuable time. Can we get a move on at all? Do whatever it is you two have to do outside while I slip into something a bit less fishy perhaps?"

Lister's top lip trembled. He developed a sort of twitch in his right eye before stepping over to the recording device on the table. He pressed the off button, ending the session. Without saying a word he rounded the table, passed Laurie and back towards the door.

"Stand down lads," he said to the two cops standing guard outside. "Get yourselves a pint of something, make yourselves scarce for fifteen, alright?"

The Devil could see the two officers outside. They looked at each other nervously and then back to Lister.

"Shift it!" the DCI bellowed.

The cops didn't need to be told twice. They scampered away from the door while Lister closed it over.

"Sir?" asked Laurie, trepidation in her voice. "I hope you're not thinking about doing anything that would get you into trouble?"

"Are you still here Laurie?" asked Lister sarcastically. "I thought there'd be some newly-widowed wifey somewhere who needs a pat on the back and a paracetamol."

"I'm serious Lister," she said.

"DCI Lister to you Laurie!" he shouted. "Last chance to take a long walk."

He moved over to the mirror and tapped it twice. Waiting for a moment, he took off his raincoat and suit jacket, throwing them on the floor. He rolled up his sleeves, eyes locked on The Devil.

"Do you know what those docs would say when they come down here?" he asked, cracking his knuckles. "They'd say that this pot-bellied streak of piss is delusional or some other piece of shit explanation as to why he's not playing ball. And you know as much as I do Laurie, that kind of snowflake diagnosis is enough to get scum off with just about everything these days."

Lister walked around behind The Devil, a sick smile on his face.

Laurie watched on, the colour drained from her ruddy cheeks.

"Sir, you can't seriously be thinking about-"

Lister pounced, a thick forearm under The Devil's chin. The DCI hauled him upwards with a savage, hard power. He pulled him free from the chair and slammed him onto the floor hard.

The Devil wasn't expecting that, he had been caught short. Before he could readjust the atoms whizzing around his Human brain he felt a heavy boot smash into his side. He was winded, rolling over, gasping for breath.

"Lister!" Laurie shouted. "You can't do this!"

"Shut up!" Lister shouted. "You're as much part of the problem Laurie. You're too soft with these bastards. Do I need to remind you that we've got a missing woman somewhere out there. A bunch of bastards have a woman, a *British* woman and this little knobhead could know where she is. And you want psych to come down here and give him an excuse to walk free!"

He punctuated his rant with another two kicks to The Devil's midsection. The policeman took a step back, catching his breath.

"Where is she?" he asked. "Where's Medina Cade?"

"I don't know..." panted The Devil. "But... I intend to find out..."

"Where is she!" Lister shouted.

The cop pulled The Devil up and gave him a slap across the face. Then he gave him another. The Devil smiled, his lip cracked and a thin trail of blood ran down his chin.

"Where is she?" Lister shouted. "Where is the Cade woman? What have you and your terrorist bastard pals done with her?"

"Lister!"

Laurie had seen enough. She ran around the table and tried to prize The Devil from the big paws of her DCI. The policeman shoved her away and shook The Devil violently.

"If you don't start talking quickly son it's only going to get worse," he threatened. "And I mean a lot worse!"

"Lister you can't do this!" Laurie shouted. "You can't manhandle suspects like this, don't you see? You're making it so he walks, police brutality, we won't get anything on him now you idiot!"

"If you don't like it Laurie you can fuck off!"

"I'm having no part in this!" she spat back and headed for the door.

"Stop right there!" Lister demanded. "You walk out that door love and I'll make sure you've got as much blood on your hands as I do."

He looked at his fists, The Devil's jumper bunched up in balls inside them. When he saw there was literally blood on them he dropped him and wiped them on his trousers.

Laurie had stopped just shy of the door. She let out a frustrated sigh.

"You're a bastard Lister," she said. "I don't care what you do to me for calling you that. It's pricks like you that give us coppers a bad name."

"Put a lid on it Laurie," he waved her off. "I don't need your Germaine Greer proto-feminist crap right now. I've got a missing woman, a ransom note from a terror cell and a suspect who's laughing at us. You can burn your bra on your own time, I'm trying to catch criminals before those Eton twats from MI5 show up."

"Well at least you've got Mrs Cade's interests at heart," said Laurie sarcastically. "I wouldn't want her distraught husband thinking you were just trying to find her to further your own career. Sir."

Lister flashed his stubby little teeth at her. He was about to chastise her when The Devil managed to breathe normally again.

"Excuse me," he said, licking blood from his lip. "MI5, worried husbands, police brutality. This doesn't have anything to do with that pack of rabid journalists and TV people outside, does it?"

The police officers exchanged an anxious, silent look. Suddenly they were on the same page. The Devil smelled blood, blood that wasn't his. And as he enjoyed doing, he went straight for the throat.

"I mean, is this Cade woman famous or something? Is she a royal perhaps? Or heaven forbid, a celebrity? I don't know," he said. "Just seems like an awful lot of fuss for a random person taken off the street. And what was this about a terror cell? Sounds to me like you two are in way over your heads. Maybe you could be doing with my help after all."

It was enough to snap Lister's temper. He brought his big, flat forehead down hard on The Devil's. Like being smashed in the face with a shovel, it made everything white for a moment, then the darkness crept back in.

"Lister, Jesus Christ," he heard Laurie saying. "You've blown this. You've totally blown this. He's not going to talk, he's a nutter, just a nutter. And even if he had done it, you can't use it. Look at the state of him, what are the beaks going to say when they get a look of him."

"We'll say he fell down the stairs," puffed Lister, getting to his feet.

"Fell down the stairs?" she asked. "Where do you think this police station is? The top of Big Ben. He's got a broken nose and god knows how many broken ribs from your little punting practice. You've totally compromised this investigation and for what? So you could be the big man? Bloody hell. A woman's life is at stake here!"

"Don't you think I know that Laurie!" Lister bellowed.

The interview room fell quiet. The Devil was gargling blood. His nose was broken, again, he could feel it out of joint. He wiped the blood on the sleeve of his jumper, coughing as it ran down the back of his throat. He looked through teary eyes at the two police officers above him. And despite the very Human pain, he couldn't help but laugh.

"Well," he said. "This is a fine welcome back. I mean, I couldn't really have asked for any more of a welcome party. A broken nose, ringing in my ears, arrested and now two rozzers who've made a complete and total balls up of what I suspect is a pretty important kidnapping investigation. I don't think I could have planned this any better myself."

Lister mumbled something under his breath. He collected his jacket and raincoat and thumped over to the door.

"Get him down to the cells," he said. "Quietly Laurie, don't let any bastard see him."

"See him?" asked Laurie. "He's all the station are talking about. We had an escort all the way from Gravesend and-"

"Just do it!" Lister yelled.

He hurried out the door leaving Laurie alone with The Devil. She stood sneering at where her DCI had been then turned back to him sitting on the floor.

"I don't know what you're smiling at," she said. "If you think he's bad, wait until you get a load of our nurse."

THE MAN IN THE DARK

EIGHT

"Ow!" The Devil winced. "Ow, stop that. Honestly, how do you people put up with this pain? Doesn't it drive you mad?"

Laurie shoved a big ball of cotton wool up his right nostril. She did it hard, deliberately he was sure.

"Would you shut up," she said. "I told you, if you think I'm bad then you're in for a shock when the nurse gets in here."

"I do think you're bad," said The Devil. "So anything other than you would be an improvement. You know I once had the misfortune of asking Andreas Vesalius how your anatomy worked. Do you know what he said to me?"

"What?" Laurie shrugged her shoulders, peeling off her rubber gloves.

"He told me it was sheer blind luck that Humanity had lasted as long as it had with the total ignorance it had shown towards its own body. And that was in your sixteenth century. Where are we now?"

Laurie closed over the small medical kit she had brought into the cell. She tried not to look at The Devil. But he could see she was curious, her eyes flickering towards him while she busied herself.

"Well?" he asked again. "Are you going to give me an approximation or do I have to sit here like an idiot?"

"I thought you knew what year it was?" she asked pointedly. "Up in the interview room, you said you could tell from my clothes, the technology."

"Yes a rough estimation," The Devil sat back on the painfully thin mattress of the cell's bed. "But that's like saying I'm *approximately* on Earth, we're *approximately* on a line of latitude. Details Laurie, I thought you were a policewoman."

"I *am* a policewoman," she said. "Believe me, I know what I am."

He detected a bitterness in her voice. She headed for the heavy metal door that led to the corridor outside. A uniformed officer was on guard. Despite Lister's instructions she had not been able to keep The Devil's movements a secret. Curiosity and worry had gotten the best of most of the cops in the station. And they'd all seen his smashed up face and hobbling Human frame.

"So what's happening now?" he said, standing up and dusting off his blood spattered jumper and training bottoms. "Are we leaving?"

"You're going nowhere mate," she said. "I told you, the nurse is coming down to give you the once over. Then some lovely people from our psychiatric department will ask you some questions and find out just what the hell is going on inside that head of yours."

"You wouldn't believe me if I told you," he said.

"Yeah, sure," she said.

The Devil took a step forward. Laurie immediately tensed. The green box of the medical kit hung like a hammer and she was prepared to use it, he could see that. He held up his hands.

"Please," he said. "If I really wanted to hurt you I wouldn't do it here and now. I'd wait until you were Downstairs and then you'd *really* suffer."

"Are you threatening me?" she asked.

"I don't do threats Laurie. Threats are for little men like your Detective Chief Inspector. Little men in little worlds desperately

 THE MAN IN THE DARK

frightened to ever venture beyond the confines of their comfort zones. No, I take action. And you can trust me when I say that I mean every word."

She stared at him quizzically. It wasn't a usual stare, or even a passing curiosity. There was a keenness, a hunger to know the truth. He supposed that was why she was a copper. He also wondered if that was why she loathed the job too.

Laurie blinked and in an instant it was gone. Like a bell being run in the back of her mind, she remembered where she was, what she was doing and why she was in a grotty little cell with a madman.

"You're staying here," she said. "And I don't want any trouble from you. No noise, no dirty protests, nothing, am I clear?"

"Dirty protest?" he twitched his nose. "What do you take me for? An animal."

"I take you for a lunatic, that's what I take you for. What kind of upstanding member of society is nicked in his flat with no ID, no documents and no record that he even exists? Eh? Answer me that wise guy?"

"Nicked? Wise guy? Where did you learn to speak like that Laurie? You're not in some bloody televised drama, this is the real world, *your* real world. Shouldn't you be a bit more, I don't know, elocuted?"

"Listen mate, I don't have time for this."

She pinched the brow of her nose, blinking hard.

"Do you know what I've got sitting on my desk upstairs?" she asked.

"Hmm, let me think," he tapped his chin. "Doughnuts and coffee?"

"No, not doughnuts, not coffee. A shit load of cases that between you and me are pretty barbaric."

At that his ears picked up. He moved a little closer, her guard remaining firmly up.

"Barbaric you say? Go on."

"That's none of your business," Laurie fired back.

"Oh come on," he said. "Everything is my business. Indulge me, it's not been the best of mornings."

He prodded the cotton wool that was stuffed up his nostrils. His whole face was on fire with a dull, irritating agony. He could feel the filthiness of his clothes rubbing off on him. And as for the shovels he'd been given as hands, the less said about them the better he thought.

"Okay," said Laurie, folding her arms. "I tell you what. Seeing as you're in such a chatty mood now, I'll give you a deal."

"A deal?" he scoffed. "With me? No, no, my dear, idiotic Laurie. *You* don't make deals with *me*. It's the other way round."

"Hey, I'm trying to throw you a bone here sunshine," she said sharply.

He sighed. Pulling the cotton wool from his nose, he examined the bright, red crimson mess. They had swollen to twice their size and he could still feel the looseness up his nostrils.

"How times change," he said quietly to himself. "Okay, a deal. Fine, if that's what you're angling for. Go ahead."

"Okay," she smirked. "I'll tell you about some of the gruesome goings on that are cluttering my desk if you tell me who you are. Simple enough, no messing. Sound good?"

"Seems reasonable," he shrugged. "But I get to go first."

She thought about the proposition. The Devil looked about for somewhere to throw his cotton wool. Seeing the dried blood stains on the floor, the unsanitary toilet in the corner and the damp creeping down the far wall, he thought the floor was as good a place as any.

"Fine," she said. "But one question at a time. Alright?"

"Of course," he said. "What's at the top of that pile on your desk?"

"Really? You have to ask that?" she said.

"Medina Cade?" he asked. "A kidnapping then. Terrorists involved; you lot don't have a clue what's going on. Yes, I got the picture. I mean what else."

"That's cheating."

"That's negotiation Laurie, come on, chop chop."

Laurie rolled her tongue about her mouth. The Devil couldn't decide if she was attractive or not. For a creature so bent on the sleazy, cheap and nasty side of Humanity, he was struggling on whether she fell into the passable category. He'd seen, danced, dated and loved some of the most beautiful women in Human history. In fact, he'd seen, danced, dated and loved *all* of the most beautiful women in Human history.

DS Laurie was something of an enigma though. She looked worn down, pushed back into the doldrums of self-preservation. Appearance clearly wasn't a priority, not practical enough. Yet there was an inherent quality about her. Nothing a good makeover couldn't fix he resolved.

"Fine," she said. "I believe next on my to do list is a robbery."

"How dull."

"Came in this morning, an old man."

"Even duller," yawned The Devil.

"Actually no, it wasn't," she said. "In fact I'd say it was far from dull."

"This isn't a competition Laurie. If it was I'd always win."

"Seems from what we can gather the old boy was heading for his morning paper when he's jumped by a bunch of local kids. Teenagers, bad bunch, he's from a shitty area in Peckham."

"I'm sure."

"But rather than just take the pensioner's wallet and scarper down to the local park to score drugs this lot decide to get creative."

She paused. The Devil could sense something from her. Anxiety perhaps, a tenseness, her body growing a little stiffer the more she thought of what she was about to say.

"What do you mean *creative*?" he asked.

"The little bastards got it into their heads that they were going to strip the old man naked," said Laurie. "So not only has the OAP been robbed of his pension for the week, but he's left out in the street starkers. Like they really did a number on this guy, smashed his face up to a pulp, bladed him, the works. He's in intensive care, docs don't have much hope for him. He's lost so much blood they're running out down at King's College. Even if he pulls through it'll take him months to recover, if he lives that long. And there's no chance he'll ever want to leave his house again. I mean, I've been a policewoman for over a decade and seen some pretty bad shit. But this, it's like there's a new brutality to the kids these days. Mental."

She stared into the space between them, lost in her own thoughts. She snapped out of it, suppressing a shiver. The Devil remained quiet.

"There, happy?" she asked.

"No, not particularly," he said. "I'm in Human form, riddled with pain and pointlessness. You'd think hearing of such mindless acts of violence would make me ecstatic. Yet here we are. Actually, come to think of it. It's not how I would have hurt that little old pensioner. But I suppose the end result is the same."

"Come on now, a deal's a deal. Name," she ignored him.

The Devil tried to straighten his new body as much as it would go. There wasn't much room in it for squared shoulders and a puffed out chest. But he tried.

THE MAN IN THE DARK

"I've had many names over the centuries," he said. "All of which I'm sure you've known in some way, shape or form. But The Devil seems to be the going rate these days. So I'm happy for you to settle on that."

"The Devil?" Laurie cocked an eyebrow.

"At your service."

He made a long, sweeping gesture with his arm and went to take a bow. Then something snapped in his back and he was stuck, halfway down towards the ground.

"Ah," he said. "I think I might have thrown the back out."

"The Devil?" Laurie said again.

"Yes," he said with a flash of anger. "Now could you please help me, I don't know how this body works yet."

He stood rigidly buckled over, bent in two and staring down at the filthy floor of the cell. He couldn't see Laurie but he could hear her. Her laughter was quiet at first but as she lost control it grew into full blown hilarity.

"What's so funny?" he said, feeling blood rush to his head.

"The Devil," she said between gulps of laughter. "You think you're The Devil? That's priceless."

"Priceless? I hardly think it's priceless that I'm standing here, quite obviously in pain and you're doing nothing about it. Don't you have some sort of professional obligation to help me or something. Don't police people take oaths?"

"The Devil," Laurie continued to laugh. "Oh that's a good one. That's really good. I mean, for a second, I actually thought you were going to come up with something creative, something original. I don't know why, I just thought better of you. But *The Devil*, man, that's so uncreative."

The Devil was grinding his new teeth. They were already pretty worn in from what he could feel. But at least he was doing something. Crippled and hunched over, he was totally helpless. And that wasn't the type of situation he found himself in regularly. If at all.

Laurie eventually calmed down. She walked over to him and tapped him between the shoulder blades.

"Alright, you ready?" she asked.

"Ready for wha-"

She grabbed each of his shoulders and pushed her knee into his lower back. With a sharp, quick tug, he was pulled upright. The agony made his head swirl but he couldn't scream or cry. Instead, he stood there, motionless, hands and arms contorted in agony.

"There you go," she said, rounding to face him. "All better your majesty."

"I'd thank you," he mumbled. "But I don't do that sort of thing."

"Oh yeah, that's right," she said. "Because you're The Devil aren't you."

She started laughing again. Wagging her finger, she walked out of the cell, leaving him standing stiffly in the centre of the floor.

"One word of advice sunshine," she said, closing the door. "You better come up with something a lot better than that if you want to ever leave this place. Because I tell you right now, no jury in the land will buy that crap."

The cell door closed with a heavy thump. The sound rang around the cell for a moment before vanishing. The Devil's pain, however, did not and he stood perfectly still while his Human body did what it had to do. This was going to be a long one, he thought. This was going to be very long indeed.

THE MAN IN THE DARK

NINE

The Devil lay staring up at the ceiling of his cell. A lattice of lines from the high window highlighted all the chips, divots and stains up there. Slowly, as the light began to fail, those lines had moved across the ceiling and made their way down the far wall. Time, he thought, just ticking away. There was no way to stop it, no way to curb it. Over and over it would go until suddenly there was none left. What would the Humans do then, he wondered? Would they even be around to see it? Or would that be so far in their future that they'd gotten bored and blown each other up before then.

Either was possible. Anything was possible. Although his money, if he had any need for the stuff, was on the latter. Aggressive, overcompensating and rude - the three must-have ingredients for an apocalyptical end.

He was boring himself. And that was really saying something. He'd been cooped up in the prison cell for hours now. There had been no sign of Laurie, nothing of the psychiatrists and certainly no whiff of the fabled nurse of doom. All the while he was growing numb and uncomfortable in the silly new body he'd been given.

Irritated, he swung his legs off the bed and felt the cold slab of concrete beneath his feet. For the hundredth time he checked his vital signs. All the bleeding had stopped and he seemed to be breathing okay - although there was an unnerving rattle with every inhalation.

He got up and walked over to the big metal door. Angrily he rapped it with his knuckles.

"Oi!" he shouted. "Am I going to get some service in here or what? This is by far and away the worst hotel I've ever stayed at. And I was at The Watergate on *that* night!"

There was nothing but silence. He hit the hard iron again, hoping for a different response.

"If you don't get that reference then I suggest you look it up!" he shouted. "It's your history after all, I wasn't doing it for the good of my health. I don't have any health to be good for!"

Again there was nothing. He ground his teeth and turned back to his cell. The light was almost gone now, little more than the faint orange glow from a summer sun finished for another day. He returned to the bed and climbed on top. Stretching as much as he could he tried to get a vantage point out of the narrow window. But it was just too high.

Defeated he slumped back down. Sucking on his gums he tasted the bitterness of dry blood and stale snot.

"This is intolerable," he said. "If I wasn't so bloody angry I'd ask to see the architect of this place. It's infuriatingly delightful."

Forgetting himself he rubbed his nose and snorted loudly. The pain made him wince and he felt his injured face. The Devil then realised that he had no idea what he looked like. Despite the grubby jumper and untidy training trousers he was oblivious to what face he'd been given this time.

"Doesn't feel very nice," he said, prodding and poking. "Then again, You would never want me to be happy in any shape or form would You?"

THE MAN IN THE DARK

He looked about for something reflective. The cell was dull, in almost every sense. Faceless concrete from top to bottom. Only the grotty looking toilet offered some semblance of hope.

"Really?" he looked up at the ceiling. "You'd really have me look at myself in a toilet pan? Come on now, that's just childish."

Without another option he dragged himself over to the toilet. Stained and marked, the metal was scratched with names and other unmentionables. A sad looking roll of toilet paper sat beside the pan and he pulled free a handful. Rubbing some of the grot, grime and slime from the top, The Devil managed to create a small patch of clear metal. He squinted, trying to get a good look at himself.

"Oh no," he said. "Not blonde!" Anything but blonde! Are You for real? You've made me blonde!"

He ran his hand through the lengthening hair. He had a large forehead and a flat nose, with lovely bruising around his pale blue eyes. His teeth were as stubby as he feared and there was altogether no shape at all to his jawline. Repulsed, he stood back up and lifted his jumper. A pot belly looked back at him, no definition where his pectorals started and his stomach ended. To add insult to his injuries, there appeared to be a little collection of moles that, if he didn't know better, which he always did, looked like a lopsided smiley face.

There was a clunk from behind him and the cell door creaked open. He turned as a po-faced little man came shuffling in carrying a medical kit.

"At last!" The Devil shouted. "You know I was beginning to think I'd been forgotten about."

"Just watch yourself with this one," said the officer standing at the door. "He's a real live wire."

The man gave a little grunt. He nodded to the cop who closed the cell door behind him, leaving them alone. The Devil lowered his jumper and outstretched his hands.

"Okay, which one are you?" he asked. "Are you here to beat me up or tell me I hated my parents? By the way, I never had any parents so you're barking up the wrong bush with that one."

The little man checked to make sure the cell door was closed and they were on their own. Satisfied, he placed the medical kit down on the floor and removed his spectacles and began polishing them on his shirt.

The Devil stood waiting impatiently. He tapped his bare foot on the floor while the little man carefully, methodically and deliberately made sure every speck of dirt and smudge was removed from his lenses. He lifted them up to the dying light before popping them back on his nose.

"There we are," he said. "Now, where was I?"

As soon as the little man spoke The Devil knew. Intuition was a fine thing. So was being in the presence of the Creator of the Universe. It came with the territory.

"You took Your time," he said, going for a walk around the cell. "I've been holed up in here for most of the day waiting for You or that copper to come down here and let me get on with business. And when You do finally show up You *still* keep me waiting with that spectacle charade."

"You sound surprised," He beamed. "I would have thought you'd learn to keep your temper in check by now. And as for waiting, well, it's all part of the job description old boy. Patience is key."

"Yeah, so is keeping up Your end of the bargain," said The Devil angrily. "Whatever happened to the 'well deserved break' I was promised? Hours, that's all I had, a matter of hours before You decided to call to check up on me. You're right, I shouldn't be so surprised. I shouldn't and wouldn't put anything past You."

He sat Himself down on the edge of the bed and opened up his medical kit. Rifling through the bandages, creams and pills, He shook His head in disbelief.

"They've been a busy bunch," He said. "I think the last time I checked on their scientific endeavours they'd only just discovered fire. Now look at all of this - pain relief, gel, tablets, ways to stem bleeding. Quite extraordinary."

"Self-praise is no praise," said The Devil, still reeling. "I would have thought You would know that."

He was angry. Just being in His presence was usually enough for that. But he couldn't help but think He was being particularly cruel this time. The beach phone call, the immediate arrest. Even the well-used body He'd given The Devil felt like a subversive pop.

The Devil, however, was too smart to get mad, especially in front of Him. He took a moment to collect his thoughts, letting Him babble on about the wonders of Human endeavour. He had a mission, a secret mission, one he'd cooked up for himself. It was vital he didn't give Him a sniff of what he was up to.

"It'll be interesting to see where they go from here," He said, closing over the box. "Oh, that reminds me, would you like anything. They've got painkillers, something for that nose of yours. It's rather red and bulbous, wouldn't you say?"

"It's about the *only* thing that's bulbous on me," said The Devil. "I mean come on, take a look at me, was this *really* the best You could do?"

He outstretched his hands. He thought about doing a little twirl but stopped just short. He didn't want to make things worse. All the while He sat giggling on the bed.

"I'm sorry," He said. "It was all a bit rushed, I do apologise. It was the best I could do at such short notice. Had you popped Upstairs when I asked I'm sure we could have come up with something a bit more to your liking."

"What? Like that sporty little golf number You had the last time I saw You?" The Devil licked his lips. "Now that was something special. If You were a million years younger and I was a billion years older then we might have had something going there. But, alas, as bad as I look it's not quite as awful as You at this moment in time."

He looked down at His large stomach. Patting it, He laughed.

"They're all beautiful, in their own special way."

"The Humans?" The Devil squeaked. "Don't make me laugh. Beauty is something that's celebrated, not the dim and dismal husks You've lumbered us with here. And that's before I get started on those psychopathic police officers I've had to deal with today. Honestly, you'd think they'd both been raised on radioactive waste or something."

"Now, now," He said.

"It's true. There's the man, DCI Lister, he's like testosterone incarnate. Punching, kicking, shouting, bawling, swearing. It's as if somebody stole my homework jotter and created a walking, talking caricature of a total and complete arsehole."

"Stop it."

"And as for the woman - man, she's got more problems than I even thought was possible for a Human female," said The Devil. "Do you know, the worst part about it all is that she's probably very good, very skilled, very intelligent. But she hides it all behind this mask of dreary self-doubt that's about as interesting as a sodden fish sandwich. I tip my hat to You though, every time I think You can't do worse You always surprise me. Always."

He sat drumming His thick fingers on the lid of the medical kit. The Devil had to catch his breath, the annoying rattle causing him some difficulties. He was always the same when He was around, he couldn't help but lose his temper. He had to keep reminding himself that there was more at play this time. He couldn't afford to let the proverbial cat out of the bag.

"I'm finished, by the way," he said. "I just had to get a few things off my chest is all."

"That's quite alright," He smiled. "That's what I'm here for."

"Please."

"I take it from your vented anger you are keen to get cracking then old boy?"

"If it gets me out of this dreadful cell and a step closer to going home then of course. I am, as always, your servant," he gave a little bow.

"Oh if only that were true," He smiled and got to His feet.

He collected His things and knocked once on the door of the cell. It creaked open but there was no police officer on guard outside. Stepping to one side, He ushered The Devil out.

"Just that easy, eh?" he asked.

"It was never locked," He laughed. "But believe me, that's only the start of it, as I'm sure you're about to find out."

"Why is it whenever You interfere I get a terrible sense of foreboding?" asked The Devil. "I thought You were meant to be the bearer of good news to all men."

"You're not a man old chap."

"True, but I'm still part of Your universe, Your creation, Your little project. Don't I get a bone thrown in my direction?"

"I got you out of that cell, didn't I?"

They walked through the corridors of the police station. The Devil sensed something odd about the place. For starters there were no police officers about. No criminals being booked, no detectives running around chasing up leads and shouting at each other. Everywhere they passed was quiet and empty.

"Wait a minute," said The Devil. "Something's not right. This place was jumping. Where is everybody?"

A grave look came across His little face. As He shuffled alongside The Devil He seemed to slow, like a grand piano had suddenly been lowered onto His shoulders. Burden, The Devil thought, that old, familiar feeling. There was nothing else like it - the burden of responsibility.

"I have to apologise to you old bean," He started. "I'm bending the rules a little just by being here. And you know I don't like doing that sort of thing."

"I beg your pardon?" The Devil said, stopping in the corridor. "You do it *all* the time!"

"Yes, well, quite," He said, continuing. "But this time I really *am* bending the rules. Bending them so far that I'm probably breaking them actually. I just… I just want to let you know that before you find out, I'm doing it for your benefit. Nobody else's. Does that make sense?"

He darted The Devil a concerned look. The nail in the coffin was when He squeezed his shoulder and carried on up the hallway.

The Devil suddenly felt very ill. He'd never seen Him like this. In all of their battles, their quarrels, their wrestling for Humanity's soul, He had always carried Himself with a jolly, almost happy-go-lucky calmness. Now, He was like a changed divine being. And that was cause for concern.

"Eh… You're not making much sense here, You do know that don't You?" he called after Him. "Do You want to tell me what's going on? Because between You and me, You're starting to scare me shitless."

He picked up his pace to catch up with Him. They wandered through the empty hallways and corridors until they were at a small foyer in the rear of the building. They stopped at a door and

THE MAN IN THE DARK

He composed himself.

"I think it's probably best that I show you first what's going on," He said. "That way it might not be so much of a shock."

"Okay," said The Devil, drawing the word out.

He nodded, His little face red with worry. Gripping the handle of the door, He pushed it open, letting a wave of heat pass over them both. The choking, sickening smell of burning rubber and petrol wasn't far behind. And with it came the distant sound of sirens and shouting.

The outside world was electrified, the night air charged with a familiar feeling to The Devil. Unrest, mass unrest, a riot even. He stared out to the skyline and saw the burning embers of fire reaching up towards the dark canvass of the sky. London was burning.

"What's going on here?" he asked. "What's with all the chaos?"

"Change old boy," He said flatly, and headed out the door.

TEN

Few sounds were quite so appealing to The Devil's ears than those of a mass riot. That sense of unrest, the drive and determination of Humans en masse to put aside their sensibilities and smash up the nearest cars, shops and buildings was truly unique. What The Devil *didn't* like was when one started and he had no idea why. Something about being ignorant to a riot's origin made him feel uneasy.

To be met with one of the biggest and busiest cities in the world tearing itself apart probably ranked amongst his worst ever surprises. It wasn't just the mass fighting and disturbance he could hear from miles away, it was the sheer scale of what was going on. The police station had been emptied, gutted from top to bottom. With him being a prime suspect, one that was being watched like a hawk to be suddenly left, spoke volumes. And he had nothing to do with it.

He walked in front of him, a few paces ahead, little legs moving with an almost cartoonish quickness. They hurried around to the front of the building and into the empty street.

"This isn't good, is it?" asked The Devil. "I mean, London having a riot isn't exactly big news. But this place is a ghost town."

"No, it's not," He said gravely. "And the worst part about it is I can't even blame you. You've got the perfect alibi."

 THE MAN IN THE DARK

"I do?" The Devil asked.

"Yes. Me."

"Thanks," he scoffed. "So hold on, I think this makes it two riots from two during my trips to this awful place. What do you know, a perfect record."

He drew him an unconvinced look. Staring up and down the street, The Devil wasn't sure what He was looking for. The high flats and office blocks that lined the road looked deserted, the burning amber of the distant fires reflecting off their polished windows. In the distance The Devil could hear the faint rumble of mass unrest. Raised voices joined in disharmony always had the same quality. Like the breaking of a wave on hard, craggy rocks, rioters were an ocean of sorts - only much more violent.

"You going to tell me what this is all about now?" he asked, growing impatient. "And what the hell this has to do with the kidnapped woman."

"Kidnapped woman?" He asked, still looking up and down the street.

"Yeah, Medina Cade," said The Devil. "I assume that's why I'm here this time. You want me to find her, save her presumably, be the hero as always."

"What? Yes, yes, Medina Cade, a terrible business, you'll have your work cut out for you with that one old boy."

He seemed strangely aloof, like His mind was elsewhere.

"Are You... distracted?" asked The Devil. "I believe I've only seen You like this once before. In fact I *know* I have. During that whole business in Galilee, remember, when we were both putting in a spot of overtime. Oh to be young in the summer nights eh?"

"What? Yes, yes, of course."

He wasn't listening. That's when The Devil knew there was something really wrong.

"Okay, come on now, no messing about," he said. "What's going on here? Mass riots, empty police stations, me in Human form. It doesn't add up. Your all-knowing smugness is, I can't believe I'm about to say this, sadly amiss. You want to fill me in?"

"There's something wrong," He said. "Something wrong with the Natural Order."

Like that The Devil's Human heart skipped at least ten beats. He wasn't sure if it was just the new body overreacting to what was a titanic wave of panic. Like the naughty schoolboy caught with his hand in the shopkeeper's till, The Devil had been caught.

"Oh," he managed, trying to think. "Really? How can You be sure?"

"I have a feeling," He said, sweating now. "I have a feeling that something really isn't right, that something fundamental has changed somewhere in amongst all the nuts and bolts old boy. Like a link in a chain has been broken but I don't know where."

"I see…"

He watched Him for a moment, his whole Human body tingling. If it decided to give up and die at that moment The Devil wouldn't have been surprised. Getting caught out by the Ultimate Headteacher wasn't something Humans were designed to cope with. Even *he* was struggling.

In a fleeting moment of worry he cursed Brutus and Cassius. Why had he listened to them? It was bound to be trouble from the start surely. Why had he been so bloody big headed and egotistical? He was smarter than that surely.

Only, there *was* something else. What was it He had just said - He had a *feeling*. That means there was nothing definite. Maybe all wasn't lost after all.

The Devil started to sweat. There was a glimmer of hope, a tiny pin prick of light in the endless canvas of black, unbearable misery

 THE MAN IN THE DARK

that *maybe* lay head. Not being somebody who would ever pass up a quick escape, The Devil jumped head-on into it, grabbing it by the proverbial horns.

"So what do you think it might be?" he asked cautiously. "You don't think it has something to do with *me*, do you?"

He didn't look at him. Instead He went into the middle of the street and got down on His knees. Licking the tarmac on the road, The Devil winced a little.

"Really?" he asked. "You have to do that, now? Couldn't You find a private moment for something like that. Disgusting."

"The atmosphere is off," He said, tasting what He'd just licked. "There's something rotten bleeding through the fundamental fabric. Have you ever seen damp crawling through a roof?"

"I beg your pardon," said The Devil. "I don't have time for such domestic drudgery."

"Well it's like that," He said, forcing himself back to His feet. "I think there may be a problem, Downstairs."

"Problem? What kind of problem?"

"I don't know yet," He said. "But I suppose it's not helping that you were whisked away here against your will at such short notice. And for that I apologise."

"Right, yeah," said The Devil. "Thanks, I guess. What's the next move, do You want me to pop back down and have a look?"

"No, no you can't do that," He said, adjusting the faint strands of ginger hair that made up His combover. "That would probably make things worse. You've been started on this journey, you have to see it through to the end. Natural Order and all that, old sport."

The unmistakable clatter of broken glass interrupted them. Far down the street a crowd appeared. There were thirty of them, maybe more, all wearing masks and scarves over their faces. Some were carrying burning bits of wood, others had golf clubs, bats and other improvised weapons. As they marched down the street they smashed up street lights and lobbed broken bottles and bricks at the offices and flats that stood on either side of the road.

"Ah, there they are," said The Devil smiling. "Your beautiful, favoured creations. I wondered how long it would take before they made an appearance."

A lump of brick whizzed past his head and he ducked. The rioters picked up their pace, dropping into a jog when they spotted the pair standing outside the police station.

"I think we should make an exit," He said, ushering The Devil back towards the courtyard.

"What's the plan then?" he asked. "Why don't You just click Your fingers and get me out of this stinking sack of misery meat?"

"Natural Order old boy, I told you," He said, fixing His glasses. "If I just pull you out of this moment and plop you back Downstairs it could do untold damage - *worse* damage."

"Oh yeah, that's right, what could be worse than a metropolis wide street riot?"

"A global one," He said flatly.

They ran around to the back of the station, The Devil outpacing Him with his much longer legs. He thought about gloating but decided it wasn't the right time. He'd keep that one in his back locker for another time.

"You have to get to work," He said, puffing and gasping for breath. "I'm going to go back Upstairs and see what's causing this sudden upsurge in violence and hatred. There has to be a reason, there has to be *something* driving all of this. It's not… natural."

"Violence and hatred eh?" said The Devil. "Two of my favourite words."

"Yes, naturally. Although even if I do say so myself, this doesn't really feel like *your* work."

   THE MAN IN THE DARK

The Devil was about to dismiss Him. Then he stopped. He felt something strange creeping up from a deep, dark pit in the bottom of his mind. A snarling, nasty little thought that he'd never known before.

"What do You mean?" he asked.

He was distracted by The Devil.

"Oh, nothing old boy, nothing at all," He said.

"No, You meant something by that," said The Devil. "What did You mean? What do You mean by it not feeling like *my* work?"

"It's nothing, honestly, just a figure of speech," He smiled weakly.

"Mass riots, violence, fighting amongst themselves, those are mine. They're classics!"

"Yes, yes I quite agree," He said. "But don't you think, maybe I'm just being a bit paranoid, but don't you think it's all a bit… I don't know. Different?"

"Different?"

"Yes," He said. "Like a restaurant you've known for a long time and the chef has retired, leaving his son in charge. They're making and serving the same food, the same dishes. But it just tastes a little… off."

The Devil felt his whole Human body tense. He couldn't work out if he was angry, confused or just imagining things. If he didn't know better, and he *always* knew better, he would have thought He was trying to goad him. However, He was in the dark - He had no idea about Brutus and Cassius' little side project.

"It's probably nothing," He said quickly. "You have to get on with trying to find Medina Cade. Have you made any progress?"

"I was banged up in a prison cell for hours before You showed up," he said sardonically. "The only progress I've made is getting out of there and into the middle of a bloomin' riot. I didn't even know what I looked like until You showed up. Thank You for that again by the way. You'd have been better giving me a corpse."

"If you don't hurry up that's what you might end up as!"

The shouts, screams and chants of the mob grew louder from the street. He mopped his brow and tapped his temple.

"I need you to work very hard on this," He said. "I need you back amongst your own kind as quickly as possible. Every moment you spend out of sync with Downstairs poses the risk of the Natural Order being upset. And we can't have that old boy, you know what that means."

"Yes, of course," he said with a bored sigh. "This Medina Cade thing, any suggestions?"

"I can't tell you," He said. "That would be cheating."

"Oh come on!" The Devil bawled. "I thought we were on the doorstep of the apocalypse here. That's what You're telling me and You can't even give me a teeny, weeny clue. It's in Your best interests as much as mine."

He stared at him silently for a moment. Then, when He'd considered all the options, he put His hands on His hips and sighed.

"Pierce Cade is Medina's loving husband," He said at length. "I can't begin to imagine what he must be going through at a time like this."

"Yeah, yeah, I get it, sob story," said The Devil. "Come on, throw me a bone, be a bit more helpful than those cops."

"Yes, such a terrible shame," He said, stepping a little closer. "I really can't imagine what Mr Cade is going through at this time. I mean, if you ever had the decency or ability to feel any compassion for anything other than yourself, you would probably be in a terrible state."

"Yes, yes, very good. Come on, clues."

"I mean, it's probably a time in his life he never would have thought would come, not to him at least," He said. "He would probably do anything to get his wife back. Don't you think?"

"It doesn't matter what I think I…"

The Devil trailed off. A big, broad smile came over his face and he tapped the end of his nose.

"You old dog," he said.

He nodded, clasping his hands together.

"Well, I must be off," He said. "I do like a challenge. Remember, it's vitally important you do what you have to as quickly as possible. There's a lot riding on this, not least the life of an innocent woman. Efficiency is key, don't waste time. I mean, it would be a shame if you didn't use that police car over there, you know, the one with the engine running and the lights already on."

The Devil looked over his shoulder. A squad car was sitting in the corner, engine puttering away, blue lights flashing on the roof. He darted Him a wry smile.

"You really know how to turn it on when You want to, don't You?"

He shrugged His shoulders and headed back into the police station. As He closed the door He called back to The Devil.

"I hear Croydon is lovely at this time of the year, particularly Green Avenue. Very quiet, very peaceful, a lovely place for a family home. Even in a riot! You might find a little voice in the car telling you where to go, it's all very handy and convenient. Wouldn't you say?"

"Yes," said The Devil. "*Very* convenient."

"And should you come across that lovely police officer, what's her name, Laurie, yes, Laurie. Try to get on with her would you? You never know, she might be quite useful."

The door shut behind Him and He was gone. The Devil didn't hesitate, dashing over to the police car and jumping in the driver's seat. As he was about to press the accelerator he paused. Staring out of the window at the alleyway that led to the road, he couldn't keep the big, broad smile from his face.

London was rioting, violence and decay everywhere. The Natural Order, those two little words that could cause such huge upset and trouble, were on the tip of his tongue. A huge relief washed over him and he drummed his hands on the steering wheel.

"He doesn't know," he said quietly at first, fearing he'd be heard. "He doesn't know a thing!"

Revving the engine, he took off, the car lurching forward in great leaps and jumps. The Devil didn't care. He hadn't been caught, that was the main thing. He could worry about learning to drive later.

ELEVEN

"Blimey, You weren't kidding, this place really *has* gone to the dogs!"

The Devil had never quite got the hang of driving. It was so *Human*. Thankfully his point and accelerate attitude went totally unnoticed as London tore itself apart.

He had very quickly lost count of the burning cars he'd passed. There were even a few police vans thrown in for good measure. For the most part the rioters were keeping themselves busy fighting with anybody and everybody they came across. The traffic was being left to glide past the pockets of disturbance quite amicably.

Being in a police car, The Devil had a special, behind-the-scenes view of what was going on. The radio didn't stop for his whole journey. If it wasn't frantic control officers trying to direct their troops to the hot spots, it was rank and file cops being pummelled by the public. Air support was being called in and there had been talk of mobilising the army. But still nothing on what had caused this mass uprising.

The Devil had a few ideas of course. The way He had spoken so gravely about the whole thing meant there had to be something iffy afoot. He could only assume it was the fact that he himself, Evil incarnate, was walking amongst the Humans. The last time had sparked some outrage, mostly protesters at the opening of HellCorp. Nothing on this scale though.

As if he needed reminding, a fleet of helicopters passed him overhead. They zoomed off towards the inner city, flanked by jets. This was getting serious.

The onboard computer had directed The Devil onto a long stretching motorway. Cars, buses, vans and trucks were all speeding along. Everyone, it seemed, was trying to escape the mayhem in the city. Tall towers of smoke billowed up from the lower levels, lining the road like great, black trees. And the night sky was illuminated with the fires of unrest. The Devil thought it all seemed very much like home. A little too much like home in fact.

"Take the next exit and drive for five miles. Keep left," said the voice.

"Yes, yes I hear you."

"Keep left."

"I said I heard you! Wherever you are!" The Devil shouted.

He hated being told what to do. Especially by some metallic, tinkered toy designed to make easy Human lives all the easier.

When he pulled off the motorway, causing a few near misses along the way, he saw that things were beginning to calm down. The further he got from the city centre the more quiet it was. High rise tower blocks and office skyscrapers were replaced with row after row of neat little houses with garages and gardens. Supermarkets and garden centres were the order of the day. Comfortable living replaced tight, cramped overcrowding and the risk of gang warfare.

Just an hour out from the police station and it was like another world. The Devil smirked to himself.

"Out of sight, out of mind," he said.

"You have reached your destination on the left," said the voice.

The Devil mashed the pedals with his feet. The police car came to an abrupt halt and he almost flew through the windscreen. When he'd settled back down and swallowed his organs he took a look about.

He was at the head of a long, straight street. Detached and semi-detached houses stood proudly to attention on either side. Two cars were parked in every driveway and a variety of hedges, trees and other assorted shrubbery marked the dividing line between neighbours.

"Nice," said The Devil to himself. "I can feel my mind turning to porridge with the boredom already. So much in fact I'm sitting here talking to myself."

He pushed the door open angrily and got out. The place was silent, a stark contrast to the clashing and clattering of central London. As he started down the street he spotted something in the distance. Cursing his new Human eyes, he squinted, trying to make out the dark shapes and figures moving around halfway down the street.

A collection of vans and cars had gathered outside one semi-detached in particular. The Devil didn't understand the words and letters on the side of the taller vehicles but he recognised the people. Journalists, lots of journalists, scuttling about with their cameras and computers. There had to be fifty of them, all in various states of their jobs. The nearer he got the more he noticed them.

Men and women, heavily made up, stood in front of large, white lights, talking into cameras in twenty different languages. Others hopped in and out of great big trucks with satellite dishes poking out from their roofs, beaming broadcasts into space and out to millions of homes. Nobody was idle and if they were, they were busy on their mobile phones. The Devil, giving logic its easiest job of the day, concluded that they were camped outside the Cade residency.

"Journalists," he said quietly to himself. "Humanity's finest."

He stopped a few hundred yards from the media circus and thought. The top of the Cades' house poked above a set of trees just out of sight. He resolved that it would probably be better going in from behind - a tactic he'd employed more times than he cared to admit.

Ducking off the street, he pushed his flabby Human body on through the darkness. Passing two cars and a garage, he slipped into the back garden of the house next door. The next step was getting up and over the fence.

"You're loving this, aren't You," he whispered, not wanting to disturb the neighbours. "You're loving me skulking about in the dark, climbing fences and getting grass stains on my trousers like a bloody boarding school tearaway. You'll pay for this Old Man."

The Devil hauled himself up onto the fence. One leg was over, then the other. But as he dropped down the other side, an almighty rip echoed about the garden. He landed on the grass and felt something draughtier about his legs.

"Wonderful," he said, examining the leg-long tear in his jogging bottoms. "Just what I needed."

As he untangled himself from the fence, the garden was suddenly illuminated. The lights were switched on inside the house, two patio doors showing the modest interior of the Cades' home. The Devil crouched down low, hiding in a rose bush. He peered through the leaves and shrubs to watch what was going on.

A man appeared in what was clearly the kitchen. He looked dishevelled, unshaven, his short hair sticking out in tufts. His eyes were red from crying and he wore a look of sadness and melancholy about him. His t-shirt was stained, jeans ragged and frayed.

"We must use the same tailor Mr Cade," The Devil whispered.

Cade was talking to someone, his lips moving. He busied himself around the kitchen, fetching two mugs from a cupboard and boiling the kettle. He looked tired, worn out, everything about him was grey and sad. The Devil had no time for moping or self-loathing. And this man reeked of it.

He moved to try and see who Cade was speaking to but it was impossible. The garden was flat and exposed, he would be seen as soon as he moved. Instead he crouched there, watching, trying to decipher what Cade was saying.

"Police maybe," he said. "Something about Medina and missing. This is useless, I'm learning nothing here. I need to be where the action is."

The Devil maneuvered himself and leaned forward. As he did so he stepped on something furry. There was a loud wail and a hiss as a dark, black cat shot out from the rose bush beneath him and took off across the garden.

Cade turned to the patio doors. He looked out, confused, eyes jumping from one corner to the next, wondering what the noise was. The Devil was in agony as he held his position, knees aching, muscles burning, his Human body locked still. After an eternity, Cade turned back into his kitchen, the bald patch of his crown glistening in the light.

The Devil unlocked himself and stifled a sigh. He carefully pushed himself free of the bush and angled along the dark perimeter of the block of light from the house. A small extension stretched out from the main building, its roof slightly sloped. The Devil rolled up his sleeves and hoisted himself up onto a window ledge before clambering onto the roof. The sheet metal was slippery with moss and he almost fell twice.

Taking tiny steps, his arms outstretched, he managed to navigate his way up to the main building. A window was waiting for him there and he examined the frame. It was thin and weak and he thought about smashing it open. Then he noticed the little gap between the sill and the frame. He gave a quick look up towards the starry night sky.

"Okay," he said. "Maybe we're even then."

He lifted the window and dropped inside. He was in a bedroom, the bed lying unmade ahead of him. Clothes were strewn about the floor and a suitcase was propped up near the door. Light from the hall reflected off the glass of picture frames hanging on the wall. The Devil took a closer look, treading lightly on the floorboards.

There was nothing remarkable about the photos - all hum drum stuff. A man and a woman, smiling at the camera. One of them in formal dress, the woman in white, the man in a tuxedo. Another saw them on holiday, both wearing what appeared to be mouse ears standing in front of a large, ornate castle. As The Devil looked closer he could see that the man was the same person downstairs.

"Cade," whispered The Devil. "And I assume this is your missing wife."

He tapped the glass on another picture, this time just of the woman. She was attractive, well groomed, someone who took great pride in her appearance. While The Devil had no real qualification in Human dynamics, he sensed a discrepancy somewhere. Looking back at the pictures of them together, he couldn't help but wonder if she could do a lot better.

"Doing well for yourself Cade," he said. "At least, you were until she was kidnapped."

The sound of raised voices distracted him. He crept over to the bedroom door and listened.

Somebody was shouting. Angry, aggressive, it was a man's voice but The Devil couldn't make out what he was saying. A woman, the tone, the sharp little sentences, Laurie, definitely Laurie, was trying to calm him down. It clearly wasn't working.

The exchange went back and forth for a moment before something broke. The Devil felt the hairs on the back of his arms stand on end. A strange sensation, he assumed it was one of danger. These bodies could be a trifle over sensitive to things like that. Fight or flight was one of His proudest achievements. The Devil saw it as little more than an annoyance.

He decided to venture a little closer. He was learning nothing standing in the dark surrounded by old memories. Stepping into the hallway, the floor creaked under his weight. He tentatively made his way down the first few steps of the staircase, the voices getting clearer.

"Would you please just calm down Mr Cade," said Laurie, muffled by the walls but audible.

"Calm down? Calm down? Do you have any idea what I'm going through here sergeant? My wife has been kidnapped. She's gone," said Cade. "And all I've had from the moment I found that out is nothing but hassle and grief from the people that are supposed to be helping me. Do you know what it's like to lose somebody you love? Do you? Do you?"

There was a pause. Then Laurie started up again, The Devil picturing her doing her very best impression of a policewoman in control.

"Sir, please, I just need you to think straight for a moment," she said. "Any clues as to who this man could be might help in finding Medina."

"You're the fifth person I've seen today, the fifth," said Cade. "Five different people have been to see me today, all from various places, the police, the army, intelligence, the government, I'm losing count. And you're all asking me the same questions, questions I don't have the answers to! I turn on the T.V and she's there - those vultures outside preying on my misery. I read the papers, I go online, she's everywhere. Everywhere except here, in our home, with me. I don't know where she is sergeant. I don't know who this man you're talking about is. I've never seen him before in my life."

The Devil pondered what was going on. He stepped down a few more of the stairs until he was almost at the bottom. Cade was still being aggressive; he could hear him walking about in the room next door.

"I came to you because I was told your department has an outstanding track record at missing persons cases," he said, exasperated. "I was told by MI5 that you and your team have tracked down people who have seemingly vanished off the face of the earth. And yet here you are, in my house, asking me about people I don't even know about. I'm at my wit's end sergeant, I really am. Now if you're not going to ask me anything else that can lead to finding Medina, I kindly ask that you leave me alone in peace."

After a short pause, there were footsteps. The Devil recoiled a little.

"Okay, fine, thank you for your time Mr Cade," said Laurie. "I understand that you're in a very difficult position at the moment, believe me I do."

"You can't understand!" Cade screamed. "How can you understand? How can you know what it's like to have videos... of your wife... videos of her being... being mutilated? How... can you possibly..."

He began to sob loudly. The Devil couldn't help but think it was all a bit dramatic. He was blubbering almost comically like a child in the next room.

"Mr Cade can I arrange for somebody to be with you tonight?" asked Laurie, always diligent.

"Get out, leave me alone," Cade snorted. "Just get out, now!"

Another short pause and then the footsteps started towards the door. The Devil realised he was in the middle of the front hall, with nowhere to go. If he leapt up the stairs he'd be caught. Anywhere else and it would be a similar scenario.

As Laurie got closer he spied a door sitting ajar close to the front entrance. Darting as nimbly as his humble Human body would go, he jumped inside and closed the door. To his relief he found he was in a small lavatory, a frosted glass window pointing outside.

Laurie passed by on the other side of the door. As she went to go she called back to Cade.

"If you think of anything, let me know right away," she said. "My superior officer has a direct line with intelligence forces and we're working on getting info from our suspect. We'll keep you updated Mr Cade. Please try and keep the faith and patience with us, we're trying to help you."

Cade didn't answer. Laurie stepped out of the front door to a blur of camera flashes. The Devil could see and hear the world's press swooping down on her through the frosted glass. Her silhouette moved like a ghost amongst the light.

Gradually it stopped. When the flurry was over, The Devil eased himself out of the bathroom. He looked about the hallway. There was nothing, only silence, light flooding out from the doorway to the kitchen. He heard a chair scraping along the floor and then its legs creak as Cade sat down. He cleared his throat and headed into the next room.

Cade was perched at the kitchen table, staring blankly at the screen of his laptop. The Devil was only a few feet from him when he realised he was there.

"Wooaah!" he shouted, getting up. "Who the hell are you!"

"Take it easy Cade, calm down," said The Devil, casually sauntering into the kitchen. "You'll give yourself a heart attack. And you're no use to either of us dead."

"Who... who are you? Laurie! Help! Help! Laurie!"

"Would you just calm down!"

The Devil's stern, hard tone seemed to strike a chord with Cade. In an instant he stopped shouting. His hands were shaking and his skin was grey. He stood in his slobbish clothes staring at the figure who had appeared in his kitchen. He was numb, blank, eyes wide and bloodshot. The Devil knew he had his attention.

"Good, thank you," he said with a little bow. "I'm only going to ask you once and I need you to be clear, concise and honest. No lies, no misleading, just straight-up, honest-to-goodness truths please. Are we clear?"

Cade nodded, his back pressed against the glass of the patio doors. He watched The Devil as he pulled out a chair from the table and offered one to him. Sitting down, he crossed his legs, hairy flesh poking out from the giant tear in his trousers.

"From the beginning," he said calmly. "I want you to tell me what happened to your wife Medina Cade."

THE MAN IN THE DARK

TWELVE

"Come on love, throw us a bone!"

Laurie ignored the shouting. She'd grown a thick enough skin in the police to handle journalists. And in her experience, if she ignored one of them then the others would quickly follow behind.

This time though it was a bit harder. She spotted all the usual crime reporters that turned up at murder scenes. They all looked the same, haggard, washed out and overweight. She knew exactly how they felt.

With the Cade case it was a different story. The normal journalists who swooped and hunted like vultures were being pushed to the back of the queue. In their place was a new breed, a wholly different kind of polished, well-groomed and good looking raft of people. Television, they had to be. No working hack could afford those kind of clothes and that amount of time for makeup. The camera crews and big spotlights on them were another clue.

Laurie hurried past them. She kept her head down while the questions were fired at her in quick succession.

"Who are you?" asked one, a hint of French about it.

"What can you tell us about the case?" came another, this time American.

"Is the British government stepping in?" a Brit this time.

"Will Mr Cade be speaking to the press?" German.

Laurie didn't dare answer any of them. As soon as they got a whiff that she was willing to speak they'd be all over her. Lister called them parasites, she couldn't really argue, even if they were only doing their jobs.

She reached her car, the camera flashes dimming and the crowd retreating back towards the front of Cade's semi-detached. She sat for a moment, hands resting on the steering wheel, the sound of her heartbeat thumping in her ears. She was tense, stressed, altogether pushed to her very limit. And she wasn't getting anywhere.

Something flashed just beyond her periphery. Laurie's senses were so shot she panicked, her arms and shoulders turning rock hard, ready to throw a punch. When she realised it was her onboard police computer she felt a little silly.

Data streams were appearing on the screen. Units requesting assistance, emergencies called, desperate cries for medical attention. The riot was spreading, getting bigger. She thought it might have been prudent to carry on with her case before she started getting her hands dirty with that. She was, after all, a Detective Sergeant. Surely she wouldn't be expected to take to the front line.

Although it was looking pretty bad now. The first calls of disturbance had come in over two hours ago. And it was still raging. She looked up through the windscreen and could see the shimmering skyline of the city. The deep, angry glow of fire made the buildings appear like jagged teeth in the night.

"Shit," she said, checking her watch. "It's after ten and they're still at it."

She started the engine and pulled away from the house - a few rogue photographers snapping as she headed down the street. Laurie had never known a case like this before and she couldn't help but feel excited. It was terrible of course, absolutely awful what they had done to Medina Cade. But it was a big, juicy mystery that

THE MAN IN THE DARK

she could get her teeth into. That was, providing Lister didn't beat her to it.

Laurie had been warned about old school coppers like him. Big, brash and bastards. They were walking, talking caricatures of a time that had ceased to exist long ago. But somehow they still managed to pull in a wage and not be thrown in jail themselves. It was a mystery, to the uninitiated. For those on the front line dealing with Wild West cowboys and self-styled sheriffs like Ken Lister, it was pretty bloody obvious why they were still in jobs. Dinosaurs had a tendency to move in herds. And there were plenty more like him in high ranking positions above and beside him to make sure little 'unprofessionalisms' were kept quiet.

When Laurie had first graduated to being a detective she'd been given some sage advice from a friend. Don't do anything that will draw attention to you instead of the job. It had seemed simple enough, she'd thought. Be a good cop, play it by the rules and reap the rewards of being a straight arrow. Except this was the twenty-first century and the more women were rising through the ranks of the police the more the old guard were grumbling into their lunchtime pints and whiskies.

This case had potential for somebody like Laurie. She could make a name for herself, be the hero cop who saves the day. The media would *love* to see her succeed, they'd probably make her an idol. But that meant jumping through hoops and angering those above her - including Ken Lister. Laurie knew all of that, she wasn't stupid - far from it. No wonder she was looking and feeling like a tired old rag. Balancing being a good police officer with internal politics was exhausting.

The loud opening chords of Walking on Sunshine by Katrina and the Waves made Laurie jump. The screen on her phone was flashing.

"Andy," she said. "Please tell me there's nothing wrong. Please tell me that on all the nights you've managed to get Matilda down to sleep first time round, that she's not got croup, that you don't need to go to the hospital and that the front door is locked, secured and you won't be going anywhere until I get back."

"Wow, that's quite a list," said Andy. "I was actually just phoning to see if my wife was planning on *coming* home and that she hadn't had her head smashed in by angry rioters."

Laurie smiled. She always smiled when she heard her husband's voice. That was why he was her husband. They were supposed to be good at that sort of thing.

"Yes, no," she said.

"Yes, no?" Andy asked. "Is that yes you *have* had your head smashed in and no you're *not* coming home. Or the other way around."

"Do you think I'd be talking to you if I'd had my head smashed in?"

"No, I don't think you would," he said. "I think you'd be so angry that some snot-nosed little punk with a brick had managed to get the better of you that you'd be in the middle of breaking his legs."

"That would be police brutality," she laughed. "And yes, that's exactly what I'd be doing."

"I knew it," he said. "So you're coming home then?"

"Yes. Is Mattie asleep?"

"I've just put her down. She was worried about her mother."

"I'm sure she was," said Laurie, a lump forming in her throat. "You didn't show her the rioting did you? That is assuming it's on telly."

"It's *all* that's on the telly, and online of course. And no, I didn't, what kind of violence hungry maniac do you take me for?"

"I'm not going to answer that my darling," she smiled. "I'm on

THE MAN IN THE DARK

my way home just now. I had to stop off somewhere to check on something."

"Oh, how cryptic of you Detective Sergeant," said Andy. "Makes you sound all mysterious. It's kind of sexy."

"*Kind* of sexy? Don't you mean *is sexy*?"

"Hmmm," said Andy. "I don't know, since they promoted you and you don't wear your uniform anymore I think I've gone off you a bit."

"Cheeky bastard."

They both started laughing. They had known each other a very long time - all through adolescence and adulthood. Laurie and her husband Andy were inseparable, joined at the hip, together all the time. He'd made sacrifices for her and she likewise. They were a team, one that worked and one that tried to keep their daughter Matilda on the straight and narrow. And Laurie knew, she *always* knew, that no matter how bad a day she was having, Andy was always at the other end of the phone or behind the front door, waiting for her.

She was thankful for his support, thankful of his backing but most of all thankful for his patience. That's why when the sudden chill of forget crept across her shoulders and down her chest like an icy shower, she knew he wouldn't mind.

"Shit," she said, thumping the steering wheel. "Shit, shit, shit, shit."

"What's wrong?" he asked. "Have you run over a rioter?"

"I wish," she said.

She patted her jacket pockets, tangling her arms while she tried to steer. A quick glance down at her bag and a rummage around the papers and files scattered over the passenger seat produced nothing. She knew, like she always did, that it was all just a pretence. She'd forgotten it.

"Dare I ask. What did you make for dinner?"

"Roast," he said. "Spuds, carrots, gravy, the works. It was delicious by the way, of course it was, I made it. Yours is in the oven."

"Can you keep it there?" she asked, wincing.

"Why, I thought you were coming home…"

He trailed off. Laurie hated pulling the rug from under his feet. While she knew he would never be angry, never be upset when work got in the way of their domestic bliss, she never wanted to push him too far. No small part of her subconscious worried that one day Andrew Laurie would finally wake up and smell the coffee he'd made for his wife, the coffee that was sitting on the kitchen table, ice cold, because she'd not come home that night.

"What a stupid bloody question," he laughed.

And instantly she was put at ease. She could picture his face smiling on the other end of the phone. She knew that face so well, seen it for so long, even the sound of his beard against the speaker was enough for her to picture him. It was the little things, she had read once, that make up a marriage. They added up to one great big thing. She loved him, more than words could describe. Even when she was a bad wife.

"I love you," she said, not really knowing why.

"I love you too," he sounded surprised. "Where did that come from?"

"I just wanted to tell you. I just always want to tell you. And I know I'm a pain in the arse and I know you put up with me, I'm sorry."

"I don't put up with you and you never have to apologise to me," he said. "Whatever you have to do, you go and do it. And I'll be up when you come home, roast and all."

"See, that's why I love you," she laughed, turning the car around in the middle of the quiet street.

    THE MAN IN THE DARK

"I know that, you don't have to tell me," he said. "You just have to promise me one thing."

"Anything," she said.

"That whatever you're going to do you're very, very careful doing it."

There was a firm but worried tone to his voice. It wiped the smile from her face and she felt that same chill come across her again. Husbands always wished their wives safety. Only this time Andy sounded worried.

"I will," she said. "I promise."

"Please, please be careful. It's a war zone out there, people are going crazy love. I don't want you put in any danger."

"I'll be fine," said Laurie, trying not to cry. "I'll be fine."

"I love you," he said.

"I love you too."

They stayed silent for a moment, the call still live. Then Andy hung up.

Laurie was left with her sniffing and the roar of her car's engine. She sped along the quiet suburban street, working everything out in her mind. She had to shift herself from home life back to hardened Met copper, underpaid and overworked. It wasn't like flicking a switch but more a strapping on of armour. Big, thick, heavy plates of armour that were painful and jagged and enough to bring her back to her senses.

The prattling and screaming from her police radio helped. While she journeyed back to Cade's house, her colleagues were fighting in the streets. Anger was rife throughout the city, she could feel it, even in her car. Being a policewoman gave her an intuition for trouble. Maybe she'd always had it, she couldn't tell anymore. A copper without it wasn't very useful. And they never lasted long.

A secret radar, a sixth sense, whatever she wanted to call it, it was going off ten to the dozen now. Every inch and fibre of her being as a police officer was incensed and inflamed. This riot, the Cade case, everything. There was trouble alright, and it felt like something a lot bigger and a lot badder than she was first giving it credit for.

All Laurie wanted to do was get home as quickly as possible. Get home, kiss her husband and child and go to bed. It would be better in the morning, it always was. The dark always brought out the worst in people. That's why it was the dark.

The glowing skyline loomed large in her rear-view mirror. And she cursed herself for leaving her work phone in Cade's house.

THE MAN IN THE DARK

THIRTEEN

"Who the hell are you?" Cade mumbled. "Who… how the hell did you get into my house?"

The Devil drummed his fingers on the table top. Something made them wet and then sticky. He looked at the ends, all round and fat, and held them up to his nose. There was a terrible smell, something strong and acrid. He pulled his hand away and gave Cade a look of disapproval.

"Aren't you house trained yet Mr Cade?" he asked. "I know animals that keep a cleaner sty than this."

He nodded over at the pots and pans stacked up untidily in the sink. The washing machine was crammed full and clothes were spilling out the dryer, making the device appear to be being sick. There were muddy footprints all over the floor and empty mugs were placed sporadically on every surface.

"Is this all meant to paint some sort of picture?" asked The Devil.

"What kind of picture should I be painting?" asked Cade.

"I wasn't talking to you," he snapped. "I was talking to… never mind. I'm not going to explain it all again. Answers, you want answers. Good, that's good, you're in a state of eager readiness. A ready Human mind is like a big, fat slab of marble just waiting to be chipped away and sculpted into a masterpiece. It's untampered and pure, lovely. You want answers, I want answers, let's start talking. Medina, your wife. Where is she?"

Cade was still pressed against the patio doors. His eyes were shifting all around the room now, always darting back to The Devil. His chest was heaving up and down quickly and his skin had gone a pale grey. The Devil started to worry he was about to have a heart attack.

"She's... she's gone," he said. "She's... she's been kidnapped."

"Kidnapped?" asked The Devil. "Kidnapped by who? Who would want to kidnap her? Who are your enemies?"

"Enemies?"

"Yes, enemies, people who swear blood oaths to have you killed or harm brought against you. You know, enemies, a nemesis, a Ying to your Yang. That's what you people go in for isn't it? It makes you feel less alone."

"I... I don't have any enemies," said Cade. "I'm just a gas engineer. Gas engineers don't make enemies."

"You'd be surprised," said The Devil. "Come on now, think. Your wife, Medina, you're happily married, have a house, pay the mortgage, walk the dog, go on holiday, cough up your taxes, the works. Why would she be the one to be kidnapped? Out of the billions of you Humans on this planet hurtling through space, why her? There must be some reason."

Cade shook his head timidly. He was still breathing heavily and he'd started clutching at his chest. Irritated, The Devil got up and grabbed one of the empty mugs. He shoved it under the tap and poured in some water. Shoving it into Cade's hands he told him to sit down.

"Pull yourself together man, you're wasting everybody's time," he said. "Now come on, think. Why Medina? Why her?"

Cade gulped down the water. He wiped his chin and pointed over to the laptop.

"Ransom," he said. "There's a ransom note in my e-mails."

"A note, fantastic, now we're getting somewhere. Now what does it say?"

"You… you can read it, it's on the screen. It's all I've been looking at these past two weeks. Over and over and over again I've been reading that bloody letter. I see it in my dreams, every time I close my eyes and-"

"Yes, yes, very good, I get the picture," The Devil waved him away. "Broken hearted, can't cope, it's all a bit obvious. The letter, what does it say?"

Cade's face flushed. The Devil couldn't tell if it was through anger or embarrassment. For a broken, bleeding hearted man, he found Cade somewhat difficult to read. He put it down to the man's bleak and utter boringness.

"I can't read it, it hurts too much," said Cade.

"You're going to have to old chum, because I can't understand a word it says," said The Devil. "And without it we're not going to get very far."

"Who are you?" Cade asked, getting to his feet suddenly. "Are you with the police? Are you another faceless suit from MI5? Let's see some ID."

"I don't have any ID," said The Devil. "And do you think a member of the secret service would be dressed like this? Please, use your brain for something other than self-pity Cade. The note, where is it?"

Cade was angry now, it was obvious. He huffed and stomped around to the other end of the table. Spinning the laptop around, The Devil looked at it blankly and shrugged his shoulders.

"Nonsense," he said. "I can't read Human writing. I'm completely illiterate."

"You can't read or write?" asked Cade, laughing a little with a snort. "You don't know what any of that says? You come in here, unannounced, won't tell me who you are and ask to see my wife's ransom note and you can't even *read*!"

"Stop focussing on the negatives Cade," he said. "It's so, well, negative. Start looking at the positives, you might live a little longer, although probably not that much. And for starters, why don't you read me what that ransom note says and we might be able to take a step closer to bringing your wife back to the land of the living. Because from what I've heard, you don't have all that many options. And surely anything new, whether it's me or anybody else, can only be a good thing."

It took Cade a few moments to process what The Devil had said. When the penny finally dropped inside his fat head, he turned the laptop back around to face him. Steadying his breath, he began to read.

"We have… we have your wife Medina, Pierce Cade," he started. "We have her and we will kill her. You are a tool of western oppression, you live and work in a country that has seen the Middle East and the territories of the Prophet as a plaything for too long and we will have our revenge. One by one you will fall and we will take back the world that belongs to us…"

Cade caught his breath. He swallowed, eyes welling up.

"I mean it goes on and on like this," he said pointing at the screen. "There are screeds and screeds of bile about who they are, what their mission is."

"Yes, I understand," said The Devil. "But I need to know the whole picture if I'm to stand any chance of finding Medina. Go on."

Cade took a long, deep breath. He wiped his eyes with the balls of his hands and then continued.

"Your wife Medina is being held as a hostage. The ransom on her head is five million US dollars," he stopped.

THE MAN IN THE DARK

Looking at The Devil, there was no reaction.

"Oh, sorry," said The Devil. "Was I supposed to react there?"

"They want five million dollars," said Cade again. "Five *million,* from me!"

"Is that a lot of money?" he asked.

"Yeah, it's a lot. You don't think five million bucks is a lot of money? You've got it just lying around do you?"

"Money is your invention, not mine. And quite frankly you lot make far too big a deal of it. Still, it's good for business."

Cade shook his head in disbelief. He was about to start reading again when another flash of anger came over him. He slammed the screen of the laptop down hard, making the table rattle.

"This is a waste of time!" he shouted. "I'm wasting time, my time, Medina's time. Get out! Get out of my house whoever you are. Get out of here!"

"Calm down Cade," said The Devil. "You're overreacting like all Humans do when there's the slightest bit of stress or tension. It's only natural I suppose, you're not built for pressure. It's a small wonder you survive so many wars, really it is."

"Get out of my house!" Cade screamed. "Get out or I'll throw you out."

The fear was gone from him now. He looked crazed, suddenly bigger. His flabby, abused body was still the same but there was a menace to him. Where there had been pathetic fecklessness there was danger now. And he looked capable of doing some damage.

The Devil chose his next words wisely. He knew he was in no state to fight, he'd already been shown that back in the police station. And that was thanks to Him of course. Once again The Devil had been handed a dud.

He decided to be cunning. It had worked for him in the past.

"Who are these people?" he asked, trying to rejig Cade's brain.

"People? What people?" asked the man.

"The people who sent you the ransom note, who are they?"

"How the hell should I know."

"Surely if you're being asked to pay five million US dollars to somebody you have to know who to give it to. They might be terrorists Cade but they're not thick."

"Some group, some terror cell, I don't know," said Cade. "I forget their name. Now get out of my house."

"Yes, but which terror cell?"

"I don't know, okay. The police, they have a list of them all, it's on there somewhere. What does it matter? My wife and I were on holiday in Dubai, she went for a walk and they snatched her off the street. Who cares what they stand for, I just want Medina back!"

A knock at the door distracted them both. Cade appeared to get taller, standing on his toes. He glanced back towards the front door and then at The Devil. He could see his mind ticking, thinking, trying to work out if he could get there in time before The Devil stopped him. It wasn't a contest, The Devil didn't stand a chance.

"Don't answer it," he said, trying to buy time. "Whoever is on the other side of that door isn't going to help you Cade. Only I can help you get your wife back."

"And who are you anyway? You haven't even told me your name," he said.

"It doesn't matter who I am. All that matters is we both want the same thing. And I'm willing, happy even, to do whatever it takes to get that. Come on now, use your brain, that's what it's there for."

The knocking distracted him again. He turned slowly to face the door and beyond it the hall. The faint flashes of light made everything out there seem almost magical. The press were back in force, snapping away at whoever was at the front door.

"Don't do it Cade," said The Devil again.

THE MAN IN THE DARK

But Cade didn't listen. He took off out of the kitchen as fast as his big legs would take him. The Devil cursed and went after him. He scrambled over the table, flapping like a duck in a bathtub, knocking everything in sight off and out of his way.

He darted out of the kitchen and saw Cade at the door. He was fumbling with the keys in the lock. Precious microseconds passed and The Devil caught up with him. But he was too late.

Cade pulled open the door and was met with a wall of camera flashes. The light dazzled The Devil for a moment and he couldn't see. He felt into the space ahead of him, desperate to grab a hold of something, someone, anyone. Then he heard Laurie's voice.

"You!" she shouted, above the din of the cameras and questions. "What the hell are you doing here?"

The Devil's vision cleared and he saw the police woman staring at him. Her face was lost between amazement, embarrassment and anger. He didn't have time for any of those things. Grabbing her, he pulled her over the doorway and brought Cade with him, kicking the door shut.

The three of them tripped and stumbled back into the hallway. Outside the camera flashes still rattled away like streaks of lightning in a midnight storm. It made the darkness jump and flitter as if they were in an old film reel. The Devil held up his hands as Laurie and Cade stared at him.

"Okay, I know what you're both going to say," he said. "But before you do, I just want to reassure you both, that's *both* of you now, that I'm still the best and most qualified person in this room, no, on this *planet*, to find Medina Cade. Okay?"

"Please tell me you know who this man is?" Cade asked Laurie. "You're a copper, I want you to tell me you at least know that."

"Yeah, I do know who he is," said Laurie, reaching around to her back. "You know that ransom e-mail you were sent, the one saying those terrorists have your wife Mr Cade?"

"Yes, what about it?"

"It was sent from an address in Gravesend, a flat even, where we found this arsehole earlier today."

The Devil couldn't see very well in the darkness, which annoyed him to no end. But he imagined the look on Cade's face was very much like his own.

"I beg your pardon," he said.

"You're not joking, are you?" asked Cade. "You mean this guy… this guy has something to do with Medina's kidnapping?"

"Well…" said Laurie.

Cade lunged forward and grabbed The Devil by the shoulders. He was stronger than he looked and he picked him up off the floor, slamming him hard into the front door.

"Where is she!" he snarled. "Give me back my wife you terrorist bastard! Where's my wife!"

"I can assure you," said The Devil between thumps. "That I'm just as surprised as you are at this revelation!"

Cade pulled a tightly clenched fist backwards and got ready to throw it. Laurie, however, had other ideas.

She sprayed them both in their faces. Immediately Cade dropped The Devil and they writhed around in pain.

"What was *that*!" The Devil shouted, feeling his eyes burning. "What have you done Laurie! My eyeballs, they're on fire!"

"Oh god!" Cade rolled around. "Oh god it hurts!"

The Devil slumped to his knees, coughing as the stinging sensation crept down the back of his throat. He could sense the others about him but he was incapacitated, defeated by the searing liquid he'd been blasted with.

"Alright you two," said Laurie. "You both need to take a time out, pull yourselves together and get thinking straight. And when you've done all that we're going to take a nice, long drive down to the station and get this thing sorted. Does that sound like a good idea?"

Neither The Devil or Cade answered. Instead they both made inaudible sounds that resembled animals - wounded animals, as they rolled around the hallway.

"Okay then," she said. "I'll take that as a yes."

FOURTEEN

"Right, I've just about had enough of all this," said The Devil, crawling about the floor. "I'm getting mightily sick and tired of being punched, kicked, trodden on, stamped, shoved, manhandled, throttled, strangled and blinded. I'm The Devil, I don't *do* physical violence. That's what you lot are for! Playthings, little toys for me and Him to push around and do as we please. It's the Natural Order, in case you didn't know. Now can somebody please stop these Human eyeballs from setting my skull on fire."

He tried to open his lids but it was still too painful. He rubbed them for the millionth time, knuckles sodden with tears. The strong taste and smell of the spray hung in the air about him like bad perfume. His throat was rough from coughing. And still nobody helped.

"I can only hope that you are in as much discomfort as I am Cade," he shouted out.

A series of whimpers and grunts met him as Laurie's other victim endured a similar punishment. The Devil stopped crawling when his head met a wall. He tried to open his eyes again but the stinging put paid to that right away.

"Laurie!" he shouted. "Laurie are you there? What is this stuff? Don't you think it's a bit excessive?"

He heard her walking up to him from somewhere in the house.

 THE MAN IN THE DARK

She stopped at his side and helped him onto his feet.

"Here," she said.

He pawed about blindly. Finally he felt a damp towel in his hands and immediately wiped his eyes. The coolness was a relief. The icy water ran across his eyes and down his cheeks like a great cleansing flood. Slowly he felt the pain receding and he opened his eyes with caution.

Laurie was standing in front of him. He squinted in the darkness, tears still streaming down his face.

"I'm not going to thank you," he said adamantly. "It was your fault in the first place."

"You're under arrest sunshine," she said, snatching the towel away. "You shouldn't be here."

"Of course I should be here, I had to meet with Cade. Where is he by the way?"

They both looked about the hall. Cade had vanished. Laurie looked panicked.

"Shit," she said. "Mr Cade? Pierce? Where are you sir! Mr Cade?"

"He told me everything," said The Devil.

"Shut up," said the policewoman. "You stay right there, I'm not letting you out of my sight."

"A terrifying thought, but I don't have time for this."

He went to make for the front door. Laurie stepped in front of him. She held up her little tube of spray and pushed it near his face.

"Do you want another blast of this stuff?" she asked. "Because it makes no difference to me how much of it it takes to get you to stand perfectly still."

The Devil held his hands up. He stepped back and watched her as she looked about the hallway for Cade.

"He was right here, how can he have vanished?" she asked.

"Are you asking me or is this a rhetorical conversation?"

"Shut up," she said. "I'm sick of the sound of your voice already."

"I thought so."

"This is a nightmare, an absolute bloody nightmare. How did you get here?" she asked. "You're meant to be banged up back at the station."

"I have enemies in high places."

"Yeah, well, you're not going anywhere now that I've got you. I tell you, as soon as we get back there's going to be hell to pay."

The Devil laughed. He sat down on the steps and rubbed his eyes. He could still smell the spray, on his hands, on his clothes. He wrinkled his nose in disgust.

"I smell like a bad Mexican restaurant," he said. "I *feel* like one too. Look at the state of this body, what an absolute shambles."

"Mr Cade?" Laurie shouted again. "Mr Cade can you come back here please, I have the suspect, he's under control."

"I'm beginning to suspect that our mutual friend Mr Cade is gone," he said. "Probably away to pine over that ransom note he was sent."

"And what would *you* know about that note?" asked Laurie, targeting him. "I thought you were clueless?"

"He told me, he read it aloud to me shortly before you showed up. I even think he was going to let me help you find Medina until you came thundering in here and ruined the moment."

"Sounds real romantic," said Laurie. "You're in enough trouble as it is mate, so maybe you should just keep quiet."

"I'm not keeping quiet and I'm not staying here," he said. "We're wasting time Laurie, you're wasting time. Why don't you let me out of here and we can find Medina Cade and stop this whole charade."

"So you know where Medina Cade is then?" she focussed on him. "I thought you said you had nothing to do with this?"

"I don't, to both of those questions," he smiled. "But I can very quickly work out where the Cade woman is if you just let me go about my business."

"We've been through this sunshine, I'm not letting you go anywhere, unless it's back into a cell and the door is *double* bolted this time."

"Believe me, that wouldn't work."

"Oh it will this time mate, I'll lock the door myself."

"No, seriously Laurie, that *won't* work. I told you, I have enemies in high places."

"What does that even mean?" she asked. "Who are you? Why do you talk like that? Is this some sort of game for you? Are you one of these posh country lads that comes to the city, pretends to be a homeless person and gets into trouble just for kicks? Is that what we're dealing with here?"

"I assure you I'm not one of those," said The Devil.

"Fine, you're a terror suspect that's under arrest," she said. "And that's just the way I want it."

"Have you seen the note?" he asked.

"The note? Of course I have," she said, looking about the hall, her spray still pointed at him.

"What did you think of it?"

"What did I think? I think it's pretty horrible. I can't imagine what Cade is going through. And I can't even begin to imagine what Medina is going through. Tired, terrified, maimed, dreadful stuff."

"Maimed?" The Devil asked. "How is she maimed?"

Laurie looked hard and straight at him. For a moment she appeared to think he was trying to trick her. Then The Devil could see that she believed him.

"Yes, maimed," she said. "The terrorists, they've hurt her. There's a video."

"A video?" he got back to his feet and headed for the kitchen.

"What, stay there! I'm warning you!" she shouted. "Get back down there."

"I assume Cade has the video on his computer," said The Devil.

He strode through the house and picked up the computer. He opened the screen and it blinked back into life. Laurie was behind him, her breathing heavy, spray still trained on him.

"Care to do the honours?"

"You're kidding me right?" she said. "You want me to show you the video of Medina Cade being maimed. On her husband's laptop, in their house, and you're a suspect in all of this."

"Every one of those sentiments is correct," he said smugly. "Now please stop faffing about and do it. I can't read and I can't work these things, these technological contraptions you all seem so fussed about. So please, Laurie, I'm asking you as nicely as I can."

He stepped to the side. She stood still, eyes peering at him like an owl staring into the night, hunting for its prey. He knew what she was doing, he could feel her trying to get inside his head. There was no chance of that. And the longer she continued the more she came to the same conclusion.

"I don't believe this," she said, pocketing her pepper spray.

"Don't believe what?"

"That I might actually fucking believe *you*."

The Devil smiled. Another one bit the dust. She pushed past him and began clicking buttons and typing on the keyboard.

"It's not your fault," he said quietly. "Everybody comes around to my way of thinking in the end. If it makes you feel any better you weren't the quickest, not by a long shot."

"That doesn't make me feel any better," she said, opening a file.

 THE MAN IN THE DARK

"But you weren't the longest either. That honour," he said, pointing to the ceiling. "As always goes to the Man Upstairs."

"Here."

The Devil watched the screen. A grainy, black and white video appeared showing what appeared to be Medina Cade. She was badly beaten, eyes black, lips cracked, her clothes torn around her chest and breasts. There was bruising around her throat and she was shaking uncontrollably.

A muffled voice from behind the camera yelled at her. She jumped, bleary eyes staring at the camera from behind her dirty, straggly hair. The glamorous, well kempt woman of the pictures in Cade's bedroom was little more than an empty husk of what she used to be. Fragile and broken, this was a woman close to death.

"Why... why are you doing this to me?" she asked, her voice cracking.

There was no answer from behind the camera. Instead a large, glistening blade appeared in the bottom of the screen. The camera moved and juggled as it drew closer to her. Medina recoiled in horror, her hands and ankles bound to the chair she was sitting on.

The camera was up close to her now, close enough to see the scores on her neck and the bruising around her eyes. A gloved hand pressed the knife against her forehead as she wept uncontrollably. Tracing a line down the middle of her head, it stopped beneath her nose and just above her lip. With one quick, precise swoop, the knife cut into her face, dark blood spitting out as she screamed in agony.

The camera shuffled, moving back and forth while the horrific attack unfolded. There was laughter from somewhere, almost lost amongst the pained moans of Medina Cade. The savagery continued for another thirty seconds, Laurie squirming beside The Devil, unable to tear herself away from the screen.

Medina passed out, her body limp, dark blood now coating her face and chest. The camera panned down to a pool on the floor. In its centre, like a macabre island in an ocean of blood, was the remains of her nose. Then, the screen went black.

"There you have it," said Laurie. "You wanted to see it. Ring any bells?"

"No, not really," The Devil sniffed. "Although the production values weren't quite what I was expecting, you can't really fault the director for getting their point across quite aptly."

Laurie laughed a little, then caught herself. She darted The Devil a dirty look.

"Was that meant to be a joke?" she asked.

"I don't do jokes Laurie," he said. "I'm above jokes. Although I should probably offer at least some sort of gratification for showing me that absurdity. At least I now know that Medina Cade is in fact kidnapped and that this isn't all some strop she's thrown in order to get attention."

"Yeah, she's been kidnapped alright. And these guys aren't messing around."

"No."

Laurie closed the laptop. As she did so there was a loud thump from the front door. They both peered out of the kitchen and saw DCI Lister storming his way through the front door. Six uniformed officers followed in his wake. His eyes immediately trained on Laurie and he marched his men towards her, nostrils flaring like an angry bull.

"Lister!" Laurie shouted, sounding surprised. "Sir, what are you doing here?"

She went to meet him. Lister ignored her, pushing her out of the way. He charged directly at The Devil, eyes white with a wild, untamed rage.

THE MAN IN THE DARK

"Sir!" she shouted as the uniforms thumped after him. "Sir, I can explain, I was about to bring him back to the station when-"

Laurie was cut off by a brightly coloured, hi-vis arm from one of the uniforms. The policeman grabbed her by the throat and lifted her off her feet. With one arm he lobbed her across the kitchen. She smashed into the countertop amongst the dirty dishes before rolling off onto the floor, covered in debris.

The whole room seemed to freeze. Nobody had been expecting that, least of all The Devil. He instinctively held his hands up, looking between Laurie and Lister.

"Okay," he said. "That's a bit of a surprise. There was me thinking you Human police officers were nothing but fat and gristle."

Lister began to laugh. The hilarity spread to his men one-by-one, like a chain. When he stopped the others stopped too. The DCI stood glowering at The Devil across the kitchen table.

"Yes," said The Devil. "Yes I'm definitely surprised by all of this. Which isn't a nice sensation as it happens. Can I help you with anything Detective Chief Inspector Lister? Or is there maybe a bone I could get you and your posse to chew on, seeing as you seem a little more feral than the last time we met."

Lister didn't say anything. He stood perfectly still, unnaturally still. His breathing was loud and laboured and the uniformed officers behind him were exactly the same. They all seemed odd, a little off, like their dimensions weren't correct. That's when The Devil began to suspect some foul play.

"Did you get them?" came Cade's voice from outside the room.

He appeared at the door behind the brood of police officers, sneaking around the frame of the door. He slunk into the kitchen, making sure he was behind the cops. His bleary, bloodshot eyes flitted around the room, drinking in all of the scene.

"You called the police," said The Devil. "How unoriginal."

"He called me," grunted Lister.

"Excuse me?"

"He called *me*."

"Yes, I know, I heard what you said," said The Devil, feeling clever. "I just wanted to make sure of something."

"What?" asked the DCI.

"That your voice is coming out of your body a little slower than when your lips move," he fired back. "And that's usually a very good sign that something's wrong. In fact, I'd say that's a stick on that something isn't quite right with you DCI Lister. I assume it's the same for your men too."

None of them spoke. Lister snorted loudly. He spat out a large, thick glob of phlegm that landed on the kitchen table between him and The Devil. It was bright green and appeared to be smoking.

"Yes," said The Devil. "I knew I was right. You know you should probably see some sort of physician before that gets any worse."

Laurie groaned from the kitchen floor beside him. He reached down and helped her onto her feet, pots and plates clattering about her. Lister and his men began to bear down on them, spreading out to fill the whole width of the tight little room. Somewhere behind them was Cade, cowering safely as the cops went about their black business.

"Laurie," said The Devil, trying to rouse her. "Now would be a good time to tell me that the patio doors behind us are unlocked.

"What? I don't know... why would I know that?" she said numbly. "What... what's going on? Lister? Lister? What... what are you doing here?"

The senior officer said nothing. Instead he began growling, a low, subsonic snarl that was like an angry dog. Or a wolf, thought The Devil.

"Laurie, I think your superior officer might be a bit on the angry side," said The Devil, easing back towards the patio windows. "So I think it might be a good idea if we gave him a little breathing space, don't you?"

The uniforms glowered at the pair. Each of them picked up something hard or sharp as they rounded the table, slowly and methodically. Knives, pots, they had the glazed look of untampered violence about them. And Lister was leading the charge.

"Yeah," said Laurie, her mind slowly clearing. "I think you might be spot on with that."

A still, serene moment descended upon the room, during which nobody moved or said anything. It was, by its very nature, all too short lived. And when The Devil and Laurie turned to break open the patio doors, it was lost forever.

The glass shattered as they both barrelled into it. They spilled out into the darkness of the garden, the breaths of Lister and the others hot on their heels. They darted across the slippery grass and vaulted up onto the fence.

Lister and the uniformed cops gave chase. They were snarling like beasts, less running, more galloping after their prey. Laurie and The Devil dropped into the next garden before making a break for the one adjacent.

"What the hell is happening?" asked Laurie, looking back over her shoulder. "What's gotten into them?"

The Devil grabbed her by the wrist and pulled her sharply to the right. They sped down the gap between a wall and the next house until they were out in the street. Far down the road the cavalcade of the world's media was still camped outside the Cade house. But in the fleeting glimpse The Devil caught of them, he sensed there was something off.

"Surely not," he said, looking at the massed group of around a hundred people. "Surely not."

"Surely not what?" asked Laurie, gasping for breath. "What in god's name is happening?"

The Devil blinked, ignoring the media throng. The heavy boots of the pursuing police officers was enough to jolt him back into action. He pulled Laurie behind him and ran as fast as he could up the residential road and back to his stolen police car.

"Get in!" he shouted at her.

"What? No! Where did you get this from?" she asked. "This isn't yours!"

"I'm aware of that Laurie but I really suggest you get in. Otherwise your old friend Lister is going to tear your throat out with his teeth."

Laurie wasn't going to be told twice. She threw open the door and clambered into the passenger seat. The Devil did the same, starting the engine. As the headlights blinked into life, they caught sight of two of the uniformed officers.

"Holy shit!" Laurie screamed. "What's... what's wrong with them?"

The cops had dropped to all fours and were charging towards them, moving like a strange cross between a horse and an ape. As they neared they leapt forward, landing onto the bonnet of the squad car.

"Get us out of here!" Laurie shouted. "Put your foot down man!"

The Devil slammed his bare foot onto the accelerator. The two uniformed cops were thrown forward, their heads smashing into the windscreen. Bright red blood mixed with the shattered lattice of the broken glass. The Devil pulled down on the steering wheel and their lifeless corpses rolled off the bonnet, cast aside like forgotten luggage.

The squad car weaved and rolled as The Devil tried to bring it under control. Laurie looked through the windows and out the back, her whole body shaking. As they tore through the suburban street and back towards the city, she felt a ball of sick and unease creeping up from her stomach.

"We need somewhere to go," said The Devil. "This dreadful Human body I've been given is beginning to wane. And I need to think."

"This can't be happening to me," said Laurie, holding her forehead. "I mean, this is like something out of those horror films you see on the telly. I hate horror films and I certainly don't want to be fucking *in* one!"

"Believe me Laurie, you haven't seen *anything* yet," said The Devil.

"See, that's exactly what I'm talking about!" she shouted. "There's always somebody who says that exact same thing and then they all get their heads chopped off or they're eaten by zombies, some weird shit like that! You've got to tell me, right now, what we just saw back there. Otherwise I'm going to spray you again with my pepper spray."

"I will tell you," said The Devil, concentrating on keeping them on the road. "But first I need to eat something. I think my body is about to shut down."

Laurie stared blankly at the cars zooming by the windscreen. She thought for a moment while The Devil's stomach began to cannibalise itself.

"I know somewhere we can go," she said. "I hope you like a roast."

The Devil smiled wryly at her.

"My dear, there's nothing I love *more* than a good roasting."

FIFTEEN

The Devil was out of breath. Climbing eight flights of stairs was as lung-busting as it got. Particularly for this body it would seem. Although he suspected two flights would be pushing it.

Laurie didn't seem to have a problem with it. And she certainly didn't think anything of The Devil's slow, wheezing breath.

"How much further?" he asked, gripping onto the banister in a vain attempt to stay alive. "Shouldn't places like these have elevators of some description? Would that be too difficult and easy to arrange?"

"We do have a lift," Laurie called back to him. "But it's broken."

"A likely excuse," he said to himself.

Laurie, mercifully, came to a stop on the tenth floor. She motioned for him to drag his crippled self down the hallway. He limped on for a little bit, passing doorways on either side of the corridor. Finally Laurie came to a stop at a rather bland, humble looking entranceway.

"Alright," she said, fetching her keys. "Let's go over a few ground rules before we go in here."

"Rules?" The Devil turned up his nose at her. "I think you might be getting me confused with one of your colleagues or a common criminal Laurie. I don't play by the rules - it's a professional responsibility."

 140

"Rule number one," she said, ignoring him. "This is my home - I *live* here, okay? That means I'm letting you into my life, my personal and private life. This is a safe place, it's my little sanctuary from all the blood, gore, murders, death, armed robberies and bad bastards of the world. And I'm letting you into it."

She shook her head and looked towards the ceiling. She appeared to be still trying to convince herself that this was the right thing to do.

"I still haven't quite worked out how you fit into all of this," she said. "You're still a suspect in Medina Cade's kidnapping. But you did save us both from Lister and whatever the hell those uniforms were. So I guess I'm trying to come to terms with just how bat shit insane this whole scenario is and how, probably, my career is over."

"Then why are you doing it?" asked The Devil. "Why are you throwing your career away on something you don't think you believe in?"

"I don't know," she said. "I don't know is the answer."

"That's not much of an answer."

"No, it's not. But it's my answer. Those coppers back there, the uniforms at Cade's place. They weren't... they weren't human, were they?"

The Devil shrugged his shoulders nonchalantly.

"Hard to tell really," he said. "You lot have a tendency to get worked up into such a state I find it hard to think of what new low you'll sink to next."

"The way they moved though," she said. "They were like animals, like dogs even."

"That's very true. But I remember Humans who couldn't stand upright and ate raw meat off the bone. Evolution has an odd way of regressing from time-to-time, ironically. Maybe they were just having a bad day."

"A bad day? You call throwing me across the room a bad day? I was up in the air!"

"Yes you were," he laughed. "With all the majesty and elegance of an elephant launched from a cannon as I recall. I must admit I did find that quite entertaining."

"And you think that's just one of our plod having a bad day?" she said. "Absolute horse shit. But conveniently it brings me on to rule number two."

"There are *more* rules?" he droned.

"My family are my life," she said earnestly. "If anything and I mean *anything* happens to them while you're here then I *will* kill you. Do I make myself crystal clear?"

"Why do you assume what happened back at Cade's house was anything to do with me?" he proffered.

"Because you said you were… you said that you were, you know…"

He raised his eyebrows and smiled. The Devil liked it when Humans caved in. He enjoyed when they parked their small-minded sense of their own reality and accepted that they had been living a lie, that they were completely wrong about *everything* they had believed in. It was a trend that had happened more and more as time had gone on. Back in the bad old days almost every one of them believed in Him, Upstairs and Down with an unhealthy fanaticism. But since they had discovered the virtues of science, that belief had been slowly eroded.

Now when he was able to convince one of them that he did in fact exist, their faces and hearts dropped like dead weights. Moreover it usually meant that he was winning. And The Devil loved to win.

"It doesn't matter," she said, without actually saying it. "Who you say you are and who you think you are doesn't mean a monkey's toss to me mate. All that does matter to me are the lives on the

THE MAN IN THE DARK

other side of this door. So when we go in you keep your mouth shut, your hands to yourself and we can try and think of what our next move is going to be."

The Devil remained tight-lipped. In the dim shade of the hallway Laurie looked concerned. He could see that she was battling conflict, an ever-growing lack of confidence welling up inside of her. And he suspected that this ran deeper than just the crisis in front of her. She was a woman with a lot of issues, clearly. He concluded that she worried herself about almost everything. Her family obviously, but also the way she behaved and acted as a policewoman. Her relationship with DCI Lister was one of total and utter contempt. And even Cade had seen fit to dismiss her. Top of the long and growing list of her issues, The Devil suspected, was her worry that her place in the world she had created for herself was constantly in jeopardy.

He had no sympathy for her. He had no sympathy for anybody.

Laurie put the key in the lock. As she was about to turn it, The Devil reached out and stopped her.

"I've just been struck by a thought," he whispered.

"Can it wait until I've poured myself a pint of gin and tonic?"

She went to turn the handle but he pulled her away from the door.

"What's wrong with you? Let go of me!" she shouted.

"Shhhhhhh," he hushed her.

He listened for a moment, Laurie watching him. The Devil held up a finger at her.

"Why is it so quiet?" he asked. "How many apartments are there on this floor?"

"A dozen," she said. "So what?"

"Twelve flats and you could hear a pin drop. That doesn't strike you as being a bit odd?"

"Not when it's after midnight. People, ordinary people, people not like you and I, have jobs to go to first thing in the morning. And that usually means they're tucked up in bed at a human hour. Not lurking about corridors and getting chased by zombie policemen."

"Yes," he said. "That's all very true. But it does lead me to believe that there might be something else going on."

"What something else?"

She sensed a change in his tone. Her eyes locked on him, glowering at The Devil, forcing him to answer her.

"What something else?"

The Devil eased her back from the door. He kept his voice quiet, constantly looking up and down the corridor at the closed doors and darkened windows.

"Look, I'll be perfectly honest with you Laurie," he said. "That little episode back at the Cade residence took me somewhat by surprise."

"It took *you* by surprise?" she scoffed. "Eh, hello, I was the one thrown across the room remember?"

"Yes, yes, of course," he flapped her quiet. "What I'm getting at is I was a little shocked at Lister and his men. And if you know who I am, even if you don't admit to it, you'll realise that's no small feat."

"So what are you saying?"

"What I'm saying is that we don't know what's waiting for us on the other side of that door of yours," he nodded at the entrance. "I'm trying to be pragmatic here Laurie. Lister, the uniforms, even the wider riot ripping this city apart, it's all a bit, well, unusual."

Laurie dropped her hands to her side. She looked once at The Devil and then over to her door. Like a starter's pistol had been fired in her head, she scrambled for the handle.

"Laurie!" The Devil shouted at her.

He tried to stop her but she was too strong. She shrugged him off and shoved the door open, vanishing inside.

"Didn't you hear what I just said!" he called after her. "You don't know what you're walking into!"

The Devil followed her inside.

"Andy!" Laurie shouted, pushing open every door she passed.

She disappeared into a room at the end of the hallway, The Devil a few steps behind. He stopped and stared at the door, half open, half closed, Laurie nowhere to be seen.

Taking a pensive step forward he used as much caution as he could. The last thing he wanted was for three Humans, foaming at the mouth, full-blown crazy in their eyes to come charging towards him. He wasn't confident his new body could handle even one of them, never mind a triple threat.

"Laurie," he said cautiously, taking another step towards the door. "Are you alright in there?"

He was met with blanket silence. The Devil prided himself on putting a positive spin on even the most dreadful and ghastly scenario. It was a common misconception that he was always in the doldrums. On the contrary, without his pragmatic positivity he would rarely be so successful in turning situations out to suit himself. Ever the optimist, it kept him in business.

But even he was struggling this time. Was Laurie dead? Had she suddenly fallen deaf? Maybe there had been an earthquake in the past hour and the whole front of her flat had collapsed. Not knowing this she had hurried through the door and fallen into the waiting abyss. Not likely but not impossible, The Devil thought.

"Laurie?" he asked again. "You know if this is some sort of comedy routine then it's not very funny. Not that Human comedy has *ever* been funny mind you. Laurie?"

The temptation was always there to just about turn and run away. Then he remembered what He had said about her. She was, despite The Devil's own better judgement and sensibilities, integral to this whole escapade.

He cursed under his breath. He made a note to take it up with Him later - providing he wasn't ripped limb from limb before then.

"Okay Laurie, I'm going to come in there," he said. "If you're a feral, snarling mess I want you to keep it in check, just long enough for me to turn on my heels and get out of here. Unscathed of course. Does that sound like a deal?"

Once again dead silence met him. Getting more than a little annoyed with being ignored and needlessly cautious, he pressed forward. This was ridiculous. He was The Devil, he answered to no man or in this case - woman.

"Right," he said. "That's it. Here I come."

He forced his way into what appeared to be the living room of Laurie's flat. Immediately he stopped. Ahead of him was the silhouette of the policewoman, her outline marked out by the aura of the hazy orange streetlight bleeding in through the windows.

The place was a mess. Clothes and toys were strewn about the floor. The curtains were half closed, letting the sickly streetlight cascade through in great chunks.

Despite the relative darkness The Devil could see that she was crying. Laurie held her hand to her mouth, her shoulders bobbing up and down with every silent sob.

"Laurie?" he asked. "What's with all the sudden tears? You're not menstruating are you? Because if you are, I can assure you I don't have the-"

She cut him off, pointing down at a couch that sat between them. The Devil straightened himself, attempting to look undeterred.

 THE MAN IN THE DARK

He slowly rounded the sofa. Something crunched under his feet. A bowl rattled with a shrill whine as he walked through the mess.

When he'd reached the other side of the sofa, he saw two figures lying flat. One was bigger than the other, both locked together in a tight embrace. He swallowed, his Human throat still tasting distinctly like tin.

"Andy and Matilda I assume," he whispered. "And they're…"

He didn't complete his sentence. Laurie was a snivelling, shaking mess beside him. The Devil suspected that she feared the worst. And even he thought it looked bad. He noticed a lamp perched on a table beside the sofa, its shade tilted to one side. He reached down to it, resolving that if he could at least see the extent of the horror he might feel a bit better about himself. Human misery was his perfect pick-me-up.

He fumbled with the switch. Immediately the room was changed, the light chasing away the darkness into the corners. And while the brightness came as a bit of a surprise, it wasn't quite as shocking as what was waiting for them on the couch.

Andy immediately sat bolt upright. The motion was so quick that The Devil let out a timid, pathetic yelp and hopped backwards, cracking a stray plate left on the floor. Thankfully Matilda burst into tears almost straight away, saving him blushes.

"Oh my god, oh my god, oh my god!" said Andy. "What… who… where am I?"

"Andy!" Laurie cried.

She barged The Devil out of the way and threw her arms around her dozy husband and miserable little girl. The Laurie family sat on their sofa hugging and crying, united in shock, horror and relief. All The Devil could do was watch and feel a bit ill.

"Oh please," he said, rolling his eyes.

SIXTEEN

Kate didn't need this crap. She had a first-class degree in multimedia journalism from a top school. She was praised to the hilt by her professors, the envy of all her classmates. She knew what made a good story, how to get to the very bottom of betrayal, corruption and a system that stunk. So why the hell was she running about a London suburb late at night trying to find a coffee shop that was open.

"Oh yeah, that's right, because *Clarissa* wanted a sugar free caramel latte," she said to herself loudly. "And what Clarissa wants, Clarissa clearly gets. Even if that means I've had to walk about a hundred miles in this dump to find somebody stupid enough to still be open this late at night. While a riot goes on!"

Nobody answered her. The street was empty. She'd walked away from the media circus camped outside Pierce Cade's house in a foul temper. No small part of her had thought that the anger might pass. But here she was, carrying the cursed caramel latte and still fuming.

London hadn't been the adventure of a lifetime she'd been promised. That had been her first mistake. Kate was learning all-too quickly that the world of frontline journalism and media was actually nothing more than a vipers' pit of backstabbers and egomaniacs. And top of the list was Clarissa Collins - news

     THE MAN IN THE DARK

anchor, philanthropist and Rear of the Year 2006, 2007 and 2008 - a personal and industry record.

Kate hated her and her buns of steel. She was obnoxious, self-centred and rude. The anchorwoman couldn't be further from her on-screen persona. In fact it was almost caricature how different she was.

Kate wasn't so green behind the ears that she didn't expect something like this. What bothered her the most about Princess Clarissa Collins was her total lack of editorial judgement.

When Kate was a senior in high school she had volunteered with the class paper. Sure it had been a resume bolstering exercise at first but she quickly learned that she had a natural knack for hunting out a good story.

That gut instinct had seen her rise and rise at college. So it was a great surprise and shock when she graduated into her first full-time TV job and found herself surrounded by people who wouldn't know a good story if it came up and slapped them on the face.

She wasn't so naive that she thought she'd just breeze in the door straight from college and take up a senior editorial position. That was just a fantasy. But there had to be a middle ground, a place where she could go and be treated like a human being. At times she truly believed there were prisoners incarcerated in penitentiaries all across the US with more human rights than her. And they didn't have to go out at all hours trying to find caramel lattes for prima donna TV presenters.

Kate had promised herself not to get wound up by all of this. In a sobering, hungover moment she had taken a good, long look at herself in the bathroom mirror of her tiny Astoria apartment. The light had flickered and the air conditioning was busted but Kate had managed to give herself a pep talk.

"No more bitching, no more whining, just keep your head down, do your job and something will come your way," she said those words aloud. "There's no use pissing people off when you're just as easily replaceable. Runners have no rights Kate. But you can be the best damn runner in the business."

She stopped and looked down at the caramel latte in her hands. Without realising it she had squeezed the paper cup enough that some of the coffee had bubbled out of the hole in the lid. She was struck by a thought.

Maybe she had been going about this whole runner thing the wrong way. Maybe the best way to get revenge wasn't by calling someone out or going on a rampage through a TV studio. Perhaps vengeance was a dish best served through knowledge. After all, knowledge was power - always had been.

She looked about the quiet, dark street. There was nobody else about. The Cade place was just around the corner but where she was standing was still and dead. A devilish smile eased its way across her face, curling her lips upwards.

Since she'd arrived in London two days ago she'd been feeling like garbage. A lot of it was psychological. The dreary British weather was definitely playing havoc with her sinuses and she was sure she was coming down with something. Ordinarily this would have been a cause for major concern. The producers hated runners - they despised those who fell ill and had silly things like lives outside of work.

In Kate's newfound determination not to sink into depression over the state of her life, she resolved to hit back at the fearsome Clarissa Collins. Giving the street another once over, she was satisfied nobody else was around.

Coughing as hard as she could onto the cup in her hands, she then proceeded to suck the excess coffee from the lid of Clarissa's latte. A thin trail of slime was left on the lid before she gave it another long, hard kiss. Kate held the cup to the streetlight to examine if there was any evidence. It was clear now, but only on the surface. The microscopic germs from her saliva were multiplying over and over again, invading the coffee with their rotten, lovely badness.

"I'm really pleased with myself," she said, laughing. "A good day's work Kate."

And she wasn't joking either. The act of petty vandalism had given her a lift. Although she suspected some of the caffeine was probably giving her a jolt too. Feeling smug she hurried around the corner. Unfortunately that smugness was almost instantly eradicated when she saw the blue flashing lights.

Kate had been taught there were only a few unforgivables in journalism. Being in the wrong place at the right time was at the very top of the list.

"Oh shit," she said, feeling her stomach tighten so quickly it hurt.

She took off into a sprint, racing past the two squad cars and a van parked outside the Cade residence. The cameras were out in force, a mob of journalists swarming from the makeshift camp a little further down the street. Kate pushed her way through the throng, watching all the while as officers stood guard around their vehicles.

A dozen of them were all standing perfectly still, faces obscured by the brow of their caps, hi-vis jackets beaming in the night. There was a commotion from the other side of the tightly packed crowd and Kate shifted to see DCI Ken Lister emerging from the Cade house.

He was taller than she was expecting, but no less intimidating. She knew all the senior Met CID officers working on the case. The flight from New York hadn't been a complete waste of her time. Not that she'd been given the chance to show off her intuition and knowledge.

The crowd around her grew too strong and she was washed away in its current and spat out at the back. Tripping as she went, she was about to draw herself together when a sharp, nasally sound penetrated her ears.

"Where the fuck have you been?"

Clarissa Collins - anchorwoman, philanthropist and as foul-mouthed as a G.I in a strip club. Kate clenched her teeth together feeling that familiar uneasiness of total hatred and not so little fear.

"I'm sorry Clarissa," she shrugged. "I was getting you your latte like you asked, but there weren't all that many places open and-"

"My latte?" Clarissa snorted. "My latte? That was half an hour ago. The cops are here and everybody has the story except us. We're the only ones without a thing on this new development and you were getting my *latte*? What are you being paid for? Why are you even here if you don't do anything useful?"

"I was getting your-"

"I'm standing waiting here for you like a goddamn fart caught in the wind. I'm ready to go and you're nowhere to be seen."

"But I was fetching you your-"

"Then the cops show up, twice, first some lowly officer comes and goes and then there's a commotion and we're all standing here. But you're gone, vanished, into thin air like a ghost or a badly dressed fairy. New York have been on at me asking where the new footage is, where my latest report is? And what do I have to tell them? That you were kicking your heels getting coffee. We. Have. Nothing, Kate. Nothing."

She waved her mic around like a wand. Her hair was so shiny it was gleaming in the streetlight. And her teeth appeared to be

THE MAN IN THE DARK

fluorescent - their American sheen far too bright for the dismal London night.

"S'up?" asked a man, sauntering up to them, camera mounted on his shoulder. "We doing this thing or what?"

"We are Chaz," hissed Clarissa. "Now that Her Majesty the Queen of England has decided to show up."

"I'm sorry Clarissa," said Kate bitterly. "But I don't understand. You're here, Chaz is here, he's ready to go with the camera. What difference does it make if I wasn't here, you can do the broadcast without me. I'm only the runner."

The whole media camp was at its peak insanity. The journalists were whipped into a frenzied froth at the sight of DCI Lister at the front of the house.

None of that seemed to matter to Clarissa Collins. For Kate there was only her, the anchorwoman's eyes so wide that the wrinkles about her face were stretched smooth. Clarissa took two steps forward so she was looming over Kate, Louboutins giving her three clear inches over her younger employee.

"Just look at me," she said through gritted veneers. "Just take a good, long look at me. Do you think I'm going on air looking like this? Do you? I haven't had my makeup touched up, my hair hasn't been brushed and I can't find my toothbrush. And you want, sorry, you *expect* me to broadcast to a hundred million people looking like this?"

She passed her hands over herself as if to present just how bad she thought she was. Kate bit her tongue. Clarissa's outfit alone could keep her in rent for a year. There was, in short, nothing wrong with her.

The anchorwoman leaned in close to her and spoke softly enough only she could hear.

"A bit of advice for you rookie," she whispered. "You might

be happy dressing like a junkie's girlfriend but I'm a bit more professional than that. And if you don't start acting like that too then you're going to be off this show and out of this industry so fast that you'll choke on your tongue stud. This refugee style fashion might do it for all the tech geeks and tramps you date but I'm bigger and better than you and all of them put together. Are we straight?"

She straightened herself. Kate could feel her cheeks burning hot with embarrassment and anger. Clarissa towered over her, a look of self-assured arrogance stretched across her surgically enhanced face.

"Now get me my fucking blusher," she sneered.

Kate said nothing. What was the point in trying to defend herself? Clarissa held all the cards. Kate should have been there and the old dragon was powerful enough and held enough influence that could make sure she never worked again. It didn't make the feeling of being two inches tall any easier to digest.

She bowed her head and dropped into a jog. Moving quickly through the parked vans of the impromptu media village she stopped at theirs and climbed in the back. Sifting through the editing equipment, batteries and other general junk, she eventually found Clarissa's on-the-road makeup toolbox.

Kate grabbed it and clambered out. When her feet hit the ground she felt a strange tingle creeping up through the soles of her sneakers. The rumbled tickled her ankles, then calves and stopped at her knees. She looked down and saw her laces dancing about wildly on top of her feet.

"What the hell?" she asked nobody in particular.

The shaking continued and things about her started to move. The trucks and vans from the media teams all rocked back and forth, their axles squeaking and groaning under their own weight.

THE MAN IN THE DARK

She thought for a moment there was an earthquake. But even her limited geographical knowledge told her that was impossible.

She started to run - not away from the unusual rumbling but back towards the gathered media mass. The closer she got to them the more she noticed something wasn't quite right. Clarissa and Chaz were still at the back of the mob and she dashed over to them.

"Hey, do you guys feel that weird rumbling?" she asked.

Her breath left her when she saw Clarissa's face. The anchorwoman, so filled with venom and hatred, was now totally blank. Her mouth hung a little open and she had a vague distressed numbness about her. Chaz the cameraman was exactly the same, as were the others all about them. Nobody moved and they all stood looking at the front of the Cade residency.

"Clarissa?" asked Kate. "Are you okay? You look a bit… spaced."

She remained silent, rooted to the spot, hands hanging limply at her side. If Kate didn't know better she would have thought her boss was hypnotised or stoned.

She looked through the crowd, past all the other human statues and saw DCI Lister standing at the front door. Between the crowd's shoulders and heads, Kate could just about see the senior cop. His lips were moving quickly, like he was reciting something. She moved a little closer to try and hear what it was he was saying.

She was too far away. A sense of foreboding rose up from the pit of her knotted stomach. The young runner turned back to her boss and took her hand.

"Clarissa I think we should-"

A piercing pain flashed across Kate's forehead, jolting from one ear to the other and back again. It was so strong she almost collapsed, hanging on to Clarissa for support. A loud crashing sound filled her head. It was like a gong, as though she was inside a great cathedral bell as it was struck by a hammer. The noise was so loud she grabbed her ears, hoping it would stop.

The gong made her teeth rattle and she dropped the makeup box, the contents shattering at her feet. The loud noises continued over and over again and she looked through the mob at Lister.

The DCI was staring right at her, his eyes firmly transfixed on her and her only. Kate moved to turn away but she couldn't. Her limbs were heavy and numb and her feet felt like they'd been baked in cement. She began to panic, her heart beating faster and faster. As she stared at Lister through the mob, the people around her began to dissolve and the world grew darker at the edges.

"What… what… what is… what is going on?" she asked, her own voice booming inside her head.

Lister didn't reply. Everything around him had faded to a dense, flat blackness. The Cade house was gone, as was the street, the police officers and their cars. Nothing remained except the lone figure of DCI Lister, a stark figure against the dark.

Kate heard footsteps echoing from ahead of her. Two figures emerged from the black. They were blurry at first, like their edges were undefined or not solid. When they reached either side of Lister they began to come into focus.

Kate was terrified. But even in her state of total fear she thought she recognised the two men who flanked the DCI. Their faces were vaguely familiar, tucked away in some long lost corner of her mind.

Before she could remember them, one of them spoke to the other, his voice so clear in her head that he might as well have been standing beside her.

"Not bad Brutus, not bad at all my lovely," he said. "You're getting better at this possession thing."

"Thank you very much Cassius," beamed the other. "You know

I've always been a quick learner. And being taught by the very best certainly helps."

"Oh you are a darling to say that," said Cassius, batting his friend away. "Your generosity is matched only by your unquenchable love for yourself Brutus. You dog."

The two men burst into hysterical laughter. That's when Kate's mind began to go blank. She fought it for a moment but there was a force there, stronger than anything she had ever experienced. Despite her best efforts the clearing took control quickly. And that's when she forgot. Everything.

SEVENTEEN

The Devil didn't know where to look. He'd seen some abominations in his lifetime. Massacres, genocides, death on a scale so brutal and unfathomable that most in the known universe would pass out just thinking about it. None of that, he was learning, compared to dinner time in the Laurie household.

"How do you people breathe?" he asked Laurie and her husband. "I mean, don't you ever come up for air once in a while? You're stuffing your faces in the most vulgar fashion. I'm surprised neither of you have choked yet."

Laurie looked at Andy. The pair of them were dissecting the remains of the roast. Between them they had stripped the bird down to its bones. Coupled with vegetables and gravy, neither of them seemed overly fussed with The Devil's criticism.

"Do you know what I had for my lunch?" asked Laurie, licking her fingers. "I had a packet of crisps."

"I don't know what that is," said The Devil succinctly. "But I imagine it's overly processed garbage."

"Yeah, that's about right," she agreed. "I had a single packet of crisps at around one o'clock and then my phone went. And do you know who was on the other end of that phone? Go on, I'll wait until you get it right."

The Devil poked and prodded the white meat scattered about

THE MAN IN THE DARK

his plate. He'd eaten some of his veg and his body was gargling as it digested it.

"Detective Chief Inspector Ken Lister I imagine," he said.

"Bingo, got it in one," said Laurie. "He was calling me to let me know that intel pointed to a certain flat in Gravesend. The tech boys had managed to trace the internet service provider and location of where the ransom note had been sent to Pierce Cade. So it was jacket on, car keys out and off to Gravesend with the blues and twos all the way. You'll forgive me then sunshine if I wolf down my husband's frankly delicious roast chicken with all the ladylike dignity of Miss Piggy."

"Miss? Piggy?" he asked.

"You know, the Muppet," said Andy, picking his teeth clean. "You've never heard of Miss Piggy?"

Laurie started to laugh. Andy did the same, the couple smiling across the table at each other. The Devil sneered. He despised Human cosiness. They always relished being on the same page and making those ignorant of their silly little jokes feel like dirt. The Devil didn't get mad though, he always got even. And he was the master of the long game.

"No, I can't say I'm acquainted with this Miss Piggy, Andy," he said. "But if I ever find a spare thirty-seconds in the next thousand years I'll make sure I give you a call and ask you to take time out of your clearly busy schedule to explain it all to me. How does that sound?"

The Lauries stopped laughing. Andy took a drink from his glass and cleared his throat.

"Sure thing," he said, a little embarrassed.

"Wonderful," The Devil beamed. "I'm glad that's sorted. I can't wait."

"Hey," Laurie said angrily. "What were we talking about outside. Mouth firmly shut."

The Devil darted her a look of total contempt. She finished her meal and pointed at his plate. He pushed it away from him and folded his arms.

"So it was a rough day then?" said Andy, gathering up the dishes.

"Rougher than you wouldn't believe love," she let out a sigh. "I don't know, there's something weird about the world."

"Of course there is, we live in Peckham."

She laughed at that. The Devil almost thought she looked relaxed. The woman who had been so utterly contemptible to him all day was hidden away now. Even the colour in her face had returned a little.

"The news was saying they reckoned the riot would go on through the night," Andy continued. "The army are on standby. The whole thing is costing billions in damage. Shops, houses, the lot. Central London is a war zone. We've been watching it on the news."

"We?" asked Laurie.

Andy paused. He stood looking guilty, plates in either hand.

"Yes," he said, although it sounded more like a question.

"You mean to say you've been letting our daughter sit and watch the world fall apart on the news with you?" Laurie had her policewoman's hat on now.

"Yes," again, Andy was unsure if he should be telling the truth. "Among other things".

"Other things?"

"Well," he said, trying to recompose himself. "We played some video games, did a bit of drawing, some homework too of course. Oh, and I let her paint my nails."

He held up his hand and waggled his fingers. The Devil peered at him sceptically.

THE MAN IN THE DARK

"You're a fully-grown man," he said sardonically. "Don't you think you're a bit too old for homework?"

"Her homework," said Laurie.

"Yes Laurie, I got that much," he rolled his eyes.

"Well, that explained the fact the flat was a tip when we came in," she said. "Honestly Andy, how many times do I have to tell you, clean up as you go along. Otherwise it gets on top of you."

"It was only a few plates," Andy laughed. "Couple of bowls, toys, dirty socks, the kitchen sink. Oh and homework. We were doing homework."

"The living room looked like a bomb had gone off."

"It was pretty exciting homework? Does that make it better?"

"Nice try," she smiled wryly at him. "But I don't want our daughter to be watching people kill each other live on the telly."

"But she wanted to," said Andy. "Shouldn't we be encouraging children to show an interest in current affairs?"

"She's in primary school Andy."

"You all have to learn some time," said The Devil.

"One more peep out of you and I'll trap your genitals in the fridge door."

She gave him a deathly stare. The Devil winced at the clumsy violence of the threat. Clumsy as it was, he still believed Laurie would stay true to her word.

"She'll be fine," said Andy. "Besides, I was there to protect her. I am a responsible parent you know my darling, my sweet."

"So responsible you fell asleep, on the couch, with our daughter, and didn't even hear us come in."

"Yes," said Andy, straightening. "Yes I did. And that's why you love me."

"Honestly Andy," Laurie groaned. "You have to think more. I thought you were both… I thought you had been…"

She tried to compose herself. Andy put down the dishes and cutlery and hurried over to his wife. He grabbed her and hugged her tight against his stomach.

"Hey, come on," he said, trying to soothe his wife. "We were okay, we were fine. We'd had a great day and we were safe. I know the flat was a tip. And yes, I probably shouldn't have let her watch all the violence and bloodshed on the telly. But we were pooped and we were waiting for mummy to come home. And now that she is, Matilda is glad. So is her dad."

Laurie sniffed and looked up at her husband warmly. He bent down and kissed her, holding her head in his hands. The Devil could feel the skin of his Human body crawling so badly that he wanted to claw it straight from the bone.

"I can't take much more of this domestic nonsense," he said. "You two are so saccharine I think it's making my teeth rot."

Andy gave a quick look to his wife. Laurie shook her head, wiping away a tear.

"And no idea how the rioting started?" she asked.

"Civil unrest," said Andy, returning to the dishes.

"Oh yeah, civil unrest, that sounds about right," she laughed. "Sounds like something those arseholes in Whitehall would come up with to keep us all on our toes."

"Civil unrest isn't a cause," said The Devil. "It's a symptom. And I can assure you both that what's happening here is absolutely nothing to do with anything your kings and queens have been up to."

"We only have one queen," said Andy. "And she's headed up to Scotland."

"Lucky her," said Laurie. "Leaving one warzone for another. You know what those jocks are like."

Again Andy laughed with his wife. He gathered up the plates

and took them to the dishwasher in the corner of the room.

"You not finishing your dinner mate?" he asked The Devil.

"Thank you, Andy, but I'd rather go hungry than eat another morsel of that."

"Hey!" Laurie shouted again. "Do I have to keep telling you?"

"Yes, yes, whatever," he said. "I need information, I need access to something that can tell me the latest on the riot."

"Do what we all do, what I've always done," said Andy. "Try the telly. Next door."

The Devil left the table, Laurie following him. They went back to the living room and she turned on the TV. She changed the channels until there was a screen with lots of moving lines of text. Video from the riot was streaming. Some shots were down on the ground, with roaming gangs of masked people lobbing petrol bombs at police officers. Others showed looting, hundreds running down streets holding boxes and all manner of items. The screen cut to a shot high above the city, the unmistakable sight of Big Ben surrounded by people, illuminated by fire.

"Jesus," said Laurie. "It really is bad."

"This isn't usual then?" asked The Devil.

"This? Thousands of people fighting in the streets at two in the morning. No, this isn't usual. Anything but. You'll get the odd disturbance out in the suburbs from time to time but it's usually contained."

"But nothing on this scale?" he asked.

She shook her head. Changing the channel there was more coverage of the misery and mayhem. The Devil watched on while the Humans tore themselves apart.

"You look uneasy," she said.

"I'm always uneasy," he said. "That's what keeps me two steps ahead of everybody else."

"I mean you look like somebody who knows a lot more than you're letting on."

"Laurie I can assure you I know nothing about Medina Cade's disappearance. That's why I'm here remember."

"I'm not talking about the kidnapping," she sidled up to him. "I'm talking about this. The riot, the violence, you know something, something you're not letting on. I know that look."

"What look?" he tried to buy time.

"That look you've got plastered across your face," she said. "I'm a copper, I know when people are keeping something from me. You know, I've got this theory about criminals, do you want to hear it?"

"If I must," he droned. "But you'll have to be quick as I fear your husband is *desperate* to tell me all about this Miss Piggy woman, whoever she is."

"I reckon there are two types of criminal in this world," she continued. "The ones who want to get caught and the ones who try to think they don't want to get caught."

"Preposterous," he said. "Why would anybody willingly want to be caught doing something wrong? It's against basic Human instinct, there's no survival trait in that."

"Very true. But there's always a reason behind somebody turning to crime. Sometimes it's financial, a quick robbery for some fast cash. Or it's to be noticed. Bludgeoning a woman's head in because she spurns your advances. Stabbing your husband's lover with a pair of scissors when you find out about the affair. And everything in between. That need for vindication, it's what's behind every crime. Or I think so anyway."

"Beautiful Laurie, really that was," he said. "Beautiful and pointless."

"You're the latter I reckon," she said. "I think you want to tell me

THE MAN IN THE DARK

what you know, you just don't want to admit it. There's that look on your face, the hangdog expression, the passive aggressive put downs, it's all a cry for attention."

"I can assure you Laurie my hangdog expression as you so bluntly put it is not of my doing," he said. "It's this dreadful flesh suit I've been crammed and sewn up into that's hanging. And it's dog ugly."

"Was that a joke?"

"A feeble attempt at humour yes."

"Feeble, yeah that's about right," she smiled. "Look I don't know what's going on inside that screwball noggin of yours. Whether you think you're The Devil or you actually are, but you've got some serious issues. I'm just trying to solve a case and look after my family. Any way you can help those two things I'd gladly appreciate it."

The Devil took a long, deep breath. The whole flat smelled of that wretched cooking. He drummed his fingers on his chin while he watched more scenes of violence and chaos on the streets of the city.

"I doubt you would understand," he said. "We should probably focus on Medina Cade. That's the priority I'm sure you'd agree."

Laurie shrugged her shoulders. She rolled her neck and handed him the remote control.

"Yeah," she said. "You're absolutely right."

She wandered back towards the door.

"Where are you going?" he asked.

"To bed sunshine," she called back to him. "Medina Cade is still going to be missing in a few hours' time. Unless she miraculously shows up, in which case the mystery is solved and we can all get on with our lives. Otherwise I'll deal with it when I've managed to get some sleep."

"And what am I supposed to do?" he asked.

"Whatever you like, it's up to you buck-oh," she yawned. "Just don't make a mess and don't talk to my husband."

She left The Devil alone in the living room. He turned back towards the television and watched as the house fell silent. Time and time again the pictures showed the devastation and misery the riot was causing across London. He leaned in close to the set to listen to what the newsreaders were saying.

Over and over they were talking about violence. And every time it made him shiver just a little. This was *his* doing, there could be no doubt about that. Rioting and mass unrest had his fingerprints all over it. So why did he feel so uneasy about the whole thing? This had been what he wanted. Hadn't it? A change in management, out with the old and in with the new. How was it the Humans put it - you couldn't make an omelette without breaking a few skulls.

While the riot played out on the screen he couldn't help but feel a little put off. This was what he wanted, spurred on by Brutus and Cassius. Yet there was something amiss, something he couldn't quite bring himself to figure out. He was in the thick of it as usual, only he wasn't, not really. Strings were being pulled that he didn't know about, buttons pressed and documents signed. He was Downstairs' lord and master. But he knew that this riot in London had been approved by somebody other than him. What worried him more was that this wouldn't be the end of it. Far from it, in fact. London consuming itself was only just the beginning.

"Are you my mum's friend?"

A voice. From behind. He turned to see young Matilda Laurie standing in the doorway. She rubbed her eyes and yawned.

"I'm not supposed to talk to you child," he said solemnly and turned back to the TV. "The rules forbid it."

THE MAN IN THE DARK

"You were here earlier weren't you?" she said. "When I woke up. You were the man in the dark."

"Yes," he nodded. "I'm the man in the dark. In fact I'm *the* Man in the Dark."

"And you're friends with my mum?"

"Friend is putting it a bit strongly."

"Dad said you were mum's friend. He said you were staying with is. Don't you have your own house to go to?"

She appeared at The Devil's side. He'd never realised how small Human children could be. She barely reached his waist, her hands and feet tiny next to his. He did his best to ignore her, pretending to press buttons on the remote.

"Do you want to change the channel?" she asked.

Before he could answer she took the remote from him. With expert ease she changed the screen. Boxes appeared, bits moving about, words there he could never understand. The scenes of abject misery and 'civil unrest' were replaced by something much more colourful and jolly. Matilda sat down, crossed her legs and was transfixed on the screen.

"What is this?" asked The Devil.

"Cartoons," she said.

"Are they educational?"

"No, I don't think so," the child answered him. "Mum and dad don't like me watching too many of them. They say it distracts me from my school work."

"Then I suggest Matilda that you watch even *more* of them," he smiled. "Your mother and father seem to be obsessed with telling people what to do. I don't listen to them. Neither should you."

The little girl laughed.

"Are all Human children as simple as you?" he asked. "Only I don't think I've ever spent this amount of time with one."

"I don't know what that means," she shrugged. "Don't you have any children?"

"No," he said firmly. "Never had any need for them."

"What about your mum and dad?" she asked inquisitively. "Did they let you watch cartoons?"

"I never had parents," he said.

"You were an orphan?"

"How do you know what an orphan is?"

"We learned about it in school," she said. "There are lots of orphans all over the world, other kids that don't have mums and dads and have to live on the streets. Is that what happened to you? Is that why you're angry?"

"Angry? Who says I'm angry?" he asked. "I mean you're absolutely right, I'm furious, completely raging. But I thought I was hiding it rather well."

"You look like you're mad at something, or somebody," said Matilda. "You look the same way mum does when she catches me watching cartoons instead of doing my homework. Or I've been given a letter home from school."

The Devil closed his eyes a little as he stared down at the girl on the floor.

"How old are you Matilda?" he asked.

"Seven," she said. "It's my birthday next month."

"Seven-years-old and already very observant," he said. "Much like your mother. I assume you want to waste your life becoming a policewoman or some other such drudgery?"

"I want to be a doctor."

That caught The Devil completely by surprise. So surprising in fact that he began to laugh. He felt his ribs ache as he guffawed all about the living room. Matilda started laughing too, watching him as he wiped tears from his eyes.

"A doctor," he said, catching his breath. "Oh Matilda, the things I could tell you about doctors."

"Matilda!"

Laurie hurried into the living room. She gathered up her daughter and took her quickly back towards the door.

"You're supposed to be in bed," she said, kissing her head. "What did you say to him, eh? What were you talking to him about?"

"We were talking about cartoons," said the little girl. "And why he's angry."

"Anything else?" she looked at The Devil this time, holding her daughter close to her chest.

"I said I wanted to be a doctor and the Man in the Dark started laughing."

"Is that right? Man in the Dark?"

The Devil took a little bow.

"What can I say," he said. "I'm a natural with children. And the child is very clever. You should be very proud. She has potential to be somebody very great."

"Okay," said Laurie. "I think you should be getting some sleep Matilda, you've got school in the morning."

Matilda waved over her mother's shoulder.

"Night night Man in the Dark," she said.

They left The Devil alone with the TV still on. He watched the bright colours and shapes on the screen for a few moments more before his Human body decided it needed some rest. He collapsed onto the couch and fell asleep.

EIGHTEEN

All things considered, The Devil actually found that he had enjoyed his sleep. Much like everything else he enjoyed, he would have preferred more of it. Nothing exceeded, after all, quite like excess.

When the loud thump above his head woke him, he sprung up from the couch and was on his feet in under a second. Even he was surprised how spry and nimble his body could be when given the correct stimulation.

While he managed to jump start his mind, the Human functions that encased him pulled themselves together more slowly. Feeling returned to his appendages, his fingers and toes wiggling. The muscles in his eyes flexed as they adjusted to the damp grey of the morning light. He heard rain teeming down outside the living room window, water sloshing around with carefree ease. The room was warm and sticky and the atmosphere thick.

His generous host, DS Laurie, was fussing around near the living room door. She had a large box down on the floor, the source of the thump, and was digging through it.

"I don't care much for the morning wake-up call at this hotel," he yawned, stretching. "You know there are resorts in Mexico who send butlers to your room with fresh tea, coffee and anything else you lot need to get yourselves restarted in the morning. Banging around with dirty old boxes isn't quite to the same standards Laurie."

"Shut up," she said, still rummaging.

"Charming."

"I'm not running a hotel service here sunshine. You're lucky I even let you kip on the couch."

"Luck had nothing to do with it," he said, feeling something in his bad back crack. "I'm as much a pivotal part of your destiny as it would seem you are part of mine. And the quicker you get used to that idea the sooner we can make some progress."

"Yeah," she said. "Progress."

The Devil noticed something about her. In the dismal gloom of the early morning light the old Laurie had returned. Stressed, under-pressure, her skin was almost as washed out as the air. She was rifling in the box with an odd intensity, like she couldn't wait to find whatever was in there.

"Lost something?" he asked.

"Well what is it? Maybe I can help?"

Laurie laughed loudly.

"You? Help? You've done nothing but cause me trouble ever since I met you buddy."

"Appreciated. But it's not helping you any by being so prickly."

"I'm not prickly."

"Yes you are."

"I'm not. I'm trying to find something."

"What are you trying to find?"

"None of your bloody business."

The Devil sighed loudly. He decided to take a different approach. Intelligence, he'd found, sometimes struck a chord with some Humans. While he didn't hold out much hope, he tried regardless.

"Adjectives in Human language, at least your language Laurie, always have to be in the same order," said The Devil.

"What?" she said, standing up. "That's nonsense."

"It's true. Haven't you listened to yourself?"

"I've got a little girl in primary school and a husband who worships the ground I walk on mate, I don't have time to listen to myself."

"Well it's a fact. One of life's little quirks as He would bleat."

"Go on then," said Laurie.

"Go on then what?"

"Give me an example."

"It's always the same order. First there's the opinion, then the size followed by age, shape, colour, origin, material then the purpose."

"Right."

"So if, for example, you wanted an ugly, little, old, rectangular, brown, Italian, leather notebook, that's what you would ask for. Make sense?"

"Yeah."

"You wouldn't ask for an Italian, old, brown, little, rectangular, leather, ugly notebook would you?"

Laurie considered this for a moment. She closed her eyes.

"I'm not so sure," she said.

"It's not up for debate Laurie, it's a fact," said The Devil. "That's how you speak, it's a hard and fast grammatical rule. And believe me, you all stick to it. In fact you never shut up."

"No," she said, rummaging about the box. "We never do. It's part of our DNA and... ah."

She produced what looked like a pistol, although The Devil didn't recognise it. Small, compact and made of a yellow plastic, Laurie examined it before finding a holster for the weapon.

"What's that?" he asked.

"A Taser," she said. "Stun gun. One zap with this thing and you're on the floor flapping about like a salmon who's been hooked and isn't going back in the river."

"A weapon then."

"Protection."

"From what?" he asked.

"Where we're going we'll need everything we can get."

She turned back to the box and pulled something else out. It was a vest of some description, black with a zip down the middle. She stood up and pulled it on over her blouse.

"The latest season?" he asked flippantly.

"Stab-proof vest mate," she said, zipping it. "Again, we need everything we can get our hands on."

"And am I to be suitably armed for whatever it is we're about to do?" he asked. "Being without my usual prowess of shaping and reshaping matter in this grubby little realm you call home, I should probably have something more than these torn trousers and a jumper to defend myself with. No?"

"I'm a copper, you're a civilian," she said, strapping on her holster. "You're not allowed to have this kind of kit."

"I'm not *supposed* to be here in the first place Laurie. Yet here we are."

"Yeah, good point," she said firmly. "But that doesn't mean I'm going to give you something you can shoot me in the back with."

"Dubious logic there," he said under his breath. "We're leaving then?"

"Yeah," she said.

"To find Medina Cade."

"No."

"No?" blurted The Devil. "Laurie, what do you mean no? Have you no urgency woman? Don't you know I'm here for a reason and that reason is to find Medina Cade! There are plans afoot, big plans, enormous plans even. And like it or not, it all hinges on you helping me find Medina Cade."

Laurie picked up her box and left the living room. For a moment The Devil wondered if she'd heard him at all. Then, realising she wasn't coming back, he decided to go after her.

"Laurie," he said. "Did you hear what I just said? I think you should probably start taking this a bit more seriously."

He followed her into the kitchen. She dumped the box on the counter and peeled a banana. Grabbing the keys of the stolen squad car she looked at him, her arms extended wide.

"Mate, my hands are tied," she said. "I know the Cade case is very important to you, it is to me too you know. But I've had the call, I've got to go."

"Got to go where?" The Devil asked. "Am I missing something here Laurie? A woman has been kidnapped by terrorists, you're one of the leading officers, there's worldwide media interest and you're *not* going to do anything about it? This is the biggest case of your career, of your life even! And you've got me to help you? What's wrong with you?"

"What's wrong with me?"

She slammed the car keys down hard on the table. Leaning against it, rocking back and forth, she tried to suppress her anger. Whatever method she was using clearly wasn't working, her face getting redder by the moment.

"What's stopping me is a call from central HQ," she said. "All officers, and it means *all* officers sunshine, have been drafted in under some cock and bull measure cooked up by the top brass. We're to report to our divisions as quickly as possible to be handed a new assignment."

"New assignment?" he asked. "But the Cade woman is

international news."

"Yeah, you'd think that would be important wouldn't you," she said sarcastically. "I mean, a young, attractive British woman is kidnapped by a terrorist organisation while holidaying in the Middle East. There's nothing *remotely* important about that at all is there? Only it seems that our benevolent leaders in the corridors of power and the House of Commons couldn't run a piss up in a brewery. And by that I mean this riot that's sprung out of nowhere is getting worse. So ordinary coppers like me are having to tool up and get ready to go for a dust up in the middle of the street."

"I thought you were a detective," he said. "Don't detectives usually get to sit back while the ordinary uniforms do the ugly work."

"Yeah," she said, grabbing the keys again. "You'd think that would make sense. And ordinarily it does. Only it seems that instead of quashing the rioters last night our commanders and chiefs have just fanned the flames. It's getting worse out there. And I have to now go kiss my husband and daughter goodbye before I head out and try not to get a brick through my face."

She slid past him and went out into the hallway. The Devil could feel his chest tightening. He couldn't shift the image of Lister and the uniformed officers from Cade's house out of his mind. And above all else he realised that this was all *his* doing.

Although it didn't all make sense. The disconcerting feeling that he was missing something, a vital part of the picture, was still nagging him. He followed Laurie as she pulled on her coat.

"I'm to come with you then," he said. "To the division station."

"I'm not leaving you here with Andy and Matilda," she said. "You're not leaving my sight until this is all over. Especially if there are psychos and nut jobs running about out there and you know what's wrong with them. Speaking of which, you feeling like telling me anymore as to what all that was about last night? Only I'm beginning to think Lister and his pals going all werewolf on us might be linked to the mass riot."

The Devil didn't say anything. She snorted to herself and headed into one of the bedrooms. He stood alone thinking for a moment, trying to methodically work out all the questions running around inside his head. Just as he thought he was straightening out the tangled mess she reappeared and threw something at him.

"Here," she said.

The Devil caught the bundle. It was a pair of jeans and trainers.

"I don't know what size you are but you'll have to squeeze or make do," she said. "Put them on and let's get out of here. The sooner I leave the quicker I can get back. Hopefully."

He shrugged. He couldn't really argue with that logic. And he didn't have a lot of options. When he was ready, Laurie pulled the front door open, a gust of cold air flooding into the flat.

"You're leaving?"

Andy appeared from his bedroom. The Devil let out an infuriated groan.

"Oh great, here we go," he droned.

"Yes, I thought you were asleep," said Laurie. "I didn't want to wake you."

"But it's only five in the morning?" said her husband, rubbing his eyes.

Laurie looked at The Devil. He stepped to one side. The last thing he wanted to do was get involved in the domestic politics of a Human marriage.

"I've got to go Andy," she said.

"Go where?"

"We've all been called in, the whole force."

"This is because of the riot, isn't it?"

The fuzziness from Andy disappeared. He straightened his sloping shoulders and a look of inherent concern made his face seem older than it was.

"I'm a policewoman," said Laurie. "I have a duty to do. You know this."

"I know I know it," he said. "But that doesn't make it any easier." He looked at The Devil.

"What's happening with him?" he asked.

"Him has a name you know," The Devil hissed.

"Oh yeah, sorry, the Man in the Dark, if Matilda is anything to go by," Andy smiled. "Are you going with my wife into the war zone or are you staying here with me and Matty to tidy this place and get the groceries?"

"Do *not* leave this flat," said Laurie. "Under any circumstances Andy, don't go outside. Don't even answer the door to anybody. It's, well, it's wild out there. People are wild."

"And I'm letting you go out there because?" he asked his wife.

Laurie bit her tongue. The Devil could see her eyes getting watery. She turned away from them both, pretending to busy herself.

"Well played old chum," The Devil said quietly.

"Look I'm sorry," said Andy. "I just mean, you know what I mean. It's not easy for me to see you go like this. Especially after all that was on the telly last night. And now you're telling me that it's so bad all the cops in London have been drafted on duty. How do you expect me to react?"

"I don't expect anything from you," she said, sniffing and turning back to face him. "I expect you to look after our daughter while I'm gone and *not* to answer this door to anybody. Is that okay? Does that work for you? If you hadn't gotten out of bed we wouldn't be having this little argument. Especially not in front of him."

They both looked at The Devil. He shrugged casually.

"When you sit through Adam and Eve boring themselves to sleep, quite literally, you can get through pretty much anything I reckon," he said. "And besides Andy, your wife is a fairly capable officer of the law. She even stood back and let her superior officer pound me to a near pulp while I was in custody. I mean, you can't go wrong with that can you?"

"That's enough," she dragged him by the arm out the door.

The Devil stumbled into the quiet landing while Laurie lingered a little. Andy shuffled up to the door, his face slack with disappointment and worry.

"What do I tell Matty?" he asked glumly.

"That her mum has gone to work," said Laurie, checking her holster. "That her daddy is looking after her today and that she's not going to school. And you tell her I'll be home to see her later tonight, like I always do."

"Yeah," he smiled sadly. "You always come home."

"I try. And no watching the news, okay. You keep that thing off. Put on some brain rotting kids shows. Anything but what's happening out there."

"Those kids shows are educational," he said.

"I meant brain rotting for you."

Andy laughed. So did Laurie. Little moments like this were what kept them together, kept them sane. They were a team. They stuck together.

"Try and keep the place tidy too," she said. "Would it kill you to run around with the hoover? I know the world is coming to an end but it would be nice to come home to a tidy flat before everything goes to shit."

"That's probably the most logical thing you've ever said," he laughed again. "I'll do my best."

 THE MAN IN THE DARK

She leaned in and kissed him on the cheek. He took her hand and squeezed it tightly before she pulled away. As she went, she shoved The Devil towards the end of the landing and headed for the lifts.

"Oh shit!" Andy shouted after them. "Love! What will I do with those flowers?"

"Flowers?" The Devil felt his Human skin prickle, like somebody had walked over his back wearing spiked boots.

"Yeah, flowers," said Laurie, unimpressed.

"You were given flowers?" he asked.

"Yes I was given flowers. Is that so hard to believe?"

"I don't know," he said. "You don't strike me as the flower receiving type."

"And what type do I strike you as? If that's not being as bloody rude as you are."

"I'm not sure," he said. "You just, you just come across as being too hard boiled for something as frivolous as flowers."

"Hard boiled? What is this? The New York Review of Books?"

"You're a reader too?"

She belted him around the shoulder. The strike was so hard and unexpected it left him with a dead arm.

"As it happens, not that you deserve an explanation or anything," she said smartly. "I was sent a dozen roses as a surprise last week. I came home from work and they were sitting outside the front door. And if you'd been able to take your head out from your own arse for just two seconds you would have seen them sitting on the hall table."

The Devil ignored the pain and raced back to the flat. He barged his way in and looked about the hall. Towards the back of the apartment he spotted the bouquet, sitting there beaming in the dreary morning light.

"I knew it!" he said, crying out to the ceiling. "I bloody knew it! Twelve white roses! You've got an absolute bloody cheek, You know that!"

"Why have I got a cheek, I haven't done anything?" asked Andy numbly.

"I wasn't talking to you," said The Devil. "I was talking to Him."

"Him? Him who?"

"Him. *The* Him!"

Andy looked at Laurie. She made a twisting motion with her finger beside her temple and crossed her eyes.

"Don't ask me."

"Twelve white roses," The Devil said again. "Why didn't you tell me this Laurie? Why would you keep this a secret?"

"Because there's nothing secret about it," she said, walking back into the flat. "I got a dozen roses, so what? Now come on."

"No, we can't go, we can't," he said.

"Mate, I don't have time for this, I really don't."

"You… husband," The Devil snapped his fingers. "Where did these come from?"

"I don't know," he shrugged. "They were delivered last week sometime, couple of days ago I think, I can't remember."

"Who are they from?"

"I don't know mate."

"You didn't get your wife these? You didn't have an inkling to get them, some divine idea out of the blue to purchase these flamboyant and quite frankly overblown flowers?"

"Nope," he shrugged.

"And the thought that some secret admirer is out there, possibly lusting over your wife and sending her bouquets of flowers doesn't sit at all odd with you?"

Again Andy shrugged. He looked at Laurie as she huffed and

    THE MAN IN THE DARK

puffed in the hallway. He smiled warmly as he stared at his wife.

"It doesn't matter," he said proudly. "If she's got a secret admirer or not, I don't care. I love her and she loves me. Flowers, chocolates, cards, I don't care. She's a wonderful person and loving wife and mum. I'm surprised she doesn't get *more* nice things like this sent to her. And I trust her, with my life."

The Devil choked back a little retch. He ground his Human teeth and felt his jaw tendons ache.

"Blind faith and trust," he scoffed. "Your logic is flawed and laughable. If I were you I'd be tearing this planet apart to find out who was trying to hit on my wife. And you've not so much as broken a frown over the whole thing."

"No, he hasn't," said Laurie angrily.

"What about the card?" said The Devil, looking amongst the flowers.

He saw the familiar white square. But as he went to lift it Laurie snatched it away from him.

"I'm getting tired of you jerking around here sunshine, now come on!" she snapped.

"We can't go Laurie, really, we can't," he said. "If you've got these roses it's a sign. And I have a suspicion you know this, otherwise you wouldn't be so uppity."

"Sign?" asked Andy. "Sign for what?"

"Nothing, go back to bed," she said sharply.

"It's a sign from You Know Who," The Devil raised his eyebrows to the ceiling. "It means you have to abandon your duty and help me find Medina Cade."

"I'm not abandoning my duty."

"You have to."

"I can't."

"But the roses."

"Sod the roses!"

"What's all the shouting about?"

Matilda appeared at her bedroom door. The little girl rubbed her eyes and yawned, her hair sticking out from her head in great clumps.

"Ooooh there she is," said Andy, scooping up his daughter. "What are you doing up, it's super, super early."

"I heard you all shouting about mum's roses," she said. "Are you fighting with the Man in the Dark?"

"They are Matilda," The Devil said. "You see, I'm trying to make sure your mother isn't killed by a horde of rampaging maniacs with pitchforks and broken bottles and she's making it very, very difficult for me."

"That's *enough*!"

Laurie stamped down hard on The Devil's foot. Her boot was like concrete, crushing his toes. He tried to scream but the pain was too great. He slumped against the wall, foot thumping in agony.

"Matilda, you stay here with daddy, maybe watch some of your cartoons today? How does that sound?" said Laurie. "Come on, let's go get the TV on."

Laurie, Andy and Matilda headed into the living room. The Devil hobbled behind them, lingering about the door. Laurie turned on the television and the screen appeared. The news channel was still on, a large shot of London from above coming into view.

"Holy Christ," said Andy. "What did that say down the bottom?"

He pointed at the rolling bar than ran along beneath the moving shot of the city.

"The rioting is happening all over the world. Says Madrid is on lock down and the army have been called in in Tokyo," said Laurie.

"There's been trouble - *big* trouble overnight. Paris, Los Angeles, Milan, they're all burning. The Prime Minister is flying out to the UN for an emergency meeting with all the other world leaders. They're calling it... hold on," he pointed at the screen. "Yeah, a global crisis. We're being told to behave ourselves but nobody is listening. It's like the whole world is going to Hell man. It's not right. It's like people have lost their minds or something."

"And there's more to come," said The Devil knowingly. "This is just the start of it and it's only going to get worse."

Laurie didn't shift her gaze from the television. Andy had sat down with Matilda, the little girl clinging on to her father's shirt tightly. The Devil could see in all three of them that familiar, harrowing look of Humans worrying. Staring at the television, none of them moved. They were locked on, dead-eyed, watching as society crumbled. There they were, a whole family, each with different experiences, memories and feelings - all united by what was unfolding on their doorstep. They were animals, The Devil thought, just animals.

"I've always said it," he sighed. "The worst thing you lot could have done was grow consciousness. Better to not know anything, ignorance is bliss."

"Are you leaving us mum?" asked Matilda.

The Devil had to make sure he didn't smile too broadly. It was so delicious he could almost hear Laurie's heartstrings being tugged.

"Maybe you should listen to him love," said Andy, speaking up. "I mean, look at what's going on out there. The city is a mess, the *world* is a mess. What difference is one more copper going to make?"

"And what if everybody said that?" she jabbed. "What if Mike or Angela said that to their families? And Lister?"

"I wouldn't worry about him," said The Devil. "I suspect DCI Lister knows exactly what's going on."

"It doesn't matter, I have a job to do."

She turned back to the television. A fleet of ambulances screamed down a road somewhere in South Africa. Then it flipped to Brazil, dark figures moving in front of huge ministerial buildings, smoke pouring out of broken windows and doors in thick, ugly plumes. Nowhere was safe it seemed. The scenes quickly cut from one spot of misery to another. Looting, large scale riots, death and misery everywhere. It was violence and blood on the streets. Mob rule.

Only there was something else. The Devil stepped forward and stopped beside her. He watched the maelstrom unfolding, information being shot at him from the garish news report. The fighting would have been normal except for the violence. One set of images showed crowds stomping on other people, viciously laying into them like they were dirt.

In another a woman was being dragged down an alleyway, screaming and clawing at the gang of men who wouldn't let her go. The image of people being thrown onto burning bonfires in the middle of empty streets was enough for Laurie to switch off the TV, remembering her daughter was in the room.

"This is terrible," she said quietly to herself.

"Yes," said The Devil agreeing. "A little *too* terrible."

His mind was heavy, he could feel it being weighed down with a million possibilities. Something had changed alright, but it felt like it was too much, too soon. He had only just started his campaign to tip the Natural Order - in fact he hadn't really done *anything*. Where was all this extra chaos and mayhem coming from?

"I really think we should be going," he said with a concerned earnestness. "Laurie, I don't normally say please but I think you should really consider not reporting for duty. Not just for my sake but for your family and possible billions of others."

"Billions?" she said, surprised. "You can't be serious."

THE MAN IN THE DARK

"No, I'm usually not, not when it comes to Humanity," he said. "But this time I think I'm making an exception. Medina Cade, the missing woman, the one captured by a terror cell and the woman you're trying to find. She's the hinge in all of this and you're the door. I can't explain why, not right now, but I'm asking you to trust me."

"Trust you?" she laughed. "And why would I trust you... if you're who you say you are."

"Call it a leap of faith Laurie."

That drew a wry, knowing smile from her. She shook her head, putting her hands on the holster of her taser. Andy and Matilda stared up at her with big eyes, watching on like an entranced audience at a really good play. The policewoman took a moment before reaching down and stroking each of their cheeks in turn.

"What if you're wrong, what if all of you are wrong?" she asked. "I'll have disobeyed a direct order. Not just any order, a three-line whip. That's a suspension, maybe even booted off the force."

"If I'm wrong then nothing will happen," said The Devil. "You'll lose your job, your family will become destitute and little Matilda there will grow up to be resentful of both of you for trusting me implicitly. And, quite frankly who can blame her."

Laurie and Andy looked at him blankly.

"But if I'm right," he continued. "Then there's a chance, a very good chance, that you could save all of your scrambling, ratty, selfish little race and we all live happily ever after. Now who wouldn't be tempted by that?"

He held out his hands and shrugged a little. Laurie took a moment to let it all sink in. Then she nodded.

"You better be right," she said, pushing him out towards the door.

"If I'm right Laurie then we're all in trouble," he said.

NINETEEN

"Something doesn't add up, it's like my judgement is clouded," said The Devil, rapping his knuckles on his enlarged forehead. "I think it's this body. I think this body is draining my intelligence away."

"You don't half talk a load of shite sometimes," said Laurie.

She concentrated on the road ahead, weaving the stolen police car in and out of all the other abandoned vehicles left behind in the wake of the riot. This section of the city appeared to be normal - or as normal as it could be. Nobody, it seemed, dared to be out on the streets, not while there were roaming gangs of troublemakers. Signs were all around them that a quick, hasty effort to get indoors and locked up as quickly as possible had been the order of the day.

It made for easier driving. Although The Devil thought Laurie was making as hard a job of it as possible. Speeding through the quiet streets was all well and good when the driver was competent. On more than one occasion he'd sucked his guts in as they whizzed past a truck or a lorry altogether too close for comfort.

"It's like I can't think properly," he said. "Like there's some sort of misty barrier between my normal working mind and the one this dreadful excuse for a body has built in."

"Maybe you're not as clever as you think you are?" she said. "I mean, if you're meant to be this big, bad cosmic super villain, how

 186

come you let yourself be caught by us rozzers?"

"I didn't let myself be caught, I was surprised," he said adamantly. "Quite literally seconds before you and your jack-booted colleagues came barging into that dismal flat, I arrived in the airing cupboard."

"Sounds nice."

"And a mere matter of moments before that I had been part of probably the biggest, dirtiest, most hedonistic party Downstairs has seen in eons."

"That doesn't sound so nice."

"Not really my taste Laurie but you have to hand it to Brutus and Cassius, they know how to hold a good ball."

"I'll bet they do," she laughed. "And you've left those two in charge then? They're running the show while you're away?"

"Not exactly," said The Devil uncomfortably. "I didn't have any time to make provisions before He decided to plonk me here with you. But it's a well-oiled, slick operation Downstairs. I'm sure it's working… yes, sure of it."

Laurie looked at him. She cocked her eyebrow and sucked on her tongue.

"Well that's hardly very convincing," she said. "You want to try again champ and make it sound like you mean it this time?"

"You wouldn't understand," said The Devil. "And it doesn't matter anyway. One problem at a time."

"So there *is* a problem Downstairs," she smirked.

"I know what you're doing Laurie," The Devil said.

"What? I'm not doing anything."

"You are. You're trying to interrogate me. And quite frankly you're making a ham-fisted job of it."

"Nothing of the sort," she said. "And I'll have you know my interrogation skills are highly sought after within the Met."

"Well you don't have much competition if DCI Lister is anything to go by."

"He's a dickhead."

"Now that *is* something we can agree on. Although I wonder just how much of it is him."

"What do you mean?"

The Devil drummed his fingers on his flabby chin. The world whizzed past the windscreen, block after block, street after street, ticking by like the hands of a clock.

"Back at Cade's house, he was quite clearly under the influence of something," he said. "I wonder if whatever it is that's gotten into his head is affecting me."

"Or maybe you're just not as clever as you think," she said. "And I mean that honestly."

"Oh come on Laurie, remember who you're talking to here. I've forgotten more good ideas than the whole Human race will ever dream of. I think I can work out what's happened to Medina Cade."

"You'd be surprised," she said, taking in a sharp breath. "I've worked on missing persons for a while now, the stats don't lie Einstein."

"Stats," he waved his hand. "You Humans are so obsessed with your numbers and quantifiable variants. It's nonsense."

"It's not mate, really it's not," she said. "The vast majority of people that go missing for any length of time never show up. And as for kidnap cases, well, they hardly ever end happily."

"And what do you think of this case?" asked The Devil. "What do you think will happen to Medina Cade?"

Laurie thought about her words. A little vein pulsed in the side of her temple and her eyes twitched back and forth across the windscreen.

"I think it's terrible what's happened to her," she said. "I think she was probably in the wrong place at the wrong time and that can happen. If I was being perfectly honest with you, I'd say the chances of her being dead are almost total."

"Interesting," he said.

"What? The fact that she's dead?"

"No, the other thing you said."

"What?"

"About Medina Cade being in the wrong place at the wrong time," he said. "You don't really believe that do you? You don't *really* believe that by sheer bad luck this woman has been captured, tortured and put up for ransom."

"Pierce Cade's statement is and always has been that she was out for a morning stroll when they were on holiday. She never came back and then he was sent that video we saw. The terror group checks out, it all seems legit. Maybe she was just unlucky, I don't know."

"Hmmm," The Devil droned.

"Well…" said Laurie expectantly. "What do *you* think happened?"

The Devil folded his arms and puckered his lips. He let out a strange groaning sound he didn't think was possible. Then he shifted restlessly in his seat, his ill-fitting clothes chafing his skin.

"I only go on what I can see," he said. "Call me old fashioned. But I've seen a lot in my time Laurie. Kings, queens, emperors, paupers, pretenders and poets, you Humans have an indefatigable knack for being incredibly uncreative."

"Thanks," she said. "That's just what I wanted to hear."

"I just don't believe Pierce Cade, I think that's what's bothering me."

"Why not? The guy is squeaky clean."

"Squeaky clean?"

"He's above board," she said. "We ran numerous background checks on him, nothing. In kidnap cases it's often the case a victim will know or have some connection to whoever it is who snatched them. You're talking about knowing people, I often find the people closest to the victim are usually suspects."

"And Pierce Cade?"

"Nothing," she said. "He's an offshore engineer. Pays his taxes, never been in debt, votes every election, the works. He's about as ordinary and plain as they come."

"How very dull," said The Devil. "I mean, most Humans are dull as that dishwater you drink but Cade sounds like a boring exception."

"And that's about as exceptional as he'll get," she said. "Nice guy, young couple, attractive wife, the media have been lapping it all up. The paparazzi and the journalists outside the station when you came in, that's it scaled back. Same goes for outside Cade's house. In the two weeks before he came back to the UK we were inundated by calls and journos all trying to get a slice of the action. Since he's been back and there hasn't been any developments it's all calmed down a bit."

"Then I showed up," he said.

"Then you showed up, yeah."

"What can I say. I like to make an entrance. And believe me Laurie, this was not one of my better ones. Do you know I was once paraded in front of a hundred thousand Babylonians who showered me with rose petals and hailed me as an all-conquering war hero. There was singing, dancing, a month of carnal excess and celebration for me returning victorious to their shores. I had the pick of any woman, or man, literally any of them, out of a whole *race* of people Laurie. Can you imagine. It was such a lovely time it even made it into the bible, can you believe that? Of course I'm dressed up as the Whore of Babylon but what's in a name anyway. It's only a label. Now *that* was an entrance."

"Yeah, cool, anyway," she dismissed him. "Our tech boys traced the internet service provider for the ransom e-mail and video. It came from that flat you were found in. Whoever had sent it had used the internet in there when sending the mail. We thought we'd struck gold when we found you."

"Think again," he said. "I'm usually more a nightmare than gold Laurie. Your worst."

"Tell me about it."

"It still doesn't explain my bad feeling about him," he tapped his forehead again. "I feel like there's something there, something right in front of me that would unlock this whole bloody frustrating thing. And it's just out of reach, just flittering on the edge of this terrible Human consciousness. Pierce Cade. Pierce Cade. Pierce Cade."

Laurie roared the car through the streets. The Devil recognised some of the buildings and looked about.

"Hold on, I know where we are," he said. "This is close to the police station."

"Yes," said Laurie. "I figured if we're going to work out what happened to Medina Cade then we need all the case files. And if I'm getting sacked I reckon the closer I am to danger the further I am from getting bitten in the arse."

They rounded the corner and the police station came into view. Laurie immediately slammed her foot on the brakes and the stolen cop car skidded to a halt.

"What are you doing?" The Devil blurted, his seat belt cutting into his shoulder.

Laurie didn't answer him. She jammed the gearstick into reverse and hammered the accelerator. With one smooth, well-practised motion she spun the cop car around and drove it on.

"Have you lost your mind Laurie?" he shouted over the wail of the engine.

"No," she said calmly, looking in the rear-view mirror. "But I think they have."

The Devil turned around in the passenger seat. He peered out through the back window and down the empty street. Only it wasn't empty, not completely. At the far end was a moving, brooding mass of bodies, police bodies, swaying from side to side with a strange, feral stance.

At the head of the throng was DCI Ken Lister. Square shouldered and smiling, he seemed to peer across the distance right at The Devil. There was a brief moment of silence, a still second that felt like only he and The Devil were all that existed in the whole universe. Then the DCI gave his order and the small army of possessed police officers gave chase.

"Ah," said The Devil, turning back around to face the front. "Do you want to say it or shall I?"

"Shit," said Laurie. "Shit, cock and bollocks."

"Yes," hummed The Devil. "That's just about the sum of it."

TWENTY

"Can't this thing go any faster?" The Devil punched his fists into the console. "I thought it was supposed to be a police car? You know, high-speed chases, running down pedestrians, that sort of thing."

"It *is* a police car," Laurie shouted back at him. "And we're doing seventy in a built-up area!"

"They're gaining on us," he said looking back out of the rear window.

A small fleet of squad cars had overtaken the mob and was now hammering down the road behind them. Lister and his army were mobilised and giving chase. The Devil wondered if some hint of their police training still existed in the possessed minds of the cops. If it did, he hoped they'd forget it soon. Otherwise he was toast.

"They're gaining on us fast."

"Do you have any idea how hard it is to drive at this speed? And that's before all the garbage and debris of a city-wide riot littering up the-"

She swerved the patrol car clear of an abandoned bin lorry. As they rounded the huge vehicle a jackknifed tanker came into view immediately behind it. Twisting and turning, Laurie somehow managed to avoid both of the massive hazards and put her foot down hard.

The Devil lolled and rolled around in the passenger seat. His stomach was churning and his Human body was sticky with sweat. None of that would matter though if Lister and his cronies caught up with them. The police weren't going to care how clammy he was.

DCI Lister had rounded up his posse and shoved them into vehicles to pursue their target. A fleet of vans, squad cars and motorbikes was now rolling and smashing its way through the streets of London. Nothing was standing in their way as they kept up their relentless pursuit. Sirens blared and the air was blue with their flashing lights. The small army was focussed on only one thing - the stolen squad car weaving in and out of danger.

"Do you have plans for outrunning this horde?" The Devil asked. "Or do you want to save us both time and just pull over so they can tear us limb from limb."

"You are *not* helping!" she shouted. "Can't you magic us up a plane or a chopper or something? Or a fire-breathing dragon to smite our enemies, some of that shit?"

"Fire-breathing dragon?" he sniffed. "What do you think I am? Merlin? I'm not some two-bit conjurer from the Dark Ages Laurie, I'm the Man in the Dark, remember?"

"Well Man in the Dark - you better pull something out of that flabby arse of yours because I'm running out of road really quickly here. We're almost at the river."

The tyres screamed for mercy as the squad car pulled hard to the left. The rampaging forces of Lister's police followed, a detachment of bikers speeding off ahead. They caught up with the squad car, two on either side and one hovering behind.

The riders wore the same feral look as the others. Foam and drool dripped from their mouths and they snarled as they bared their teeth. There was an other-worldly air about them, detached

 THE MAN IN THE DARK

from the Human world but still very much there. Possession, thought The Devil, he should have known better. He'd never seen it on this scale before. The thought made him angrier than he thought possible - the power it would have taken to create this chaos.

"Do something!" Laurie shouted, distracting him.

"Like what?" he asked. "Offer them a handkerchief for that rabid problem they've all got?"

The rider closest to him came hurtling towards the car. He was broad and heavy and the thud echoed about the cabin. Staring at The Devil with glazed eyes, he drew his head back and smashed it into the window, splintering the glass.

The blow was enough to send him tumbling from his bike. Two thuds where his body was broken beneath the squad car's tyres and he was gone.

"Christ almighty!" Laurie shouted, trying to control the car. "What are they *doing*?"

The rider behind them took her colleague's place. She sidled up to the squad car before punching through the window. She grabbed at The Devil as he recoiled from her.

"Get us out of here Laurie!" he shouted. "If they get us we're finished. And if I'm finished then *everything* is finished!"

"I'm trying my best... I'm trying to..."

She trailed off when she saw the rider. Through the matted hair and growling fangs, Laurie recognised the policewoman she used to be.

"Angela!" she said. "Angela... Angela Morrison! No! No, not you!"

"Who's Angela Morrison?" asked The Devil, doing his best to dodge the rider's attempts to grab him.

"She's... she's..."

The cop who used to be Angela snagged The Devil by the wrist. With inhuman strength she pulled him as hard as she could. He flew forwards, only the door stopping him from flying out the window.

"Laurie! Help!" he shouted. "I don't care if it's Angela or Archimedes, get this thing off of me!"

Laurie hesitated. The Devil tried to fight back, slapping, punching, swearing at the rider. Nothing worked and she held on with a deathly grip that almost pulled his arm from its socket.

"Laurie! Kill it!" he shouted. "Run it over! It's not Angela, not anymore! Just kill it!"

The plea seemed to snap Laurie from her hesitation. She blinked and gripped the steering wheel a little tighter. She angled the car at speed towards the row of parked vehicles that lined the road. With one quick, brutal hit Angela and her motorbike were gone - smashed to bits by a parked ice-cream truck.

The Devil recoiled quickly into the car, gasping for breath. But the respite was short lived as the third rider picked up speed. He was about to warn Laurie when the cop leapt from his bike.

His frame was heavy and hard enough that the squad car's door buckled in its frame. Laurie let out a yelp as she tried to keep them on the road. The rider pawed at the door until suddenly it fell away, almost taking him with it. He hung on to the frame, tendons standing up at unnatural angles in his hands as he gripped on to the chassis.

"Kick him Laurie!" The Devil shouted. "Get him, he's just there!"

The DS did as she was told. Two big kicks to the rider's head were enough to break his nose but not his grip. He held on, legs useless as they were dragged along the road at great speed.

"He won't let go!" she shouted. "He's too strong. He won't let go!"

                    THE MAN IN THE DARK

"Just get rid of him!" The Devil cried.

Laurie lined up another kick when the rider's head began to quiver. His jaw dropped open, cracking loudly above the groan of the engine. He tilted his head back, taking aim. The Devil knew what was coming next but he was too slow to react.

A jet of rancid, white liquid shot out from the bike cop's mouth. It doused Laurie in the face and she let out a single, agonised scream. She let go of the steering wheel and grabbed at her smoking, burning face in horror.

The Devil tried to reach the steering wheel but it was too late. He didn't see the wall of the river embankment come racing up towards them.

The squad car smashed through the barrier in an explosion of brick, mortar and broken bones. The bike cop vanished somewhere amongst the debris as the squad car flew majestically through the air.

For a carefree moment it was elegant and graceful, defying gravity with ease as if it had been designed that way. Then reality bit back hard and it was payback time. The roaring police cruiser smashed into the river with a mighty splash, white crested waves of dirty brown water lapping against the bank twenty feet away.

The cabin filled immediately, the filthy river pouring in through the open door and the whole car tilting on its side. Laurie writhed in agony, holding her burned face while they began to sink. All The Devil could do was watch the world vanish below the waterline as the car was swallowed whole very quickly with a forgettable gargle.

"Shit," he said, the roar of water filling his ears. "I probably should have learned to swim after all these years."

On the banks of the river DCI Lister stood watching where the car had sunk below the surface. About him was the gathered forces of the possessed Met Police. They stood in silence, twitching behind their leader. When the final bubble popped and the river was still again the hundred strong mob began to laugh in unison. And somewhere beyond the realms of space, time, reality and Human imagination, two traitors sat and congratulated themselves on a job well done. The Devil was gone and they were ready to take his place.

TWENTY-ONE

He had never known Upstairs to be like this. Not in all of time. And that was really saying something. Since the beginning there had always been a neatness to His kingdom. He supposed it was part of His own makeup, His obsession with tidiness. No loose ends, nothing left hanging, everything as it should be. Not now.

Now there was a new feeling about the old place. And it wasn't welcome. He had never been against change, far from it in fact. He had always seen himself as a father figure to the Humans, whether they liked it or not. Indeed, whether they knew it or not was a totally different argument.

When the time came for them to take their next step forward, to reach that new milestone, He never stood in their way. From the moment they had uttered their first word to when the time was right to start things over, He had always offered His own guidance and opinion on what was right and what was perhaps a little off.

But He had never stopped them. As much as He would have liked to at times. That was what being a good parent was all about. Letting them make the mistakes they had to in order to learn.

Although what they were doing now was anybody's business. Except, it wasn't. It had to be *somebody's* business. And when that was the case, He was where the proverbial buck stopped.

He sat in His office, brooding. Eternity stretched above Him, the most perfect summer's sky going on forever. Clouds of brilliant white hovered peacefully amongst the ocean of pure, unfiltered blue. It was lovely. Of course it was.

He wished He could say the same for the inner workings of His mind. That was far from peaceful. The phones hadn't stopped ringing all day. If it wasn't one corner of the kingdom reporting mass hysteria and chaos it was another. The only phone that hadn't rung was The Big One. He knew that as soon as the call from that one came in then there was a chance something could be going right for a change.

A knock at His door distracted Him. He manifested Himself into a form more suiting the Creator of the Universe and clicked a desk into existence. Why He bothered with all of this formality He never quite knew. Especially when the old troublemaker Downstairs seemed so strict on these sorts of things.

"Come in," He said, trying not to sound too distracted.

The door creaked open. A timid looking man poked his bald head through the gap. A long, fuzzy beard stretched down from his chin all the way to his belt, polo-shirt neatly tucked into a pair of comfortable if slightly stuffy slacks.

"I'm sorry to disturb you Great and Wise Creator, Lord of All Existence and Bringer of Peace," he said weakly.

He beckoned the man in. He closed the door behind him, drowning out the unfiltered sound of panic and commotion. The bearded man cautiously walked up to the desk, a floor appearing beneath his feet just before every step.

"Peter," He said. "You don't have to use that great, long-winded style every time you address me."

"No Oh Great One, of course, sorry, please accept my deepest, most humble apologies for being so rude and clumsy in Your

THE MAN IN THE DARK

presence. I didn't want to-"

"Peter," He said with a gentle firmness. "You're rambling."

"Yes Oh Great One. Sorry. Again."

"I've asked a lot of you over the years. But I don't think I've ever, *ever* wanted you to tell me some good news quite so much as I do now."

He smiled warmly at one of His most loyal servants. But Peter didn't know how to react. Pious to the end, he nervously fumbled with his hands, trying his best to put some positivity on what he was about to say.

"You can't raise him, can you?" He asked.

"I'm afraid we've tried every possible outlet Great Ruler of Reality," Peter gushed.

He had thrown His servant a lifeline. Now that he had a grip he couldn't turn off the apologies.

"Transcranial communication seems to be blocked by something and the pockets of faith we still have in service are so jammed with calls and requests that our whole system is overloading," he said. "It's almost as if… as if…"

"We've been cut off," He said.

"Yes My Lord and Master Forever, exactly that," Peter bowed his head.

He let out a concerned groan. Getting up from His desk, He looked down at His feet. He hadn't really thought about what form He was taking. He was rather surprised when He saw His slightly yellow, fungal toes poking out from His sandals. He shook His head, beads rattling in His long dreadlocks.

"Very concerning old chap, very concerning indeed," He said. "And you're sure you've tried every conceivable way of trying to reach him?"

"Yes sir, we have," said Peter. "Some of Upstairs' best people have been working on it for the better part of, well, you know how long time is. It's like he's dropped off the face of the planet. Actually, sorry my Darling Saviour, it's almost as if he's been wiped from all of creation!"

There was something about Peter's words that greatly disturbed Him. For a man who had spent his entire Human life in servitude of His message, and even longer afterwards, there was a desperation about him. Peter was as loyal as they came - a true believer right to the last. Yet even He wondered if he had reached his breaking point with the task He had set him. Indeed, trying to find the antithesis of everything he believed in was a test even Peter would find trying.

"The Man in the Dark," He said.

"Pardon me?" asked Peter.

"It's a name that he calls himself, at least he was called it. I'm not sure where it came from but I keep hearing it, calling out to me, words," He said. "I'm not quite sure what to make of it. Perhaps I'm latching on to something that really isn't there. Hope I suppose."

"Hope Sir? Hope for what?"

"That he's alright."

Peter was a pale-faced man behind the long, grey curls of his beard. What colour he did keep in his old, time-fashioned looks appeared to disappear immediately.

"You… you hope he's well?" he stammered. "But, forgive me, he's… he's… well, evil!"

"Completely," He smiled, tying His dreadlocks back in a loose ponytail. "But that doesn't mean I don't care for him. You should know that more than most Peter. Everybody deserves a second chance."

"Yes I know that, of course I do but…" said Peter. "I mean, there's a second chance and then there's, what, a millionth chance, trillionth maybe?"

    THE MAN IN THE DARK

He laughed a little to Himself. Humans had always caused Him a little hilarity. While they were built in His image they always proved to be far from as forgiving as He was.

"And what's wrong with giving someone another chance?" He asked playfully. "Turn the other cheek, love thy neighbour, all good stuff wouldn't you agree?"

"Yes, of course, I'm not arguing that. But I mean, it's *him* we're talking about."

"Yes, I know it's him, that's why I'm so concerned."

He marched out of His office and into the maelstrom outside. People were running up and down the long hallway of the main building of the golf club. There were a lot of worried faces there, looks on people He would never have imagined would be bothered by this sort of panic. Upstairs was unique in its approach to the way things were done. Everybody who was there was meant to be on the same page.

"Sorry about this oh Just and Generous One," said Peter, as if sensing His disappointment. "We're just working very hard to figure out what's going wrong with the Humans. I'm sure it will return to normal as soon as we know."

"No need to apologise Peter, I'm just a little surprised is all," He said philosophically.

"Calm and tranquil, those are the words I normally associate with this old place. This is most certainly neither."

"I think there's a bit of panic. I think there's a worry that this could all be leading to something… else."

He stopped His walking. Turning to Peter, His friendly, warm eyes took on a darkness.

"What do you mean?" He asked. "Something else?"

What little of Peter's colour remained was now banished for all eternity. He was going to wear his fingers down to their bones with the worrying fumbling he was doing. Over and over they went, getting faster the more he panicked.

"It's just… well… I think we could all be doing with a little reassurance is all," he said feebly. "Myself included. We've been trying to find that awful beast for you and drawing nothing. Then there are the riots."

"Riots?" He asked. "I thought there was only one?"

"No, it appears to be spreading," said Peter. "London was first. Now there are mass unrests in Rome, Paris, Los Angeles, Tokyo, Izmir, Buenos Aires and I believe a place called Sydney which is in Australia."

"I know where Sydney is old pip," He said knowingly. "When did this happen?"

"Within the last day or so Human time," Peter swallowed a dry gulp and almost choked. "They're all following the same worrying pattern. Mass hysteria, ultraviolence, a distinct lack of care or courtesy to even the most basic of Human functionality or decorum. It's quite unsettling and, as I say, a few of us are, well, worried."

"Have you tried the usual procedures?" He asked. "Visions, apparitions, manipulation of fate and consequence."

"Yes Your Ultimate Highness, everything," gulped Peter. "But so far the Humans don't seem to be paying any attention. It's almost as if they've been forced to ignore us."

"And what about our old friend? You said there was nothing from him?"

"Nothing at all," said Peter. "We've seen neither sight nor sound of him anywhere. Which is, quite frankly, terrifying."

He started walking again, this time much more briskly. Not hearing from The Devil was to be expected. He was on a secret mission of good faith on His instruction - lost amongst the

Humans. The problems, He thought, would arise if he had been in some way caught up in the hysteria. Or worse yet, killed.

He reached the main reception to find it much busier than usual. The sun beat in through the huge panoramic windows as a large gathering, thousands in numbers, milled around the infinite space of the foyer.

The receptionists of the club were furiously processing the next in line. Gone were the pleasant exchanges, the reassuring welcomes, the brief explanations as to what was going on. A little bit of the chaos the Humans liked to call their own was seeping into the atmosphere of Upstairs. And He didn't like it at all.

"This is getting out of hand," He said, getting as close to angry as He dared show. "Peter you have to bring this under control. I can't be worrying about bureaucracy when existence is falling apart."

"I know. I'm terribly, terribly sorry about all this. We're working as hard as we can to get everyone reassured and moved on to their next step as quickly as we can. But there's been a rather large increase in numbers."

"From the riots?"

Peter nodded. He cast a quick, all-seeing glance over the gathered crowd. It seemed the unrest was taking no prisoners. Humans of all ages, shapes, races, classes and creeds were gathered there - victims of the violence they had created for themselves.

Only He didn't believe that. He knew there was something afoot, something at a very basic, fundamental level that was causing all of this. Was it simply that The Devil wasn't holding up his end of the bargain? Or did this run deeper - much deeper than He had first suspected.

"Have you had any contact from Downstairs?" He asked suddenly, turning to Peter.

"Downstairs?" said the old man. "Good grief no, I would never dream of speaking with those abominations. I mean, we're all Your creations but Downstairs is just-"

"Do me a favour would you old chap?" He said, keeping His voice level. "Get some of our people to give some of their people a quick call. Nothing formal, just a little catch-up to see if they're as busy as we are. If the course is being flooded then I would have thought they would be just as busy. And see what HellCorp is doing."

"HellCorp, yes," Peter nodded furiously.

"Keep it quiet old man, nothing to shout about. If people are on edge I don't want them to be panicked any more than they have to."

"Yes sir, of course," Peter bowed over and over again, his bald head shining with sweat and his fingers red.

He turned away from Him to join the throng of people running to and fro along the corridor. He stopped and turned back, a quivering finger lifted timidly into the air.

"Sorry about this," he said. "But, may I ask, what are You going to do? You don't have to answer that if You don't want to. Of course You don't, You are You after all."

He thought about not answering. As Peter had just said, He didn't have to do anything He didn't want. And it felt like there was something rotten in the air, something big, bad and about to get worse.

But He wasn't about to start turning on His own people. Peter was timid and frightfully dull. However, his faith and loyalty were second only to his devotion to his job. He smiled warmly at one of his closest allies and patted him on the shoulder.

"I have every faith in you old sport," He said. "I know this is just a little glitch in the system, a bump in the road. And what do I always say when things seem to be getting out of hand?"

"These trials are sent to test us," Peter said, like a well-trained child.

"That's right."

"So you'll speak to us, all, to put our minds at ease."

"Well, that's not *exactly* what I had in mind," He said. "After all, I chose you before to spread the good word. And I'm choosing you again Peter to be my messenger. You have to reassure my people, *our* people, that everything will be alright. You see, if I make a grand entrance and take to the stage, then they'll *really* think there's something wrong. After all, do you remember the last time I did that?"

Peter thought for a moment. Then he remembered.

"Oh dear," he said. "The war, the *wars*. Yes I remember My Lofty Liege, dreadful times for all involved."

"Exactly," He lamented. "Now we don't want to repeat those dark days do we?"

"No we don't. We certainly don't want to do that. I mean the suffering, the anguish, the sheer scale of it all. I never thought we were capable of such dreadful acts of cruelty to each other."

"Yes Peter, I remember."

"But *he* had a hand in all that, You remember that of course."

"Yes I remember that too," He said wisely, gently nudging Peter away.

"I will do my very best, You can bank on that my Dear and Wonderful Master."

"I know I can."

"And You'll be in your office?" he asked in hope. "If anything gets out of hand or Downstairs decide to be a little... prickly?"

He hesitated.

"Perhaps best if I stay under the radar for a little while," He said. "As I said old chap, don't want to blow things out of proportion."

For the first time in their history, Peter looked less than convinced by Him. Residual damage from what was going on He supposed. Faith was never questioned more in times of crisis. And this was fast becoming more than just a crisis. It had a danger about it of growing into *the* crisis, the crisis to end them all.

Peter bowed once again and joined the melee. He waited for a moment to make sure His loyal servant was out of sight. Then, when nobody was looking, He disappeared.

TWENTY-TWO

The world around The Devil was moving, despite the fact he was paralysed. Stuck motionless lying on his back darkness flowed all about him. Occasionally a streak of lightning punctuated the landscape. But there was very little to see in this place.

He didn't know where he was or, indeed, what was happening. This world he'd been sucked in to wasn't anywhere he'd been before. There were slivers of comfort about it though, little hints that it was Down rather than Up. Although he couldn't truly say he believed he had been sent home. That would be too easy - far too easy. And he was too shrewd to be led on by false promises.

What concerned him more was a voice echoing from the distance. It was faint but getting louder. And the stronger and clearer it got the more The Devil recognised it.

Alice. His loyal secretary, the one woman in all of existence who probably had control over him - his most faithful servant and cruellest tormentor. Her voice rang out every few seconds, the same terrifying cry for help over and over again.

He continued on the wild path as the darkness fleeted past him. There was no way he could determine how fast he was going or in what direction. But the urgency of movement was clear. He was going.

"Help!" Alice screamed again. "Help!"

"Alice!" he shouted back. "Where are you? What's going on here?"

His voice was distorted and broken, like the sound was new to his ears. There was a slight delay and he thought he could hear the words being said back to him in reverse. He knew then that he was no longer amongst the Humans and that this was some sort of temporal portal.

That could mean only one thing.

"Are you there?" Alice called to him. "Is that you?"

"Alice! Yes I'm here!"

The Devil tried to move but there was nothing. He looked down and there was no body, nothing underneath him. He was consciousness only.

"Well, here in spirit anyway," he said. "Where are you? What's going on? Has somebody done something to you?"

The lightning grew more intense. The Devil winced with its ferocity, deafening crackles echoing about the endless void of the strange world he was in.

The beams and streaks appeared to be focussed. They zapped and sparked together, congregating in one spot on what appeared to be the horizon. Erupting from an invisible point, the long, twisting beams of pure, white-hot light formed a broken and distorted pallet. The lightning grew more intense, sprouting out of the darkness like a mangled, twisted bush. The Devil stared on, narrowing his view of the light display.

Amongst the blazing beams he thought he could make out a face. More lightning bolts shot down from above, making the pallet a bit more intense. Alice's face appeared amongst them, etched with worry.

"Did you miss me you old rotter?" asked his secretary, immediately relieved.

"I can honestly say I've missed you probably more than anything else. Ever. Full stop."

"You're such a charmer," she said. "You always know exactly what to say to a wicked girl."

"What are you doing here?" he asked. "I mean, this, a vision, it must be using up a tremendous amount of power. Power I didn't think you had my darling, my sweet."

"I can't stay for long," she said. "But I had to speak with you. I had to speak to someone. You see, it's a matter of urgency."

"Urgency? You're never urgent," said The Devil cautiously, staring into the intense white centre of the bush of lightning. "In fact you make it your business that you're *never* urgent. What is it you always say? You come around at the exact right moment."

"I do say that," Alice said with a wicked laugh. "Only this time it's different. You see, I, we, need your help."

"My help? Since when have you ever needed my help Alice? Let's be honest here, you can manage just fine without me."

"It's Cassius and Brutus," she said.

Immediately The Devil was overcome with what he could only imagine was panic. Unashamed, unadulterated panic. The two names, the Romans, echoed about inside his mind, bouncing off of the walls and each other.

"Cassius and Brutus," he said. "What about them?"

"They've… they're…"

"They're what? Alice? Are you there?"

The bush distorted again. Snaps of lighting flew from its edges, the image of Alice's face drawing in and out of focus.

"Cassius… Brutus…"

"Alice!" The Devil shouted. "Now I know they can be a handful. And I've got them working on a little side project for me. I won't be away for much longer, I'm working on it, I promise. But He's got me stuck with a moron policewoman you see and now I'm having to deal with another cretin who's gone and misplaced the skeleton he calls a wife. It's just a total omnishambles Alice, I could be doing with having you here to crack the whip. And to sort things out too - wayhay!"

Alice didn't react. Her face was static amongst the crackling streaks of lightning. The Devil then sensed that something was really wrong. It brought him out in a cold sweat. Or it would have if he was at all corporeal.

"Alice?" he said. "Is the signal broken? Alice can you hear me?"

"I can't stay for much longer," she said earnestly. "But I had to warn you. I couldn't not warn you."

"Warn me? Warn me of what? Alice? What's going on? Are you safe?"

"Department J…" said Alice. "Has fallen."

"Fallen? What do you mean fallen? Departments Downstairs don't fall, they can't. Alice. What are you talking about?"

"Cassius… Brutus…"

The image of Alice's plump face, her glasses pressed up her button nose, hair tied back tightly, began to falter. The intensity of the lightning was lessening - beams splintering and vanishing into the darkness. They whizzed and spiralled away into nothing, like pieces of string burned to their ends.

"Alice!" The Devil shouted. "Alice! What's happening, what's happening Downstairs!"

"You have to hurry…" said Alice, her mouth moving but her voice getting fainter and fainter. "Cassius… Brutus… Department J has fallen… ramifications are enormous… irreversible changes… Judas… Judas…"

"Judas!" The Devil shouted. "What about Judas! Alice!"

What was left of the lightning bush erupted in a great ball of light. The Devil was propelled backwards, the sense of movement returning. He raced through the darkness with only the faint outline of the lightning left imprinted on his mind.

"Alice!" he shouted, but his voice was lost.

He sped backwards as if a hand was pulling him from the brink of the abyss. The darkness retreated until suddenly, everything seemed much more real again.

TWENTY-THREE

The Devil sat bolt upright. Something held him back. He was tangled up, caught, like he was bound tightly around his chest, arms and wrists. The more he struggled the worse it became. Eventually he gave up.

Lying back down he took in his surroundings. Everything was suspiciously bright and, above all else, dry. There was no stolen police car, no filthy river water and no Laurie. The whole place had a sterility to it, well cleaned but lacking imagination. Across the room was a window, the bright and clear sky of a summer afternoon shining in. A television was mounted on the opposite wall. The news was on, with more scenes of violence and misery plastered across the screen. He tried to roll onto his side but the cables and pipes attached to his body wouldn't allow it.

The Devil was in hospital. A private room but definitely a hospital. He didn't know how he'd gotten there. Not drowning in a river and not plunging through an eternity of nothingness seemed altogether too lofty for this place. A hospital. Always a hospital he thought.

To add insult to injury there was a little wooden cross on the wall above his bed. More last laughs than last rites.

He tried to sit up again but it was too painful and awkward. He realised then there was a great plastic tube poking out of his mouth. He tried to swallow and felt it go all the way down into his chest. Every time he moved he could sense it deep inside of him. A nasty experience even by The Devil's high standards. Torture, it seemed, was the Human price for surviving.

He lay perfectly still and stared up at the ceiling tiles. No matter how hard he tried he couldn't shake the vision of Alice from his mind. Her face, her words, Brutus, Cassius, it all made him so angry and enraged that he thought he might explode.

The Devil wasn't stupid though, he knew exactly what was going on. If hindsight was a valuable thing, foresight was even more of a commodity. And the Humans always paid dearly for it. He only wished he'd taken some of his own medicine, all puns intended.

He didn't have to ask why - he knew exactly why things had unravelled the way they had. Was he shocked that Brutus and Cassius had betrayed him? No, of course he wasn't. They were two of the worst parasites in all of existence. And he was perfectly aware of what they were capable of. Asking why was a typically Human thing to do. Even their old boss Caesar had asked that question as they'd plunged their daggers into his back. Clinging on to the last vestments of a life well lived, a life that would be written into the annals of time, he still couldn't reason as to why his close allies had shafted him.

The Devil wasn't that sentimental. Brutus and Cassius were the very worst Humanity had to offer - greedy, violent and selfish. That's why they'd gotten where they had Downstairs. That they had betrayed The Devil almost wasn't their fault. Leopards couldn't change their spots after all.

No, what angered him the most was the fact he hadn't seen it quicker. It all made perfect sense now. The violence, the riots, the sheer brutality that had befallen the Humans was evil alright. Just not *his* kind of evil.

This was a new breed - a clumsy, in-your-face style that lacked the usual panache, dignity and subtlety of The Devil's own work. It was painting by numbers when what was required was the deft touch of an Old Master's genius.

PR stunts and statistics and The Devil had fallen for it. He might not be able to read and write Human language but he was still a sucker for a headline. Worst of all he'd *known* he was falling for it. Vanity was a powerful drug and there was a reason it was his most tempting ally. It was the oldest trick in the book. Nothing made a creature feel better about themselves so quickly. The Devil had, of course, made sure that was the case.

He looked up at the cross again. Simple, plain and wooden, who could ask for more? You couldn't really argue with that sort of branding and goodness, no matter how hard he had tried.

The door opened and he was distracted. A slender man in a tight-fitting shirt with sleeves rolled up beyond the elbows came striding in. His dark skin shone with sweat beneath the hard light of the hospital room. Bags were under his eyes and his breath stank of coffee. He checked the file of notes at the bottom of The Devil's bed and smiled at him.

"You're awake," he said. "Good news. How are you feeling?"

The Devil wanted to say something sarcastic but the tube down his throat made that impossible. The doctor quickly moved on.

"You've had a lucky escape from what I've heard," he said. "Very lucky indeed. I think I heard one of the policemen saying it was probably one in a million that you survived the crash let alone the sinking."

Police. Suddenly The Devil grew anxious. When he tried to move the young doctor soothed him. Two nurses came into the little room. They stood on either side of the bed, like bodyguards around the medic.

 216

"Steady on, you've been through the ringer," he said. "Tell you what, let's get this thing out of you shall we? Just relax now."

He nodded to the nurses who sprang into action. They reached for the tube poking out from The Devil. Working together with a familiar efficiency, they started to ease the tube from his throat.

Of all the experiences The Devil had been put through in Human form, this was by far and away one of the worst. The discomfort was almost unbearable. As the nurses worked more and more of the pipe from inside him, he could feel every inch as it left his body. On and on it went, tears rolling down his cheeks. At last the end came out and he coughed up a little sick. The nurses cleaned him up as the doctor hovered around the bed.

The Devil's throat was raw and tender. He was desperate for a drink.

"Water," he rasped, barely able to get the words out. "Give me water."

"Not at the moment," said the doctor succinctly. "Just try to take it a little easy".

The Devil thought for a moment that the young medic was trying to be funny. He considered, briefly, if he'd make a good torturer Downstairs one day. If Downstairs existed that long.

The nurses reappeared and offered The Devil what looked like a small sponge on a stick. He shot it a quick glance and cocked his eyebrows.

"I don't want a bed bath," he croaked. "I want water. And… and…"

He coughed a little. While he wasn't quite used to his new Human voice yet, something was amiss. Even in his strange ears he sounded odder than usual.

"What's wrong with my voice?" he asked. "What is this place? Some sort of chop shop for body parts?"

The nurses dabbed at his mouth with the sponge lollipop. It was wet and went a little to relieving his dryness. Obviously distressed, the doctor called off his staff from the patient. They retreated from the room, muttering to themselves as they went.

"Police," The Devil rasped. "Where are they?"

"They're outside," said the doctor. "I think they want to speak to you about the crash and what happened. Do you think you're up to it?"

"No!" he rasped, his voice still unbearably weak and scratchy. "No! Absolutely not!"

"Okay, okay, take it easy, no problem. I'll tell them."

The Devil's head was spinning. He was finding it difficult to focus. He tried to get out of the bed but the doctor stopped him gently.

"Get out of my way," he said. "Let me go."

"Just try to rest, you've had a pretty tough time of it," said the medic. "I think you should just calm down for a moment and get your strength back."

"I don't have time for that," said The Devil. "I need to get out of here, I need to find Medina Cade and then I need to get my kingdom back before…"

There was a knock at the door. Another nurse appeared, this one pasty-faced and timid.

"Is he awake?" she asked.

"Yes, he's just coming around," he said.

"I'm already around," snapped The Devil. "And I have to get out of here."

"Is he okay to see some visitors?"

"Visitors?"

The Devil froze. The doctor picked up on his tension and gently touched his shoulder.

"Are you alright?" he asked.

"What visitors?"

"There are two gentlemen here to see you," said the nurse. "They seem very worried about you, they insisted on coming to say hello. It could make you feel better? Is he strong enough doctor?"

"I'm not sure," said the medic. "What do you think? It would do you the world of good to see some familiar faces yeah?"

"No," said The Devil flatly. "Any faces familiar to me would put the shits right up you and Matron over there."

"I think it would do you the world of good," said the nurse.

"The world of good," said the doctor.

"The absolute world of good," they both said at the same time.

The Devil started to think he was in a spot of bother. He remained perfectly still, half in the bed, half out of it.

The nurse and the doctor both smiled at him numbly before stepping to one side. Two shambling tramps came staggering into the private room. The smell of stale urine, dried up booze and decay followed them like a cloud. The stench was so thick The Devil thought he could see it as they moved.

"Well, well, well," said the first one, grinning a gap-toothed smile. "There he is."

"There he is indeed," said the other, pushing back his ragged and torn cap with a filthy hand. "Never thought I'd see him like this."

"No, neither did I."

They might have looked and smelled differently but The Devil knew Cassius and Brutus when he saw them. Despite the shabby clothes, gnarled faces and vile odour they still carried with them a pompous grace and arrogance.

"Now you'll have to tell me which one is which," said The Devil calmly. "Because quite frankly you're both as bad as each other."

The tramps let out a loud cackle of laughter before erupting into fits of coughing. They stooped over, leaning on each other for support. They wretched and coughed up thick, black grog, trails of blood running down their cracked lips and into their stubble and scars.

"He's still got it Cassius," said the one with the cap.

"You never lose it, that's what they say isn't it Brutus?" said the other.

They pulled themselves together. They passed the young doctor and the nurse by the door, both Humans locked in a blank-faced trance. Brutus clapped his hands together once and the pair turned on their heels and left. They closed the door of the room behind them, leaving The Devil alone with the Romans.

"I can't even begin to imagine the strain this is putting you under," he said, trying to remain level-headed.

The urge to lunge forward and gouge out their eyes was almost unbearable. But he hadn't become the Man in the Dark by acting solely on instinct. Even in his nauseated state he knew he had to be clever. Don't get mad, get even.

"It's been hard work," said Cassius. "I don't think either of us knew just how difficult it could be running the whole show. Did we Brutus?"

"No we certainly did not," said Brutus. "In fact, we're almost a little envious of you for doing it so well all of these years."

"Are you now?" asked The Devil. "So envious that you're happy just to hand power straight back over to me?"

That made them laugh. He knew it would. While they slapped each other on the back and guffawed about the room, coughing and spitting, The Devil's mind was ticking over. He cursed the fuzziness of Human consciousness. He cursed Humanity in general.

"No, no, no," said Butus. "It's not going to be that simple I'm afraid."

"Then again, whatever is?" chuckled Cassius.

"You didn't take long," said The Devil. "I was barely out of the room and you were having a right good go at making things as uncomfortable as possible for everyone."

"A stroke of luck really, wasn't it Cassius?"

"Absolutely Brutus. I mean, we couldn't have ever thought that you wouldn't even make the bottom floor of Department J before taking us up on our idea. Quite remarkable, if we do say so ourselves."

"Which we do," laughed Brutus.

"I wouldn't be so self-congratulatory gentlemen," said The Devil. "Sometimes there's more than a little divine intervention when it comes to how the universe plays out."

"Indeed," smarmed Cassius. "But it seems that intervention and, dare we say it, the Natural Order are on our side. Wouldn't you agree Brutus?"

"I most certainly would Cassius."

"So what do I owe the displeasure of this visit?" asked The Devil. "Did you bring me grapes at least? Or a bottle of that bright orange liquid the Humans seem to ingest by the gallon when they're in these places?"

Brutus and Cassius both smiled. They split apart and shuffled over to The Devil, one sitting on either side of him, their grubby, dirt covered feet dangling off the edge of the bed.

"We're not here socially I'm afraid sir," said Brutus.

"No, it's not a social call," said Cassius. "As you said, it takes an incredible amount of power to have us here, back amongst the living."

"Yes, indeed," said Brutus. "In fact it might well have caused some considerable damage to the workings of Downstairs just having us here."

"You'll agree we don't look at our best."

"No we don't."

"But vagrants, the bottom of our society was just about all we could muster."

"And even then I'd imagine it's burning up unfathomable energy," said The Devil, his teeth clenched. "Energy that I wouldn't have thought would go unnoticed."

"No," said Cassius. "Quite right."

"Combine that with the possession," The Devil continued. "And you've got to be talking about a universe sized hole in the balance sheet. So big, I'd say, that it's going to attract some unwanted attention from You Know Who."

"Yes, quite," said Brutus. "But you see, we did the maths, totted it all up and concluded that the risk was worth the reward."

"And what reward would that be?" asked The Devil.

Cassius looked at Brutus, who did the same across The Devil's chest. What had started as a little curio was now really getting on his nerves.

"Well, we hadn't quite anticipated on you being... what's the best way to describe it?" asked Cassius.

"Good at being Human," said Brutus.

"Yes that's exactly it."

The Devil couldn't be sure how deliberate all of this was. While he duly gave Brutus and Cassius credit for being master politicians and venerable geniuses in the dark arts of manipulation and treachery, he couldn't help but feel he had underestimated them. It would take something very, very special to get under his skin quite as badly as they were doing now. He couldn't be certain if it was intended that way or they'd passed a threshold and were now just lucking out.

"It seems that your little dip in the water wasn't quite enough to put you to sleep," Brutus continued. "In fact, quite the opposite."

"Yes, we were congratulating ourselves in getting rid of you when, nope, out of the blue, up you popped," said Cassius.

"Dead to the world but still, infuriatingly, breathing."

"You know me," said The Devil. "Bad penny and all that."

"Still, it was a shame what happened to your friend," sighed Cassius.

"Laurie?" The Devil yelped. "What happened to her?"

In all the confusion and anger he'd forgotten all about the policewoman. The last he'd seen of her she was writhing in pain, her face burned off by the poisonous bile of a possessed colleague.

"Humans Cassius, how ever did we get so durable?" asked Brutus.

"Must be in our creation," said Cassius. "We're tough nuts to crack."

"Ah, yes, cracking nuts. That reminds me."

Brutus tip-toed his fingers up The Devil's arm. He marched them all the way to his shoulder before grabbing him by the mouth. Cassius moved behind him, forcing him back onto the bed. Machines bleeped and whirred as he tried to fight back, the cables still attached to his chest and arms.

"Now please don't struggle, you'll only make it worse!" shouted Cassius over the din.

"Yes, be a good Human and let Brutus and Cassius take care of everything."

TWENTY-FOUR

The two tramps were much stronger than their brittle, thin bones appeared. While Cassius pinned The Devil to the bed, Brutus reached into the inside of his filthy coat. Cockroaches dropped from within the crevasse of dirt and foul stenches, scuttling away beneath the bed. He managed to scoop one of them out and held it up to the light.

"Now I'm sure you know what this is," he said, smiling.

The Devil stared at the insect in his hand. It was larger than the other roaches with a thick, black shell covered in a thin layer of slime. Its antenna weaved in circles above its head, eyes transfixed on Brutus like it was waiting on orders.

"Straight from the back drawer of creation," he said. "A little treat that's quite out of its time. About sixty-five million years in fact. You should have seen the effort it took to get him here."

"And while it might not be poisonous, when it gets inside your head sir, you're going to know about it."

The Devil struggled again. Cassius pinned his shoulders down while Brutus mounted him, flattening his legs. He whistled and kissed the air in front of the huge insect, its head twitching before locking its sights on The Devil. Slowly Brutus leaned down and let the roach onto the bed beside The Devil's head. He clamped his filthy hands on his temples and held him still.

"You can't do this," said The Devil. "If I die you don't know what will happen."

"Oh but we do, we do," said Cassius. "With you out of the picture, permanently, we'll have free reign to do exactly what we want."

"We have the know-how, the manpower and above all else, *your* blessing, at least, that's what Downstairs and your legions of supporters will be told," said Brutus, nudging the roach towards him.

"While you gallantly decided to continue to try to do His bidding with the Humans, we'll merely be continuing your good work in your absence," laughed Cassius. "It's perfect really. But to succeed we have to be sure that you're not going to… put a fly in the ointment."

"Or a cockroach," said Brutus.

The Romans laughed with glee. The Devil clenched his jaw tightly shut. He felt the antenna of the roach probing at his ear lobe. Then its claws. It moved tentatively at first, testing the grounds before quickly starting to burrow into his ear canal, slime lubricating the way.

An agonising jolt of pain coursed through his head when it started to bite the flesh. The tender skin and tissue was no match for its sharp appetite. He let out a terrible wail of pain, eons of poetic justice flooding into his mind.

Brutus and Cassius slowly clambered off of him. He grabbed at his ear but the roach was too far in. Struggling to his feet he tried to focus, tried to ignore the agony that was now gripping his Human body. He whirled around the room wildly, bouncing off the walls and yanking cables from the machines beside the bed.

All the while the Romans watched on in glee. They shook each other's hands and delighted in his misery.

"You... you..." The Devil snarled.

He staggered towards them but they evaded him easily. Despite their old, broken bodies they were still too quick for him. The room spun as the agony increased inside his head. He held on to his temples, begging for relief while the roach burrowed further and further in, heading for his brain.

"I... I... can't die like this," he said. "It's not meant to be this way... it's not... meant... to be... this... way!"

Cassius stepped forward and stopped him from spinning. He looked at The Devil with odd coloured, bloodshot eyes and smiled.

"But it *is* this way," he started to laugh. "Goodbye."

"Goodbye," said Brutus.

They shoved The Devil backwards and he tripped over himself. He landed flat on the floor, pulling with him the monitors and machines he was still hooked to. They clattered down beside him as he lay writhing in pain, every muscle tensed, his blood boiling deep inside of him.

Could this really be it? Could this actually be how it all came to an end for the Man in the Dark, the embodiment of evil, Downstairs' lord and master? In all the eons of natural and unnatural time he'd never given it much thought. He never really felt like he had to. Beginnings and endings were His thing. It was The Devil's job to make the moments in between as miserable for others as possible. Whether He liked it or not.

Now here he was. Half-naked scratching about the floor stuck in Human form while a prehistoric bug feasted on his mind. He'd seen the darkness that awaited him, lightning bushes and all. And there wasn't a single thing he could do about any of it.

Something moved above him, distracted him just enough from his agony to look up. The door of the private room opened up and in strode a middle-aged woman in a hand-knitted jumper. She was reading through a stack of notes when she stopped and looked up at Brutus and Cassius.

"Who are you?" the Romans said in unison.

"Oh I'm sorry," said the woman in a thick Northern Irish accent. "I thought this was the… what's it called, the thingy-ma-jig."

"Thingy-ma-jig?" said Cassius.

"This is a private room good woman," said Brutus. "Now kindly fuck off!"

The woman gasped. She took a step back before realising The Devil was on the floor. She pointed at him.

"What's wrong with this one?" she asked. "Is he alright?"

"What did we just tell you?" asked Cassius. "Get lost!"

"I think he might be in a bit of trouble," she said. "He looks like he's in agony."

She kneeled down beside The Devil. He tried to speak to her but the tendons in his jaw and neck were so tense he couldn't move. He reached out to her, hands shaking violently, and grabbed her by the jumper.

"You know I think he's in pain," said the woman.

"We told you politely to leave this place!" said Cassius, stomping forward. "Now if you don't go we'll be forced to cave your head in and-"

He put a hand on her shoulder. There was a bright flash that filled the whole room followed by a short, sharp ripping sound. Cassius was lifted off his feet and thrown across the room, faster than any Human was ever designed to go. His broken tramp body smashed through the window, passing through the glass with as much ease as scissors through silk. He flew so far he became a dot on the clear blue palette of the sky before dropping into obscurity.

Even in his pained state The Devil knew what had happened. For Brutus is took another few seconds to work it out. And that was too long, as it turned out.

"You shouldn't be so quick to judge," She said, getting up quickly and moving, seemingly instantly, to Brutus' side. "It really is a bad habit to get into. Because you see old chap, you never know when you're going to get caught out."

Her hand reached for Brutus' throat. Rather than grab at his scarred, ragged neck, it passed straight through the skin. The Roman's tramp body shuddered for a moment, bloody and black froth gargling from deep within him like an acrid volcano. His eyes rolled back in his head and he turned to face Her.

"It's already started," he said, voice deeper, darker, more distorted than before. "The wheels are in motion, the game is already won."

"I know," She said calmly, smiling a little. "But that doesn't mean I won't at least try."

She reached further into Brutus' neck until Her whole arm had disappeared. With a sharp tug, She pulled herself free. There was a hiss before his body erupted into a fountain of black, grainy sand. From the centre a white dove appeared, flapping its wings clear of the filth. The bird cooed once and flew out of the window.

She dusted Her hands clean and smiled as the dove disappeared. The Devil groaned as loud as he could, crawling over the damaged equipment and tangle of pipes and tubes he was still connected to.

"Oh yes," She said, remembering why She was there. "Hold still would you old chap. This is probably going to hurt."

She took his head in Her hands. Staring at him with a soft smile, She muttered something under Her breath. The Devil felt an intense heat behind his Human eyeballs. The burning pushed its way out of his skull, down through his ear canal and out into

THE MAN IN THE DARK

the air. A little spark puffed from his ear and his nose filled with the smell of burning hair.

"Bugger," She said, clapping his head. "Looks like I might have left you a little bald there. Sorry about that."

The pain inside The Devil's head was instantly relieved. It was so great a relief that his whole body went numb. Every muscle relaxed and he rolled onto his back, gasping for air. He was covered in sweat, blood running from his ear, but at least he was alive.

"Come on old chap," She said, helping him onto the bed. "You've had a bit of a time of it haven't you?"

"People keep saying that to me," he croaked, wiping sweat from his top lip. "It really doesn't do what I've been through any justice."

"Justice, now there's a funny old thing," She said. "Everybody wants it but only a few are ever truly owed it. Strange, don't you think, how the Humans never quite latched on to that idea."

"You would know," he said. "You invented them. Every. Single. One."

She let out a hearty giggle that made Her belly jiggle. She patted him on the back and sat down beside him on the edge of the bed.

"I thought hospitals were meant to be safe havens," said The Devil. "The last couple I've been in I've been left a sack of bones on the floor. It's becoming a nasty habit that I don't want to continue."

"There might not be much left to continue with at this rate."

She nodded up at the television. Somehow the screen had evaded The Devil's whirlwind of destruction. Soldiers were marching down roads in some distant land. Tanks were firing into cities and people were running for their lives.

"The story is the same," She said. "All over the world. Violence, greed, debauchery. It wasn't like this in your day."

"This *is* my day," he said. "At least it was until You showed up."

"And just as well I did."

The Devil wiped his face dry on his hospital gown. He looked at Her.

"Do I detect a sense of urgency about You?" he asked. "I don't think I've *ever* known You to be urgent. I didn't think You were capable of something so…"

"Human?"

"Yes, I suppose."

"Of course I'm urgent, you've seen what's going on out there. We're in a spot of bother old boy. And by a spot of bother I mean a-"

"Great big gaping hole of a clusterfu-"

"Yes, exactly," She said gravely. "Do you think you can walk?"

The Devil rolled his shoulders. He wriggled his toes and nodded. She began detaching him from the machines, tugging at hair and skin in the process.

"Your clothes are in that cupboard," She nodded at the cabinet beside his bed. "You might want to bring them with you."

"Where are we going?" he asked.

"To collect DS Laurie."

"Laurie!" he shouted. "You mean she survived the sinking of the Titanic too?"

"Of course she did," She said. "I told you, she's special."

"Everybody is special to You," The Devil said darkly, collecting his things. "I take it You had more than a hand in getting us out of that jam."

"On the contrary old pip, absolutely nothing," She said.

They slipped out of the room and into the busy corridor. Hospital staff were running around, nervously, anxiously, the sense of dread hanging about them gloomily. This was a place of crisis, like a war zone, not an urban hospital.

"How come this lot aren't under the influence?" he asked as they hurried down the hall.

"Safe haven," She said. "I've got a perimeter up around me, a mile or so, all I could manage without drawing attention to myself."

"I've heard that before," he said. "Our old pals Brutus and Cassius tried something similar."

"It wasn't enough, they don't know what they're doing."

"I don't know," said The Devil.

They walked past an old man, his face covered in blood. He held his hands up, as if begging for mercy while nurses tried to clean him up.

"They seem to have this chaos and misery thing down to a tee," he said. "Not bad work actually."

"That's what I'm afraid of," She said.

She called a lift and it arrived instantly. The door opened to a melee of action. Two porters pushed a bed out surrounded by more nurses and doctors. Another medic was up on the bed performing emergency CPR, a dying patient lost somewhere amongst the IV drips, blood bags and tender care. The bed was wheeled out quickly, its entourage almost running them over. When they were gone, they headed into the lift and closed the doors.

Alone, The Devil felt a sudden panic. He didn't like being out of the public eye with Her. That usually meant there was bad news on the way. Or a good hiding. And even he couldn't argue that he didn't deserve both. Not after Brutus and Cassius' so far successful insurrection.

"I know what you're thinking you know," She said, a smug look on Her face. "I'm not deaf."

"I didn't say anything," said The Devil. "Although I'm also totally aware that that was a futile thing to say."

"I should probably say that I'm not angry with you," She said.

"Angry with me? I'm not Your child, I can see, think and do as I please."

"You're not a teenager either old sausage," She said. "But I'm not angry with you. I'm more… disappointed."

The lift started to go down. The Devil hesitated for a second. Then remembered that he didn't have to put up with that sort of telling off.

"You know, I'm not the only one to blame here," he said, thinking offense was as good as a defense. "I mean, it's not like I'm omnipotent. Incontinent maybe in this ridiculous body You've put me in. But I can't see *everything* that's going on, ever. I don't have that gift, remember. Out of the two of us it's probably *You* You should be disappointed with."

She didn't answer him. She stared blankly at the lift doors.

"You have your argumentative hat on," She said. "It's only natural. You're angry, you're upset. You've had the rug pulled out from under your feet in a big way old chap, I can't blame you."

"You can't blame me? Well that's a first," The Devil snapped. "I kind of want to get a picture of this moment to keep it fresh in my mind."

"You should have known better," She said. "You know what they're like."

"Yes, I know what they're like. And I *do* know better. That didn't stop them from shafting me though, did it."

"No, it didn't," She sighed. "Still, you should have known there was a chance of it happening. After all, you struck a deal with them. Didn't you."

The Devil felt his mouth hang open. He tried to close it but found he wasn't able to do so. There was no mystical force stopping him. He was just gripped with panic.

"I… that is… we didn't… I had…"

The lift stopped suddenly. The light above them flickered. She looked up at it inquisitively. Growing at least an inch, she reached

THE MAN IN THE DARK

up and tapped the plastic cover over the bulb. The light flickered before fixing itself.

The Devil should have used those precious seconds to come up with an excuse. Or at the very least a lie to try and worm his way out of getting caught red handed. But he didn't. He blamed the sluggishness of his mind encased in a poorly put together Human body. What he didn't admit was the feeling he refused to acknowledge. That perhaps he had wanted to get caught all along.

"Natural Order old boy," She said, shrinking back down to Her previous size. "It's what keeps everything ticking over. I know you don't like it, I know it gets right up your goat. To be perfectly frank with you, it's not a perfect system. But it's just about as close to perfect as we can get. And you don't do too badly out of it, do you?"

The Devil shook his head. If that was going to be the worst of it he thought he hadn't done too badly. Only he knew that would never be the worst of it. Not really. It never was when She was involved.

"I guess I had a rush of blood to the head," he said humbly. "I think that's what the Humans call it. A rush of blood to the head. Stupid really, of course they've got blood in their heads. They've got blood everywhere. And it *gets* everywhere when they start to leak. How typical of them."

"Quite the analogy," She said. "Given where we are."

"It's not that I don't respect the Natural Order, of course I do," The Devil continued. "Respect is one of the cornerstones of my ethos. You know that. Without respect we're little more than… well, *them* aren't we?"

"Debatable," She nodded.

"I think I was just curious is all."

"Curious?"

"Yeah, curious," he started to pace about the lift. "I mean, don't

You ever get curious sometimes? Of course You don't, You're *You* after all. When You get curious You simply conjure it all up and let it go with the flow. I don't have that luxury. Not on the same scale at least. Maybe I just thought I might, maybe, do a better job of things."

"You mean *different* job of things old pip, different."

"Semantics," The Devil waved a hand around. "Different, better, it's all change in the end. I suppose Brutus and Cassius were just good enough to pick up on that and run with it."

"And boy did they run with it," She said.

She let out a little, almost inaudible sigh and wandered over to the wall of the lift. Leaning on it, She tapped Her palms against the hard metal. The rhythm was soft and steady and The Devil felt a strange, alien sensation come over him.

"What's that?" he asked.

"What's what?" She asked back.

"That, what you're doing."

"I'm not doing a thing."

"Yes you are, that tapping," he pointed at Her hands. "What's that all about?"

"It's nothing," She asked. "Is it bothering you?"

"No it's not bothering me, it's… it's…"

"It's?" She asked.

"It's soothing."

She smiled. She knew as well as anybody that soothing wasn't something The Devil was familiar with. Part of the job meant that he couldn't ever really be soothed. He was too busy, too angry, too energetic to ever slow down. The tap, tap, tapping on the lift wall was at just the right pace, just the right tempo and pitch that it got right inside his twisted, warped brain.

"You're doing that deliberately," he said. "You're messing with my head."

"I'd do no such thing," She said with a knowing smile. "I'm not at liberty to go about jumping inside people's minds willy-nilly. That's more your sort of thing old bean."

"Well stop it," he said. "Just stop it."

"Why," She said, continuing to tap. "Is it working?"

The Devil gritted his teeth. He clenched his fists and rapped them on his forehead. No matter how hard he tried he couldn't chase away the feeling his Human body was starting to relax. Tap after tap after tap, the rhythm was just right, just perfect enough that he could feel himself getting heavy with fatigue.

"This isn't helping you know," he said. "You need me at my optimum, You need me at my best."

"What I need you to be is clear, focussed and ready for what lies ahead," She said. "I need you to put aside what petty, squabbling differences we have and I need you to be in a state of alertness."

She stopped. The Devil instantly felt better. He could feel the life returning to his arms and legs. His mind sharpened, even his eyes felt like they'd been given a new lease of life. The Human senses he'd struggled with were quicker now, smell, touch, taste, everything. Like waking from a long, tired sleep he could feel an energy within him he'd never known possible in Human form.

"What have You done to me?" he asked. "Is this some sort of… this is cheating isn't it?"

She tapped the end of Her nose and clicked Her fingers. The door of the lift opened. The hustle and bustle of the hospital was gone. The outside world waited for them. Warm, summer air blew in and about The Devil and he could smell the thick musk of freshly cut grass.

"This is definitely an upgrade," he said, flexing his hands and feeling his paunch. "But I'm starting to suspect that it's because I'm not heading back Downstairs any time soon."

She stepped out of the lift. The laws of architecture clearly didn't apply, not when She was in the mood. They were out on the street now with a car sitting parked next to the pavement, the engine running quietly. She walked up to the passenger door and stooped down to look in the window. The Devil followed her and saw a figure sitting the passenger seat.

"Laurie?" he asked.

"The very same," She said. "Don't worry, she's out for the count at the moment. Heavily sedated. I should think you've got about thirty minutes before she comes around."

The Devil looked in at the policewoman. Her head was tilted away from him. Even still he could make out that she had been badly disfigured by the biker's attack. Thick gauze was taped across half of her face and she was an unhealthy shade of yellow everywhere else.

"She's alive then," he said.

"Just about," She answered succinctly. "It seems she has Brutus and Cassius to thank for that."

"You didn't answer my question," said The Devil. "I'm not going Downstairs? I'm not going to boot their arses from here to eternity and stop the whole of existence from falling apart around our armpits?"

"No, you're not," She said.

There was something about the tone in Her voice that implied She wasn't prepared for any further questions. The Devil, however, was never one to take a hint lightly. And with the apocalypse knocking on his door, there was no time to stand on ceremony.

"Why not?" he said angrily. "I thought we were neck deep in it this time? Surely this whole charade with Medina Cade and whatever Laurie has going on can wait?"

"That's the real trick though old bean, it's the little things that add up," She said.

"The little things?" he blurted. "You've got to be kidding me. Brutus and Cassius are causing merry hell all over the planet and You're worried about a missing housewife?" What's the point in taking her along, she'll just slow me down. Especially if she's hurt."

She drew The Devil a long, hard look. He'd known Her long enough to know when not to argue. And he was skating on thin ice as it was. Not that She would ever say that. She didn't have to with looks like that.

"Regardless of what you think of the Humans and DS Laurie, you still need her help," She said firmly.

"Fine," he grunted. "But I still don't understand why You can't just bring an end to this ridiculous goose chase and send me back Downstairs with an army. If You did that I can guarantee this whole mess would be over and done within a matter of minutes. Seconds even."

"I only wish that were true," She said, sighing softly again. "But even I think the damage may already be done."

"What? Surely not," he said. "You, *You* not looking on the bright side? I told You I wished I had my camera. Now I *really* wish I did."

She shook Her head. She stared longingly at nothing, time and space seemingly passing behind Her eyes. She was wistful and morose, more than he had ever seen Her. A cold sweat made his clothes sticky and he felt a surge of panic make his calves tingle.

"Look, it can't be *that* bad, surely," he said. "I mean nothing's ever that bad is it? We always come out on top in the end. Don't we? I mean we fight a lot and hate the sight of each other."

"I don't hate you," She said.

"Yeah, that's what I said, I hate the sight of You."

He forced a laugh. She smiled sadly. He nudged Her in the ribs, trying to josh and play with Her. But even The Devil knew when he was licked.

"Medina Cade," he said. "She's still missing I take it."

"Yes," She said. "Firmly missing. If you find out what happened to her then you can return Downstairs. And then, maybe, we might be able to get around the table or something. I don't know old boy, I really don't know."

She pushed off from the side of the car and started walking away, Her hands in Her pockets and head bowed towards the pavement. The Devil tried to push the uneasiness from his mind, tried his hardest to convince himself that this was all part of Her great, grand scheme.

"Where are You going?" he shouted. "You know there's plenty of room in the back of this thing for You to tag along. If You like?"

She stopped. Turning back to face him, The Devil could see that She was crying. Tears wet Her puffy cheeks and She wore a look of such abject sadness that he felt his whole body convulse with what he assumed was pity.

"Thank you old chum," She said, voice cracking and broken. "But I think I'll head home to see what I can do."

"Upstairs?" he asked.

"Yes," She nodded. "Hurry, won't you. There really isn't a moment to waste. Not anymore. Maybe not ever."

With that, She turned away from him and walked up the street. Before She could reach the end of the block She had vanished, gone, like She had never been there.

THE MAN IN THE DARK

TWENTY-FIVE

Laurie didn't want to open her eyes. She was happy where she was. So happy, in fact, that she wanted to stay in this place forever.

It wasn't fancy, it wasn't even somewhere new. That made it all the more tangible and all the better. Everything was just where it should be. Natural, in order, perfect.

Light snow was falling outside the living room window. It had been like that all night. Little mounds had formed on the rims and edges of the panes and the glass was frosted from the cold air meeting the warmth of the house.

There was a roaring fire that made the whole room unbearably hot. Not that anybody would ever dream of saying so. The Christmas tree in the corner, gently blinking its lights on and off was like a silent bouncer in that regard. The festive season meant one thing and one thing only. No fighting.

Laurie liked it that way. She always had. There was plenty of trouble at work and every other day of the year. Christmas was a day off in so many ways. But she particularly liked that about it.

She moved around the living room, taking everything in. She could smell it all, sense the fibre of every conversation, every voice, every moment that had happened in there over the past seven decades. The world could end a million times over outside the front door and this place would still be the same. It was safe, it was peaceful and for the majority of her life it had been home.

The table was set in the middle of the cosy living room. There was just about enough room around the edges to get in and out without knocking something over. Five chairs, five plates, five sets of cutlery and hundreds of crackers. The odd shaped candles, burned down at different lengths, had been rolled out too. They were lit, despite every light in the house being on. That drew a smile from Laurie.

She walked, with some difficulty, all the way around the table. When she reached the television she squeezed her ample frame in tight. The Queen was on, delivering her annual message to the people. The sound was down and Laurie was alright about that. She stopped at the window and cleared some of the condensation.

Snow, everywhere. The front garden, the main road, nothing but white. All of the houses chugged a little smoke from their chimneys, some more than others. Bernadette and Malcolm's was spewing big, black clouds. Beside them old Francie had barely a whisp. The village was filled with little copies of each other, all poking out from the blanket of white stuff that levelled everything off like a cake.

Laurie laughed to herself and drew away from the window. She drank it all in, letting everything seep into her pores. She couldn't get enough. Even when she was a teenager, leaving school, going to college she still longed to be back here, with her grandparents. Home was always home. She'd always known that, always been made to feel that was the case. Gran and Grandad had made sure that was what was best for her. Especially after her parents had disappeared.

And now she was back.

The living room door opened a little. A small, well-groomed head poked around the edge.

"Matilda," said Laurie.

Her daughter, her only daughter, came trotting in. She was younger than Laurie remembered, no older than three. She carried a beaten up, worn down stuffed rabbit, its ears wet with saliva. When she saw her mother she ran for her, arms wide open, little feet thumping on the old floorboards.

"I love you my darling," she said as her daughter wrapped her arms about her.

"Matilda?" a voice shouted from the hallway. "Matty, where have you gone? You've got to get dressed for dinner!"

Andy came striding into the living room. He was carrying a little red dress and striped tights. When Laurie saw her husband she could feel her heart swelling. Again he was younger than she knew him, much younger. His hair was long, down past his ears, kissed at the end by the sun. He had a rough, thin beard and shabby, loose-fitting clothes, his feet bare beneath his jeans. He looked exactly how he did the night they had first met. Lean and happy with a playfulness that seemed to fill the whole room.

"Are you running away from me?" he smiled a big, broad grin. "Are you running away from your daddy? Yes you are. Yes you are."

He pretended to creep up on Matilda. Big, over-the-top steps made the little girl gargle with excitement. When he reached his daughter, he tickled her under the arms and she screamed with delight.

"Merry Christmas love," he said, leaning in to kiss Laurie on the cheek.

"Merry Christmas Andy," she said.

The contentment was real, even if she knew that none of this was. She'd tried to convince herself to let go, to forget that this was clearly some sort of dream, but she just couldn't do it. And strangely, that didn't make her sad or disappointed. If anything, it meant she could enjoy everything about it. Her grandparents' house, Matilda being so young and Andy still fresh-faced and hip.

It was a tailor-made fantasy plucked straight from the nether regions of her mind. Even the faithful recreation of Christmas all around her. She was certain she could hear Greg Lake's I Believe in Father Christmas playing somewhere in the background. It was perfect, too perfect and that was why she couldn't stay forever. Even if she wanted to, she knew this wasn't for her.

She buried her nose in Matilda's hair and smelled the aroma of her young daughter. She kissed the little girl tenderly before handing her off to her father. Andy took Matilda and sat her down at the table. He took his place beside her, the two of them pulling a cracker, laughing and joking, happy and free.

There were voices from the kitchen, Laurie knew who they were. Gran and Grandad, fighting over the gravy, clanking pots and plates around, fighting like cat and dog. They'd be there for another hour bickering and battling. Then the turkey would arrive and everybody would be stuffed like pigs.

Laurie cherished it all as she made her way from the living room and into the hall. Her coat was hanging on the stand, hat, scarf and gloves all bundled around it. She pulled them on, carefully, feeling every fibre of wool on her fingertips. When she was ready she took a long look at herself in the mirror on the wall.

Twenty-something years of change that mirror had seen. Her face, her haircut, everything had moved on. She stared at herself and picked apart every little detail. Crow's feet, wrinkles on her forehead, her flushed cheeks that were puffier than they should be.

She leaned in closer and saw something else. Down the side of her head the skin looked different. She touched it and it crinkled, like the crepe paper she'd used to make Christmas cards in school. The more she pressed the more marked it became.

Her contentment began to vanish, replaced by the worry and fear of reality. Like sand being blown from a table top, her old, recognisable face vanished. And in its place was a new one, the latest one, the one she'd be stuck with. Damaged, burned, deformed.

The front door flew open and a bitterly cold wind came rushing into her grandparents' house. It lifted the rug and the telephone table and sent them spinning past her. The worn out floral wallpaper was stripped from the walls and the carpet uplifted. Snow and ice darted down the hallway, stabbing at her like a million tiny daggers. Laurie tried to shield herself but it was all too strong, too much for her.

She pressed herself against the wind as it grew stronger and stronger. Something inside of her urged her to give up. But Laurie had never given up on anything in her life. She'd never backed down, never conceded. When she was told she couldn't do something that made her want it all the more. She was a pain in the backside, a contrarian and a bloody good policewoman. No feral wind was going to beat her.

Her feet slipped a little as she tried to move towards the door. Laurie ducked her head and pushed on, fighting against the powerful gale that was battering and blasting the corridor. Step by step she edged closer and closer to the door. The wind grew stronger but she kept going, determined as ever to reach her goal.

She reached out and grabbed a hold of the door frame with the very tips of her fingers. It was enough to give her leverage and she pulled herself up and through the entranceway and into the blizzard.

Then everything went white.

Laurie could feel her whole being tingling. The wind was gone, replaced with a comfortable silence and stillness. She stood perfectly still and just listened. The quietness felt like a warmth in her ears.

She knew, of course, that she was still dreaming. But there was something else, some other force just behind what she could see and feel. Laurie couldn't explain what it was, only that it was benevolent and kind.

A detached haziness crept into the corners of her conscious mind. She could feel herself very gently being guided away from this fantasy world and back to reality. Her time in her dream had been one she would cherish, always. But nothing lasted forever and she knew she had to go back. Back to a world filled with darkness, misery and death. Back to a world that wanted nothing more than to consume itself in a painful, drawn out torture. Back.

Very slowly she opened her eyes. The whiteness retreated and she felt her limbs again. Only there was something different, something blocking her now.

She was in a car, the world racing past the window at an altogether too fast speed. It made her jumpy and alert and she sat up. Beside her was The Devil, a hard look on his face, feet mashing the pedals like he didn't really know what he was doing.

"Where are we?" she asked.

"London, England," he said succinctly. "We had a lucky escape."

"Lucky?" she said, feeling every limb and joint in her body ache. "It didn't feel like lucky from where I was sitting."

"No," he said. "Then you won't be so shocked when you look in the mirror."

Laurie could almost feel the ice cold sweat push itself from inside her. Her stomach lurched once, then again and finally for a third time as the memories of what happened hit her like a boot to the mouth.

She pulled down the sun visor and hesitated for a second, hand

THE MAN IN THE DARK

quivering over the plastic cover of the mirror. Sucking in air, she slid it open and caught sight of her damaged, burned face for the first time. At least she would have if she could see through the gauze.

"Great," she said. "That's all I need."

"I told you," said The Devil. "You're not going to have a fit are you? Because we really don't have time for amateur dramatics Laurie. Something big has happened, huge in fact. And I need you to focus and concentrate as much as that prattling Human brain of yours can."

"I think I'd rather be at Gran and Grandad's," she said.

"What?"

"Never mind."

TWENTY-SIX

"We go to Cade's house, shake him down and find out what he's not telling us. Sound like a plan?" asked Laurie.

"I think that's probably the best idea you've ever had Detective Sergeant," said The Devil. "In fact I'm tempted to say it's the best idea you're ever likely to have too. Although judging by the way things are going, that might not be much of a compliment."

The Devil was still struggling with the controls of the car but he was beginning to think he had the hang of it. How hard could it be anyway? The Humans had invented it, there wasn't anything complicated with pointing, pressing and steering.

The route to Cade's house was impressed on his memory. A strange quirk, he thought, given the relative slackness this body had shown him so far. Although when he thought about it, he suspected there had been a little help from a certain Mistress of the Cosmos.

One thing The Devil wasn't so sure about was Laurie's sudden keenness. As the purveyor of 'if it's too good to be true it usually is' mantra, he decided to call her on it.

"You seem awfully enthused suddenly," he said. "What's the matter with you?"

"What's the matter with me?" she grunted. "Have you seen my face? Look at me!"

"I didn't particularly want to look at you in the first place Laurie," he winced. "I've spent more than my fair share of time in the company of some of Humanity's most beautiful men and women. Cleopatra, Alexander the Great, Harrison Ford, you name it. I'd ask for forgiveness but even you would agree you're not quite in that league."

"You're such a dick," she said. "Here I am happy to help you."

"Finally."

"Happy to help you and all I'm getting is a torrent of abuse."

"I'm only asking," he said. "You've not seemed very enthusiastic up until now. And suddenly you're coming up with plans left, right and centre. I'm just curious as to why you're so eager to kick on when you could be, say, back at home with your family."

Laurie was silent. She pulled the sun visor down again and looked at her face. She began to peel the gauze from her damaged cheek, wincing every time the glue and tape got caught.

"What are you doing?" he asked.

"I want to see what's happened to me," she said. "I want to see what your pals have done to me. So that I know."

"Know what?"

She freed the gauze to reveal the extent of the damage. The skin across the whole of the right side of her face was burned and scorched. Large, bloody blisters oozed and wept from the damage. There was no whiteness in her right eye, although she could still see through it, despite the blood. She didn't react. She looked at it from every angle, taking everything in with a military, robotic efficiency.

"I needed to know," she said. "How much pain and misery I'm going to inflict on the bastards who have maimed me."

The Devil smiled. His whole Human body shivered a little with excitement.

"Oh my," he said. "It's been a while since I was given a little cheap thrill like that. You make me want to take back what I said about you being unattractive Laurie. That gave my pencil a jolt of lead there."

Laurie flipped the sun guard back up and cracked her knuckles. She rolled her neck and shoulders like a prize fighter ready for the final round. The Devil didn't even realise he'd pressed the accelerator more. He was filled with a strange, ungainly sensation he assumed was hope.

The late afternoon sunshine was still strong when they pulled into the Cade's street. Taking things extra cautiously, they parked up at the end of the road and made their way onwards on foot.

When they were within sight, The Devil stopped Laurie. They sheltered beneath one of the large trees that lined the sleepy avenue and peered up towards the Cade residence.

"This is a bit odd," he whispered. "Where have all the news crews gone?"

Laurie searched the street herself. It was empty, save for the parked cars in the driveways and next to the kerbs. There was no media circus, no police presence, nothing. It looked, for all intents and purposes, like an ordinary suburban street.

"I smell a rat," she said. "There isn't even a sentry. Nobody's guarding Cade's door."

"I agree," said The Devil. "As much as it pains me again Laurie, you're right."

"You think they've been, you know, possessed?"

"I think it's safe to assume that all of your police colleagues will be under Brutus and Cassius' influence," he said. "When I spoke to them they admitted as much. Although the amount of power and energy that must be taking up makes my head spin just thinking about it."

248

"You've met them?" she asked. "You mean, since it all kicked off?"

"I'm afraid so," he sighed. "And it was about as unpleasant as you can imagine. Mostly for them right enough. I came out of it totally unscathed of course."

Laurie looked him over with a sarcastic glint in her eye. She took in every inch of his pitiful state. She knew who he was, what he was. But even in this light, with everything that had gone on, she had to hand it to him. There was something ever so slightly heroic about The Devil.

She hadn't seen it before. Not until now.

"What did they say?" she asked.

Laurie seemed more focussed now on the bigger picture. The Devil wondered if She hadn't had a quiet word with her when she was sleeping.

"They said as much as any Human traitor who's been dead for two thousand years. Nothing."

"Nothing? I don't believe that for a second."

"It doesn't really matter if you believe it or not Laurie. The fact of the matter is they've taken over your pal Lister and all of your cronies and they're bent on making sure we're snuffed out as quickly and no doubt as painfully as possible. Did I mention the cockroach?"

"Cockroach," she shivered. "What cockroach?"

"Never mind."

They watched the street for a few moments, waiting for any sign of life. The place was perfectly still, a little slice of serenity amidst the crumbling decay of Human civilisation.

"Wait a minute," said Laurie. "What's going on there?"

She pointed towards the far side of Cade's house. A small van had its back doors open. A man was lugging boxes and dumping them untidily in the back. He was sweating in the heat and appeared to be grumbling something under his breath.

"Police?" asked The Devil.

"No," said Laurie.

"How can you be sure?"

"He's lifting things up and tidying them away," she said. "No copper would do that. We don't need to. We get the public to do it for us."

"Touché," he replied, and stepped out from behind the tree.

"Where are you going?"

"To ask him what's going on?"

"You mean just like that?" she bleated. "What if he's, you know?"

She pointed at her mutilated face. The Devil had the courtesy not to wince. He didn't need reminded of the terrible wounds she had suffered.

"Then we'll soon find out, won't we."

"Fine," said the policewoman. "But we do it on my terms. Okay? You might be the Man in the Shadows."

"Man in the Dark," he corrected her.

"Whatever. I'm still a police officer. If I stop him he'll speak to us. If you do it he'll knock you spark out."

They waited until the man was around the other side of the van before hurrying up the street. They hid on one side and heard him on the other, swearing, and banging things on the ground.

Laurie held a finger to her mouth and crept around towards the open back doors. The Devil was her shadow, staying an inch behind her as she went. They heard footsteps from the man coming around. The Devil felt the hairs on his arms stand on end, the anticipation making his Human heart thump that little bit faster.

"I should be retiring," grunted the man as he reached the back of the van.

Laurie sprung forward. She shoulder-barged the open door with enough force to send it swinging into the man. It clattered against him hard and he let out a yelp, dropping a heavy case. The policewoman grabbed him while he was still reeling and twisted his arm up behind his back. She kicked the back of his knees and he sank down to the ground.

"What the bloody hell!" he shouted.

"Shut it," she said, wrenching his arm.

"You'll break my bloody arm!"

"That's right, I'll break your arm sunshine. Just calm it down, okay?"

The man held his free hand up and nodded furiously. The Devil watched on as Laurie brought him under control.

"Very impressive," he said. "One might even think you had a passion for this job Laurie."

"Yeah, well, I try," she said. "Now you - Van Man. What are you doing?"

"I'm not doing anything!" he said, his accent Welsh. "I'm just loading up the van."

"Who are you?" asked The Devil.

"Mal. Malcolm Brody."

"And who are you Malcolm Brody?" asked Laurie. "What are you doing here?"

"I'm a labourer," he said. "I just tidy up. Load up the van."

"Load up the van with what?"

"Equipment."

"What equipment?" Laurie looked in at the boxes and cases stacked up in the back of the van.

"Cameras and that," said Mal. "Mics, booms, cables, everything for the network."

"Network?"

"The TV channel - the network. I'm a labourer for the network, have been for the past six years. I just do the driving, the loading. Manual labour."

Laurie looked at The Devil. He shrugged his shoulders.

"What do you think?" she asked him.

"About Mr Malcolm Brody here? I don't think there's any suggestion that he's under any incantation," he said. "He says he's a labourer, we've seen him labouring, albeit lazily. I think you could probably release your death grip. Unless you really do want to pull his arm from his socket."

Laurie was satisfied with him. She let Mal go and helped him to sit on the lip of the van. He wheezed and rubbed his shoulder, reaching for a packet of cigarettes in his shirt pocket. He lit one with a shaking hand and puffed away.

"Where is everybody?" asked The Devil. "I thought this was a media hot spot, the world's finest journalists and photographers camped out in front of Pierce Cade's house in the hopes of spotting white smoke or something."

"Eh?" asked Mal blankly.

"Reign it in sunshine," said Laurie. "Your bosses, where are they?"

"I don't know," said Mal. "I just got the order to pack everything up."

"When?"

"Would have been this morning, I think," he scratched his chin. "I left last night, went home for my dinner and locked the door. You know how it is these days, of course you do, you're a copper. So I went to my bed. Got up this morning, told we were packing up and that was that. I showed up here earlier and there wasn't a soul in the street."

"Everyone was gone?" asked The Devil. "No Americans,

Chinese, those annoying Brits with the rotten teeth and bad boob jobs?"

"Not a soul," Mal sucked on his cigarette. "So I started lugging the stuff. The presenter, what's-her-name, the good looking bird, she wasn't here but her camera and mic and all that game were left behind. So I'm just doing my job. You can't nick me for that, can you?"

The Devil growled quietly. He beckoned Laurie a little way away from Mal.

"You smelled a rat," he said. "I smell a bigger one. And it's coming from Pierce Cade's house."

"You think he's in cahoots with Brutus and Cassius?" she asked. "You think he might be involved?"

"What? Cade? No chance," The Devil scoffed. "That mindless moron is too... too Human."

"Thanks..."

Laurie trailed off. The Devil sensed a change in her. Even the red from her wounded face turned a little pale.

"Hold on a second," she whispered.

"What is it?" he asked.

"When did I say to Mal that I was a copper?"

The Devil noticed a concerted effort in his own body to be shocked. He was just getting used to the sensation when he was clattered around the back of the head with something heavy.

He fell to the ground. The air was knocked from him but he still tried to get up, arms wobbling. There was a commotion above him and he heard Laurie shout some obscenity. Then there was something else.

An equal mixture of pain and anguish, Mal let out a horrid howl. The Devil didn't need to look at him to know something wasn't right. He rolled over and got back to his feet.

"A little help?" asked Laurie.

She had Mal by the wrists and was holding him at arm's length. The labourer was snapping his teeth at her, trying to get a bite. The Devil, a little bleary from the blow to the back of the head, stumbled forward and tripped. He barged into both of them, breaking the lock.

Mal was first to react. He was on top of both of them in an instant, snarling and frothing at the mouth. The Devil did what he could, flailing his arms madly as he tried to bat off the labourer. He managed one quick, well placed punch to his face but it didn't stop Mal. He twisted his neck with a gruesome crack and sank his teeth into The Devil's shoulder.

"Fuck!" he screamed.

The pain raced through his whole left side, crippling him. Mal hung on, snarling and snorting like a dog.

"Laurie!" he shouted. "Do something!"

Blood was seeping into his sweater now around Mal's mouth. The labourer was livid, eyes bulging as he clung on, teeth sinking deeper and deeper into The Devil's shoulder. He tried to push him off but the grip was too great. And the pain was rendering him almost completely incapacitated.

A big, black box with heavy metal edging flew in out of nowhere. It smashed into Mal's head and ripped him free from The Devil. The equipment box smashed open, spilling camera parts out onto the pavement. The Devil reeled backwards, clattering into the van as he grabbed at his bloody shoulder.

Laurie pounced on Mal. She pinned him down on the ground, knees digging into his arms and stopping him from moving. The labourer's face was smashed up, his nose little more than blood and gore in the centre of it. He snarled and spat at her but she was in total control.

"You alright?" she gasped.

The Devil winced. He looked at the blood on his hand, a thick, dark patch now staining his sweater. He grabbed at the wound again and tried to stem the bleeding.

"I'll live," he said. "Although I wouldn't recommend it."

"What are we dealing with here?" she asked. "Is he one of Brutus and Cassius' lot?"

"Well unless he's developed a sudden taste for cannibalism I think it's safe to assume so."

"Where's Cade?" Laurie asked Mal.

The labourer snapped his head backwards and forward, clunking it off the concrete. Laurie stopped him, pulling at his hair. His wild, feral eyes focussed on her, black froth and blood mixing around his mouth into a wicked grin.

"Where's Cade?"

"You two really don't know when to give up, do you?" said Mal, his voice distorted into a low, agonised growl.

Laurie looked up at The Devil. He hobbled over to her, wincing with every step. He kneeled down beside Mal who stared straight up into the early evening sky.

"Bad pennies," he said. "You can't get rid of us."

"Indeed," Mal giggled. "Quite a knack you both have for surviving. Of course, it's not helped when you have Friends in High Places."

"Friends is a very liberal word," said The Devil. "But at least She doesn't stab me in the back at the first opportunity."

Mal began to laugh. He was animated and pronounced.

"Brutus and Cassius?" Laurie whispered to The Devil.

"So it would seem," he said. "Even when they're crammed into the one body they're still unimaginably irritating."

"That hurts," said Mal. "That hurts a lot."

"Where's Cade?" Laurie asked, flipping back into policewoman mode.

"Cade? We have no idea," said Mal. "We don't have time for such trivialities. Only for making your life a living hell Detective Sergeant Laurie. Or perhaps, maybe it's your husband and that lovely little girl of yours. What's her name now... oh that's right. Matilda."

The Devil swore he could feel the raw heat of rage coming from Laurie. She stiffened on top of Mal who was grinning. Her hands retracted into the tightest fists he had ever seen. She recoiled a little like a prowling tiger and prepared to strike.

"Calm yourself Laurie," said The Devil. "Just take it easy now."

"What have you done with them?" she seethed. "If you lay one finger on them I'll-"

"You'll do what?" Mal's head snapped up towards her. "You can't do anything. You're nothing, an insignificant speck of dust on the surface of this planet. You're Human DS Laurie, a pale, paltry Human that has absolutely no control, no say and no effect on us. We're the masters of the underworld and soon all of reality. You work for us now. All of you do. And there isn't a single thing you or your cantankerous friend there can do about it!"

"What have you done to them!" she screamed.

"Laurie," said The Devil. "Don't do it!"

"What have you done to them!"

Mal started to laugh. He laughed and laughed and laughed until the sound coming from him wasn't Human anymore. He gargled and growled, barked and howled - body convulsing. Blood and dark, black liquid poured from his mouth then his eyes and his ears. Laurie clambered off of him and The Devil moved her back.

Mal's skin began to bubble and hiss. Everything flesh, bone and muscle in him started to dissolve and his clothes caught fire. Soon there was nothing of him left except a burning pile of fabric and ash.

The Devil pinched his nose, the smell insufferable. Laurie turned and started running for the car.

"Laurie! Wait!" he shouted after her. "You can't go! We have to find Medina and Pierce Cade!"

"Matty and Andy, I've got to be with them!" she shouted back. "If they're hurt I'll never forgive myself."

"You don't know anything's happened to them!" The Devil shouted. "It's Brutus and Cassius, this is how they work. Divide and conquer, seeds of doubt, they're trying to distract us from our goal long enough for them to grow in power."

Laurie stopped. She leaned against a tree and started to sob. The Devil joined her. He didn't know what to do. And it wasn't just with Laurie. In all of his time in existence he had never been so pulled apart, so drawn in as many directions as he was now. If this really was the end then he could see why it had been a long time coming. The effort put in by all involved was immense.

"What's happening?" she asked, bent over. "What's happening to us?"

"It's not supposed to be like this Laurie, it never was," he said solemnly. "But we have to keep fighting, have to keep up at least some semblance of... what's it called. Hope. Yes, hope. I mean listen to me, I'm starting to sound like Her."

"I thought it was Him," she said, standing back up.

"Him, Her, it makes little difference anyway," The Devil shrugged. "What can make a difference is me. I can stop all of this and believe me, I wish I was doing it right now. But unfortunately I can't do it on my own and for some unknown reason you have to help me. That's why you're still here and not fish food at the bottom of a river."

"There's a compliment in there somewhere I'm sure," she said, wiping a tear from her burned cheek. "But what about Andy and Matilda?"

"I don't know," said The Devil. "It's as simple as that. No lies, no cheating, just the truth Laurie. I don't know what's happening or happened to them. What I do know is you'd be wasting your time heading back to them. Whatever Brutus and Cassius have planned they'll already be there. So you either go to them and play right into their hands or you stay with me and stand a slim chance of being able to save them. It's your choice of course, I can only advise you, as I've done to so many in the past, present and formerly future."

He shrugged at her.

"But I don't get it," she said. "I mean, you're The Devil, The Devil for god sake. Why can't you just, you know, turn into whatever it is you are and snap your fingers or something. Surely fixing something like this is child's play to you. I thought that's how this all worked?"

The Devil let out a small, sad laugh. He shook his head and looked towards the sky.

"You know something, I've asked myself that question more times than I can ever care to count," he said. "But put simply Laurie, I can't."

"What do you mean you can't? Wouldn't it make it all a lot easier."

"Yes of course it would. But that's not how it works, how existence works. Natural Order is what we call it, fundamental rules by which reality is governed. And barring a few short, sharp exceptions, this is never tampered with, by me or You Know Who."

"This has got to be one of those exceptions though," she said. "I mean, look what's happening here, if not now, when?"

 THE MAN IN THE DARK

"I'm not sure," he said. "It's just the way of it I suppose. Whether it's for some greater purpose She has in mind or She just doesn't fancy bending the rules a bit more, I can't be sure. When She gets something in Her mind, there's no stopping it usually. Either way, the fact remains. I'm in Human form to solve this case. I agreed to it, in a roundabout sort of way. And until it's done, you are stuck with this less than strapping form of Evil incarnate you see before you right now. Like I said before. You're in the driving seat. It's your call as to what we do now. Part of the deal."

Laurie said nothing. She sniffed and wiped her running nose on her sleeve, blood and pus from her wounded face trailing along with it. She took one quick glance at the burning embers of Mal beside the TV van and nodded.

"You better be right," she said.

Then she headed for the front door of the Cade house.

TWENTY-SEVEN

Laurie kicked the front door hard and it fell off its hinges. It landed with a satisfying thump that echoed throughout the house.

"Cade!" she shouted. "Cade, are you in here?"

She stepped into the front hallway, The Devil by her side. The house was silent. Nothing was on. There was a sense of loss about the place, an absence that hadn't been there before. And there was something else.

"Can you smell that?" she said, sniffing the air.

The Devil smelled too. He nodded.

"Barbeque," he said firmly.

"Barbeque?" she asked. "Indoors! Are you sure?"

The Devil stopped in his tracks. He slowly turned to her, his face deadpan.

"Yes Laurie, I'm sure," he said. "If there's one thing I know about, it's roasting things in searing heat. Call it a by-product of my occupation."

"Point taken," she said. "But indoors? That's a bit odd isn't it?"

"I have my suspicions that Pierce Cade is an odd fellow. Odder than we've been giving him credit for."

"Yeah," said Laurie, looking around. "I know what you mean."

"You think he's odd too? Why didn't you say something?"

"I didn't really think it was worth saying," she stepped into the

THE MAN IN THE DARK

living room.

The place was a mess. Glass was scattered across the floor from a broken coffee table. The couches were ripped and torn, stuffing strewn about like entrails. Large scorch marks covered the walls and the television set was smashed to pieces.

"Not the behaviour of a man grieving," she said. "I don't know. I told you before that most kidnap cases know who their kidnapper is. Jilted boyfriends, jealous lovers, angry parents, that sort of thing. Pierce Cade should have been the number one suspect. But we had a ransom note and video that checked out."

"And you never thought to question that?" asked The Devil, glass crunching under his feet.

"It's been a delicate case," she blew out a long breath of air.

Laurie stopped when she spotted something under the debris on the floor. She brushed away some broken glass and picked up a picture frame. She handed it to The Devil. Pierce and Medina Cade were on holiday somewhere. He was bare chested, shoulders and forehead burned red raw with the sun. She wore a skimpy bikini and was pouting for the camera. Posing like a movie-star or a supermodel, she hogged the limelight.

"Delicate?" asked The Devil. "I suspect there was nothing delicate about Medina Cade. She strikes me as a woman who always got what she wanted. And when she didn't she made everybody's life a living hell, pardon the pun."

Laurie smiled then winced, her face sore.

"That's about the gist of it," she said. "Celebrity lifestyle on a modest income. More and more of it these days. At least, that's what the counter-terrorist boffins at MI5 said. When the Whitehall mob start messing around with cases it gets ugly. And, more importantly, it takes much, much longer. Foreign diplomacy, top brass politicians, they're all just hurdles in the way of cracking the case and filing it away. Believe me sunshine, I wish she'd been bumped off by her husband. It's open and shut then."

"I can imagine," he said, handing her back the picture. "Although what she ever saw in him I'll never know."

"I don't know," Laurie shrugged. "He's not bad looking. Nothing special I suppose but he would be on a good wage. Working off-shore has its advantages for her too."

"Ah," The Devil smiled broadly. "When the cat is away the mouse can play. Am I right?"

"As a police officer it's not my place to sit in judgement of people's private lives, least of all victims," she said, dumping the picture. "But as a working mum I'd say you can bet your life she had somebody or *somebodies* out there she could nip round to for a shag. Good looking woman like that, no job to go to, of course she was at it. Problem was we couldn't ever prove it."

"No?" he asked.

"Like I said, delicate. If she'd vanished in Shropshire or Merseyside or anywhere at home it would be no bother. Phone records, e-mails, we'd have the lot. But as soon as anything happens to a Brit abroad then you've got about a hundred Foreign Office departments and sub-departments all nudging in on the action. A nightmare. I'm surprised you don't already know about it."

"I've got people that deal with the details Laurie. I'm too important for details…"

"I bet you are," she laughed.

"Hold on," he said.

"What?"

He stood in the centre of the room, staring blankly into the space between them. He pinched his fingers together, like he was trying to feel the air.

"What did you say?" he asked.

"About what?" she asked back.

"Just then."

"I said lots of things just then," she said. "What are you rabbiting on about now? I thought we were in a hurry, Cassius and Brutus and all that game. They'll know we're here surely."

"Yes, yes, yes, of course," he said. "But just now, what was it you said about Pierce Cade? Something about ordinary."

"Yeah he's just an ordinary guy," said Laurie. "Nothing special."

"Nothing special," said The Devil quietly. "Nothing special at all."

"I don't follow you," she said.

"He's nothing special, nothing out of the ordinary," said The Devil. "He's as clean as a whistle, you checked him out. No outstanding arrest warrants, not so much as an unpaid bill, nothing."

"Absolutely nothing," she confirmed. "What's your point?"

"Pretty awful then that his wife was kidnapped out of the blue, don't you think?" he said. "I mean here's a man, a hard-working, upstanding member of your society who does all he can to please his demanding wife. Day in, day out he goes to work, dutifully bringing home the bread so they can go on holiday, buy expensive clothes, live in a nice neighbourhood. Then suddenly, wham!"

He clapped his hands together. It made Laurie jump.

"She's gone. But not just gone, kidnapped, by an extremist terror cell who are bent on mutilating this westerner with as much brutality and malice as possible. Really very extraordinary, wouldn't you say Detective Sergeant?"

"Just unlucky I guess," she said.

"Luck, hah! Don't make me laugh," he scoffed. "Luck is overrated."

"Do you think Brutus and Cassius are to blame?" asked Laurie. "You think they've been at it behind your back?"

"I *know* they've been doing that Laurie," he said glumly. "But it depends on how long for. It was *their* idea that I come up here to sort this mess out. A good public image exercise they'd said. And I fell for it. None of us are perfect I suppose - except for Her obviously."

"Obviously."

"It still doesn't make a great deal of sense though," said The Devil, puzzled. "I mean, they are proper snakes in the grass. But it's all a little too advanced for them and for what they had at their disposal at the time of the kidnapping. And as for the video, well, that's really not their style. They're still struggling with possession - hence all the rabid police officers and roadies we've been running into."

He rubbed his shoulder. The blood had stopped but he was still in agony. Some things never changed.

"No, I can't fully believe it's been them all along," he said. "It fits together too perfectly and it would be far too easy if that was the case. It's like there's a missing link somewhere, a bit of the puzzle that's nowhere to be found. And it's just outside my grasp."

"Aren't you all about the easy way out though?" she asked. "I thought it was all quick fixes, no hard work, let somebody else do it with you and your kind."

"My kind?" he asked. "Careful now DS Laurie. Otherwise you could be treading into borderline racial territory and I-"

There was a thump from upstairs. The Devil and Laurie exchanged a knowing look before they both bolted out of the living room. They jostled and fought as they leapt up the stairs, taking them three and four at a time. They stopped in the upstairs landing, four doors facing them.

"Where did that come from?" she whispered.

"I'm not sure," he replied. "That one there is the master bedroom."

He pointed at the one he recognised.

"How can you be sure?"

THE MAN IN THE DARK

"Because that's where I broke in the first time. Remember? Just before you and Lister appeared and it all kicked off."

"What about the others?"

"Anyone's guess."

He waited for a moment then stepped towards the main bedroom door. Laurie grabbed him.

"Are you nuts?" she said, straining to keep her voice low. "What if it's another one of Brutus and Cassius' little pet projects?"

"And what if it's Pierce Cade?" asked The Devil.

"And what if Pierce Cade has gone mad like everybody else we've come across? I know you don't believe in luck but believe me, we're lucky we've gotten away from them every time."

"I'd hardly call your face or my shoulder lucky Laurie," he said.

"Thanks mate," she said. "Means a lot."

"You know what I mean."

"I know you're obsessed with trying to get us killed."

"Believe me Laurie, that's the *last* thing I'm obsessed with."

There was another thump. It came from behind the door.

"That's it," he said. "We're going in."

He pushed the door open and froze. The messy bedroom was the same as he'd last seen it - clothes all about the floor, the bed unmade. Across the room something twitched. The Devil missed it at first but he caught it the second time. He held a finger to his mouth and pointed. Laurie crept into the bedroom behind him.

A tall cupboard took up all the back wall. The doors were all closed save for one. A small, pink finger was sticking out of a gap, curled around the edge to keep it closed over enough to conceal whoever was hiding inside. The Devil and Laurie eased their way up to the door and stood on either side of the gap.

He counted down from three silently. Then he shouldered the door as hard as he could. A yelp came from inside and he pulled the cupboard open. A young woman spilled out onto the floor clutching at her hand.

"Don't hurt me!" she shouted. "Don't hurt me please!"

Laurie grabbed her and threw her down on the bed. The young woman recoiled, shielding her face from the others. She started to cry.

"Alright," said Laurie. "Who are you? And I'm warning you now. If those bloody Romans are in your head just tell me now. I'm beginning to get a bit pissed off with this 'are they or aren't they' bollocks."

The Devil looked into the cupboard where the woman had come from. There was a camera. He leaned in and picked it up, a screen coming to life on the back. He mashed buttons with his thumb and saw Pierce Cade.

"Laurie," he said, handing it over.

The policewoman took the camera. She scrolled through the images. They showed Cade and Lister and the rest of the media circus gathered outside the house. The crowd were still, all pointing towards the front door. As Laurie progressed through the pictures, she saw them disperse, leaving Cade alone outside.

"You took these?" she asked the woman.

"Yes," she said. "Yes I took them. My name's Yip, Samantha Yip, I'm a snapper."

"Snapper?" asked The Devil.

"Photographer," Laurie explained, going through the camera. "What were you doing in here? You know that's breaking and entering? I could charge you."

"The window was open and it seemed like the safest place to be," said Sam. "And besides, I've got a mortgage to pay. I need the money."

"I've heard that before," The Devil laughed a little.

"Bloody press," said Laurie, sucking in air through her teeth. "You're just lucky I've had the day I've had and the world is coming to an end."

"The what?"

Sam began to cry again. The Devil rolled his eyes.

"What is it with you Humans and crying?" he snapped. "Honestly it's a wonder you ever learned to walk."

"When did you take these?" Laurie asked.

"I don't know," said the photographer. "It's been such a blur. I've been hiding up here for hours I think, all night anyway. I didn't want to leave, I couldn't. I was too terrified after what… after what happened to them?"

She clapped her hand to her mouth to try and stop herself from blubbing. Laurie's hardness began to crack. She sat down on the bed beside Sam and put an arm around her shoulder. Carefully she pulled her in closer and rubbed her arm.

"Come on love, chin up," she said. "All over now eh?"

The Devil watched the two women on the bed, his mind ticking over. He scrolled through the pictures again, looking for any clue, any little detail that might help them.

"You're feeling okay, aren't you Sam?" Laurie asked.

The photographer nodded, still holding on to her shoulder and chest like a terrified infant.

"You're not going to want to claw my eyes out or spit acid in my face or anything?"

"What?" Sam sniffed.

"It's fine, don't worry about it," she nodded at The Devil. "She seems alright. Any ideas why?"

"Why?" he laughed. "Why anything Laurie. Why does the sun go down and still come back up in the morning. Why do the seasons change and the tides go out, why are there people living, dying and fighting across this city. Why anything anymore?"

"Okay," said the policewoman rolling her eyes. "I wasn't quite expecting that philosophical insight. I was just wondering why Sam here seems to not have had your pals inside her head raising bloody hell."

The Devil groaned loudly. If there was one thing that annoyed him it was having to explain himself.

"I don't know is the short answer Laurie," he said. "Sometimes possession can be a bit off."

"A bit off? We're talking about people here, not eggs."

"It all depends on the person I suppose," he ignored her. "If somebody wants to be possessed then it's going to be easy. If they don't then there's bound to be resistance. Not for me right enough, it's still fairly easy for me. But Cassius and Brutus aren't me of course."

"Not yet anyway," said Laurie.

The Devil puckered his lips. He clicked his fingers at Sam.

"You there," he said pompously. "What's your name again?"

"Sam," she said timidly. "Sam Yip."

"Sam Yip, let me guess," he said. "Strict upbringing, religious, doesn't really matter which one. Church every week, fear of You Know Who put into you. Make donations to charities, try to live a good, clean lifestyle, don't dabble in any hard drugs, alcohol or music that features the word baby? Am I about right?"

Sam's mouth hung open a little. Laurie watched her, silent in anticipation. The Devil loomed over them both, supremely smug.

"No, not really," said Sam.

The Devil's face dropped six inches. Laurie had to stop herself from laughing and gloating. Sam looked confused.

"What?" he said.

"No, I never was very religious," said Sam. "My parents are

doctors, they're strict scientists, top of their fields in Hong Kong. I was brought up on maths and chemistry, physics, biology, all of that. And as for drugs and alcohol, I don't do anything hard, maybe a little smoke of something exotic now and then and a glass of wine with dinner. I give to charity though, when I can. You were right about that part."

"Perfectly normal then," said Laurie.

"Yeah, I suppose so," said the photographer. "I don't understand though. You two, you're talking about possession and what happened outside like it's normal. It's not normal, it's not normal at all. It's really *not* normal!"

She started to cry hysterically again. Laurie pulled her back in close and tried to calm her down. The Devil stood stewing by the door.

"You Humans," he said over and over again. "You just can't wait to pull the rug from under my feet at every opportunity. You're as bad as She is."

"Hey, come on, focus," said Laurie. "Matilda and Andy, remember? We need to stay on track here."

"Yes, yes, yes," he flapped. "You, Sam. Did you see where Pierce Cade went?"

Sam peeled herself from Laurie's shoulder. She shook her head.

"He came back into the house when everybody outside left," she sniffed. "I panicked, didn't know what to do. He looked like he was in charge or knew who was. I didn't want him to find me so I came in here and jumped in the cupboard."

"What did he do when he came back in?" asked Laurie.

"He was downstairs for a long while, I think," said Sam. "There was a lot of noise, a lot of shouting. He sounded angry. There was breaking glass and loads of bumps and loud bangs. I thought he was fighting with somebody or something. But it was just him."

"How can you be sure?" she asked.

"I didn't hear the door open," she said. "Except when he went out the back. He was gone for maybe about twenty minutes then he came back in."

"And he was on his own?" asked The Devil. "The whole time."

"I think so," she said. "If there was anybody else I would have heard them. I didn't want to climb back out the window, he would have seen me from the kitchen."

"How do you know he was in the kitchen?" asked Laurie.

"He had the oven on," said Sam. "It was on for hours, I could hear it humming away. And the smell. It was like he was roasting something.

"Barbeque," said The Devil. "I told you so."

"I fell asleep though," said Sam. "I can't remember when that was. It was dark, the middle of the night. Then I heard a thump from downstairs and it woke me up. So I went to see what was happening."

She took her camera from The Devil. Sliding through the pictures she showed him and Laurie what she had taken.

"He's gone," said Laurie.

"Long gone by now I imagine," said The Devil.

"And you have no idea where he went?"

Sam shook her head. The Devil looked at the pictures on the camera. He narrowed his eyes on Cade leaving his house. The photos showed him heading to his car. The Devil tapped the screen.

"What does that say?" he asked.

Laurie squinted.

"It's nothing, just a logo," she said. "It's a branded bag."

"Yes I know that but is it nothing specific?"

Laurie groaned loudly. She took the camera and tried to fathom it out.

 THE MAN IN THE DARK

"I can't make it out."

"Here," said Sam.

She began tapping buttons on the camera. The picture was enlarged and made brighter. With hardly any effort she'd made the image clearer. They could make out the corporate logo, a globe with a giant shipping container embossed across it.

"Bailor Oil," said Laurie.

"What does that mean?" asked The Devil.

"It rings a bell," she said. "At least, I think…"

She quickly fished her mobile phone from her pocket. She furiously started skimming through the files and her e-mails. When she'd found what she was looking for she snapped her fingers.

"It's his company," she said. "He's a topographic surveyor for Bailor Oil, I knew that name was familiar."

"He's gone back to work?" asked Sam. "After everything that's been going on? With his wife and the riot?"

"It wouldn't be the first odd thing he's done," said The Devil. "And besides, I have a suspicious feeling that he's not going to clock in and do a shift. And do either of you know what happened the last time I had a suspicious feeling?"

The two women didn't answer him.

"That's right, Mars. The planet Mars my good ladies. Mars."

"Wow, wow, hold on here," said Laurie, getting up. "These pictures don't prove anything. He could be going anywhere, quite literally anywhere. How can you be so sure he's gone back to his job?"

The Devil sucked in air through his brittle Human teeth. It made them hurt and he vowed never to be so stupid again.

"You're a policewoman Laurie, you live on evidence and proof, yes?" he said.

"Of course I do," said Laurie. "That and copious amounts of tea, coffee and any other stimulants I can lay my hands on. Legal ones."

She nodded at Sam who smiled.

"What's your point?"

"Evidence and proof is all well and good. But I know Humanity. And I know that you lot love to rely on this so called gut instinct thing you've attuned yourselves to. So why don't you trust my gut feeling and go with me on this one."

"So what, you think he's just gone back to work like nothing's happened? Need I remind you that the city is tearing itself limb from limb out there. Nobody is going to work, it's mob rule."

"You needn't remind me," he said. "But I don't think Pierce Cade is going back into employment simply to collect a pay cheque. Nor do I think he's of high moral fibre that he would be diligent enough to go back for the good of his health. No, far from it."

Laurie ran a hand through her greasy hair. She paced around the bedroom, wrestling with her own thoughts.

"We're wasting time," she said. "Every second I spend arguing with you is another second closer to god knows what."

"I completely agree with you," he said calmly. "So why don't we plough right ahead with the only lead we have."

"Pierce Cade going to his car with a company branded bag isn't a lead. It's not even half a lead."

"True," said The Devil. "But it's the closest thing we've got to anything even remotely productive."

Laurie gritted her teeth. The tendons flexed in her damaged cheek, forcing a little fresh blood to the surface. She dabbed her face on her sleeve and grimaced.

"Has anybody ever told you that being on a case with you is a real nightmare," she said, heading for the door.

"Yes, actually," he laughed. "Frequently."

THE MAN IN THE DARK

"What… what about me?" asked Sam, still holding her camera.

"You're a fully grown woman," said The Devil. "We're not your nursemaids. Get on with it like everybody else."

"Hey, shut up," said Laurie angrily.

She took Sam by the shoulders and looked into her glassy eyes.

"I need you to keep your head down Sam, do you understand me?" she said. "You need to find a place where you can ride all of this out. You've been given a lucky escape love, a really lucky escape. Stay off the main roads and try and avoid the police as much as you can."

"Avoid the police?" she asked. "But… I thought you said you were police."

"I am," said Laurie. "But they're not all like me. Not at the moment anyway, they don't know themselves. Just find somewhere, a little dark hole in the back end of nowhere and stay put. You'll be fine. You've done a good job here. But now it's time you looked after yourself."

Sam nodded. The young girl held back more tears as they hurried out of the house and down the street. Laurie saw her off and got into the car, watching in the rear-view mirror as they pulled away.

"She'll be fine won't she?" she asked The Devil.

"What? Oh her, well, that depends," he said.

"Depends on what?"

"Depends on whether you want me to tell you the truth or not."

Laurie was about to chastise him but then thought better of it. She stared out the window as they raced through the city, heading for the docks.

TWENTY-EIGHT

"I really don't think we have time to get this wrong Laurie," said The Devil. "We have one shot at this and then that worm Cade is gone."

"We don't even know he's done anything wrong," said Laurie, fiddling with her phone. "You're putting all our eggs in the one basket."

"I'm going with all we've got. Everybody else might have given up, which on an ordinary day is usually very good for me. But as it stands I'm the sole champion of determination. Now what does that say about everything."

"I don't want to think about it," she said. "Left here."

The Devil wrestled the car around the corner. They chewed up ground with ease, the traffic laws now non-existent. Night was falling quickly and the burning embers of the burning city were once again taking charge. Following the course of the Thames they headed for what they hoped was Cade's dock.

"Says here that Bailor Oil operate out of Dagenham," she said.

"Dagenham? How do I know that name?" he asked.

"I have absolutely no idea," said Laurie. "Dagenham is about as famous as the arse hole of the moon."

"I know it somehow."

"It's a dump, believe me. It's where Romford Chavs go for a holiday.

You can get any street drug you want as long as your preference is to have it over eighty percent cut with washing up powder."

"Sounds like my kind of shit hole," he said. "High death rate? Crime through the roof?"

"Oh yeah, you can bet your last fiver on that sunshine."

"Good. About time I was treated to some of the finer parts of London. My visit here this time has been distinctly bland, boring and altogether bloody."

"Hey, I let you sleep on my couch you ingrate."

"Sleep is hardly what I'd call that Laurie," he yawned and cracked his neck. "More like just not being awake."

"You just can't please everybody," she said. "Take the next right."

She was following an interactive map on her phone. The Devil tapped his hands against the steering wheel. He was starting to get anxious.

"How long?" he asked.

"Says seven minutes."

"That's too long," he pressed the accelerator. "If that odd little crying woman..."

"Sam," said Laurie sharply. "Her name was Sam."

"Yes, whatever. If she was right about Cade leaving he has a good hour on us. Maybe more. It's going to be a tight push."

"We shouldn't have left her like that," said Laurie. "We should have brought her with us."

"I don't think where we're going is the best place for a Human who's had a lucky escape," said The Devil. "In fact I'm pretty much expecting there to be one giant road block in the shape of Brutus and Cassius' burgeoning army standing in our way. In fact, those two snakes have probably been building two huge statues to literally stand in our way - just because they're so arrogant and smug. I tell you something Laurie, I simply cannot wait to get out of this flesh and flabby prison you call a body and to kick their proverbial arses all across eternity."

"You sound so sure that you can do it," she said.

"And why wouldn't I be sure?" he asked.

"No reason I suppose," she said. "Except, for all the times I've seen you with them you've hardly left your mark. I mean look about the place sunshine. They're running the show, the whole show, this is all their doing. Have you ever known London to lock down like this. Look at the streets. This is the docklands, eight o'clock at night. It should be mobbed, people on the streets, cars, traffic, haulers, you name it. And we haven't passed one soul on our way here."

The Devil watched the empty streets rolling by as he drove them on towards the port. He hadn't really noticed how quiet it was. Perhaps he didn't want to. By doing that it was like a secret admission of defeat. He suspected Cassius and Brutus were up to something big, something grand. A huge, cataclysmic gesture that they'd use to herald their arrival and ascent to the master of Downstairs role. And with every passing second that didn't happen The Devil grew more and more fraught with worry.

"Pierce Cade better be here," he said quietly. "For all of our sakes."

"And what if he's no help? Have you thought about that?"

"I try not to think of my own fallacies Laurie," he said. "Haven't you heard of positive mental attitude?"

"PMA? From you? Are you kidding me? You're kidding me right?"

"Don't look at me like that," he said. "You've got to believe in something. So why don't you do something useful with that fangled contraption of yours and check to see if we're even on the right track."

"I'm trying," said Laurie. "But there must be something wrong with the network - it's as slow as a week in the jail."

"Time is relative," said The Devil. "Never has a truer word been spoken by your kind Laurie. Which reminds me actually. I don't think I ever caught your first name."

Laurie didn't answer him. Her eyes were locked on her phone. The bright blue glow highlighted the puckered and burned skin of her cheek. The Devil looked away.

"You know, as much as I hate to admit it," she said. "I think you might be onto something."

"You sound surprised."

"Not surprised, more angry that you're not wrong."

"I'm not?" he asked smugly.

"I've got the port schedule here. Says there are a dozen ships booked in for today. Top of the list, departing ten minutes ago, the Valiant."

"Valiant," The Devil laughed. "How totally ironic."

"Any guesses who owns the Valiant?" she asked.

"Hmm, let me see here," he pretended to think really hard. "It's a difficult one. Do you know, it's times like these I really wish I'd gone to police training college and learned how to be a detective. Because quite simply put I don't know how anybody would be able to work out that the Valiant was owned by Bailor Oil."

"Dickhead," she said. "Left here."

A bleep chirped from Laurie's phone. The Devil peered through the dusk and saw a set of gates up ahead. The port was ringed by a chain link fence, ten feet high. And beyond it, standing dark against the burnt orange of the sky, was a huge container ship.

"It's here!" Laurie shouted. "The ship, it's here."

No sooner had she clapped her hands together in joy when a large, loud horn sounded out. The whole road seemed to quiver under the vibrations of the boom. The buildings around them shook too, glass rattling in frames of the stubby little buildings and apartment blocks. Another loud honk and the dark shape very slowly began to move.

"Oh come on!" The Devil screamed. "Couldn't we catch just one break? Would that be too much bloody trouble to ask?"

He sped the car up as fast as it would go. They smashed through the barrier of the port authority gate and skidded on the tarmac that led to the river. The stern of the ship loomed large above them, fifteen stories high with the Bailor Oil logo painted across the back.

"Shit," said Laurie. "Now what do we do?"

The Devil was certain he couldn't think this fast before. Something about the quick pep talk with Her Upstairs had cleared away all the cobwebs from his sluggish Human mind.

As a result he could see his surroundings in a totally different light. The port was broken down into tiny parts, highlighted every time he looked at them. Like a puzzle that was solving itself in front of him, he slammed on the brakes and the car stopped.

"What are you doing?" asked Laurie.

"Get out, quickly," he said, throwing off his seatbelt.

"What are you doing? We've missed the boat, literally."

The Devil rounded the car. He checked again what he had seen, mind clicking everything into place. The Valiant was pulling away, over half the ship now clear of the port as it headed down the river. Laurie clambered out of the car and shuffled up beside him.

"How are your feet Laurie?" he asked.

"My feet? What about my feet?"

"As in are they capable of running?"

"They're as capable as yours are mate. In fact I'd say I'm probably in better shape to run than you - judging by the size of your belly."

The Devil nodded towards the ship.

 THE MAN IN THE DARK

"You think you're up for catching this boat?" he asked.

"Didn't you hear me? And can't you see? The boat's gone sunshine, we've lost him."

"If you ever learn anything from your time with me Laurie," he said, starting to run. "It's that I'm never, ever counted out."

Laurie bolted after him. They hurried along the dockside, the Valiant picking up speed. Its huge metal hull towered high above them, lights glowing from inside. The Devil ignored the boat, that wasn't the problem, not yet. First they had to get some height.

A stack of brightly coloured containers took up the far end of the dockside. Piled on top of each other, the heavy metal boxes looked like huge steps. The Devil, through his newfound clarity, was going to use them exactly like that.

"Where are we going?" Laurie shouted behind him.

"We're getting on that ship," he called over his shoulder. "Just follow me. And get ready."

"Ready for what?"

The Devil picked up speed. He ran as fast as he could directly at the nearest container. When he was a foot away he jumped as high as he could. He vaulted through the air, his hands catching on the lip of the box's roof. He kicked, trainers skidding off the corrugated side. Then he was up.

"You've got to be shitting me!" Laurie shouted, sliding to a halt. "I'm not getting up there."

"Come on!" he reached down for her. "Time is pressing, we've got a boat to catch!"

Laurie hesitated. He clapped his hands at her. She took a step back and then jumped. He caught her and felt the muscles in his arms burn.

"Bloody hell Laurie!" he shouted. "You're heavier than I thought."

"Cheeky bastard!" she shouted back.

He pulled hard and she rolled onto the roof of the container. The Devil was up instantly, his policewoman companion a little slower.

"That was the easy one," he smiled.

"There's more?" she gasped.

"Just a few," he pointed towards the ship rolling past them. "And then there's that thing there."

She followed his finger towards the skeletal frame of a crane. The shock was enough to get her on her feet instantly.

"Absolutely not," she said, looking upwards. "You're expecting me to... us to get up...there? Have you gone completely mental? Is that it?"

"Don't ask questions you don't want to know the answers to."

He grabbed her by the wrist and made off across the roofs of the containers. They leapt the small gaps between the huge metal boxes and scrambled their way upwards towards the crane. Laurie gasped for breath and was beginning to tire when they reached the crane.

She leaned against the hard metal beams that made up the central shaft, looked down and saw they were already halfway up its height. The dockyard stretched out below them, the car still sitting with its lights on.

"You ready?" asked The Devil, getting a foothold.

"You're not serious are you?" she asked. "You want me to climb this thing?"

"All the way to the top," he said. "Then it's a short walk along the gangway and down onto the boat. A piece of cake."

"I'd murder you right now for a big bit of cake," she said, climbing through a gap in the lattice and mounting the ladder. "Or gateau, a great big wedge of Black Forest Gateau, with gallons

THE MAN IN THE DARK

of fresh cream and maybe a cherry on top. And I'd eat it in one bite and…"

She trailed off. The Devil, sensing she had stopped talking, paused his ascent. He looked down at her.

"What's wrong? Keep moving Laurie, chop, chop."

"What's that?" she asked.

"What's what?"

"That, down there, at the gates?"

The Devil wiped sweat from his eyes. The sun had faded and darkness lay across the city like a cloak. The burning glow of the riot was behind them and out along the port the streetlights created a gridded lattice map of roads. Only the grids were getting fewer and fewer.

First one block went out and then another. Another followed it, then another and another. On and on it went until the last block by the gates of the port was extinguished. The Devil could feel his teeth beginning to itch as he stared at the encroaching darkness.

"The lights," said Laurie below. "They're going out."

"No they're not," said The Devil. "They're just disappearing."

"Disappearing from where? The street?"

"Disappearing beneath the mob."

He started to climb faster. Laurie strained her eyes as the shadow reached the docklands. The closer it got the more she realised it was moving. This wasn't simply a shadow. It was a throng of people - hundreds wide and thousands deep.

A distant din of growling and shouting hung over them. The outriders dictated the building speed of the throng, barking and galloping on all fours.

"Laurie!" The Devil shouted from high above. "You better get your arse into gear. Otherwise that baying mob of your colleagues, friends, family and total strangers down there is going to swallow you whole!"

Laurie didn't need any more motivation. She began to climb the ladder as quickly as her tired arms and legs would take her. Up and up she scrambled, all the while watching as the mob flooded the docklands like a rabid, black tide.

Their car was gulped down, the headlights flashing long shadows of the shambling mob - every one of them possessed and willed forward by perverted motivations. Laurie climbed and climbed, catching up with The Devil's feet. He pushed onwards, up and up as fast as he could, trying to put as much distance between him and Brutus and Cassius as possible.

At last they reached the top. A cold wind whistled in his ears as he helped Laurie out onto the gangway. He glanced back down to the docklands a hundred feet below them. The mob swarmed like ants ejected from their nest. They had reached the containers and were climbing over them, bent on catching them up.

"A small piece of advice Laurie," he said, his greasy blonde hair blowing in his eyes. "Don't look down."

"Why not?" she said.

"Because I think it would be the end of you," he said. "Just know that you're in a precarious position here my dear. There's no way back and the path forward has a pretty high chance of killing you."

She grabbed his shoulder. He yelped. They made their way slowly out onto the gangway that ran the length of the crane arm. The wind picked up the further they went as they rounded each section of the metal lattice. Below them the Valiant was passing beneath the end of the arm. There wasn't much of the ship left and The Devil knew they were running out of time.

"This is going to be down to the wire!" he shouted back at Laurie. "Come on. Death or glory."

                    THE MAN IN THE DARK

"I don't like the sound of either of those!" Laurie cried over the wind.

They reached the end, a big beacon flashing red every two seconds. The Devil eased himself around so they were standing on either side of it. Below them they could see the deck of the Valiant passing underneath.

"Shit!" she shouted. "It's too far down! That's a forty foot drop! We'll break our necks!"

"Hold on, hold on!" The Devil shouted back. "We just need to wait until the bridge gets closer."

He pointed back towards the stern. The command tower that housed the bridge was coming up fast. Radar dishes and aerials were dotted about its roof. More importantly it was only fifteen feet of a drop.

The Devil smiled and laughed a little. He gave her the thumbs up.

"See!" he shouted over the billowing gale. "I told you I always w-"

The crane lurched violently beneath them. The sole of his trainer squeaked as it slipped off the gangway. Everything pulled him downwards and he realised he'd let go of the hard, comforting metal of the crane. He was about to scream when Laurie caught him.

But he was too heavy for her. She slipped too. As she fell she had the foresight to try and grab something. By sheer luck she caught hold of the lip of the gangway. They swung for a moment before settling.

"Oh my," he said.

"Oh my?" said Laurie through gritted teeth. "Did you say oh my?"

"Yes, I think so."

"That's the best you can come up with? Dangling in mid-air while my arms are wrenched out of their sockets hundreds of feet above the Thames? Oh my?"

"I suppose it's just whatever comes natural in these sorts of situations."

He dangled there, lost between safety and danger. Laurie was struggling to hold him, the sweat on her hand making everything slippery. Then the crane began to move.

Through the darkness The Devil could see the mob. They'd reached the control cabin, some fiddling with the levers, while others made their way along the gangway towards them. The whole arm jerked every time they did something wrong and a few fell off the edge, splashing down into the water or splattering with a clang on the containers.

The arm groaned as metal gears whirred into action somewhere out of sight. The crane began to very slowly swoop away from the passing Valiant, edging further and further in land.

The Devil looked through his stretched out arms. The ship's bridge was still ten feet away. But at this rate they were never going to meet. He looked up at Laurie who was crying with the pain.

"What's your faith like Detective Sergeant?" he asked.

"My faith?" she blurted. "Don't you think this isn't the right time for that sort of question?"

The growling and snarling of the mob was now within earshot. More were venturing out along the arm. Slowly, menacingly, they were creeping closer.

"I never thought I'd say this but I think I'm being tested," he said. "I don't know how much influence She has anymore. But I suspect that if She has any then She's asking us to put some faith in Her. And by faith I mean our lives. And by our lives I mean my life. And by my life I mean all of existence."

THE MAN IN THE DARK

"That's a lot," she grimaced, spit flying from her mouth, blood and pus dripping from her damaged cheek.

"Yeah," he said. "It is, isn't it? It's really not on."

The crane arm kept moving, the ship kept getting further and further away. If he was going to go, it had to be now.

"Shit, cock and bollocks," he said. "I'm too old, too wealthy and too fed up for all of this. Are you ready?"

Laurie hesitated. She gave one last glance above at the approaching mob and then down to the boat.

"What do you think is going to happen?"

"I have no idea," he said. "But I think that's the whole point, knowing Her as I do. Maybe we just wait and see."

"Yeah," said Laurie. "That sounds like a good plan. Let's just wait and see."

With that she released her grip on the lip of the crane. The weightless elegance of flight took hold. For the faintest of moments, the most fleeting of split seconds, The Devil knew what it was like to feel sheer and total Human tranquillity. He'd only ever known a feeling like this once before. And he doubted he ever would again. Especially when gravity took hold.

His whole body slumped downwards at an alarming speed, Laurie somewhere beside him. He closed his eyes and thought that he'd better scream or something. If this was the end he wasn't going to be silent. He'd never been silent before. And this was no time for turning over a new leaf.

TWENTY-NINE

The Devil thought he knew pain. Clearly he didn't. The agony in which his body was now flooded was something totally new and harrowing to him. The dramatic irony wasn't lost either. Eons of inflicting suffering on an endless amount of souls was now clearly catching up with him.

He somehow managed to roll over onto his side. His lungs were working, barely. Every morsel of his Human body seemed to be on fire. Or at the very least thinking about catching fire.

"Even the tips of my fingers are sore," he said to himself. "How is that even possible?"

In all the pain and suffering he forgot to realise that he was still very much alive. A groan from behind him signalled that somehow Laurie had survived too.

"Brilliant," he coughed. "And there was me thinking I was finally going to get that holiday I've been desperate for."

He forced himself onto his hands and knees. Something wasn't right, he could feel it inside of him. Like a bridge with a screw loose or a car with a flat tyre, he might have survived the fall but his Human body wasn't indestructible.

He coughed loudly. A load of pink phlegm dropped from his mouth. Blood, he was certain of it. As if time wasn't already at a premium he began to fret that the inner workings of this Human body might be shot.

Laurie groaned again, distracting him. She slowly got up, rubbing her head.

"You made it then," he said sarcastically.

"What happened?"

The Devil looked about them. The radar dishes and aerial arrays of the command tower were all around.

"I think we might have lucked out," he said, getting to his feet. "Although just how much She had to do with it I'm not so sure."

"Friends in high places?" she asked.

"Hardly," said The Devil.

A sharp, stabbing pain streaked through his sternum and into his chest. He doubled over, unable to breathe.

"What's wrong with you?" asked Laurie in a panic.

"Nothing," he said, teeth bloodied. "I'm alright."

"You're bleeding."

"I'm always bleeding," said The Devil. "That's just what I do. I bleed."

She got up and tried to help him. He pushed her away, hobbling over towards an antenna.

"We need to find Cade," he said. "We're running out of time."

Laurie didn't seem convinced. She knew by now that it was useless arguing with him. Instead she clapped her hands against her thighs, clouds of dust erupting about her.

"I supposed we need to get into the boat for that," she said.

"That might help," said The Devil, the pain easing. "Don't go down through the bridge though. We don't know how far the mob has spread."

Laurie looked about the roof of the command tower. She spotted a small ladder disappearing over the edge. They started to climb down and headed for the main deck.

The Valiant was a huge, sprawling ship designed for the harsh weather of the North Sea and English Channel. Even in his brief time onboard The Devil could sense its hard working, salty roots. He was still gripped with pain but his augmented senses were picking up life from the rusted metal hull.

He could feel something else too. A strange, tingling sensation that wasn't going away. Like an ice cube being dragged slowly down his spine, everything was acutely sharp and aware.

"There are thirty people on board this ship," he said to Laurie as they dashed between the huge stacks of containers piled high on the deck. "And one of them is Pierce Cade."

"How can you be sure?" she asked.

"I'm not quite sure I can answer that," he said, rubbing his head. "It's like I'm caught between two worlds. This one and Downstairs. Some of my residual powers are eking through in dribs and drabs. But I can't focus on them and make them work like I normally can."

"You think it's Brutus and Cassius?" she asked. "You think they're trying to get in your head?"

"No," he said. "They're nowhere near that powerful. Even now. That mob back at the port, they're amassing Humanity in huge numbers. But it would take a power greater than all of imagination to crack this nut."

He tapped the side of his head. Laurie gazed out at the water. They were in the middle of the wide river, the shore a distant dark line. The lights of the streets and houses were little more than pricks in the darkness. And slowly they were going out.

"Looks like we didn't shake them," she said, nodding towards the distance.

"We won't, not now," said The Devil. "This is do or die, death or glory, remember."

 THE MAN IN THE DARK

"Yeah, I remember. Only I don't really fancy dying if you don't mind."

"I'll try to remember that."

They pressed on, hurrying down the length of the Valiant until they reached the other end. They slipped inside the ship and descended down the stairs into the bowels of the floating hulk. The place was deserted, no sign of any of the crew. It made The Devil wary. He preferred to see his enemy up front. Cloak and dagger tactics were his forte, nobody else's. But he was too tired to get enthused.

On and on they went, weaving through the narrow corridors and further into the bowels of the ship. A pulse kept pressing against the inside of The Devil's skull. Like an inbuilt compass he followed it, always keeping it in the centre of his forehead. The deeper they penetrated the ship the stronger it got. Until finally it settled across his whole forehead.

"We're here," he said.

A long corridor with doors on either side stretched out ahead of them. It was narrow, barely wide enough for two people to walk down side by side. Laurie looked about for a sign as to where they were.

"You sure?" she asked. "Why here?"

"I'm sure," he said.

They started down the corridor. The Devil stretched his hands out so he could touch both walls at once. They passed the doors on each side, one after the other, until finally he stopped.

"He's here," he whispered, pointing at the door on his left. "This is the one."

Laurie took a deep breath. She cracked her knuckles and rolled her neck, preparing for the worst.

"Okay," she said. "How are we doing this? Good cop, bad cop?"

The Devil gave her a dry look.

"Alright, bad cop, bad cop. Suits me just fine."

Laurie booted the door of the cabin hard. The wood buckled but didn't budge. She gave it another good, hard kick and this time it gave way. The second of hesitation, however, gave Pierce Cade a chance to prepare. He was up on his feet when The Devil and Laurie came barging in.

"Cade!" The Devil shouted.

Cade grabbed what came to hand first. He launched a lamp at Laurie who barely got her hands up in time. He used the confusion to make a bolt for the door but The Devil was ready for him.

He fired a hard shot into Cade's stomach. The force was enough to buckle him over with a loud, painful wheeze. His legs gave way from underneath him and he slumped down onto the floor beside his bunk.

Laurie regrouped. She grabbed Cade by the scruff of his shirt and pulled him to his feet. She shoved him hard against the wall and patted him down for weapons. When she was finished she forced him onto a seat and caught her breath.

"Alright sunshine," she said. "Time to start talking."

Cade started coughing. He held his stomach with both arms, his face pale beneath his grotty stubble. He rocked back and forth.

"I don't feel well," he said. "I need a doctor."

"Don't give us that crap Cade," said Laurie. "There's nobody else here. Just me, you and him over there."

She thumbed at The Devil. Cade looked at him and sneered.

"What's *he* doing here? I thought he'd kidnapped my wife," he spat.

"Kidnap is such a strong word Cade," said The Devil. "It's also one that's banded about far too easily by liars like you."

"I'm not a liar!" Cade shouted. "I'm a victim. My wife's been kidnapped by terrorists! They've mutilated her, probably killed her by now. And it's all your fault!"

"Let's cut out the grieving husband act, shall we Pierce?" said Laurie. "It's growing stale."

"I *am* grieving!"

"Then what are you doing here, on this ship?" asked The Devil. "Getting away from it all? Taking a little pleasure cruise down the Thames?"

"I'm at work," he said. "I came back to work to get my mind off of everything. I'm allowed to do that, aren't I? A man is allowed to earn a living."

"Yeah, sure," said Laurie. "But it's all a bit too early, don't you think? I mean, we don't even know for sure Medina is dead do we? What if the terrorists get in touch with you, say, in the next five minutes? Are you going to tell them you can't come to the phone because you're in the middle of a shift? Doesn't really add up Pierce. Does it?"

Cade said nothing. He didn't look at either of them. He bit his fingernails, thinking. The Devil leaned in closer to him.

"You want to know what I think?" he said, his voice steady and brooding.

"No, not really," said Cade. "Why would I want to know what you think? You're a nobody. A nobody who probably knows where my wife is."

"I don't know where your wife is Pierce," he said. "But I think *you* do."

"Bollocks!" Cade screamed. "I don't need this. I don't need to be accused of this. You're both in trouble, big fucking trouble. This is harassment. My lawyer is going to have you both for every penny you've got!"

"Money," said The Devil. "Is the root of all evil. Do you know who said that? Anyone?"

Nobody answered him.

"Paul, Saint Paul if you want to use his Sunday name. Although he had a good few. A dreadfully dull man, couldn't ever figure out if what he was thinking was actually what he was thinking or just going along with the crowd. Anyway, not that it matters. He was spot on with the whole cash obsession you lot have. Sweat, toil, hard work or a semester at HellCorp, it all boils down to cash. And you, Mr Cade, didn't have enough of it."

"Piss off," said Cade. "What do you know about my money? You know nothing."

"I know that you were constantly being badgered by your wife for more and more and more," The Devil pointed at him.

"How could you possibly know that? You don't know me and you don't know Medina."

"He doesn't have to," said Laurie. "I don't have to either. It's all over your house, your social media, everything. You and Medina, married couple, living a normal little life, getting by as best you can. Only she didn't want to be normal. She wanted to be special. She wanted, wanted and wanted. That's why you were in Dubai. Home of footballers on holiday, celebrities cashing in. She wanted everything and you couldn't afford it."

Cade was starting to get anxious. He was moving more and more, hands flexing, his face reddening. The Devil was a master tactician and he knew when a Human was on the ropes.

"I'll be honest with you Cade, I don't blame you for feeling the pressure," The Devil sounded philosophical. "Do you know how many people have begged for my help over the centuries just to keep their yapping partners at bay? Too many to count. It's a nice and easy bit of business for us Downstairs. And if you'd just asked I'm sure we could have come to some sort of arrangement."

THE MAN IN THE DARK

Cade looked across at Laurie. He cocked his eyebrow at the policewoman.

"Is this guy for real?" he asked.

"You're asking the wrong person there mate," she said. "But I'm not going to ask you again. I'm too sore and tired to keep this up all night. Where's Medina?"

Cade sneered and scowled at both of them. He paused for a moment. The Devil watched him carefully. There it was, he thought, that hesitation. It's a split second, a fragment of time, but it feels like an eternity for all Humans. Fight or flight, keep lying or confess, battling away constantly, two opposing sides vying for supremacy.

"Medina is a bitch," said Cade at last.

The Devil wanted to jump for joy. But he stopped himself. There was more at stake than just his ego.

"She's always been a bitch, even when we were at school. Queen bitch, if you were being kind. Everybody knew it. That's why she doesn't have any friends. Never has done."

"She had you though," said Laurie. "That's something."

"I love her, that's why," said Cade bitterly. "I'm the only one who's loved her. Her mum and dad never wanted anything to do with her. She was a mistake, when they were sixteen. Her brothers and sisters were all planned. And they went on to do things. Nurses, engineers, everything. Medina does nothing, never wanted to do anything. She knew early that if she looked the right way, acted the right way, she could get whatever she wanted. And she does. Up to a point."

"And you still love her?" asked Laurie.

"I loved her from the moment I set eyes on her," he said. "That doesn't make life with her any easier. Harder in fact. Do you have any idea what it's like to pour all of your love, all of your life into somebody you know doesn't love you back? Somebody who only keeps you around because you're paying for her clothes, her car, her holidays in the sun? Do you know how that makes somebody feel? Do you?"

Laurie didn't answer him. She couldn't. The Devil leaned against the wall.

"Do you?" Cade screamed.

He was crying now, his eyes bright red. Snot and spit flew from him as he slammed his fists into the arms of his chair.

"Cut to the chase Cade," said The Devil. "You're not the first man in history to be taken for a ride by a beautiful woman. It's a very large and not very exclusive club. You're a sap, we get it. Where is she?"

Cade's mouth was curled into a frown. He wiped his eyes and swallowed his snot.

"I thought the holiday might do us some good," he said. "Don't ask me why. It wasn't like it was our first holiday this year. She constantly wants to go away, always wants to be on a beach somewhere so she can take a picture and put it online. I swear to god she spends every waking moment with that phone of hers in her hand. I used to tell her she'd hurt her neck the amount she looked at it."

"Used to tell her?" Laurie asked. "What do you mean *used* to tell her?"

Cade shook his head.

"Can't say she was hugely surprised. Can't say I was either to be honest," he said.

"Surprised with what?" asked Laurie. "What are you trying to say Pierce?"

He looked down at his hands. They were shaking and pale. He was silent, his knees hopping up and down. Then he looked at

Laurie and then to The Devil. He smiled a sad smile and shrugged his shoulders.

"I killed her," he said flatly, nodding. "It was me. I killed her. Dead. She's dead. I killed her."

The small, confined cabin was silent. It was only broken when The Devil clapped his hands together loudly.

"I knew it!" he shouted. "It's *always* the husband!"

THIRTY

The cabin felt like it was getting smaller. The bland walls, the bunk, the cupboard and the desk weren't moving. The Devil could feel them though, all pressing down on him and Laurie as Cade sat weeping in his chair.

The Devil ignored his growing paranoia. The pain making its way across his chest and back again should have been enough to distract him. He kept his trembling hands hidden beneath his folded arms, leaning against the wall for support. He had to hold on.

Laurie was in charge now. He could see her relishing the chance to twist the knife into Cade. And he sensed this was more than just a victory over the man who'd murdered his wife. This was something more for her, a vindication perhaps, over a bigger, greater foe. Even her bleeding face couldn't dampen her spirits. She marched around the room, looming over Cade with all the grace and glory of a gladiator and his opponent.

"Why the ruse?" she asked.

"What do you mean ruse?" asked Cade, rubbing his forehead.

"A kidnapping? I mean, that's a bit much isn't it? You could have just bumped her off and come up with any old story."

He slammed his fist into the desk beside him. Laurie backed away.

"Hey, just calm it, okay," she said. "Don't make this any more difficult."

"You think I would have just been able to stroll back here, go back to work, if I'd just said she'd died? You're meant to be a copper, you know how these things work. It's always the husband."

"Always," said The Devil.

"I needed time to think. And believe me I had plenty of it. Kidnapping, it happens all the time, you read about it in the papers, online, documentaries on TV. People are taken every day while they're on holiday. I figured it was just as easy to come up with something to buy me some time."

"Time for what?" asked Laurie.

The anger left Cade for a moment. His shoulders sloped forward and he laughed a little.

"Cade?" she asked. "Time for what?"

He rolled around some spit in his mouth. Then he spat it at her feet.

"Have you ever seen fear in somebody's eyes before?" he asked. "I mean really seen fear. It's a look, it's a real, actual look that they give you. It's terrifying actually, really not a nice thing to have to see. I saw it. In her eyes, those eyes that I loved for so long, decades, a good portion of my adult life. I saw that fear when I cut her nose off. I saw it when I sliced her throat. And I saw it vanish when she died in my arms. There's nothing else like that. Not anywhere in life. It's a rush. I know that sounds sick and it is, believe me, I know it is. But it's true. That power, that sense of actual power, that you control how somebody feels, how they react, how they prepare for what it is you're about to do to them. It's strange man, it's like nothing else."

"Jesus Christ, listen to yourself Cade. Are you high?" asked Laurie. "Are you a junkie, is that it? Out of your face on something all the time? Did you down a load of pills and booze before it?"

"He wasn't high then, and he isn't now," said The Devil, stepping forward. "And he was perfectly sober when he murdered his wife."

"How do you know that?" asked the policewoman.

"Because I know exactly what he's talking about. And I've seen that look of his a million times before. Emotionally detached faces telling stories that you wouldn't want to even read about, let alone experience. It's got many names Laurie, a hundred of them you Humans can't even pronounce. But it's commonly know as evil."

"Evil," said Laurie.

She shivered. She stared at Cade who still had his head bowed. He rolled his thumbs over themselves, his knees bobbing up and down.

"That's why you weren't affected by Lister and his cronies," said The Devil. "Isn't it Pierce?"

Cade looked up at him. He wore a smirk on his face like it was a badge of honour. He snorted at The Devil.

"Don't know what you're talking about mate," he said.

"Oh I think you do," The Devil smiled back. "I think you know *exactly* what I'm talking about. See, it's been niggling away in the back of my mind. You didn't seem phased at all by what was going on. Lister and the other police officers, all walking in unison, laughing when he told them to laugh, totally mechanical. DS Laurie here was thrown across the room, smashing up your kitchen. It all happened right in front of you and you didn't even flinch. You feel nothing for anyone except yourself. Now ordinarily I'd say that level of coldness and unwillingness to give a toss comes from making a deal with yours truly. But I'm quite certain we've never met before."

"He's working for Brutus and Cassius?" Laurie yelped.

"No, I don't think he is," said The Devil. "I don't think he has anything to do with them - not directly at least. But *they* certainly know all about *him*."

Cade kept smirking.

"You've always known it. Deep down inside of you there's been that little burning flame of something. It's not hatred, it's not anger, it's something that combines the two. You've always had it, always been aware of it, that's why you've been able to keep it under wraps for so long. And it's what you put to good use when you mutilated your wife. Where did you do that by the way, warehouse? Garage somewhere?"

"Apartment bathroom," said Cade.

"Of course," The Devil snapped his fingers. "I thought the whole room looked too white and clean. Easily cleaned up too I imagine. What's a bit of blood on the floor of a hotel bathroom. Could be anything. Only it was your wife's nose and then, presumably, her life. Am I painting the right picture here?"

Cade sat back in the chair, a smug grin spread across his face. He was gloating at them now, his tears long since dried up.

"You're proud of this, aren't you?" said Laurie. "You're pleased with what you've done, what you did to your wife."

"And why wouldn't I be?" he laughed. "I've had the world's press camped outside my door for almost a month. Every morning I get up and I'm on the news again. If it's not been me giving a press conference, it's been pictures of Medina plastered all over the newspapers, websites, the TV, everywhere. And not just here, America, Dubai, the whole world. She's a superstar, *I'm* a superstar. It's all she ever wanted. A bit of celebrity, a bit of fame."

"Jesus Christ," said Laurie, blowing outher breath. "You're saying you did this for *her*?"

"No," said The Devil. "He didn't do anything for her. He did this for himself."

Laurie looked at him and then to Cade. He shrugged again, his eyes full of unashamed glee.

"Medina was a pain in the arse," he said. "But I did love her. I really did. She wanted to be famous. I've made her famous, made her a global superstar where everybody knows her name. The fact I'm spoken about with her, hey, that's only natural."

"And if it means you don't have to work another day in your life then that's a happy coincidence. One last jaunt to clock in, get out into the big blue. What's another shift, am I right?" asked The Devil.

Cade held his hands out wide.

"A guy's gotta eat."

"But you're back at work anyway, so you obviously didn't cash in too much", countered Laurie.

A large smirk crept across Cade's face as he stared unblinking at the detective.

The Devil let out a laugh. He ran his hands through his hair and smiled.

"You know something Pierce Cade," he said. "If this was any other scenario I would probably shake your hand. Murdering your wife to make you both celebrities is certainly a new low for me. And believe me when I say this - that is *really* difficult to do. I mean, it's almost kind of genius. Seriously. If I was in a better position I'd probably promote you to one of the better jobs Downstairs."

"Eh, hello?" said Laurie, clearing her throat. "Time and place sunshine."

"Yes, yes, of course," said The Devil. "It's just unlucky for you Pierce that I'm not in charge. Not at the moment anyway. And that means you're subject to strong arm of Detective Sergeant Laurie here and the full weight of Human law and order."

Cade took a long, deep breath. He held up his arms towards Laurie and showed her his wrists.

"Go ahead copper," he said. "You can try but who's going to believe you? It's your word against mine and the only witness is this ranting and raving bloke you found squatting in that shit hole flat I rented in Gravesend. That's right, it was mine. You'd be surprised how easy it is to rent a place in this city with cash in hand and a false name. Almost as easy as pinning the whole kidnapping on a bunch of wannabe bombers out in the desert."

"I assume then you have no connection to that terror cell - just another part of the ruse," said The Devil.

"Hah!" Cade laughed. "You're kidding right? I just Googled obscure terrorists and plucked a name and badge out of nowhere. It's not like they're going to come after *me* is it?. I'm doing them a favour. I've made *them* famous!"

He smiled and waved his wrists at Laurie again.

"So come on then. What are you waiting for? Or do you know as well as I do that without a body, you don't have shit on me."

Laurie was fuming. She was chewing on her lips, her eyes burrowing into Cade's across the cabin. The Devil felt a stab of pain across his forehead again. He rubbed it and spied something sitting on Cade's bunk.

He forced himself over to beside the bed. The large bag he'd seen Cade carrying from his house was there, zipped up and closed in the middle of the bunk. He touched it and pulled on the handles. He felt something creep up his arm. One by one the hairs stood up, like an encroaching wave, all the way up to his shoulder. It was a strange sensation, almost other-worldly. Evil had a tendency to leave its mark in the Human world. And this bag was reeking of it.

"Tell me Mr Cade," he said. "Do you always travel so light for two weeks at sea?"

Cade sat up a little in his chair. The Devil could sense the tension in him. Like a shark smelling blood, he felt his whole body tingle. The Devil had him now.

"First rule in the murderer's handbook," he said smugly, unzipping the bag. "Never, ever, under any circumstances, think you can outsmart *me*."

He opened the bag and the cabin was immediately filled with the hot, musky smell of charcoal and petrol. Laurie and The Devil began to cough as it caught in the back of their throats.

They wiped tears from their eyes and looked inside the bag. There, stacked up neatly like a weekly grocery shop, were bones. Human bones, blackened and brittle like they'd been burned for a very long time. At the bottom was a skull, smiling a toothy, eyeless grin. The Devil could almost hear it yelling 'surprise'.

"Medina Cade I presume," he said. "Finally we get the chance to meet."

Cade shot up from his chair. He barrelled into Laurie and threw her against the wall. The Devil tried to react but he was too quick. He jabbed him beneath the nose and then chopped at his ribs. The Devil screamed in pain and slumped to the floor, paralysed. Cade grabbed the bag and jumped over him, bolting down the corridor.

"Fuck!" Laurie shouted. "He burnt her!"

"No," said The Devil, being helped to his feet. "I don't think he did. I think it's much worse than that."

"How can this get any worse?" she asked as they gave chase.

"Believe me Laurie. It can *always* get worse. And when it does, it really, really does."

THE MAN IN THE DARK

THIRTY-ONE

Laurie led the pursuit through the ship, The Devil lagging sorely behind. He was trying his hardest to keep up but there just wasn't enough breath in him. The more he pushed himself the worse the pain got. He was wet with sweat and he needed to hold on to the walls and railings just to stay upright.

Laurie was getting further and further from him. She was invigorated now, pressing herself hard as she tried to run down Cade. His headstart had been chopped considerably. And there was only one place he could logically go. Topside.

The Devil gritted his teeth. The pain was getting worse. He was choking down great gulps of vomit and coughing fits. He knew if he stopped he'd probably collapse. And if that happened then it was game over for everybody. He climbed the stairs through the insides of the ship, up and up he went until at last he reached a door.

The night air almost blew him back down the steps. He held on to the door frame by his fingernails. Stumbling out onto the deck, he saw Laurie in full pursuit, Cade only a few feet ahead of her. He was heading for the bow of the Valiant.

"A lightning bolt wouldn't go amiss right now if You're listening," said The Devil, trying to catch some breath. "You know what happened, You heard him. He's admitted killing her. Medina

Cade is in that bag. Her husband did it. Now release me and we can sort out this mess."

The wash of the river kicked up some water onto the deck, soaking The Devil. He shook off the filthy wetness and shambled onwards.

"You never make this easy, do You?" he asked the night sky.

Hurrying as best he could along the deck. The pain in his chest was now unbearable. Every step he took he felt like he was going to die. He grabbed at himself, hoping the pressure would relieve the agony. But nothing was going to stop this. Even with his limited knowledge of Human anatomy outwith the brain and genitals he knew that things were failing. Death was close, closer than it had ever been.

"Stop right there Cade!" Laurie's voice distracted him.

She was just ahead of him. Five feet from her was Pierce Cade. He stood close to the railings at the bow of the ship, his bag hoisted high above his head. He watched them both, a savage smile on his face.

"Don't do it!" she shouted. "It won't make a difference whether you dump the bones or not. You're caught bang to rights. We'll get DNA evidence from your flat. If those bones have been in there we'll find something. Do yourself a favour and leave them be. For Medina."

"For Medina?" he started to laugh. "Do you have any idea how much I did for Medina! I gave her everything. *Everything* I had I gave to that woman. And she took and took and took."

"She was your wife man, it was your job," said Laurie, shouting over the engines and wash.

"Don't stand there and tell me what I did and didn't have to do for that woman! I did everything I could for her. And I'm still bloody doing it!"

 THE MAN IN THE DARK

"She deserves a proper funeral Pierce," said Laurie. "You loved her, you said you loved her. Doesn't she deserve that? You dump her bones over the side and she's never going to get that."

Cade's smile dropped. His eyes went teary again as he stared beyond Laurie and The Devil. The wind caught his tears and lifted them off his cheeks. He lowered the bag.

"What… what have I done?" he asked blearily.

Laurie looked at The Devil. He shook his head, struggling to focus over the pain.

"What… what have I done here?"

"What do you mean what have you done?" Laurie shouted. "You've killed your wife. You killed her to make her famous, to make *you* famous. You admitted that."

Cade looked over the edge of the ship. Laurie eased herself a little closer to him. He looked confused and dazed, like he'd only just woken from a deep sleep.

"I… I killed her," he said. "I slit her throat, after I made that video. It all… it all got out of hand so quickly. And then I… then I brought her home."

"You brought her home?" asked The Devil. "How?"

"In our suitcases," he said. "I carved her up, chopped her up in the apartment. There was so much… so much blood. She was only small, she weighed nothing, but there was so much blood. And I put her in our cases."

The Devil snorted some salty air. He hobbled up to Laurie and balanced himself against her.

"How did you get through customs?" she asked.

"It was perfect," he laughed a little, still crying. "After the press got involved, who was going to stop me? I mean, the media met me off the plane, they even stopped me before *you* got to me."

"I don't understand," said The Devil. "Don't you people have rules and regulations going between countries?"

"Yeah, but what customs officer is going to have the bollocks to stop a grieving husband whose wife has been taken by terrorists?" said Laurie. "He could have brought back as many duty free fags and bottles of vodka as he wanted. Nobody was going to check, were they?"

"I see," said The Devil. "Very clever Cade, very clever indeed. Like I said, if I wasn't in so much agony I'd congratulate you."

"I still don't follow though Cade!" Laurie shouted at him. "Medina - she's in the bag. But it's her skeleton. What happened to her muscle, her skin? Her organs?"

Cade didn't answer her. He stood looking down at the contents of the bag, sobbing uncontrollably.

The Devil squeezed Laurie's shoulder. She looked at him, confused.

"I don't get it," she said.

"Remember that smell in his house?" he asked. "And what the photographer woman said when she was hiding upstairs."

"She said he had the oven on for hours. Yeah, so..."

There was only a few seconds between Laurie realising what had happened and her throwing up. She spewed all over the deck while The Devil held onto the side railing. She was doubled over, coughing and spluttering for minutes as the true horror of what had happened dawned on her.

"You... you ate her?" she said, wiping her mouth.

Cade said nothing. He held the bag up close to his chest and hugged it like it was a person, like it was his wife.

"You ate Medina's remains? You ate everything?" she asked again.

He didn't need to answer her. The grief, shame and guilt on his face was enough of an admission. The Devil couldn't fight back his smile.

"I told you Laurie," he said. "It always gets worse. Much worse. It doesn't matter how long you live, how far you've been about, it never gets old. Humanity, I'm afraid, will always find a way of outdoing itself. Whether that's in science, innovation or murder. You lot really are disgustingly beautiful in a savage sort of way."

Laurie was about to throw up again when the whole ship groaned. It shuddered violently and the air was filled with a terrible screeching sound.

The deck dropped beneath their feet, slipping away at a steep angle. The groan continued as metal screeched and screamed. The Devil was thrown against the side barrier, Laurie barrelling into him.

"What the hell is going on?" she asked. "Have we hit something?"

"I think so," he said. "I think we might have run aground."

The ship ground to a halt. The whole deck was slanted, the Valiant tilted above them. Water from the river crashed against the rocks beneath them as they headed along the railing.

"Where's Cade?" Laurie shouted. "Where did that bastard go? Did he fall over the side?"

"Shit!" The Devil shouted. "We need him. We still need him Laurie!"

"He was at the bow. Just there, he was -"

She grabbed The Devil and pointed at the front of the ship. Cade was there, stumbling around. He held on to the barrier, staring down at the crashing water and rocks. He climbed over the barrier and Laurie took off.

"No!" she shouted.

It startled Cade. He tripped and fell off the barrier. Laurie leapt forward and caught him by the hand. There was a thud as he hit the side of the ship.

"No you don't!" she shouted at him. "You're not getting out that easy you fucker!"

The Devil managed to edge his way along the barrier. He grabbed at Cade and helped pull him back over the edge.

They worked their way to the bow of the boat and climbed upwards. As they reached the other side they peered over the edge and saw the dockside. The Valiant had crashed into the river wall, smashing through the flood barriers. The river was spilling onto the dockside amongst the wreckage. But there was something else down there.

"The mob," said The Devil.

The water was gushing in from the broken barrier but the throng, a hundred thousand strong, was there, moving, hunched over, flailing their arms like wild animals. They all looked up at the boat, dead, lifeless eyes transfixed on the three of them.

"They found us," he said. "They caught us up. That's it Laurie. This is the end."

Laurie pushed Cade up and over the edge of the boat. Then she grabbed The Devil.

"What are you doing?" he asked.

"Come on," she said. "We're going down there."

"Didn't you hear what I just said. It's over Laurie. They've won. Brutus and Cassius, that's them down there waiting for us. It's finished, we've lost. I've lost."

"Yeah, I heard you loud and clear," she said. "And you're right, I don't doubt for a second that you're right."

She stared right at him, her wounded face leaking and bleeding.

"If this is the end then I'm going out on *my* terms," she said. "I'm not running away only to be shot in the back. I've never run away from anything. I've stood my ground and tried to be a good policewoman, a good wife, a good mum and above all else a good person. Plenty of people have tried to stand in the way of all of those things sunshine, yourself included, and pigs like Cade here.

But I won't run now, like I didn't then. If this is my time to go then I'll face up to it head on, with my dignity intact."

She began to lower herself and Cade down the side of the Valiant towards the docks.

"You can do what you want," she said to him. "I don't know anything about Upstairs, Downstairs and everything in between. All I know is all I know. And I'm going to die with dignity damn it. That's something you and your pals can never take away from me."

Laurie and Cade eased themselves down the side of the ship. It lurched a little as more of the broken flood barrier gave way, making the angle less steep from them. The shift of the huge hull was enough of a distraction for Cade to strike. He wrenched his wrist free from Laurie as she struggled to keep her balance. With a cackle, he slid away from her.

"No!" she shouted after him.

The murderer was too far away for her to catch him. He hurried down the side of the ship, barrelling towards the dockside. Laurie was about to go after him when she spied the mob down below.

They'd seen Cade, all one hundred thousand of them. Every twitching head followed the cannibal as he raced towards the docks. And when he hit the ground hard, the crack of his ankles resonated throughout the whole crowd.

The dockside fell silent. Every rasping, barking mouth was closed. Fangs clenched tightly together as they stopped and watched Cade writhing in pain at the foot of the ship.

"Help me!" he screamed. "My legs! I've broken my legs!"

Laurie and The Devil were frozen still. From his vantage point at the top of the buckled ship, he could see the mob slowly shambling towards Cade. They walked with a terrible, menacing inevitability - like an incoming tidal wave ready to consume a coastline. Slow and deliberate, slow and deliberate, on and on they went until they surrounded Cade.

"I have to get him," Laurie shouted.

"No!" The Devil yelled. "Stay right where you are!"

He eased his way down towards Laurie. Grabbing her weakly, he kept her in her place, far away from the dockside.

"He deserves to face justice! Death is too good for him! He ate that poor woman!"

"I know what he did Laurie," he said. "But you can't do anything for him now. Don't move a muscle!"

She watched on helplessly as the mob of feral Humans encircled Cade. It was only a matter of time before they engulfed him. Although The Devil couldn't fathom why they didn't simply consume him.

"What are they doing?" she whispered.

Slowly, those closest to Cade raised him up onto their shoulders and then over their heads. He screamed in agony, arms and broken legs splayed wide. The mob passed him from one to another, taking him further and further from the edge of the ship.

The Devil watched on with a morbid fascination. He'd never seen anything like this before, a mass control of Humanity all working in sync with each other. Like a great talisman they eased Cade over their heads until he was at the centre of the mob gathered on the dockside.

"Remarkable," he whispered.

"What are they doing?" asked Laurie.

"I have no idea," he said. "But it can only be to do with the purity of his evil. I mean, a virus doesn't attack its own cells, cancer doesn't get cancer, does it?"

"What are they going to do with him?"

As if answering Laurie, Cade was stopped. Even through the

THE MAN IN THE DARK

gloom they could see the terror in the cannibal's eyes. He caught sight of them across the thousands of heads now between them. With all of his might, he cried out to them.

"Help me!" he shouted. "Help me!"

His screams for aid were like a starting pistol for the mob. The tranquillity and peace of their feral nature was abandoned in an instant. Like the huge mouth of a whale coming to the surface of the ocean to feed, the throng consumed Cade in one, giant gulp. His screams echoed for a few, brief seconds before there was silence.

"Oh God," said Laurie, grabbing her mouth. "Have they, have they eaten him?"

"Yes," said The Devil. "Feasted even. Like he was one of their own. Strangely fitting, don't you think?"

The stillness of the mob remained and they all turned from the centre of the pack to face The Devil and Laurie in unison. The companions stood still in the darkness for a moment. They were waiting for them. This was it, thought The Devil.

"Ah," he said quietly. "Remember what you were saying about dignity."

Laurie nodded.

"Do you still think it's a good idea?"

Tears were welling in her eyes. She sniffed and looked down at the bag of remains slung over The Devil's shoulder.

"I caught the bad guy," she said. "It might not have been the type of justice he deserved. But justice is justice. And nobody can take that away from me."

She reached out and took his hand. Squeezing it tightly, she nodded down towards the dockside. The Devil looked out at the gathered mob waiting for them. Embracing the pain for what he suspected was his final journey, he started to ease his way down the side of the ship and headed off to meet his destiny.

THIRTY-TWO

The Devil was moving slowly. He wasn't trying to make an entrance, he just couldn't manage anything quicker. The bag containing Medina Cade weighed him down and he could feel his Human organs failing him with every passing second. His head was light and he was dizzy, the fringes of unconsciousness biting at the edges of his mind.

He knew if he passed out that would be it. Yet somehow, some way, what Laurie had said to him about dignity was resounding inside his head. Suddenly it made an awful lot of sense.

He was The Devil, he always had been and always would be. That's how the Natural Order worked. He had a place in the known universe and he'd enjoyed that role more than anybody ever could.

He also knew that nothing could last forever. Everything had an end. It seemed that his was coming up, very quickly. Every shambling footstep in ill-fitting trainers down the nearly horizontal side of the ship was taking him closer and closer to that moment. After all the things he had done, all his devious planning, inventions, scheming and hijinks, this was where it was all to come to a close. On a dockside in London, torn apart by a possessed mob bent on the whims of two of Humanity's greatest traitors.

There was an irony in there that he should have been enjoying

                THE MAN IN THE DARK

more. As it happened he couldn't find anything to enjoy, not in his final moments. He could only hope that his body would fail him long before Brutus and Cassius could carve him up.

The dockside was steeped in darkness. A row of flashing blue lights was all that highlighted the gathered thousands who had come to finish the job. The strobes danced off their faces, highlighting every nostril, every glare, every snarl. Police, journalists, butchers, bakers, politicians, school teachers, business people, they were all there. The professions didn't matter. Only that they were under the spell of the two Romans who wanted it all.

They neared the edge of the ship. The broken river wall was only a few feet away from them now. The mob was starting to twitch again, barks and howls sounding out from its near endless depths. They could smell him getting closer, their excitement building. They were happy for him to come to them, walk right into their waiting claws and teeth.

The Devil and Laurie stopped right at the edge, where the ship met the dockside. This was it, the final step. The mob stayed firm, hopping, growling, screaming with anticipation.

"Why don't they come for us?" she asked.

"An incantation, I imagine," said The Devil. "A little joke on Brutus and Cassius' part, to prolong our agony. Still, I might get lucky."

"Lucky?" she said. "How do you figure?"

"Maybe I'll die before I make this last step. Maybe this Human body will actually give out and I'll be dead before they even lay a finger on me. That would be nice."

"For you maybe," she groaned. "What about me?"

"I'm far too important to worry about you Laurie. You know that."

"Yeah, I suppose you're right," she said sarcastically. "My only regret is that I didn't realise that sooner. This truly has been a blessing to know you."

"Regrets, I've had a few," said The Devil.

"But then again, too few to mention," sang Laurie.

He looked at her strangely.

"What? You don't like Frank Sinatra?" she asked.

"I don't know what that is," he said. "But I'm sure you'll have plenty of time in whatever machinations Brutus and Cassius have cooked up for you Downstairs to think about it. Eternity, my dear, can be a very long time."

"So what happens now?" she asked, nodding at the mob. "After they rip us limb from limb like Cade."

"I don't know," he said. "I've never lived through an apocalypse before."

The pair of them stood silently facing the hundred thousand packed into the dockside and beyond. Laurie squeezed The Devil's hand.

"I'm scared," she said quietly. "I'm scared that I'm never going to see Andy and Matilda again. I'm scared, even after everything you've told me, that there's nothing that comes next. Nothing except pain and suffering and two Roman twats who want us dead."

"Fear," said The Devil, coughing and wheezing. "Is all relative Laurie."

"That's all you've got to say?"

"That's all I've got to say. Pathetic really, given it's the last thing I'll probably ever say. Still, better than nothing I suppose."

That made her laugh. She sniffed loudly and wiped her nose on the back of her sleeve. Taking a deep breath she took one last look at the creatures waiting to devour her.

"Do me one last favour would you?" she said, panic in her voice.

"What would that be," he croaked.

"Don't let go of my hand."

The Devil turned and smiled at her. Laurie smiled back. Then, like they had telepathically told each other to, they both stepped down off the ship and onto the flooded dockside.

A fearsome roar went up from the mob. They all lunged forward as a collective, ready to devour their prey.

But before the first fang could pierce flesh, a great gust of air billowed out from beneath The Devil and Laurie's feet. The shockwave passed through the baying mob, its force knocking each of them onto their backs like dominoes. In an instant, they were all flattened. Only The Devil and Laurie remained standing on the dock.

"What's going on here?" Laurie said, breathless. "What's happening?"

The Devil didn't have an answer for her. He didn't even have something sarcastic to say. He felt let down by his lack of verve. He looked out across the dockside at the flattened mob.

Relief quickly gave way to suspicion. He stepped forward, nearing the closest Humans who had, until a few seconds ago, been ready to eat his face.

He looked down at them. They were all the same, still and serene. Only there was something different about them now, something that had been missing before.

"They're... normal," he said.

"What?" asked Laurie.

"Look, at their faces, look at them."

He pointed down at the nearest to them. A young man, in his early twenties. He was sound asleep, with a peaceful and calm look on his features. It was the same for the two old women on either side of him. And for everybody else in the vicinity.

"They just… fell asleep?" she said. "Just like that?"

"Yes," said The Devil. "Just. Like. That."

"What did you do?"

"Nothing," he said firmly. "Nothing at all."

"You must have."

"I didn't do a thing," he said.

"But they just… I mean. They just stopped. If you didn't do anything, then who…"

The Devil's top lip twitched. It was involuntary, like a nervous tic his Human body, even in its dying state, couldn't help but do. He was about to speak when the sound of a hundred thousand people waking up from a sleep they didn't know they were taking, interrupted him.

The crowd slowly started to get to its feet. There were a lot of confused faces. And plenty of yawning. People greeted each other and started to talk. They asked the same questions and were met with the same lack of answers. All across the dockside, the once rabid mob was confused. And sleepy.

"I don't think I can take much more of this," said Laurie. "I don't know what's going to happen next."

"No," said The Devil. "For once I have to agree with you. I don't think I can take much more of it either."

The blue lights in the distance started to move. Ambulances, police cars, emergency services began weaving their way through the gathered crowd.

"Laurie!" came a voice through the gloom.

There was a slight commotion directly ahead of them then the crowd parted. A single figure came walking out from their ranks.

"Lister," Laurie said bitterly. "I don't believe it!"

DCI Ken Lister strode purposefully through the confused mass. The water didn't seem to phase him, nor did the hundred

THE MAN IN THE DARK

thousand strong mob all trying to work out why they were where they were. Even the wreck of the Valiant couldn't break his superior demeanour.

"Laurie," he said again. "What are… where are we? How the bloody hell did I get here?"

"Are you feeling alright sir?" she asked. "You don't have any sort of, well, urges, to do anything rash?"

"Urges," the old detective barked. "The only urge I have around you Laurie is to put a rocket up your arse to do some work for a change."

He looked around him at the others. Stretching his arms out, he shook his head in disbelief.

"I don't understand Laurie, what is all this?"

She gave a quick glance at The Devil. He remained stoic, his insides turning to mulch.

"Truth be told sir, I don't really know myself. There're strange things going on in this city, strange things all over the world. I think this might just be another one of those. Like Pierce Cade."

"Cade!" Lister snapped his fingers. "Pierce Cade! The kidnapped wife! I remember. I remember that name, that woman. We were… we were on to her. We were on to her before my mind went blank. Something came over me, I felt like I was in a coma. But I remember Cade. And his wife, what was her name again, Medina! That's it. Medina! Jesus Laurie, they must have killed her by now."

"You're half right sir," she said.

Laurie took the bag from The Devil.

"Half right?" he asked.

She threw the bag at her superior.

"What's this?" he said, unzipping it. "Sweet Jesus," he said, recoiling instantly. "It smells like a fucking takeaway kitchen on a Saturday night."

"With all due respect sir," she said. "That's Mrs Medina Cade you're talking about."

"Holy Hell," said the detective. "What the bloody bollocks happened to her?"

"Cannibalism," said The Devil flatly.

"What?"

"He ate her," said Laurie. "He killed her on holiday, brought her body parts back in suitcases and cooked her."

"Who?" asked Lister, retching. "Who did this?"

"Cade," she said, with more than a little pride. "Cade did it. He was going to throw the bones out at sea, that's why he came back to work sir, back to the ship. Thought he'd just sail away into the night amongst all the madness. But he didn't. He didn't get that far."

"Where is he now?" said Lister, zipping the bag shut. "Where is the bastard?"

Laurie seemed a little uneasy. The Devil, despite his declining state, never shirked the chance to be as cold and callous as possible.

"Dead," he said flatly. "Eaten by you and your cronies."

"By me… and my cronies… Laurie what's he talking about I-"

"It's a long story sir, too long for tonight," she said. "But I think you should probably get looked over by a doctor. Probably as soon as possible."

Lister scratched at the hard, bristly stubble that dotted his cheeks.

"Yeah," he said, staring down at the bag. "Jesus Christ. Ate her. That's horrible. It's always the husbands. Am I right Laurie? Still, they normally put poison in the missus' diet tablets. Or strangle her with the cheese cutter or whatever it is these middle class twats use. But eating her. Christ alive. That's grim."

"Yes sir."

"And the video? The old…"

He whistled as he tapped the side of his big, round nose.

"All staged," she said. "He also rented the flat in Gravesend, where the video came from."

"How do you know all this?"

"He told me," said Laurie. "Before he died. And I had a little, help, shall we say."

"But why?" he asked. "Why do it? Why eat your wife?"

"Evil," said The Devil. "Evil, DCI Lister. For no other reason than the fact the man was born rotten to his very core. And while you may think you've dealt with his type before, I can assure you, there is likely nothing of his sort you will ever encounter again. That is, until, the impending doom consumes us all."

"Eh?"

"Yes sir, like I said," Laurie interjected. "I had some help."

She smiled at The Devil. Lister cocked an eyebrow in his direction, unconvinced. The old detective shouldered the bag and slung it behind him. He nodded at both of them.

"I don't know what's going on here," he said. "I don't know why I'm not tucked up in bed with a copy of Auto Trader and a cup of Horlicks. But I know when I've seen good work. And as much as it pains me Laurie, I reckon you might have done some good work here."

Lister nodded to himself again. He wagged a finger at her and smiled as best he could

"There's probably going to be a promotion in this for you then. Who would have thought it, eh?"

He turned and walked off into the crowd. He clung tightly on to the bag, shouting over the din for some poor, unsuspecting uniformed officer to help him. Laurie scratched the back of her head.

"And get that face seen to!" the DCI shouted back at her, before disappearing among the others.

"Yes sir," she said.

Her mouth hung open, her face a picture of worry and confusion. She pointed after them.

"What's going on?" she asked. "Is this really happening? Are they all really back to normal?"

The Devil dropped to one knee. He mumbled something but blood spilled from his mouth. He tried to catch it but there was too much. He felt everything start to go numb, from the ends of his feet all the way up through his chest and towards his fingertips. She managed to catch him before he fell face first into the water.

"Hey!" she shouted. "I need a medic here. I need an ambulance!"

She held him close to her as she screamed for some help. The Devil wanted to close his eyes, even though he knew that would be the end. But a voice inside his head told him to hold on.

"Just for another minute," it promised. "Just one more minute."

The Devil hated being told what to do. And even at the end he was tempted just to die. That would have been so him, a last little jibe at all of creation. What a way it would have been to sign off. No greater revenge.

Breaking the habits of a lifetime was among the hardest things to do. The Devil didn't have the energy to try now. He was a coward at heart. And he always would be.

THE MAN IN THE DARK

THIRTY-THREE

"You just don't expect to see boats crashing do you? It's not the done thing."

The Devil snorted a little, like he'd been snoring. He blinked and tried to crank his mind back up and running.

"I mean, it's like something you read in those tabloid newspapers isn't it? Like something from a film."

The Devil was confused, and not for the first time. He went to speak but his mouth was numb, tongue lolling around inside like a beached whale.

"I tell you what though, I don't envy whoever it is that's going to have to clean up this mess. Not me mate, not me at all."

He couldn't turn his head. A thick, plastic neck brace was keeping it locked in place. Instead he turned his whole torso to meet the anonymous voice.

"How you feeling mate? Any better?"

An old man with a silvery, white beard sat on a trolley in the back of an ambulance. He slurped tea from a flask loudly, a blanket wrapped loosely about his shoulders. He winked and drained his cup.

"Can't beat a good cuppa," he said. "Good for what ails you."

"Yes," said The Devil with great difficulty. "Yes I've heard that's the case."

The old man stood up with a groan. He took off his blanket and folded it neatly down and left it on the trolley. He eased his way past The Devil who was sitting on the step at the back door of the ambulance. When he hopped down he pulled a flat cap from his pocket and pulled it on.

"I wasn't really hurt," he whispered. "Just fancied a free cuppa. Be seeing you mate, stay lucky."

He wandered off, whistling a tune only he knew. The Devil, wracked with pain and stiffness, wasn't quite sure if he was dreaming, having a nightmare or a total psychotic breakdown.

The dockland was a flurry of activity in front of him. Ambulances, police cars, fire engines, just about every emergency service out there, all scurrying about the wreckage of the Valiant. Cops were directing long lines of people to and from the port while the medics set up emergency treatment rooms in tents. Huge spotlights had been directed at the buckled hull of the ship and a helicopter buzzed around the night sky above them.

"You know, if I didn't know better, I'd say there was a full-scale recovery operation going on here," he said.

He looked about expecting a response. There was none forthcoming. He watched the Humans buzzing around in front of him like nothing had ever happened. And that, ironically, raised more questions than it answered.

"I can never work these new devices they swear by," came a vaguely familiar voice from behind.

A young paramedic with long, braided hair and rich, dark skin stepped around him, head buried in a phone. She tapped the screen then let out a gentle sigh.

"Bring back buttons is what I say. You can't go wrong with a button. If it breaks you can replace it. If it jams, just wiggle it off and put in a new one. They will insist on these touch sensitive screens. Still, at least they haven't mastered telekinesis yet, then we're really in for it old sausage."

"You're remarkably chipper for somebody who's whole life's work is about to come crashing down about them," said The Devil. "And You've changed again. You've had more costumes this time than a bloody pop diva."

"Is that a popular culture reference?" She smiled. "Because it sounded very much like it."

"I'm in too much pain to argue with You," he said. "Although I suspect You know that already and are simply prolonging the agony."

She smirked a little. Reaching down She unfastened his neck brace. He could breathe and speak properly again and he rubbed his throat. He was weak, his arms and legs still tingling. He didn't try to stand up, there was no point.

She fiddled around with Her phone before giving up. She shoved it into one of the pockets of Her NHS jumpsuit and pulled out a little torch.

"Say ah for me," She said.

"I'd rather not."

"Just say it, come on, be a good sport."

"Ah."

She shone the light in his eyes and blinded him. He blinked them clear and shook his head.

"What's the verdict then doc?" he asked. "Time to be put down?"

"I would have said that centuries ago but then again, you know me."

"Don't I just."

She laughed and leaned against the ambulance. She nodded out at the recovery operation unfolding in front of them.

"What do you think then? Not bad for a last minute effort?"

"Stunning," he said sarcastically. "You want me to pat You on the back too or can Your arms reach around there enough already?"

"I managed to extend the safety field about fifteen miles," She said, ignoring him. "Tens of thousands have been saved as a result - most of those who were about to have their wicked little way with you and the good constable."

"You certainly took Your time."

"You didn't think I'd let anything happen to you, did you?"

"I'm not going answer that," he said. "Let's just say I wasn't making too many plans."

"I never thought you did that anyway."

"Touché," said The Devil. "Fifteen miles, that's not a lot. What about the others?"

A grave look made Her face age a little. She shook Her head.

"Not pretty," She said. "I'm afraid Brutus and Cassius' bad work has spread now to every corner of Downstairs. Only a few pockets of resistance remain but their influence has turned good proportions of this planet into a dog's dinner, for want of a better expression old boy."

"So what am I still doing here?" The Devil asked. "I did what You wanted, exactly as You asked. I even had to suffer that blubbering murderer Pierce Cade for half an hour longer than I needed."

"Yes, strange one that," She said. "I must admit I didn't see it coming. The whole eating part. Very macabre."

The Devil stared up at Her. He closed his eyes until they were slits.

"You really don't give a shit, do You?" he asked.

She kept watching the emergency operation. Cranes were being brought in to help stabilise the hull of the Valiant. The ship had now sunk below the waterline of the river. Only its bow was left above the water, half perched on the dockside.

"Pierce Cade, Brutus, Cassius, me, it's all pretty meaningless to You, isn't it? It's just an inconvenience to whatever it is You want to be doing all day."

"Pierce Cade is an outlier," She said calmly. "You don't get a lot of them. Not anymore. A real throwback, as the kids say these days. Evil like him is reserved solely for the rare occasions. And when it does appear, well, there's normally a good bit of collateral damage."

"Collateral damage, that's what we're calling it then?" asked The Devil. "We're sitting on the precipice of the greatest war existence has ever known and You're calling it collateral damage? You're something else, You know that. Of course You know that. You're You."

"I know you're upset," She said calmly. "But shouting at me isn't going to change anything. All we have left is what's ahead of us."

The Devil groaned loudly. He sat forward, easing his aching back into a comfortable arch. He stared at the ground beneath his dangling feet. The water was oily, a rainbow of swirls reflecting off the spotlights and strobes. He could have watched those shapes morphing and changing forever. Like the fabric of the galaxy that was spinning the Earth around at unsurmountable speeds, it was endless and forever. At least, it used to be.

"What's the use in arguing eh?" he said. "I've done that with You for millennia and look where it's gotten both of us. Me with a broken back and You struggling to keep everything ticking over. What a joke!"

"If I was feeling in a more savage mood I'd take that sentiment as a come down," She said, clapping him on the shoulder. "But as it happens, I'm taking a leaf out of your book and being the eternal optimist for a change."

She stepped forward so he could see Her. He forced himself to sit up, everything burning. She sucked on Her tongue, flipped Her long hair back and put Her hands on Her hips.

"We need action," She said. "But the flaming sword, blazing chariots led by stampeding stallions isn't going to work old boy. You know that and I know that. Brutus and Cassius are far too clever for that sort of thing."

"Not to mention too powerful," he said. "I can't really see any of Your pals wielding axes and machine guns to blast away the heathen hordes. Can You? Imagine Peter at the controls of a machine gun - a Vulcan cannon even. Blimey, we'd be safer with the enemy."

She let out a little laugh.

"He tries his best," She said. "But violence has never been his strong point."

"I detect from Your tone of voice that You have a plan."

"I *always* have a plan," She smiled. "But first things first, there are a few loose ends to tie up."

She stepped to one side. Across the dock was another ambulance. Standing by its door, The Devil saw Laurie sipping from a mug, a silvery foil blanket wrapped tightly about her.

"Do I have to?" he asked. "I mean I've had to put up with that woman for days now. Couldn't we just quietly disappear into the night?"

"What do I always say?" She asked. "If a job's worth doing then it's worth doing properly."

"I don't think I've *ever* heard You say that," he said.

"First time for everything," She smiled.

She helped him onto his feet and made sure he could walk. Then She sent him on his way.

THE MAN IN THE DARK

THIRTY-FOUR

"Is this ambulance taken?"

Laurie looked up and smiled. It was the first time she'd been relieved to see The Devil. Although she couldn't really understand why. Maybe she didn't want to. There was plenty of weird stuff happening that she couldn't fathom. The longer the night went on the more she was realising it was better just to let it slide.

"Are you feeling any better?" she asked him. "You were at death's door not an hour ago. Thought I'd have to call an undertaker."

"No, not really," he said. "In fact I doubt I'll ever feel well again. But hey-ho, what does my happiness count for anyway?"

"I take it all of this is part of your handiwork," she pointed at the clean up operation. "You might not be feeling better but these folk certainly are. Nice to see some of my emergency service colleagues not wanting to tear out my throat and use it as a headband."

The Devil eased himself down onto the step of the ambulance. He tried to stretch his legs but the pain was too much. Laurie sat down beside him and offered her cup. He refused. She ran a hand through her hair and touched the fresh dressing on her cheek.

"You sure know how to show a girl a good time," she said.

"That's not the first time I've been told that," said The Devil. "And I highly doubt it'll be the last."

They sat in silence, catching their breath. Laurie was restless, he could feel her getting antsy. The Devil hated fidgeting. He ground his Human teeth, hoping she'd take the hint.

"Here's the thing right," she said, turning to him. "I've been wrestling with this the whole time I've been with you."

"Great," he groaned. "You might as well spit it out, while you've got the chance."

"If you're The Devil right, how come you're not just snapping your fingers and sorting all of this shit out right away?"

"It's not the first time I've heard that either," he said flatly. "Simply put, it's not that easy."

"Yeah, so you said."

"This is nothing but a temporary blip, a glitch in the system, it'll be fine."

Laurie looked at him. He ignored her.

"A glitch in the system, yeah right," she laughed. "Who are you trying to convince with that chat sunshine. Me or you?"

"No comment," he said.

She pulled her blanket tighter around her shoulders.

"Alright, seeing as I might never get another opportunity to ask," she began. "Maybe you can help me."

"I severely doubt that," he yawned.

"I'm a copper right."

"So you keep saying."

"I see a lot of bad shit on a daily basis. In fact, I see it on an hourly basis. Murder, death, mutilation, the works. How come that happens? How come we're still tearing ourselves apart, doing more and more bad stuff to each other. I mean, we've been doing it for thousands of years. Aren't we bored of it by now? Haven't we got it out of our system?"

The Devil let his head bob in her direction. He rolled his eyes.

"Yes Laurie," he said lazily. "You lot have really gotten it out of your system. That's why there are still wars, that's why you've got old pensioners being beaten to a pulp and left naked by horny teens. That's why we're staring into the face of an eternal abyss. I think you answered your own question."

"But I mean, we've been like this for so long," she said. "Don't you guys have a way of like, you know, making us wake up and smell the coffee?"

"We're not allowed, *I'm* not allowed," said The Devil. "Strictly forbidden to directly interfere."

"Oh come on," she smiled. "You're trying to tell me The Devil has never broken the rules? I'm a bit unimpressed."

"I've not been here to impress you Laurie. I was here to find Medina Cade."

"But it's a bit of a let-down, don't you think? The ultimate bad guy, this great embodiment of evil, hasn't even broken a rule."

"I don't have to," said The Devil. "That's the beauty of it. You lot do it all of your own accord. You can't help yourselves."

"I don't agree."

The Devil mopped his brow. When he looked at his hand it had turned white with dust. He tutted loudly, not even attempting to tidy himself. What was the use.

"I was once approached by a man, a Human man," he said to Laurie. "He was old, a pensioner, pushing eighty according to my records. He'd lived his life, paid all his bills, never had a penny more than he could spend. A humble life, married at twenty, three children, grandchildren, the height of tedium that you Humans so desire."

"Sounds like Pierce Cade."

"This old codger, he was happy."

"If he was happy why was he speaking to you?"

"There was an unpleasantness," he said.

"Unpleasantness," Laurie scoffed. "That's usually half-baked toff talk for getting caught with your pants at your ankles in a brothel."

"Not quite. When he came to me his beloved wife of a half century had been attacked, mugged, her pension swiped and left in the hospital. Not unlike our friend back in the station."

"It happens, unfortunately."

"Anyway, our man, our straight as an arrow, dutiful and law-abiding citizen asked if I could help."

"Let me guess," she sat up. "He wanted you to smite down his enemies, bring them to justice and see that their souls were forever damned."

That drew a smirk from The Devil. He steepled his fingers.

"Absolutely not," he said. "If he wanted justice he would have gone to your lot. Or, heaven forbid, Him Upstairs. No, no, no my dear Laurie, our man wanted something much more interesting."

"Interesting?"

"Absolutely interesting. You see, our pensioner was so disgusted with what these thugs had done to his wife, hospitalised, dignity robbed, money gone et cetera, that *he* was the one who wanted justice. *He* was the one who wanted to get his own back. And *he* was the one who wished to carry it all out. I've given a lot of Humans what they wanted over the millennia, but this old chap sticks out as being so determined, so focussed on taking revenge for his wife and being the one who took it that he always springs to mind. Humans, Laurie, you like to pretend that you're a higher creature, bigger and better and more civilised than animals. But really you're just beasts of instinct that can hide it well."

Laurie was silent. The Devil let her chew over his parable. Eventually she came around to him.

"Did you help him?" she asked. "Did you give him what he wanted?"

   THE MAN IN THE DARK

"Of course I did," The Devil sniffed. "A little influence straight from Downstairs let him think he was twice the size he was, twenty years younger and had no fear."

"And what happened?"

"He was killed by the thugs who robbed his wife," he said flatly. "Straight up murdered in a back alleyway somewhere, found a bloodied pulp by a dog walker the next morning. That's what happens when you try to take on men a quarter of your age armed to the teeth with knives and sharp things and you're pushing eighty. He's now a doorman Downstairs, has a nice little number that doesn't particularly offend anybody."

Laurie let out a whistle. The Devil laughed at her.

"There's no such thing as a happy ending when you deal with me Laurie," he said. "Well, I say that, no happy endings for you lot anyway. I always win. Always."

A tall, lean looking paramedic with long, braided hair strode up to the side of the ambulance. She cleared her throat gently and The Devil stood up.

"It's time," he said with a smile.

"Time for what?" asked Laurie.

"Time I was gone."

"Gone? You're going? Going where?" asked the policewoman.

"Oh please don't," he said, wincing.

"Don't what?"

"Don't go start crying or anything. You lot get so attached to me. The indignity of it all makes my skin crawl. I'm off, end of. No long goodbyes, no sloppy, heart breaking departure speeches. I'm going, to sort out the mess that's been unfolding in front of our very eyes. And I don't need a blubbering Detective Sergeant Laurie."

"Esther," she said.

"Come again?"

"Esther. You asked me what my first name was, earlier in the car. I never told you. It's Esther."

The Devil chewed over an expletive and then looked at the paramedic.

"Esther," he said to her. "Really? You ever think about becoming a little more subtle in your old age?"

The paramedic shrugged. She had a warm, comforting smile on her face and didn't say a word.

"Do you guys know each other?" asked Laurie. "Or am I missing out on some sort of in-joke."

"We go back a long way my dear," said The Devil. "Too long to count. Anyway. Must be off, universes to save and all that jazz."

He went to hobble away but Laurie reached out and took his hand. He felt something pass into it and looked down. A crumpled bit of white card with washed out ink was staring back at him. He held it up to the light, unable to decipher the writing.

"It says I wasn't to tell you I knew who you were," said Laurie.

The Devil was confused.

"It came, with the roses. You know, the ones that you saw in the flat. Remember you were asking about them, asking where they came from, if there was anything with them. Well, there was. That card."

"So you knew," he said, blowing out his cheeks. "You knew all along who I was, what I was? And still you had Lister do a number on me, had your officers beat me up. Made me sleep on the couch and suffer your quite frankly insufferable patter for days on end. You *knew*."

"I didn't *really* know," she shrugged. "I just kind of had a feeling. Like a little uncomfortable knot in the pit of my stomach. I figured the card had something to do with you and that for whatever

 THE MAN IN THE DARK

reason I was in the middle of all of this. I still don't know why, to be honest. I mean, why me? What's so special about me?"

The Devil tapped the card and handed it back to her. She took it and stared down at it for a moment, smiling.

"Beats me," he said. "I don't think you're anything special at all Esther Laurie. Then again, maybe that's the point."

"Mummy!"

Matilda rushed past him and into Laurie's open arms. She scooped up her daughter and whirled her around, holding her tight.

"Esther!"

It was Andy's turn to hug the policewoman. He wrapped his arms around his wife and daughter and the three embraced each other warmly. They stood for a long, quiet moment drinking in each other's company, each other's presence. A family reunited, amongst all the misery, chaos and carnage of the crashed ship, the ruined dockside and beyond it the city in chaos.

"This is making me feel quite sick," said The Devil.

"It's probably just the meds you've been given," She said quietly, hands tucked behind Her back. "I've pumped you full of goodness knows what to keep you alive that little bit longer."

"You mean this isn't it?" he spluttered. "This must be the longest death ever. I mean seriously, what else could possibly be taking more precedence than heading back Downstairs to kick arse and crack some skulls."

"We have to get there first," She said.

"Thank you!" Laurie shouted over to both of them, Matilda on one arm, Andy on the other. "Thank you for all of this."

"A pleasure," She said. "Oh and I'd leave that dressing on your face for at least a week. Then be very careful when you take it off. You never know, it might be a whole lot better if you just give it time."

Laurie nodded and smiled. She turned and took with Her The Devil, an arm resting on his shoulder.

"Fifteen miles you said," he whispered to Her. "From what I recall her flat, that family of hers, they were a lot further away than fifteen miles."

"Give or take a few spots. Here and there," She said smugly.

"What use are rules if you don't break them, eh?"

"I couldn't possibly comment old chap. Couldn't possibly comment."

They walked quickly away from the hurly burly of the clean-up operation. While the police policed, the medics doctored and the fire brigade secured the wreckage, nobody really knew how lucky they were to be within the safety zone. Outside, the world was being ripped apart, turned inside out, burning itself to the ground. But for the moment, at least, there was some tranquillity and peace in London.

And nobody noticed when The Devil and She vanished. It was like they'd never been there at all.

THIRTY-FIVE

Smoke billowed out across the ancient rooftops and historic skyline of Edinburgh. The tower was coming from the blazing inferno in the grounds of the castle. Perched high above the city, the thick, black smoke looked like a dirty, nasty scar on the crisp, clean summer sky.

The streets should have been busy with tourists and locals. Travellers from all over the world flocked to the Scottish capital, desperate to soak up the atmosphere, the sights, the sounds and the shortbread. Hundreds of thousands of them would get their pictures taken on the Royal Mile, buy cheap kilts and stagger from one pub to another, ready to leave when they'd felt that little bit more Scottish. They'd even convince themselves that the bagpipes sounded good, only to get home and wonder just when they'd play that CD ever again.

Now, the whole city was a war zone. Like every other capital around the planet, fear stalked the streets. Amateur comedians and dozy students should have been punting bad shows and plays in Edinburgh. Instead - terror was the new biggest attraction. And hellish law was enforced for anybody who dared venture outside.

Screams and cries drifted through the once bustling streets. The sounds of pain and anguish hung heavily in the air. The Devil could hear them from his perch on Arthur's Seat. And he knew She could too.

The huge, grassy peak was at the opposite side of the city from the castle and its fire. But the view was perfect. He shielded his eyes from the sun as he watched the smoke pour up and out from the esplanade, carried by the wind towards the sea like a victory flag.

"It's getting worse, isn't it?" She said.

The Devil puffed out his cheeks. He stopped short of blowing a raspberry. Even he thought it was inappropriate.

"I'd say so. But I don't think You need to know what I think. You probably know already anyway."

She hummed in agreement. The distant chorus of chaos and mayhem drifted up and about them both as they stood looking out across the city. The Devil knew it was a similar picture across the planet. The irony, he thought, was that the whole of the Human race was, at last, all singing from the same hymn sheet.

They were united in discord. Sure they were tearing themselves apart but at least they were all doing it. And that included those they had just left in London. What would happen to Laurie and Lister and everyone else at the docklands was anybody's guess, The Devil supposed. But he decided not to voice his concerns to Her. It didn't seem fair somehow.

"You think they'll ever be the same again?" he asked.

"I can't imagine so," She said. "This isn't really the sort of thing one gets over very easily. I can't tell how they're taking it to be perfectly honest. You know what they can be like. They internalise everything."

"Internalise? Them? You're pulling my leg aren't You?" said The Devil. "You should take a look at the spreadsheets for this place. I'll let you in on a little secret. They internalise *nothing*."

    THE MAN IN THE DARK

He thumbed at the huge, towering skyscraper of steel and glass that loomed high above them. The black streak of smoke shimmered and reflected off the windows - the windows that weren't smashed up.

The Devil stood in the car park at the front of the building and tutted. He knew there would be sacrifices. But he had secretly hoped that HellCorp would have remained unscathed.

"The sign though," he said. "What kind of sick, twisted individual would change it to HellCrap. I mean, that's not even funny is it? Am I the only one who thinks that's just bloody petty?"

She covered Her mouth. The Devil could still see a smile poking between Her fingers. He adjusted his tartan tie and fixed his cuffs. He was feeling much better now that he'd been allowed to take on something closer to his old self.

"And I don't know what You're laughing at. You could have at least changed for the occasion."

She looked down at Her paramedic outfit.

"What? You don't think this is appropriate?" She said. I thought I'd try out something a bit more casual for a change. A little less exotic."

"You, My Dear, wouldn't know exotic if it jumped up and started licking that stupid bloody smile off Your face."

He cursed silently under his breath. He'd been in Her company less than a Human hour and already he was regretting it.

"Come on then," he said. "Let's get this show on the road."

He led the way. They walked purposefully across the car park and towards the main entrance of HellCorp's international headquarters. There were no doormen and even the sliding doors were on the fritz. The Devil pushed one of them aside and She squeezed Her way through.

The inside wasn't much better than the out. The main lobby of the building was scattered with papers. Files and sheets fell over the balconies and upper levels of the skyscraper like bureaucratic snow. A small fire had been lit on the far side of the courtyard and there were printers, desks and smashed up chairs littered about the place. The walls were etched in graffiti and what looked like brown paint. Although on closer inspection The Devil suspected it was something much worse.

"I love what you've done with the place," She said. "It's got a real end of the world feel about it. You really captured the whole 'we don't care anymore' vibe."

"I can assure You, this is *not* what it's supposed to look like," said The Devil.

He made a point of noting just how embarrassed he felt. This was his pet project, his retirement legacy, the place he'd striven so hard to get up and running and off the ground. Now She was finally here - seeing it as a colossal dump. Sure, She knew that Brutus and Cassius had been up to their old tricks. But that didn't diminish the embarrassment The Devil was feeling. Not for the first time he vowed to exact every last microsecond of revenge on them when he got back Downstairs.

"I assume there's a portal in the basement," She said, pointing towards the stairs.

"Naturally," said The Devil.

They walked across the courtyard, sidestepping the mountains of damaged office supplies and equipment. He took a look up towards the glass ceiling forty floors above. It was smashed to bits of course, the Edinburgh sky peering back at him like a giant eye.

"I assume everybody has been sent home," She said.

"I would have thought so. Although they're probably prowling the streets somewhere on their hands and knees, frothing at the mouth. It seems to be the fashion these days."

They headed downstairs. On The Devil's instruction, the building was twice as big below ground as it was above. There was nothing sinister in the planning, he just knew he'd be able to get the room and permission - especially after a Papal signature.

Eighty flights of stairs later they reached the bottom. She stopped and caught Her breath.

"Human lungs aren't built for that sort of descent," She puffed.

"You will insist on staying in that form."

There was only one door down here. He stepped to one side to let Her go first. She hesitated, just for a fraction of a second. The Devil smiled.

"No booby traps," he said. "What do you think I am, the Man in the Dark or something?"

"That title won't stick," She said, pushing the door open.

A loud groan erupted from the other side of the door and a wave of stifling hot, foul smelling air washed over the pair. Thick, black soot bubbled through the opening, wisping and curling all around their feet and legs. She gave a quick glance at The Devil who stood smiling.

"Just a little bit different to what You're used to old bean," he said with glee. "But it gets the job done just as well."

With that, She stepped through the door and was consumed by the swirling cloud of thick, black smoke and dust. The Devil waited a moment before looking to the ceiling.

"Oh how the mighty have fallen," he said, before following Her into the cloud.

THIRTY-SIX

Darkness reigned supreme. The lights had been tampered with. The Devil always knew when somebody had been messing around with the settings. He always had it exactly the way he wanted.

Now they were all off. He only wished that was the worst of his problems. Downstairs had, quite literally gone to hell.

They had emerged on a small mountaintop overlooking the central city.

"Oh you've got to be kidding," he said.

He walked through the ash spread out across the ground like fresh snow. A billowing, boiling wind was whipping up from the cauldron of the city far below them. The constant, grinding din of the place was loud and uncomfortable. And in the distance a row of fiery, lava spewing mountains were doing their best to disrupt the dark, swirling sky peppered with white streaks of lightning.

"Have they been reading from a five-year-old's version of scripture or something?" he asked Her. "This place looks like a bloody stereotype!"

"I told you you wouldn't be happy," She said, hardly hiding a smile.

"You're enjoying this aren't You!" The Devil snapped. "You're absolutely loving seeing me on my hands and knees. There's some

THE MAN IN THE DARK

sick, twisted and perverted pleasure You get from watching me suffer isn't there? I tell You what, I shouldn't be so surprised."

She folded Her arms across Her chest. The Devil stalked around Her, muttering to himself, running his hand through his more familiar hair. He unfastened the top button of his shirt and loosened off his tartan tie.

"I'm losing it, I know," he said. "You can't blame me for that. It's just very difficult when you've been building up to this moment for what feels like forever and it finally comes. And when it does you're met with something so abysmal, so heartbreakingly ugly that it makes my insides turn to mulch. You can forgive me for being a little tetchy."

"I haven't said a word," She said. "It's you who is making yourself tetchy old pip, not me."

"Yes, fine, I know," he said, turning back to face the cauldron. "But come on, look at this place. Everything's just so... so Roman."

He looked out at the ruins of the city. The buildings were decaying, diseased looking and ill. The gridiron structure he had painstakingly created was littered with rubble and protruding fountains of fire and brimstone. The sense of loss and atrophy hung heavy in the sooty, thick air. And as for the ash storm blowing about them, it was all very typical.

The Devil didn't do typical. In fact, he detested it almost as much as stupid questions.

"Wait a minute!" he shouted, stepping over to the edge of the mountain. "What's that? What's that going on down there?"

"Down where?" She asked, joining him.

"Down there, in the heart of my city," he pointed. "Right in the centre, where the Bell Tower used to be. Where the Bell Tower *should* be. It looks like... like..."

"Ah yes," She said knowingly. "It would seem that's where Cassius and Brutus have decided to have their monuments built."

"I beg Your pardon," The Devil blinked. "Did You say *monuments*?"

"Yes," She agreed. "You see if you look closely you can just about make out the two sets of legs that have been built already."

"Built?"

"Built, yes. I had my boys Upstairs do a little bit of research ahead of our trip."

"Research? And You didn't think to tell me before now?"

"It seems Brutus and Cassius decreed that they wanted the monuments built in the old-fashioned way. Slave labour old chap, proper Roman style. No black magic or conjuring. And they're being erected on the site of what used to be Department J, I believe. They wanted to go 'old school'. That's the term of choice these days. Very Roman of them."

"Don't," said The Devil.

"Don't what?"

"Don't You speak like that. It was bad enough listening to the Humans but You are a totally worse kettle of fish."

He stared down at where the monuments were being built. The Devil knew anger, it was like an old friend and companion he could always rely on. Some of his best work had come about when he was in the throes of a rage. What filled him now was something much worse, much more powerful and all consuming.

"I'm not happy," he said ominously. "I'm really not happy. And I don't know what You've got in store to try and get this shit show in order but I'm telling You right now. I'll bring a terrible vengeance down on those two low-life, conniving, sneaky, backstabbing, treacherous Roman bastards even if it's the very last thing I do."

She nodded. The Devil was expecting a telling off or at the very least a stern warning that he was dangerously close to overstepping the mark. Nothing was forthcoming, giving him a sense of just how big a job this was going to be.

"Shall we get to work then?" he asked.

"Yes, I think we should," She said. "But first there's somebody we have to collect."

She walked away from the edge of the mountain, wading through the inches of ash that had fallen from the storm. The Devil was confused.

"Somebody we have to collect?" he called after Her. "What is this? A carpool?"

She stopped at a large mound of boulders and rocks that were stacked up towards the rear of the peak. The Devil followed Her, keeping his distance.

"Could we hurry this up please," he said impatiently. "Can I remind You that You were the one who said I'd been arsing around for too long with the Humans. Now You're hitting out with mini-mysteries all over the place."

"Watch and learn," She said.

She reached out and touched the ash covered boulders. Wiping it clean, The Devil squinted and saw what appeared to be a face beneath the surface of the rock.

It was a man. Not only that, a man he recognised very well. A man that, somewhere in the back of his mind he'd noted to throttle if he saw him again. He squinted, making sure he was right.

"No," he said calmly. "If he's coming along for this jolly then I'm not."

"He deserves another chance," She said calmly.

"No, absolutely not, not a chance. He's incompetent and blithering and that's on a very good day."

"He's paid his debt to society."

"He *is* payment to society."

"He's sorry."

"He doesn't know the meaning of the word!" The Devil yelled. "In fact, hold on a moment. He's one of the many, *many* reasons we're standing here in Deep Shit Arizona! If anything it's all his fault!"

She drew him a long, unimpressed look. He licked his lips.

"Yes, well, I said he was one of the reasons," he said.

"He's waited a long time for redemption," She said with a sad sigh.

"And this is when he gets it, is it?" The Devil sneered. "Of all the times and places, of all the scenarios that have unfolded in thousands of years, this, *this* is when You want to give *him* a chance to pull his act together and actually make a difference?"

"He already made a difference," She said.

"Yeah, and how did that work out?" he pointed back down towards the crucible.

The Devil let out a frustrated growl of anger. He clenched his fists and was about to stomp his feet. This wasn't the glorious homecoming he had been hoping for.

"I'm sorry this wasn't what you were expecting," She said, reading his mind. "And I'm sorry we're not doing things your way. I know how angry you are with Cassius and Brutus. That's why I'm trying to placate at least some of that bloodthirst for revenge by formulating a plan that works quickly and efficiently, without too much collateral damage."

"Collateral damage," he said. "There's that term again. It's fast becoming my most hated phrase of all time."

"You're better than an all-out war with these Romans old bean," She said sincerely. "And you're better than falling out with me over

     THE MAN IN THE DARK

a silly little tiff."

"Tiff? Silly?" he sighed. "I don't think I'll ever understand You. In fact, I know I won't. I don't think I want to."

"Then we'll agree to disagree. Like we've done so many times before."

The Devil clicked his tongue. He knew he wasn't going to win this one. Picking your battles was all part of the game with Her. And this was one he would never win. So what was the point in trying? It was just wasting time.

"Before You free him," said The Devil. "Just answer me one thing. One simple, little question."

She crossed Her hands across Her waist, a look of peaceful serenity on Her face.

"Of course," She smiled wryly.

"Are You bringing him along just to annoy me?" he asked. "I mean, there must be thousands, hundreds of thousands of people You could choose to resurrect to help us out. Dictators, military geniuses, just plain old clever folk. But him, him! He's beyond worthless as he's already shown. That's why he's stuck frozen in time in a rock in the back arsehole of Downstairs where nobody would think to look. He let Cassius and Brutus put him there! How bad is that!"

In true, typical fashion, She remained tight-lipped. She turned back to the boulder with the face peering out and rolled up the sleeves of Her paramedic outfit.

"Yeah," said The Devil. "I thought so."

She concentrated, fingers outstretched. The Devil stepped back a little, making sure She was between him and the boulder in the event the thing blew up. He prepared himself for something spectacular. But all that happened was the massive rock disappeared. There was a little pop sound and it was gone.

The man slumped to the ground. His robes were ragged, hair long and shaggy. He coughed and spluttered, gasping for mouthfuls of air. He gripped the ash beneath his fingers, gathering it up and smelling it.

"It's a miracle," he croaked. "I thought… I thought I'd never be free."

He began to sob with joy, smearing ash across his face. When he opened his eyes and saw who was standing in front of him, he let out a pathetic yelp. He cowered, retreating away from them, kicking up ash with his sandals.

"Oh god!" he shouted. "Oh god, I'm so sorry. I'm so, so sorry!"

"I think he's talking to you," She said softly.

"You think?" said The Devil, sneering. "Sounded more like he was apologising to Your Good Self."

"Please forgive me. I didn't… I didn't know what they were going to do. I didn't know they were going to go crazy. The power, it went to their heads. I thought… I thought they were on my side, I thought they were on *our* side! I'm sorry… I'm so, so sorry. I'm-"

"Enough!" The Devil shouted.

His voice seemed more powerful suddenly, the mountain quaking beneath their feet. He took a few steps towards the man who cowered and wept pathetically.

"Judas!" he said. "Judas bloody Iscariot. What am I going to do with you? I'm very, very, very disappointed in you. You've been a naughty boy and you've let me down."

Judas peered up through his hands. Even he hadn't been prepared for that kind of telling off. Sensing that he might not be handed the wrath he was expecting, he let his guard down. And that's when The Devil struck.

"I'm going to kill you Judas! I'm going to kill you!"

He grabbed the Ultimate Traitor's throat and started choking

THE MAN IN THE DARK

him. He wrung Judas neck, his head wobbling back and forward like a rag doll's.

"I'm… sorry… I'm… sorry!" Judas kept saying.

"Sorry isn't going to cut it boy-oh! You've flushed us right down the cosmic toilet with this one!"

The throttling went on for minutes, The Devil enjoying every moment. He'd wanted to do this for what had felt like a thousand lifetimes. He was just getting into the rhythm of it when She decided playtime was over.

"Okay, that's enough," She said, stepping between them and breaking them apart.

The Devil retreated. He composed himself, fixing his suit to make it look at least half presentable. Judas was sprawled out on the ground, gasping for air with deliberate, over the top, martyred gulps of air.

"Are you both finished?" She asked. "We have rather a lot of work to do and a long journey ahead of us. So if you're both done with playing around in the dirt like children we could get on with putting things right again."

The Devil sneered at Judas who tried to avoid catching his eye. The traitor picked himself up and dusted off his robes and beard. He rubbed his neck and nodded humbly.

"Yes My Lord," he said, looking for sympathy. "Whatever You wish I'll do my utmost to make sure that it is done."

"Oh please," The Devil droned. "You never speak to me like that."

She smiled and nodded.

"Good, that's settled then," She said. "Now come on, we've got a bit of a trek if we want to get down into the city."

"Trek?" asked The Devil as She and Judas walked past him. "What do You mean trek? Why can't we just, You know, appear?"

"And where would the surprise in that be?" She said knowingly, starting down a winding path that snaked down the side of the mountain. "I told you, there are little pockets down there still sympathetic to the Natural Order. We can't really go about attracting attention to ourselves. Otherwise the toxic twins will be all over us. So come on, get your hiking boots on, we're going for a walk. And besides, the exercise will do you the world of good."

The Devil could feel his face contorting. He wasn't happy, he was pretty much as far from being happy as was possible. His kingdom was a mess, run by two low lives bent on erasing him from history. He was being forced, under huge protest, to give a second chance to one of Humanity's most vilified and untrustworthy characters. And that's who She was trusting to help the situation.

On top of all that She didn't appear to be leaving any time soon. The longer The Devil spent in Her company something invariably always ended up going wrong for him. Like some cosmic restaurant, the greater the time the heftier the bill.

"This is it," he said to himself, staring out across the crucible at the ruins of Downstairs, his Downstairs. "I've hit rock bottom. I can't stoop any lower. I've finally done it."

"Aren't you coming old sausage?" She shouted after him.

The Devil ground his teeth and looked about the mountaintop to make sure nobody was watching. When he was satisfied, he stamped his feet twice like a scolded, spoiled brat and tried to make himself feel better.

Unsurprisingly, it didn't work.

The End… but not as we know it!

ACKNOWLEDGEMENTS

This is the part that's always so difficult. Seriously, plot holes, character development and weighing up how the forces of good and evil will do battle is EASY compared to this.

However, I know it's only this way because I have so much support, help, belief and encouragement from so many people. And quite frankly there isn't enough time left in the universe for me to thank them all individually. They know who they are and I am, as always, grateful and eternally humbled for everything they do.

I'd like to extend a special thanks to the wonderful Urbane team, Matthew Smith and Kerry-Jane Lowery specifically, who have given me so much backing, so much faith and support in bringing the infernal to the real world. And also for their tireless efforts in weeding out my (millions) of spelling mistakes!

Family, friends and foes alike - I thank you all. You're all in this book and my writing in general in some way or another.

Without you I wouldn't be able to do what I do. So don't ever change. Thank you.

Jonathan Whitelaw is an author, journalist and broadcaster.

After working on the frontline of Scottish politics, he moved into journalism. Subjects he has covered have varied from breaking news, the arts, culture and sport to fashion, music and even radioactive waste - with everything in between.

He's also a regular reviewer and talking head on shows for the BBC and STV.

Man in the Dark is his third novel, a sequel to second novel *HellCorp* (also published by Urbane), and following his debut, *Morbid Relations*.

EVEN THE DEVIL
NEEDS A HOLIDAY

HELLCORP

JONATHAN
WHITELAW

Life is hard for The Devil and he desperately wants to take a holiday. Growing weary from playing the cosmic bad guy, he resolves to set up a company that will do his job for him so the sins of the world will tick over while he takes a vacation. God tells him he can have his vacation just as soon as he solves an ancient crime.

But nothing is ever easy and before long he is up to his pitchfork in solving murders, desperate to crack the case so he can finally take the holiday he so badly needs...

This is a perfectly pitched darkly comic crime novel that is ideal for fans of Christopher Fowler and Ben Aaranovitch.

Urbane Publications is dedicated to
publishing books that challenge, thrill and fascinate.
From page-turning thrillers to literary debuts,
our goal is to publish what
YOU want to read.
Find out more at

urbanepublications.com